Going for Jazz

# Going for JAZZ

## Musical Practices and American Ideology

### Nicholas Gebhardt

The University of Chicago Press
Chicago and London

Nicholas Gebhardt is music director of Radio 2SER-FM in Sydney, Australia, and holds a Ph.D. in American history from the University of Sydney. He has published interviews with Wynton Marsalis, Steve Lacy, and Philip Glass, and is himself a saxophonist.

The University of Chicago Press, Chicago 60637
The University of Chicago Press, Ltd., London
© 2001 by The University of Chicago
All rights reserved. Published 2001
Printed in the United States of America

10 09 08 07 06 05 04 03 02 01     1 2 3 4 5
ISBN: 0-226-28466-2 (cloth)
ISBN: 0-226-28467-0 (paper)

Library of Congress Cataloging-in-Publication Data

Gebhardt, Nicholas.
    Going for jazz : musical practices and American ideology / Nicholas Gebhardt.
        p. cm.
    Includes bibliographical references (p.    ) and index.
    ISBN 0-226-28466-2 (cloth : alk. paper)—ISBN 0-226-28467-0 (paper : alk. paper)
    1. Jazz—History and criticism.   2. Music—Social aspects—United States.   I. Title.
    ML3506 .G43   2001
    781.65'0973—dc21
                                                        00-012300

Knowledge about the character of creating and created
objects is at present in a state of conceptual infancy.
Its illumination will require a richness of work far
beyond the frame of any single study: like the activity
of "making," the activity of "understanding making" will
be a collective rather than a solitary labor.

Elaine Scarry

That music, it was like where you lived. It was like
waking up in the morning and eating, and it was regular
in your life. It was natural to the way you lived and
the way you died.

Sidney Bechet

The very element that raises music above ideology is
also what brings it closest to it.

Theodor W. Adorno

# CONTENTS

# ACKNOWLEDGMENTS

Many people were involved directly or indirectly in the process of my writing this book. I hope to have done justice to the richness of their ideas and their shared understandings of the world. Doug Mitchell is as wonderful an editor as anyone could hope for. His faith in the project has never wavered, and whatever success there is here, is surely a tribute to him. For their efforts in bringing this book to fruition, I extend my sincere gratitude to Leslie Keros, Ryan Li, Robert Devens, and Mark Heineke of the University of Chicago Press, and to my superb copyeditor, David Bemelmans. For their support and inspiration over many years and in many different ways, I would like to thank Shane White, Graham White, my dissertation examiners Robin D. G. Kelley, Ronald Radano, and David Goodman, my friends and colleagues at Radio 2SER-FM in Sydney, my musical comrade Ion Pearce, and last but not least my family—Peter Gebhardt, Christina Gebhardt, Sophie Gebhardt, Anna Gebhardt, Lois Wilkinson, Leslie Gebhardt, and Ron Chuck.

Institutional support came from the Department of History, University of Sydney, the staff at the Institute for Jazz Studies at Rutgers, the State University of New Jersey, and the Schomburg Library in Harlem. For their extraordinary generosity during my research trips to the United States, I am indebted to Adam Reingold, Nathaniel Stevens, Mary Priscilla Stevens, Sam and Ellen Stevens, Joan Phelan, Ann Phelan,

Sally Whitely, and Mark Johansson. Without their assistance, the task of gathering material would have been an arduous one. The research for this study was made possible by an Australian Postgraduate Research Award and a number of travel grants from the University of Sydney. I am also indebted to Avigdor Arikha for permission to use his image of the saxophonist.

Finally, most of the credit for what follows should go to my dear friends Laura van Tatenhove, Roland Kapferer, and Maria Kontis. Without their fine sense of humor and a passion for all things artistic and intellectual, this would have been a poorer work indeed. This book is as much a result of their efforts as it is my own, and so to them it is truly dedicated with the utmost thanks and respect.

# Introduction

This book posits a *historical relation* between jazz and American ideology. It is not, however, a history of jazz in the usual sense. Nor is it a strictly musical analysis. Rather, it is positioned between the two. In taking this approach, my aim is to develop a critical framework for analyzing the creative character of the "jazz act"—by which I mean the musician's practice of playing a musical piece—but also to grasp more fully the social structures in the context of which such creative acts are made. To posit a specific *historical relation* between music and ideology is to highlight the problem of *mediation;* that is, our task is to define a theory capable of analyzing the relations between two structurally distinct dimensions of human being, without reducing or subsuming one into the other.[1] Indeed, it is not a question of deciding on either the primacy of musical acts and practices or their ideological context; nor is it a matter of arguing for their ultimate equivalence, that one is merely a reflection of the other. Rather, I argue that musical practices and their ideological context are related *disjunctively,* and that only at this point of disjuncture does our critical work really begin.

How will this critical work proceed? In a fine essay on musical production, the philosopher Theodor Adorno argues that the purpose of musical analysis is "to articulate the social meaning of the formal constituents of music—its logic, in short."[2] Following Adorno, this study proceeds phenomenologically through as precise a delineation as possible of the "logic" of the musical act as revealed in the social situations of three jazz saxophone players: Sidney Bechet (soprano saxophone), Charlie Parker (alto saxophone), and Ornette Coleman (alto saxophone). The social situation of each musician is analyzed in terms of its ideological frame, while musical phenomena are analyzed as elements in what I define as the practical logics of musical making. The phenomena of music (melody, harmony, rhythm, and so forth) is designated by the phrase "musical material," while the human act of transforming that material is denoted "musical making." I explain the dialectic of human agency and social determination by considering the jazz musician's "musical ways," a phrase that denotes the attempt to grasp the *social existence* of the musical act at the level of its *virtuosity*. To propose a theory of jazz virtuosity is one of my primary concerns.

This introduction is divided into four parts. In the first I take up the historical emergence of the jazz act and its significance to a study of American capitalist society. The second offers an overview of the three chapters that follow and the critical problems raised in each. The third part outlines my theory of musical virtuosity, which is used to refer to a specific domain of human being that is designated as *musical* and to a form of human consciousness that is analyzed as *musical consciousness*. In the fourth part, I stress the significance of a theory of ideology—or to be more precise, the relevance of ideological criticism—to the study of jazz practices.

The musical ways of Bechet, Parker, and Coleman form, respectively, the focus of each of the three chapters that follow. Bechet was born in New Orleans in 1897 and played a formative role in the creation of the hot jazz form; Parker was born in Kansas City in 1920 and became one of the key figures in what was known as the "bebop revolution" of the 1940s; while Coleman, who was born in Texas in 1930, was central to the free jazz movement of the 1960s.[3] My aim in each chapter is to analyze the *social content* of their jazz acts, to situate the creative character of those acts and their specific musical dynamic in relation to the changing forms of the capitalist society of which they were a part, and to demonstrate how those acts of musical making were indicative *and* transformative of the key elements of American ideology.

My argument in each chapter is that the jazz act, prior to any process of individual self-expression, is already a social act. That historians and critics continue to reduce the jazz act to a privileged mode of individual self-expression, however, merely functions to reproduce the very *ideological* terms on which the jazz act depends for its economic and historical value *as commodity*.[4] Although the act's ideological frame cannot be separated from the making of the act, I suggest there is a specific dimension to the act that complicates the social and political efficiency of this ideological frame and that cannot be reduced to pure ideology as such.[5] This dimension is the virtuosic.

Before I explain the relation between the virtuosity of the jazz act and exceptionalist ideology, I want to emphasize the reasons for concentrating on the "jazz lives" of these particular musicians. First, Bechet, Parker, and Coleman can each be considered as part of a historical series that exemplifies the influence of the saxophone on American musical practices.[6] All three musicians made profound contributions to the practice of saxophone playing and the instrument's centrality to jazz and to American music in general. Second, their jazz lives *coalesce* within the same capitalist *modernity*. This coalescence complicates the evolutionary schema that divides jazz into a series of progressive stages that reflect the "progressive" stages of the history of the American state. Third, the structural homology implied *between* their musical practices and the social context *of* those practices results from the coexistence of forces that continually struggle for possession of the jazz act. My task is to demonstrate the logic of that struggle, the structure and form of those forces, and how, in spite of the fragility of their musical material, Bechet, Parker, and Coleman managed to produce significant and lasting jazz acts as a consequence of precisely such a struggle. Finally, each "musical life" is symptomatic of a key ideological development in the larger historical formation of the American state. The structure of this relationship—among jazz life, the virtuosity of the jazz act, and the act's ideological dimension—is discussed at greater length below.[7]

Aside from the musical ways and acts of the three jazz saxophonists, my broader concern is with the historical forms of human action and, in particular, the making of musical acts within a capitalist social order. As the political theorist Paolo Virno suggests, there is no question so vexed or enigmatic today as the question of what it means to act. While Virno's focus is primarily political, his analysis opens up several important avenues for the investigation of musical production. By pointing to "the kinds of people whose work involves *virtuosic performance*," Virno suggests that what is at stake in the study of musical acts is the production of the forms of human subjectivity.[8] In other words, the very manipulation and transformation of the material world through a person's *virtuosic* movements, through his or her embodied motions, is constitutive of, and constituted by, the relations of domination and exploitation specific to the division of labor in capitalist society. For Virno, the meaning of action, and its subsequent postmodern crisis, lies in the possibility of maintaining a certain excess, that is, an irreducible gap between working and acting; a gap that is, however, already inscribed in the form of the class struggle itself.

To enter more fully into the analysis of human creative action and its relation to ideology, I rely upon a number of critical concepts. I have tried not to use these concepts gratuitously, but rather to mobilize them in retracing the existential path of our object. Thus, the overarching purpose of this study is to analyze social relations between human beings as they are established in the concrete musical situations of the jazz act; that is, to emphasize not only the modes of production and the ways of working that determined the American social order, but also, to focus on ways of existing and co-existing, on human relationships.[9] Lewis Erenberg, in his study of big band jazz in the 1930s, suggests that the social basis of jazz production depended on the assertion of a radical egalitarianism; that, for jazz musicians, "[w]hat counted was the way you played."[10] The very assertion of the *way* you play as constitutive of jazz production involves a statement about how, with whom, and what kind of relationships are formed through the dynamics of the musical act. In the ensuing pages, I outline the appearance of the various critical concepts as I use them to analyze the social character of these *musical* relationships.

## Black Music and Historical Situations

Black musical practices emerged in the United States during the nine-teenth century from the productive relations of social labor and social organization that characterized the struggle between black and white Americans. The dynamics of those relations of production, and the social and political struggles that issued from them, characterized both the struc-ture of the southern states' plantation system and the emergent industrial society in the North.[11] How and under what conditions these musical practices emerged has informed several fine studies of slave and nonslave communities, alongside a number of excellent studies of black music, the most comprehensive of which is Eileen Southern's *The Music of Black Americans*.[12] Although somewhat schematic, the importance of Southern's study lies in her attempt to align all the various and, more important, irre-ducible strands of black musical practice within the specific circumstances of the New World, and understand the logic of these practices on the basis of particular sociohistorical situations. Her enterprise is invaluable to the study of jazz, American ideology, and human creative practices.

Following Southern's lead, a range of historical and musicological studies has uncovered a sense of a distinct and original musical purpose among enslaved and free blacks in finding meaning and value in their own and others' musical acts.[13] Equally, such studies have offered evidence of the manifold social processes through which black and nonblack communities actualized their sense of those acts as meaningful expressions of social consciousness. If Southern's study proves exhaustive in many respects, its shortcomings are indicative of a general weakness in music history in analyzing and explaining the structuring of the ideas and actions of human beings and, in the case of music, the orienting aspect of human creative practices and the sense of social value incumbent upon and derivative from those practices. To redress this weakness, further attention must be directed to the "situated practices" of jazz musicians and the manner by which those practices were considered historically significant—that is, how they were constituted by and constitutive of human social and political realities.[14]

My concern is to situate the jazz act in terms of the historical logic of the American state in its global political phase, a phase that began with Theodore Roosevelt's imperial designs on the Philippines (1898–1902) and continues on an enlarged scale today.[15] Indeed, one must confront not only the immediate social and political practices and ideas that oriented and, likewise, were oriented by jazz musicians, but also the larger complex of practices, institutions, beliefs, and productive techniques that constituted the ideological forms of the American state. David Stowe's analysis of 1930s big band music during the rise and fall of Franklin D. Roosevelt's New Deal society offers one of the more persuasive arguments for analyzing the social dynamics and the ideological frame of jazz production:

> Historians must regard the score or recording as merely the sign of a large field of social forces that provide the ground for those texts. In other words, the arbitrary distinction between a musical performance and its origin or source can be abolished. Swing would be understood not as a collection of written arrangements or recordings but as the field that makes such texts possible. In short, we should view the music not simply as text but as social practice.[16]

The correlations between a musical practice and its conditions of production, in this instance expressive of what Stowe calls "swing ideology," reveal a certain mimetic or illustrative quality in relation to larger social or political combinations or constructions.[17] To claim otherwise would be to preclude the influence of dominant ideologies from the act of making music and, likewise, attribute a scientific transparency to the act of listening to and judging a music's social value.

Even the most formal operations among a people require the dynamic of social being and consciousness, however logical these operations are thought to be. In spite of an argument for jazz as social practice, however, Stowe's emphasis on the plurality of the jazz act's reception, where the value of each jazz performance is defined by the range of responses to it, tends to reify the jazz listener as the ultimate focus of musical practice. As a consequence, his analysis displaces the logic of those practices onto the privileged viewpoint of the listener (and, ultimately, the music critic). Not only does this undermine the orienting power of musical acts, but it also circumscribes the logic of the act within the limits of its response and then rationalizes the response as symptomatic of a period, thereby erasing the complex social dynamic of the act *qua* act. The problem with such theories of reception is highlighted by Adorno: "Sociological research that would prefer to avoid the problems of analyzing production and to confine itself to questions of distribution or consumption remains imprisoned in the mechanisms of the market and hence gives sanction to the primacy of the commodity character of music. . . ."[18]

To avoid a series of reflective correlations—hot music and rising prosperity, swing and big government, bebop and alienation, free jazz and liberation—I have aimed to approach them from a different position, without discarding the force of those correlations and their practical import for musicians in the making of their musical acts.[19] So where Stowe hastens to find in the jazz act evidence of its reception as a social practice, I am interested in the form of the jazz act's situation and the orienting of such situations in time as practices that had social and political consequences and that were, likewise, socially and politically consequential. In other words, in the analysis of the musical situation, the sense of the act's essential being relies upon the prior historical struggle over the social consequences of an act's form. While the distinction may appear academic at best, undue emphasis on jazz's reception risks cutting the virtuosity of the musical act off at the pass, reducing it to nothing more than an amalgam of all possible views at all possible times.[20]

With a situational analysis, several points have to be kept in mind. Both Clyde Mitchell and Bruce Kapferer emphasize that such an approach maintains "an aversion to using practices merely to illustrate abstract theoretical or cultural ideas."[21] Although their respective analyses are of fundamentally different societies, Mitchell's of southern Africa and Kapferer's of Sri Lanka, their arguments can offer important challenges to, and developments in, the study of musical practices in Western societies.[22] To use their terms in this context one might indeed propose that jazz practices were socially creative acts entirely relevant to and formed within industrial capitalist conditions.[23] The significance of group improvisation for jazz musicians, the adaptable modes of jazz performance, and the musicians' use of ragtime, spirituals, popular song, and brass band music—in relation to what LeRoi Jones (Amiri Baraka) calls the "blues impulse,"—were constructed entirely within the context of these conditions, and not prior to, or independently of, existing realities. Likewise, the historical and political emphasis on African antecedents and stylistic consistency in black music is as much a part of the dynamic of capitalist industrial reality as is the urban society from which it, and the musical practices themselves, emerged.[24]

An analysis of the framing and reframing of human creative action has critical repercussions for understanding jazz practices, lending to historical study what we might identify as a situational imperative. In Mitchell's view, the situational imperative

> consists of selecting from the vast set of current activities and interactions (or social phenomena in general) a limited set of events which the analyst has reason to assume may be linked together in some way and be capable of being interpreted logically in terms of a general understanding of the way in which social actions take place. . . . The general perspective then is that the behavior of social actors may be interpreted as the resultant of the actor's shared understandings of the situation in which they find themselves and the constraints of the wider social order in which they are enmeshed.[25]

The subsequent relation between the situational immediacy and social orientation of the musical act, and its simultaneous historical orientation within American industrial capitalist society, constitutes the dynamic of jazz practices in time. In this sense, the study of jazz as a social act encompasses not only the discrete situations in which such acts were made and remade, valued and revalued, embraced or discarded, posited or withdrawn, but also encompasses the constraints and inducements, the contradictions and inconsistencies, in short, the whole multiple series of determinations and contingencies generated by the institutional and ideological forms of the American state.

The following brief overview of the three chapters that follow clarifies how I establish the practical logic of the musician's social situation in relation to these institutional and ideological forms.

## Chapter Overviews

The first chapter analyzes *Treat It Gentle,* Sidney Bechet's elegant and evocative autobiography.[26] The significance of Bechet's narrative for the history of jazz practices and, specifically, for the historical logic of Bechet's own musical acts, lies in his attempt to provide jazz with a foundation myth and to inscribe that myth within the history of jazz practices and the wider social developments in black and Creole communities in southern Louisiana after the American Civil War.[27] At the same time, the narrative functions to legitimate the historical course of Bechet's own practices and the direction of his life as one of the first generation of jazz practitioners. The historical problem specific to Bechet's text is the social value of the jazz musical act in New Orleans; that is, its relation to the musical traditions of slave and ex-slave communities, the subsequent legacy of emancipation in shaping the direction of black music, and the creation of jazz as a significant step in the formation of a sense of the value of black social practices and social consciousness.

When I refer to the dynamic of a black social consciousness and social practices and culture, I am following the work of Ira Berlin, E. P. Thompson, Barbara Fields, and Herbert Gutman on the formation of a working class and racial consciousness specific to industrial capitalism. In Berlin's terms, the making of a racial consciousness was a complex historical process that was irreducible in time and space to a single mode of existence, or to a prior essence, carried over intact from Africa. Rather, the making of the slaves' and ex-slaves' racial consciousness was thoroughly entwined with the development of the American state and the emergence of a class consciousness. It was made, therefore, from both "the volatility of experiences that collectively defined race" and from social "experiences that differed from place to place and time to time and not from some unchanging transhistorical verity."[28] As with the social and political practices through which Africans oriented themselves to the exigencies of their enslavement, slaves' and ex-slaves' consciousness was not just made, but continually remade, in vastly different historical contexts and in a whole range of historically situated ways. Hence, Herbert Gutman's influential attempt to analyze the structure of the slave experience and uncover "the passageways through which the experience and beliefs of these people traveled."[29]

The dynamic between nineteenth-century black musical practices and the emancipation of the slaves was the ground for Bechet's practical orientation as a Creole musician from New Orleans. It was also the basis of his sense of legitimacy as a jazz performer and his feeling that he carried within his music some of the original impulse for jazz creativity and its collective praxis.[30] In this light, the causal logic underlying the narrative in *Treat It Gentle* can be seen to have been formed in the process of trying to understand the transition from slavery to freedom, from the world the slaves made on the southern Louisiana plantations to Bechet's success as a professional musician dependent on large urban black and nonblack populations for his livelihood and for musical recognition. Moreover, this logic was constituted by the overarching framework of American exceptionalism, its corresponding social formations, and the combined forces of industrial productivity, monopoly capital, and state expansion that characterized the processes and conditions of emancipation after the Civil War.

In analyzing the situational imperative of Bechet's narrative, I argue that the value of the jazz act to Americans is inextricably bound to the value of the slave and the historical understanding of the southern slave world. This argument is made primarily through an analysis of Melville Herskovits's ground-breaking study *The Myth of the Negro Past*. Herskovits's study brings to the fore the problem of how to explain the historical importance of the "middle passage" between Africa and the New World, and the correlative issue of "African survivals" in black music throughout the New World colonies. I also draw on Edith Wyschogrod's and Bruce Kapferer's respective uses of the notion of a "remythologization" to explain the purpose of Bechet's narrative and its significance for our understanding of black Americans' struggle for social and political recognition within industrializing America. For Wyschogrod and Kapferer, a remythologization pertains specifically to the historical logic of industrial society and to the ongoing systemic crisis for those excluded from, or struggling against, the material limits and the technobureaucratic determinations of the dominant state capitalist social order. A remythologization, in these terms, seeks to restore life, to overturn the "death space" of the slave system, and grasp the emancipatory powers of human being and human social practices as practices of making and remaking in time. It is, more than anything, a meditation on the collective structure of human artifacts.

By interweaving local folklore and legend, discussions of the music business and black society, by elaborating on kinship and musical lineages and reflecting on the transformative qualities of the slaves' and ex-slaves' musical acts, Bechet finds, in the musical practices of blacks and Creoles, the form of their social struggle to make sense of emancipation and give renewed meaning to their lives beyond the plantation system. Wyschogrod argues, however, that "this remythologization does not restore, nor can it restore, the mythological wholeness of pre-technological societies. It can only borrow from the material and spiritual culture available to it, treating the detritus of that culture as older mythic systems had treated natural existence."[31] Bechet's narrative, as I see it, is one such remythologization and, arguably, is crucial to understanding the collective virtuosity of the jazz act and the influence of the jazz act on other musical practices. It points to the struggle to define and value not only jazz practices among jazz musicians, but also the social and political context in which that struggle took place and was pursued.

While Bechet's jazz life raises the problem of the value of the slave, the impact of emancipation, and the musical consequences of freedom, the bebop saxophonist Charlie Parker was pivotal in directing jazz practices toward a radical self-consciousness of the jazz act and the act's implication in the making of black social practices that were specific to urban industrial society. While it cannot be in any way argued that Parker was solely responsible for this shift, his significance in terms of explaining the dynamic of jazz practices and social situations is overwhelming. Many pages have been devoted to Parker's musical adventures, not the least to his unruly, sad life. Most, however, alight on the brilliance of his playing, on his astounding capacity for improvised creativity, only to then turn, with tabloid fascination, to the intractable events of his short career. As one observer put it: "At 12, he was a man of the world. At 15, he was a heroin addict. At 20 he was master of his instrument. At 26, he was a mental and physical wreck. At 30, he was a living legend. At 35, he was dead."[32]

In the second chapter, my aim is to clarify the influence of Parker's practices in terms of key changes in American ideology and social consciousness, and to analyze the orienting force of his struggle, both with the limits of the jazz group and with the very possibilities for blacks to act creatively within the institutions and conditions of postwar American society.[33] While the use of such a source may seem unusual in a study of jazz, the late-nineteenth-century historian, Frederick Jackson Turner, features prominently in this chapter.[34] The ongoing preoccupation with the western frontier from the early days of the colonial era was used by progressive historians and politicians, from the 1860s, to identify the unique historical experience of the American people. This same preoccupation also underpinned the search for the practices and definitions of an American art adequate to the nature of such experiences. The later crisis (and, indeed, the paranoic intensification) of American ideology during the Cold War, of which Turner was an influential and exemplary antecedent, inflected on the meaning and value attributed to Parker's musical acts. If we are to explain the dynamic between jazz practices and industrial society, then a consideration of the influence and direction of Turner's argument and his role in articulating the limits and imperatives of American ideology at a time of great social and political crisis is essential.[35]

Turner's argument was notable for its insistence on the idea of repetition as the underlying principle of American capitalism. However, we must be precise about the ideological character of this repetition. To understand the movement of westward expansion one has to understand the proposition that the frontier, as the threshold of individual experience, was something that repeats itself to infinity in a multiplicity of contexts and modes, as an encounter between the free individual and the wilderness. Hence, Turner made it quite clear that the impending geographic closure of the western frontier—that is, the end of free land identified in the 1890 census—was a pivotal point in that it signaled the end of that on which the democratic experience relied for its perpetuity.[36] In Turner's understanding, the crisis of democracy that emerged from the closure of the frontier also marked the moment of transition to a new stage of historical, cultural, and thus, national development. The challenge was, as F. Scott Fitzgerald later described it, to find "a way out by flying, maybe our restless blood could find frontiers in the illimitable air."[37]

To identify the terms of such a transition, Turner argued for a theory of the state that privileged an American historical consciousness grounded in the struggle between the emergent forces of industrial capitalism and the disappearance of an original frontier "spirit." The form of this struggle, shaped by the individual's encounter with the geographical and the existential frontier, as well as the limits of the industrial state, was defined by Turner (and his progressive historical protégés such as Charles and Mary Beard) as the essence of the modern democratic experience. It was this experience that he subsequently reified within the structures of industrial productivity and governmental organization as the guiding principle of the free individual's social value and of the state's historical progress. And yet, while arguing that the history of American settlement was the "exemplar of the universal process of social evolution," Turner also sought a resolution to the antinomies of time against which that historical experience was formed and through which it gained legitimacy and permanency. In this sense, his theory granted a logical finality, an end to world history, concordant with the aims and assertions of a generation of progressive politicians, business leaders, educators, scientists, and the like, who invested their faith and their fortunes in the consolidation of monopoly capitalism, in the new modes of industrial production, and in the state's bureaucratic expansion.[38] Thus, the significance of Turner's schema in setting up the ideological terms of the American state's *material and spiritual limit* adds a further dimension to how we analyze the historical processes by which black musical acts were defined and valued.

From an analysis of the ideological dimension of Charlie Parker's jazz life, I turn my attention in chapter 3 to the alto saxophonist, Ornette Coleman, and, more generally, to the musical and situational problems that emerged for the generation of jazz musicians such as Cecil Taylor, Steve Lacy, Abby Lincoln, Max Roach, John Coltrane, Charles Mingus, Eric Dolphy, and so on, who began to dominate the avant-garde jazz scene in the 1950s and 1960s. In this final chapter, my aim is to grasp the situational dynamic and the musical structures of what is referred to as the free jazz act, and, in particular, the development and organization of Coleman's quartets and trios from 1959 to 1965. The massive economic, military, and political transformations in America after 1945 formed the conditions for a profound struggle over the meaning of human freedom in capitalist society. At stake in this struggle were the very *forms* of human creative action. The specific character of Coleman's musical ways challenged precisely those forms and the terms in which they were conceived and valued. Our task here is to define the creative character of the free jazz act, and to delineate in what sense and what terms (if any) free jazz involved a resistance to and transformation of its ideological frame.

A brief description of some of the analytical problems encountered in chapter 3 will clarify the social meaning of Coleman's musical ways but also suggest how they were related to those of Bechet and Parker. To begin with, I argue that the *form* of Coleman's jazz act was inseparable from the organization of a group of musicians who could play together with few, if any, of the melodic, harmonic, or rhythmic criteria normally identified with bebop, swing, or hot jazz. To explain this shift in jazz practices, I suggest that the virtuosity of the free jazz act extended, not only to the technical capacities of the players, but to the daunting problem for the musicians of where to start and how to end their performances. The challenge was to continue the act of musical making once the series of harmonic relations was displaced onto melodic development and the rhythm was no longer divided by a regular swing beat. In other words, the central problem for Coleman was to find the means to a melodic form and a unity of expression without recourse to the objective forms of jazz production. I suggest that in the very manner by which they de-structured and remade these objective forms, Coleman and his contemporaries offer remarkable insights into the processes and structuring of human actions and the forms of musical consciousness. Instead of merely demonstrating an innate capacity for self-expression—a purely subjective relation to the act—a critical analysis of Coleman's quartets and trios directs us toward the social conditions of musical action, that is, the long and difficult historical process in which jazz practices were fought for and won over time. Understood in this way, the virtuosity of the jazz act implies a monumental absorption by the musician in the collective structuring of the act, in terms of the relation to one's musical instrument, to the logic of the group's efforts, and to the form of what one hears of and in other's musical ways.[39]

This book proposes a theory of the jazz act, and involves a definition of the *form* of the act and the act's *historical conditions* of possibility. By conditions of possibility, I mean the particular historical conditions under which a new musical form is effectively produced and the process through which it acquires its social value.[40] In terms of the study of jazz, this process of social evaluation relies upon a crucial distinction between the jazz form and the jazz act, even though there is no form that does not also become an act, and vice versa. Thus, the jazz form is qualified or divided by the historical conditions in which the jazz act appears as such. The act, in this sense, is an attempt to realize the jazz form, which remains buried or virtual within the act as its existential limit, as its impossible-utopian point.[41] As Charles Rosen argues: "The music is only partially conceived in terms of what can be heard: it resists a complete translation into the audible."[42] The structure of this resistance means that the musical acts of Bechet, Parker, and Coleman are all accomplished within the same form—the jazz form. Thus, the basis of their historical relationship is one of *repetition* in terms of the musical material—the attempt to make the jazz form audible—and one of progress within the state—the political and economic struggle over the legitimacy of the jazz act.

The historical series that runs from the jazz acts of Bechet to Parker and then from Parker to Coleman is exemplified by two sociosymbolic orders: the ideological and the virtuosic. These two orders, as I have explained, are the objects of my analysis. Within the ideological order of the act, the history of jazz is defined by a continuity of "progression" that places an ultimate value on the individual's "jazz life" as the ideal *form* of the act. No jazz act is authentic that does not at the same time express the individual terms of the jazz life. As Nat Hentoff writes in *The Jazz Life:* "[t]he music reflects the man. . . ."[43] Thus, what differentiates the historical relation between each jazz life is the degree to which it is self-expressive; in other words, the jazz life is the very *form* of individual self-expression, of which the musical act is merely its medium.[44] In this way, the jazz act becomes a synonym for a privileged form of individual self-expression—the jazz life—that *in ideological terms* appears inevitable.[45] The result of applying such a progressive schema to the jazz life is to neutralize the very historical struggle from which the jazz form emerged and to suppress those elements interior to the act that do not reinforce the efficiency of the jazz life's ideological frame.

Contrary to the progressive schema of jazz history, I want to posit the significance of the second order of the act: the virtuosic order. From this perspective, it is the virtuosity of the act that articulates the practical relations—the logic of intentionality—between the jazz form and the jazz act. However, I have argued that all musical acts are, by definition, already ideological. The challenge to our theory, then, is *in what sense* the ideological and the virtuosic orders are related, and *in what terms* we can begin to grasp the dynamics of the act.

To this end, I follow LeRoi Jones's path-breaking study of black American music, *Blues People.* For Jones, the *sense* of the relation between the virtuosity of the act and ideology of the jazz life is one of an irreducible social antagonism, and the *terms* in which we must grasp the dynamics of this antagonism are those of the *blues impulse.* Jones states the problem in these terms: "The blues impulse was a psychological correlative that obscured the most extreme ideas of assimilation for most Negroes, and made any notion of the complete abandonment of traditional black culture an unrealizable possibility. In a sense, the middle class spirit could not take root amongst most Negroes because they sensed the final fantasy involved."[46] In Jones's analysis, the blues impulse was the barrier to the jazz act's assimilation to American "progressive" ideology, even though the pressure to assimilate was already a *possibility* inherent in the act. We can reformulate Jones's proposition in this way: through the blues impulse, the real antagonism of racial and class struggle in the United States was manifested *symbolically* in the effort to prevent assimilation, but in the sense that assimilation *had already taken place.* The external opposition of whites to blacks, the very form of the antagonism between black and white Americans, was already internal to the jazz act.[47]

As I mentioned at the outset, our critical work begins at the point of disjuncture between musical practices and their ideological context, that is, at what we will now identify as the act's impossible-utopian or nonideological point.[48] As stated above, the historical process that produces this disjuncture is that of the act's repetition. In other words, what is repeated in the jazz act is the *attempt* to actualize the jazz form under the specific historical conditions of a racist, capitalist society.[49] What is a stake in any act is its future form, but always in relation to an appeal to what that form *might have been* under different circumstances. The jazz form, therefore, is a virtual form and, as such, it is impossible to fully or adequately realize.[50] I use the concept *virtual* in the sense developed by the philosopher Susan Langer in her book *Feeling and Form*.[51] For Langer, all musical acts create "an order of virtual time, in which sonorous forms move in relation to each other," and which is unrelated to the conditions of their actual appearance.[52] This virtuality of the musical form is to be distinguished from the social logic of the musical act, from the sequence and structure of its actualization. In the course of being actualized, however, the virtual form is still inseparable from the movement of its actualization.[53]

The historical struggle to actualize (or symbolize) the jazz form—which is also already an ideological struggle between black and white Americans—constitutes the outer limit of the jazz musician's virtuosity. The force of this struggle creates a critical break in time, a moment of suspension, in which the jazz musician seizes on a blues impulse or "riff" as a mode of subjectification within the capitalist society.[54] The character of this impulse or riff—as a form of struggle *and* as a mode of subjectification—is critical to understanding the logic of American society's processes of assimilation and the ruling class's powers of domination.[55] What Jones calls the "blues impulse" is the very virtuosic dimension that enables the jazz musician to invent, through the repetition of his or her act, a new relationship to the act's social conditions of production. This is the sense for Jones in which black music is "always radical in the context of formal American culture."[56] A critical analysis of the jazz act relies upon a correct understanding of Jones's claim: it is not the jazz *act* that is radical; rather, it is the jazz *form* that is radical *in its very impossibility*. The jazz act, in this sense, is never radical enough.[57]

To grasp the dynamics of this relation between an act and its form, I argue that jazz is but a single, continuous form involving what I define below as three acts of virtuosity: the virtuosity of construction, or harmony; the virtuosity of speed, or rhythm; and the virtuosity of illusion, or melody.[58] The historical relation between Bechet, Parker, and Coleman is therefore as much *virtuosic* as it is *ideological*. Each musician repeats the founding gestures and figures of New Orleans jazz, but according to different instrumental and harmonic terms, and, thus, on the basis of a different virtuosic act: in Bechet's New Orleans hot jazz, the virtuosity of speed and that of illusion are subsumed into a radical virtuosity of *construction;* in Parker's bebop, the acts of construction and illusion depend on the virtuosity of *speed;* and finally, in the free jazz of Ornette Coleman, the construction and speed of the act are remade through the virtuosity of *illusion.* This triad of construction, speed, and illusion informs not only the structure of this book, but operates within the interior structure of the jazz act itself.

## Virtuosity and Human Creative Acts

Over the course of this book I define the social basis of the ways in which jazz musicians act on their musical material as the *virtuosity* of the jazz act, and I do so by attending to the development of a specifically musical consciousness. Three studies have guided my research into jazz virtuosity and musical consciousness: Elaine Scarry's *The Body in Pain,* David Sudnow's *Ways of the Hand,* and Jean Baudrillard's *Seduction.* Their combined influence, in dialogue with two fine ethnographic studies of jazz practices—Ingrid Monson's *Saying Something* and Paul Berliner's *Thinking in Jazz*—suggests that the dynamic and structure of the jazz act is to be found "in the historical particularity of the 'ensemble of social relations' and not in a particular form or ritual isolated from these."[59] That is, the *form* of the jazz act was made from the social "situating" and "orienting" of musical practices in time as an act of virtuosity. When I describe the virtuosity of the musical act, what I mean is the particular stance or attitude that gives the act its practical coherence and social meaning.[60]

Berliner has gone the farthest into this matter of virtuosity in relation to jazz, and it is in response to his work that much of the present one is addressed, although often indirectly. His concern, to chart the "learning, creativity, and the development of an extraordinary skill," intersects with the problems outlined below. I also build upon a definition provided by the contemporary Italian composer Luciano Berio. For Berio, "music cannot detach itself from gestures, techniques, ways of saying and doing—but it's not exhausted by them."[61] In his terms, a virtuosic act is made through the continual tension between "the musical idea and the instrument, between concept and musical substance."[62] In this sense, virtuosity refers to several dimensions of the musical act at once and is, in fact, constitutive of the act's social existence. To define a musical act as *virtuosic* is to point to particular historical conditions for human action that rely upon a musician's directing his or her imaginative, technical, physical, and musical capacities into a particular way or manner of musical making. In these terms, a distinction can be made between a musical virtuosity—that is, his or her skilled musical ways—and the virtuosic dimension to the musical act—that is, the social basis of the act. Neither aspect can be understood, however, without reference to the other.

The term *virtuosity*, of course, has acquired a somewhat pejorative sense, used to denote a heightened technical ability on the part of practitioners that appears mechanical at best, "soulless" at worst.[63] However, I want to argue that it is worth retaining and developing precisely this skilled sense of the act, if only to uproot naturalistic interpretations of musical production that privilege certain musical modes or scales as primordially given independently of human action and consciousness.

I now want to return to the authors acknowledged above to be influential in directing my work in this book and discuss how I use certain of their concepts to analyze the virtuosity of the jazz act. Scarry's study of the character of human acts of material making is one of the more remarkable books I have encountered in the course of my research. Her discussion of the dynamic and structure of torture, physical and mental pain, and the strategies of war pursued by modern states, followed by striking analyses of the Hebraic genesis myth and Marx's *Capital,* entails a critical procedure for analyzing forms of human action and sentience. In the study of human being and human intention, Scarry focuses on developing a "complete account of the interior structure of the act of creating as it is objectified and made knowable in the hidden interior of the created object."[64] Her work has directed me to the particular attitudes and the elaboration of values that constituted the making of the jazz artifact from the 1920s to the 1960s. It is from Scarry that I take the phrases "musical making" and "musical ways." Indeed, such descriptive phrases are essential to defining the existential arc of the jazz act and to establishing the act's larger significance within the processes of human material making.

The relation that underpins Scarry's analysis, and which will prove decisive for my own, is that established between act and object, between the processes of making and the object of that making. On this basis, I will argue that the virtuosity of the act constitutes the relation between the jazz musician's act of "making" and his or her skilled musical "ways," while at the same time constituting the social basis of the act, or, in other words, the act's objective meaning in history. The logic of these relations should, however, in no way appear intrinsic nor given. Rather, the virtuosity of the musical act arises from the effort to realize, in the very form of the act itself, the musical ways on which the act depends.

Turning to Sudnow's study of improvised conduct, his analysis, in its fine phenomenological detail, proved both invaluable and consistently challenging. It suggested how I might orient my analysis toward the materiality of the jazz act, but in terms of the sociohistorical conditions in which such acts unfold. At the same time, I decided to test Sudnow's terminology against that used by other jazz musicians to describe their own acts. To study the processes of "going for jazz," as I came to think of the work of making jazz, meant also finding a way to demonstrate the "indicative articulations of human practices."[65] Sudnow's concentration on the dynamics of the act, the bodily motions of musical playing, and the "protracted struggle" to learn to play well suggested how these articulations both oriented and were oriented by the historical and social framework in which jazz is made.

The title of this book—*Going for Jazz*—is drawn from Sudnow's book. Throughout his study, as with Scarry's analysis of pain and imagining, the emphasis on human agency and its relation to the discrete structures of musical activity was manifest in and modified by the human intent on the part of the act's practitioners. To use the word *going* underlines the intentions with which human beings have approached musical making in time; that is, the specific consciousness of musical practice that was formed in the process of wanting to make jazz, of learning to play jazz, and of trying to do it well—in other words, the processes of establishing its value as a social practice. At the same time, I use the term *going* to invoke the situational limits of the musical act. In other words, in going for jazz, a musician, when he or she decides to play a musical instrument, or sing, or beat out a rhythm, comes to that decision as part of a complex field of choices, beliefs, and assumptions about the value and purpose of musical acts that are already, at a conscious and an unconscious level, socially and politically determinant and orienting. To encompass the making of jazz, and the structures of feeling through which such acts of making occur, within the intentional trajectory of "going for jazz," is to stress the social context of the act. The skilled ways of the jazz musician's musical making, the motivations for his or her musical acts, and the values attached to this kind of making and acting all emerged in relation *to* something.[66] As Scarry asserts, it "is impossible to imagine without imagining something."[67]

My argument, then, is that the meaning and value of the jazz act is inseparable from the intentional aspects and the changing character of the musician's social and political relations in time. In pursuing this argument, I take up Scarry's further point that the "making of an artifact is a social act, for the object (whether an art work or an object of everyday use) is intended as something that will both enter into and itself elicit human responsiveness."[68] This process of entering into and eliciting human responsiveness thus constitutes the outer limits of the act's "intentional frame" and the basis of its objectification.

Throughout *Ways of the Hand,* Sudnow's aim is to clarify "the nature of the human body and its creations."[69] His method for undertaking such an analysis is to describe the relationship of his own hands to the piano keyboard and, thus, to document and explain how his everyday hands became his piano-playing hands:

> . . . I want to offer a close description of the handicraft
> of improvisation, of the knowing ways of the jazz body. I
> want to review the acquisition of jazz hands, on the way
> toward the closer study of the human body and its works:
> in jazz piano playing we have an occasion of handicraft of
> elaborate, elegant dimensions, a fitting place to explore
> perhaps our most distinctly human "organ."[70]

The historical movement from a person's early efforts to play jazz to his or her acquisition of jazz-playing hands constitutes the interior structure of what I seek to analyze in the musical practices of Bechet, Coleman, and Parker. At the same time, I locate those practices in relation to the larger social and ideological framework of the jazz act.

As I have explained, the term I use to denote musical agency is *virtuosity,* and its social form is denoted by the *virtuosic act.* Some further clarification of the term is in order, however. Aside from Berliner and Monson, scant attention in other than the most general terms has been paid to this dimension of the jazz act. But an essay on the pianist Glenn Gould by Edward Said is of help. For Said, Gould's virtuosic performance was one of *extreme occasion:* "Gould always seemed to achieve a seamless unity among his fingers, the piano, and the music he was playing, one working by extension *into* the other, the three becoming indistinguishable from start to finish. It was as if Gould's virtuosity finally derived its fluency from the piece and not from a residue of technical athleticism built up independently over the years."[71] And yet, this very process of bodily extension also hints at the ambiguous status of the virtuosic act: "The orchestral piece that begins [Richard] Wagner's only comic opera [*Die Meistersinger*] is seen by Gould as no conductor or orchestra has ever played it: it becomes a compendium of eighteenth century contrapuntal writing displayed for an audience with a sort of anatomical glee by Gould, who plays the piece with such a neat virtuosity as to make you forget that human hands are involved."[72]

We can summarize the ambiguity of the act in this way: while the musician's virtuosity relies upon the inner complexities and sentient tissue of the "piano-playing hands," his or her musical act's expressive power derives from the subsumption of those same hands into the interior of the act.[73] Pierre Boulez explains this process of subsumption by dividing the musical form into the three acts of virtuosity I have already described: the virtuosity of construction (the ways of musical making), the virtuosity of speed (the skilled musical ways), and the virtuosity of illusion (the music's social value).[74] And again, each virtuosic act likewise corresponds to a specific musical dimension: construction to the harmonic or sonorous dimension; speed to the dimension of rhythm; and illusion to the dimension of melody, which in turn emerges from the distribution of harmonic and rhythmic material. To be considered so, a musical performance requires all three virtuosic acts to occur *simultaneously*. It is thus the specific concentration of each act through the effort of musical making that then defines the musician's relationship to a musical form.

Said's argument can be restated in this way: to define a virtuosic performance as an "extreme occasion" refers to the particular concentration of these virtuosic acts in relation to the given musical form. At the same time, the concentration of the three acts into a single performance alters the intentional frame of the event itself. Far from preceding the act, the musician's virtuosity appears as a consequence of the act, as internal to the act's form. The musician now feels as if he or she is being acted upon by the musical form, that, in an uncanny sense, he or she is being played. In a critical passage, Sudnow describes the reversal of his musical sense, and the subsequent objectification of his hands: "I see my hands for the first time now as 'jazz piano player's hands,' and at times, when I expressly think about it, one sense I have from my vantage point looking down is that the fingers are making the music all by themselves."[75] Indeed, the process by which his "jazz piano player's hands" are subsumed into Sudnow's jazz act informs the very structure of his text.

The first part of *Ways of the Hand* is taken up with finding the melodic and harmonic pathways specific to his ways of piano playing. He focuses on the movement from note to note, from chord to chord, and from musical phrase to musical phrase. In this section, Sudnow describes the ways in which his hands perform the "voicing" of chords, their adherence to tempo, the bringing of his hands' connective tissue into action, and the arraying of his fingers along the keyboard. Slowly, he begins to develop a certain attitude or stance in relation to the piano—his body's "way of handfully being in the terrain." Finally, he recognizes that he is playing the instrument in "jazz ways."[76] "Doing melodying, going for particularly pitched transactions, in this phase of play thus had a characteristic unevenness, 'me' trying to have the hands say this in particular, the hands saying something of what I took them to say but not everything, and then saying things of their own rather inappropriate choosing."[77] This notion of "melodying" conveys in a precise sense a form that is only ever realized through the relations of the act to its own conditions of making; in other words, the musician's "melodying" is the virtuosic power of the act returning to itself.

The second part of Sudnow's study focuses on the practice of "going for jazz," of putting his "melodying" to work. After years of trying to develop the "right" course of musical action and the "right" set of procedures for making the hands work well in jazz ways, Sudnow describes how, in a certain course of pianistic action or certain musical phrases, "I saw jazz piano player's hands a bit at a time."[78] This part of his book turns on an encounter Sudnow had with the pianist Jimmy Rowles in a New York City bar. From his isolated efforts at practicing, Sudnow describes how the virtuosity of the jazz act emerged, in the end, out of the social structuring of Rowles's actions:

> Listening to him, taking notice for the first time of ways
> of moving at the keyboard, beginning to play slow music,
> bringing attention for the first time, peculiar as it was and
> so much a part of my isolation from the occupation, to a
> careful regard for the presentation of a song, giving that
> sort of a care to the beat which his bodily idiom displayed,
> I began to develop a fundamentally different way of being
> at the piano.[79]

Few discussions contain such a "lived" sense of the interior dynamics of jazz practice, and even fewer enliven our understanding of how the processes of musical making have actually eventuated over time. For this reason, I consider a number of Sudnow's terms essential for delineating how the making of the jazz act is created and subsequently transformed by its virtuosic appearance. His argument that "there is no melody, only melodying," is particularly apt in terms of describing the logic and intent of the musician's virtuosic ways, as is his argument that to "get the time into the fingers, hands, shoulders, everywhere, was to develop mobile ways with the terrain. . . ."[80] The dynamic interplay between timing and melodying, between the purposive motions of the hands and the determined conditions of the musician's skilled musical ways, accentuates Sudnow's claim that "to define jazz (as to define any phenomenon of human action) is to describe the body's ways."[81] Embarking on such a process of definition has led to the present analysis of Bechet, Parker, and Coleman.

Taking up Jean Baudrillard's analysis in his book *Seduction,* I argue for the virtuosic motions of the musical act as the art and practice of seduction.[82] While what follows in this regard is in no way a thorough-going commentary on Baudrillard's analysis, nor even an adequate critique, I find much in his work to be deeply suggestive. In short, Baudrillard opposes the art and practice of seduction to the vast, inexorable logic of capitalist accumulation, progress, growth, production.[83] These seductive arts and practices are, however, constantly endangered, threatened by their own entanglement with power, with the law, with desire, and with their contradictions; in other words, with their relation to historical struggle. Social historians offer substantial evidence for how and by whom musical acts were made, while musicologists rely upon a glossary of persuasive terms for understanding the formal properties of the work itself. However, practitioners of both often resort to abstractions or caricature when asked to explain in more detail the relations between the processes of musical making and the formal structures of musical virtuosity. Mindful of these theoretical weaknesses, Baudrillard's analysis enables me to explain the active tension between the historical effort that constitutes the act's musical making and the musician's musical ways, and the radical artifice of the act's virtuosic appearance, or what Boulez calls the virtuosity of illusion.

In *Seduction,* we find a terminology for defining this virtuosic illusion: the critical moment when the jazz act appears to consume and denounce the very conditions in which it is made. Thus, against the historical eventuation of the act's making there

> is neither a time of seduction, nor a time for seduction, but
> still it has its indispensable rhythm. Unlike instrumental
> strategies, which proceed by intermediary stages, seduction
> operates instantaneously, in a single movement, and is
> always its own end. . . . The cycle of seduction cannot
> be stopped. One can seduce someone in order to seduce
> someone else, but also seduce someone else to please
> oneself. The illusion that leads from the one to the other

is subtle. Is it to seduce, or to be seduced, that is seductive? But to be seduced is the best way to seduce. It is an endless refrain. There is no active or passive mode in seduction, no subject or object, no interior or exterior: seduction plays on both sides, and there is no frontier separating them. One cannot seduce others, if one has not oneself been seduced.[84]

By focusing on how the arts and practices of seduction are constituted through "an endless refrain," Baudrillard provides the terms for grasping the virtuosic dimension of the musical act and its complex relation to the circumstances and intentions—that is, the ideological conditions—of the jazz musician's making and going.[85]

This relation, between the real historical conditions of musical production and the seductive motions of the jazz act, leads us to ask what it means to act *musically* in a capitalist social order. All the great historical accounts of the "jazz life"—from LeRoi Jones to Lewis Erenberg—demonstrate unequivocally the effects of racism, capitalist production, and mass consumption on the jazz act. Indeed, the development of the "Fordist" logic of the American state and the creation of jazz are, as David Stowe's study of "swing ideology" so clearly demonstrates, inseparable.

What these studies miss, however, is some further account of the *form* of the social struggle waged within the act itself; that what is at stake, in each attempt at musical action, is the very framework that determines the act's *musicality.* This struggle is, in every sense, an ideological struggle, but also one of virtuosity, such that the act's musicality is, in every instance, purposive and yet undecided, oriented and yet unknown. Indeed, what is at stake is the jazz act's *radical impossibility,* by which I mean "a structure that can never be realized in sound."[86] Indeed, this realm of impossibility constitutes the seductive logic of the act, such that this logic has no way of being properly articulated *outside* the prevailing ideological-political framework. At yet, it is precisely this seductive logic that disturbs the social unconscious that supports this underlying ideological-political framework, and thus changes the very parameters of what is considered musically "right."[87] This was what the pianist Thelonious Monk meant when, unhappy with an improvisation, he finished it with the statement: "I made the wrong mistakes."[88] Monk's statement exemplifies the virtuosity of illusion through which the *form* of the jazz act effects its own seductive ways. This virtuosity short-circuits the ideological efficiency of the process whereby the jazz act is required to both reflect and contribute to the material productive capacity of the American state. The jazz act, by Monk's definition, is already a mistake, is already "impossible," within the conditions of its own making.[89] Understood in this way, the jazz act no longer refers to the reality to which it is forced to correspond, but to the *form* of the struggle with that reality. In the section below, I take up the form of that struggle within the act in terms of the ideology of the American state.

## Ideology

In the *Phenomenology of Perception,* Maurice Merleau-Ponty argues that "there is history only for a subject who lives through it, and a subject only in so far as he [or she] is historically situated."[90] Into this movement, between a conscious subject and his or her historical situation, Merleau-Ponty inserts a "lived ambiguity"—the dynamics of social existence—that works to destabilize those attempts to reify either the historical situation or the individual subject as privileged objects of analysis.[91] Given this understanding, the study of the making of jazz practices and jazz acts produces a "lived ambiguity" in relation to three fundamental aspects of American history: the struggle between masters and slaves; the influence of the frontier on American historical consciousness; and the significance of musical practices to questions of human freedom. Each of these constitutes an existential limit against which the jazz act is continually pitched, and in relation to which the act acquires social and historical meaning. The combined effect of these historical dimensions on the form of the jazz act is to mark out the existential horizons of American exceptionalist ideology.

In analyzing American exceptionalism I explain the ways in which that ideology "interpellates" itself at the level of jazz production. The term *interpellate* is used by the philosopher Louis Althusser to refer to the demand placed on the social subject by an ideology, but also its role in generating subjectivity itself.[92] What I refer to throughout the text as the "jazz life" is, quite simply, the existential form of this interpellation, while the concept of self-expression is the *differential* through which the value of the act is generated and against which it is measured. In other words, the jazz life is the existential mode through which exceptionalist ideology is materialized in jazz musical practices, and through which those same practices acquire a social meaning determined by the institutional forms of the American state and its capitalist relations of production. Broadly speaking, the jazz life is, in the words of the critic Nat Hentoff, "the total existence of its players."[93] Upon closer inspection, however, such statements generally function to neutralize the specific critical and historical terms of their discussion. Thus, we must not confuse the conception of the jazz life and its relation to self-expression, which we wish to define and analyze, with a single theory about its form and contents. In short, our definition of the jazz life cannot properly assume those same ideological elements toward which our analysis is directed.

The impetus for an ideological critique as I use it extends from Karl Marx and Friedrich Engels in *The German Ideology,* through a range of critical and historical arguments. The effect of these is to explain the social basis of human consciousness *as a form of social struggle,* and to develop a critical analysis of how and for whose benefit social practices are valued and enforced within a given historical order or epoch.[94] At stake in these analyses, therefore, are the practices of power and consciousness through which human relations are constituted, and on the basis of which specific means and relations of production and domination are legitimated and maintained within a social order. An ideological critique thus takes for its object the form of the social struggle as it is produced in human consciousness through the dominant relations of production. By this, I mean the *form or specific manner of the relation* between "the social agents of production" on the one hand, and the "material means of production" on the other.[95] This social struggle is not to be confused with those notions of "intersubjectivity" or pluralism that privilege individual agency as the primary mode of human exchange.[96] In fact, in the conclusion to this book, I propose a critique of the intersubjective or pluralist model of social relations of production as it is applied to the jazz act.[97]

My aim is to find, in the *form* of the musician's relation to the American state, the imaginary and symbolic foundations of the jazz act's reality. In this view, ideology is materialized in a range of ideological practices, forms, and institutions that function to naturalize the social mechanisms that regulate its efficiency.[98] While precedents for this type of critical approach are abundant in other areas of American historiography—one immediately thinks here of Richard Slotkin, Eugene Genovese, Eric Foner, Barbara Fields, and Joel Kovel—there has been little significant consideration on the part of scholars of jazz. In following this line of analysis, I have relied upon the arguments developed by Slavoj Žižek in *The Sublime Object of Ideology.* Žižek's analysis is of particular interest here because it argues that what creates and sustains the identity of a given ideological edifice, beyond all its possible variations, is the domain of the unconscious.[99] In other words, what is usually left out of ideological analysis is "the level on which ideology structures social reality itself."[100] My argument then is that ideology is the *historical* systemization of human consciousness. It is the way that social subjects in different historical contexts orient·their social practices, their desires, their attitudes and values, and so give productive meaning to their lives as situated subjects of a given social order.

Under this view, the task of an ideological analysis of the jazz act is to demonstrate how the historical processes of musical making are worked out in the virtuosic struggle between the forms of American exceptionalist ideology and the material forces of the American state, and what elements bring unity to this ideological field. That the ideological form is more than just a misrecognition of the facts on the part of human subjects (which the historian can then happily correct), that the ideological form in fact structures the very reality to which we refer, means that we cannot avoid the ideological conditions of the jazz act. But nor can we define the act as a mere reflection of those conditions. A fundamental purpose is to establish how the social struggles that centered on slavery, the frontier, and freedom formed the existential horizon for jazz acts and oriented the musical ways of jazz musicians. To do this is to demonstrate that not only does each of these specific ideological configurations constitute a *given element* in the larger framework of American exceptionalist ideology, but that each element, like the human acts on which it confers ideological meaning and value, also transforms the reality on which it depends.

So when I refer to the ideology of slavery, or the frontier, or that of human freedom, I mean all the various social practices and institutions, the ideas and emotions, that cluster around these terms and produce their ideological form as the form *most like America,* but I mean as well to refer to an irreducible dimension that cannot but exceed that very likeness. In taking up each of these ideological elements, I have been influenced by Richard Slotkin's trilogy on the myth of the frontier in American history. In particular, I follow his assertion that "the different forms in which ideology is voiced have their own special powers and properties, which affect the substance of the ideological communication and the way in which it will be received."[101] Slotkin's reference to the special powers and properties of ideology offers a means of grasping the dynamic relation between the immediate properties of human action and the existential powers that frame and, in fact, orient those properties. It is to these special powers and properties that I wish to direct my attention.

As I have said, each chapter corresponds to a specific ideological element as it is materialized in the "jazz life" of a musician. The difficulty for historical analysis resides, however, in clearly discerning the relations between the individualized "jazz life" and the ideological-symbolic formations through which that life is interpellated as a subjective position. To address this difficulty, each chapter is structured to proceed dialectically between the making of a given musical act and its ideological-symbolic frame. I suggested at the outset that this kind of analysis requires consideration of the *process* of mediation, a process that is usually ignored in formal musicological analysis or suppressed in more descriptive musical history. The process of mediation can best be understood, in Fredric Jameson's terms, as the means to an *indirect* or *disjunctive* connection "between the various series of phenomena, or the various levels of data (the psychological, the oratorical, the political, the economic, the geographical, and so forth) of which a given historical event is composed."[102] In this instance, the task of the critical or dialectical analysis of the jazz act is to demonstrate in what sense the *form* of the relations between the various series of musical and social phenomena or the various levels of data is already internal to the jazz act itself.

Accordingly, I define the making of the jazz act in relation to the ideological form of American exceptionalism as part of a chain of ideological significations that encompasses the influence of slavery, the closing of the western frontier, and the idea of freedom. The identification of this chain permits me to grasp how the act's reification—as a privileged mode of individual self-expression and as a function of mass culture—also mystifies its social and historical value. The articulation of an ideological frame, however, should not be confused with the social logic of which the ideological frame is a specific dimension. Although the ideological frame is constitutive of social reality as such, it is not just another term for social reality. Indeed, it is crucial to my argument to recognize that an analysis of American ideology is not a reduction of the act to the merely subjective and to the status of a psychological projection of the surrounding reality.[103] It is only by showing how the very struggle to make music is thoroughly embroiled in and activated by the larger struggles of human society that we can appreciate the "moment of suspension," the virtuosic moment, when the jazz artifact emerges from the endless multitude of symbolic forms.

Having posited a relation between an act's virtuosic and ideological dimensions, I now want to clarify what is meant by the term *American exceptionalism*. I use the term to denote the ideological doctrine of the state that emerged after the American Revolution and through which Americans have framed their sense of republican destiny.[104] A fascination with this exceptionalism has dominated the study of American history and society. How this notion of an exceptional liberal capitalist state informed, and was itself formed by, the identification and legitimation of jazz practices and jazz performances depends on positing a shift in the dynamic of social practices and social consciousness. The structure of this shift is linked to specific social and historical conditions of industrial labor, a centralized economy, and mass consumption that characterized American life in the 1920s.[105] To paraphrase an early critic, jazz, like cinema and the dollar bill, was recognized as one of the privileged signs of American power.[106] The basis for this recognition is the common view that the history of jazz "parallels the course of 20th century American history with eerie accuracy."[107] As I argue, however, the actual basis of this relation between jazz and the state is an ideological *and* a virtuosic one that deserves further investigation.

The phrase *American exceptionalism* constitutes the outer limit, the ontological horizon, that organizes the formation and perpetuity of the American state. The field of ideological meaning specific to this state is characterized by several recurrent symbolic forms within the exceptionalist framework. Each of these symbolic forms functions to bring an ideological efficiency to the historical reality of which it is constitutive, to transform the discrete and contingent historical circumstances of European conquest and settlement in the New World into a universal, self-evident ideology of American global power. This ideology of the America state is not, however, monolithic, but rather the form and object of a continuous social struggle over those same historical conditions. American exceptionalism thus refers to both the *historical process* of European settlement in the New World and the mythico-ideological *explanation* for the social and political forms produced by that historical process.

The central assumption on which the American ideological system is based is that of the exceptional role of "America" in the history of seventeenth- and eighteenth-century European imperial expansion. As Slotkin argues, the

> root of American exceptionalism rests on the fact that
> American society originated in a set of colonies, abstracted
> and selected out of the nations of Europe, and established
> in a "wilderness" far removed from the home countries.
> These colonies in turn were able to expand into the
> continent by reproducing themselves in subcolonial
> settlements, projected at a distance and abstracted from
> their own body politic. The American colonists therefore
> had a special relationship to the processes of development
> that were modernizing their European homelands. . . .
> Local factions arose out of economic and political

interests peculiar to the colonies' select composition and
physical circumstances, and these were often of more
importance in the shaping of government policy than
the partisan differences of the home country. Moreover,
these colonial governments had to contend not only with
competing local interest groups, but with two external
centers of power: the Metropolitan government and the
native tribes.[108]

How the logic of competing interests and relations of production among
the colonists was transformed into a symbology powerful enough to constitute a revolutionary consciousness, and then to provide the symbolic
forms and conceptual terms adequate to the formation and organization
of a liberal capitalist state, is the critical ideological problem for American
studies. In other words, any study of the American state must address the
structures of belief underlying the conception of that state as both an exceptional object of desire and a primary means to subjective legitimation.
In *The Rites of Assent,* Sacvan Bercovitch offers a precise summary of the
form of this ideological belief:

> It was a web spun out of scriptural myth and liberal
> ideology that allowed virtually no avenue of escape.
> Technology and religion, individualism and social
> progress, spiritual, political, and economic values—all the
> fragmented aspects of life and thought in this pluralistic
> society flowed into "America," the symbol of cultural
> consensus; and then, in a ritual balance of anxiety and
> reaggregation, flowed outward again to each independent
> unit of society.[109]

Bercovitch defines American exceptionalism as a "ritual of consensus."[110] Since the American Revolution in 1776, the forms in which
such a ritual is cast, and the limitations of a consensual order on human
actions, has determined the social and political value of those actions.
At the same time, this consensual order diffuses the transgressive power
of the act in the name of transgression itself. For Bercovitch, the ritual
of consensus is thus constitutive of social and political acts in the sense
that, through its very structure, it restricts the terms of any social struggle, "symbolically *and substantially,* to the meaning of America."[111] Even
transgression, or dissent (as Bercovitch calls it), is maintained by the state's
ideological frame as a principle of social cohesion. In fact, the "very act of

identifying malfunction becomes an appeal for cohesion."[112] The result is that "American ideology has achieved a hegemony unequaled elsewhere in the modern world."[113]

The symbolic and substantive form of the American exceptionalist framework relies upon a "chain of signifiers" for its ideological meaning.[114] Underlying the logic of consensus, and yet constituted by that same consensus, is the unchallenged primacy of the propertied individual, the metaphysics of self-interest and independent selfhood, and a faith in the creative powers of human reason and endeavor. This progressive "individualism"—what Christopher Lasch termed "American progressivism"—was not only subsumed within the redemptive focus of the Massachusetts Puritan's "errand in the wilderness," but it was suffused with the primal myth of the frontier as the site of human regeneration and dependent on an immovable belief in the ascendant powers of Anglo-American bourgeois civilization.[115] The object of this progressive individualism was freedom, and the means to this freedom was a social contract—the legal contents of the liberal democratic state—that mediated the unruly passions and conflicts of self-interest through an equality of opportunities. In was out of these historical conditions that the colonial state built its ideological power and legitimacy, and through which it institutionalized the laws of capitalist exchange and a "natural identity of interests."[116]

In the wake of the American Revolution, however, the basis of that ideological power and legitimacy was centered on the concrete level of the struggle over slavery, the influence of the frontier on American consciousness, and the definition of human freedom. What we find materialized in each of these historical elements is an argument concerning the very ideological character of the modern American state: (1) the struggle over slavery exemplifies the *form* of social relations within the order of capitalist production; (2) the influence of the frontier on American consciousness refers to the *form* of the capitalist state itself, that is, to its material and spiritual limits; (3) and, finally, the value of freedom constitutes the *form* of the relation between human action and human consciousness within such a capitalist state. As I have said, each chapter of this book will analyze one of these elements as constitutive of a musician's jazz life. This is not to say that any one of them is prior to the others. Rather, each is simultaneously taken as an effect of the jazz life to which it refers, and as the ideological form through which the jazz musician transforms his or her subjective relation to the state.

My understanding of the term *state* is informed by the work of the political philosophers Antonio Negri and Michael Hardt, but also by

Bruce Kapferer's discussion of Sinhalese sorcery practices in *The Feast of the Sorcerer* and Pierre Clastre's study *Society against the State.*[117] When I use the word *state,* therefore, I do not simply mean governmental agencies or various institutions of bureaucratic organization. As Kapferer argues, the "*state* refers to a complex of dynamics that are part of formal organizations of government that will be described as states. But the term *state* applies to dynamics of power that can be discovered or repeated in other structures that may or may not be relevant to state political organization as such."[118] In other words, the term *state* denotes a modality of power that is permeated by, but also permeates, other modalities of power and being, and other historical acts and social structures. A historical analysis of the form of the state, therefore, is not simply an explanation of a particular style of government nor of the personalities of politicians. Rather, such an analysis seeks to explain the universal workings of power and its relation to human consciousness in terms of social and political practices. Given this understanding, the state form is neither the natural destiny of every society, nor simply an effect of power, but is part of the lived dynamic of human organization and hence integral to the making and remaking of human acts.[119]

To suggest a fundamental relation among the jazz act, American historical consciousness, and the state requires a critical appraisal of black music in terms of industrial modes of production and the dynamics of American social life since 1865. The study of black music, like other creative practices, can lead to profound insights into how social consciousness is formed and how human beings constitute their social and political realities. To further refine the theoretical framework for this analysis, I want to examine the level at which musical practices articulate ideological and ontological assumptions and, at the same time, I intend to demonstrate that these very ideological and ontological assumptions continually transform the practices through which they gain their conscious reality and historical specificity. The structures and structuring of social acts is denoted by the phrase *the logic of practice,* which refers to the ways in which human actions and modes of consciousness intersect to constitute a practical and orienting consciousness of the social world.[120]

Attention to the "practical logics" specific to the history of jazz practices requires that we must also define what is meant by *a practice* and its relation to the historical eventuation of a *practical consciousness.* Pierre Bourdieu's argument is a useful starting point: "Practice unfolds in time. . . . Its temporal structure, that is, its rhythm, its tempo, and above all its directionality, is constitutive of its meaning. . . . In short, because it is entirely immersed in the current of time, practice is inseparable from temporality, not only because it is played out in time, but also because it plays strategically with time and especially with tempo."[121] Bourdieu's argument demonstrates the significance of concepts of rhythm and tempo to our understanding of how musical practices are transformed by, and transformative of, human consciousness and human actions.[122]

To define the specific logic of jazz practices involves close attention to the meaning and value of jazz in the political economy of American society. A study of jazz that fails to address the system of which jazz is an integral part fails both jazz musicians and critical analysis. As Fredric Jameson argues, "[E]ach system—better still, every 'mode of production'—produces a temporality that is specific to it. . . ."[123] To analyze the *creative character* of the jazz act, and to grasp that character through the historical logic that produced such creative acts, is the task ahead of us.[124]

# 1    Sidney Bechet

## The Virtuosity of Construction

> [T]he history of humanity consists of innumerable passages
> from slavery to freedom.
>
> Roberto Rossellini

In his autobiography *Treat It Gentle,* New Orleans jazz saxophonist Sidney Bechet outlines the making and remaking of musical practices by freed blacks living in the American South between 1865 and 1900.[1] His narrative also situates black Americans' musical activities within a larger cosmogony that anticipated, in the creative practices of the black musician, a fundamental renewal of American life and culture. In this sense, *Treat It Gentle* is as much a narrative about the making of a black consciousness as it is about the origins and essence of the jazz musical act. Bechet's effort to understand how the passage from slavery to freedom was lived and transformed by blacks provides a social and mythical counterpoint to the historical dynamics of emancipation, the gains and failures of Reconstruction and, finally, the institutional racism and state violence of the post–Civil War period in American history.

In this chapter, I argue that Bechet's narrative enables us to understand, precisely, how the making of jazz practices in New Orleans during the 1880s and 1890s intersected with the ideological framework of the American state. I also suggest that *Treat It Gentle* crystallizes the social logic through which a new unity of the musical act is produced. I define this social logic as the *virtuosity of construction* and the new unity of the act as the *jazz form.* As I hoped to make clear in the introduction, the making of the jazz act and its relation to social situations is a major concern of this book. The ideological basis of this relation cannot be detached from further consideration of the political and social problems confronting blacks in the South after 1865, and particularly, how the masses of freed men and women were effectively recomposed and reoriented, primarily by legislative and economic coercion after the Civil War, into a new laboring class of wage-dependent sharecroppers and artisans.[2] As Eric Foner argues, for the "large majority of blacks who did not fulfill the dream of independence as owners or renters, the plantation remained an arena of ongoing conflict."[3] Our attention here is directed toward how the form of the jazz act that emerged in New Orleans between the 1880s and 1900 was situated within and as a consequence of this conflict, and how that form was indeed a means of challenging and shifting the prevailing terms of such conflict.

Several late-nineteenth-century popular and traditional musical practices contributed to the structuring and orientation of the early jazz act. The influence of these practices on jazz has been more than adequately addressed by several fine studies such as Burton W. Peretti's *The Creation of Jazz,* William J. Schafer's *Brass Bands and New Orleans Jazz,* and Donald Marquis's *In Search of Buddy Bolden,* among others.[4] However, a brief summary of these nineteenth-century practices is useful at this point because it details the range of musical possibilities that Bechet encountered in and around New Orleans, from which he gained a sense of how, with whom, and under what conditions he could attempt to play music. Of the numerous musical styles, the blues, ragtime, and the minstrel songs—with their emphasis on polyphony and syncopation—were the direct precursors to jazz, capturing the interest of large segments of the rural and urban black populations (both as practitioners and audiences). Likewise, the prevalence of the local brass bands in nineteenth-century American cities and towns provided a comprehensive model, among blacks as much as whites, for musical training in a variety of techniques and styles. After the Civil War, the popularity of the minstrel shows, circuses, medicine shows, and religious revivals across the southern and the western states produced a new class of mostly itinerant, and often highly skilled, black musicians. These musicians' careers usually began on the road with the traveling companies, and just as likely ended up in particular towns or villages as church organists, opera house accompanists, or band leaders.[5] It was from the marching bands and touring orchestras, however, whose many performative practices intersected with a whole range of social events—from festivals to funerals—and whose musical dynamics established the precedents of ensemble playing, that the early jazz players would draw most. As Schafer points out, in New Orleans "the brass band was a powerful influence on the new jazz music that developed around 1900. Brass bands gave jazz its instrumentation, its instrumental techniques, its basic repertoire. Habits and attitudes of brass bandsmen carried into jazz, shaping its music for decades after it was apparently dissociated from the military tradition."[6]

New Orleans was a notoriously musical town. By the 1800s, a range of "cultivated" middle class and "vernacular" working class musical practices were in abundance in the city, as were the numbers of ensembles, organizations, and societies—some amateur, some professional—devoted to musical performance and appreciation.[7] Black and Creole musicians of all classes were involved in a range of musical events, from the ring shouts in the churches to the Congo Square slave dances, to European opera, concert music, the 'Quadroon Balls, and the many annual parades. The end of the Civil War, however, brought about a number of significant changes for the city's musicians, particularly regarding with whom, and what kind of music, they played. One such change was prompted by the wide availability of Confederate army band instruments, provoking a fashion for brass instruments and bands; another by the huge influx of rural blacks into New Orleans' three already overcrowded and segregated black districts.[8] As Schafer argues, the "stimulus of Emancipation, the prolonged presence of Federal troops and military bands in the city, the promise of social and political equality for black people contributed to the style and content of the music."[9]

The promise of the Reconstruction period in the South (1867–1877) was short lived, destroyed by segregation legislation (the Jim Crow laws), by a hostile and remobilized white planter class, by waves of antiblack violence among poor and lower class whites, by economic depression and chronic unemployment, and by the massive expansion of industrial modes of production in the North. The social impact of the various Jim Crow regimes—both at the state and federal level— transformed every facet of post–Civil War black life, including the social conditions in which musicians played and on which they depended for livelihood.[10] By the 1880s, forms of racist legislation were entrenched by city and state politicians, by businesses, and by an aggressive judiciary, such that the employment opportunities for black and Creole musicians were increasingly limited to particular audiences and venues.[11] As Peretti notes, black musicians "could play in certain downtown regions, but were kept out of many halls and saloons, and black customers were strictly segregated into clubs in all-black neighborhoods. Creoles were caught in a marginal state somewhere . . . between racial and economic polar opposites."[12]

The making of the first jazz practices thus occurred in a period of great social and political transition in the dynamic of the capitalist state and in the lives of blacks as they sought to reposition themselves, and were in turn positioned, in relation to the institutional practices and productive forces of the state. How we analyze the historical basis of this transition in the South, from a slave-labor to a wage-labor society, from agrarian capitalism to industrial capitalism, will in turn affect how we analyze the making of jazz practices, and vice versa. As E. P. Thompson argues, the stress of the transition from one social order to another "falls on the whole culture: resistance to change and assent to change arise from the whole culture. And this culture expresses systems of power, property-relations, religious institutions, etc., inattention to which merely flattens phenomena and trivializes analysis."[13] Thus, to prevent such a flattening and trivialization of the social order, it is crucial to analyze how the social dynamic of the passage from slave labor to industrial labor shaped conceptions of human action in the postwar South, and how such conceptions reoriented and reframed musical practices and consciousness.

In this chapter, I define *Treat It Gentle* as a mythic text, intended to account for just such a reorienting and reframing of human action. I also want to argue that the narrative structure itself offers profound insights into the structures of belief and consciousness that inform the dynamics of the jazz act. To this end I have cast Bechet's narrative as a form of "remythologization," a concept that, as I pointed out in the introduction, is taken from the work of Edith Wyschogrod and Bruce Kapferer. While each uses the notion in a very specific sense—Wyschogrod for her study of human-made mass death and Kapferer in his analysis of state and insurrectionary violence in Sri Lanka—the combined effect of their usage helps demonstrate the critical role of jazz autobiography in situating and legitimizing the experiences of black musicians, particularly vis-à-vis the ideological forms of the American state. As an example of a remythologization, *Treat It Gentle* provides not only an account of the events of Bechet's life but also a discourse of legitimation. By "discourse of legitimation," I mean the terms in which Bechet's jazz ways were constituted, in their practical reality, as collective acts of musical virtuosity and, likewise, as an authentic form of black consciousness. As Kapferer contends, the issue is not whether the particular discourse of legitimation is true or false, but rather "the fact that they have an effect: an effect which is a property of the discourse itself and not merely a function of the agencies and political and social relations through which it also gathers force. These agencies and relations do not stand independently of the discourses which they produce and support."[14] In this sense, the problem is not so much whether Bechet's text accurately depicts his grandfather's slave life or the events of his own childhood in New Orleans between 1897 and 1912. Of major concern, however, is how the disparate logics of black folklore, of trickster tales and slave legends, and the dynamics of social practices and manual labor were reconstituted by Bechet into a generative discourse about the conditions from which black American musical practices emerged.

Both Kapferer and Wyschogrod pose fundamental questions about the meaning and force of folklore and customs, and the form of mythic consciousness, within the technical and rational basis of modern capitalist states. Their analyses have critical implications for how we value and analyze the cultural forms, the beliefs, and the social practices of disenfranchised, marginal, traditional, or immigrant sections of a given state's population. Such distinctions, of course, are politically and historically charged and constitute the social terrain upon which human interests are legitimated and pursued within such states, and through which the struggle, both to describe and to imagine other social ways and other human realities, takes place. By focusing on antecedent habits and customs, the social relations, and the practices of ritual and belief, a remythologization thus provides an encompassing structure of meaning "in a world demythologized and fragmented in the processes of secular rationalism and . . . capitalist/technical transformations. . . ."[15]

This debate over folklore, custom, and myth is central to understanding the forms of American ideology and the structural dynamics of the post–Civil War capitalist state in breaking apart the agrarian forms of the colonial period (as well as pre-Columbian forms) and bringing about industrialization on a massive and effective scale. The debate over *slave* folklore, *slave* customs, and *slave* myth is even more intrinsic in the attempt to understand the free blacks' struggle for economic, social, and political influence in the period after slavery was ended. In this regard, our argument will rely on the influential work of W. E. B. Du Bois, Melville Herskovits, Herbert Gutman, Eugene Genovese, Barbara Fields, Stanley Elkins, Joel Kovel, and Lawrence Levine. Together they provide an understanding of the effects of the slave system on the slave, a common slave culture that actively resisted and transformed the conditions of enslavement, and the structures and ideology of American racism as it was formed from the remnants of the slave system after 1865. I find their analyses particularly useful for articulating a theory of musical action and the form of that action within the framework of the "slave event," by which I mean the logic of relations established by the state (and carried over by historians) among the slave system, the movement toward emancipation, and the aftermath of the slave economy and social order.

On this basis, I want to show that, although Bechet's jazz life included, in its collective experience and shared history, the enormous impact of the "slave event" on the making of black musical practices, his discourse is not, however, a simple affirmation of the progressive ideology of emancipation, nor of the so-called liberatory dynamics of industrial capitalism, nor even proof of his significance to the emergence of the jazz form. Instead, I suggest that the tensions within his narrative— between the desire for commercial success and the virtuosic aims of collective improvisation, between slavery and emancipation, between Bechet's musical ideas and those of other jazz musicians, between a musician's musical practices and his or her social situation—constitutes the very form of the struggle by blacks to orient and value their acts of musical making. In this way, the narrative actualizes a mythic black consciousness that expresses, through the specific dynamics of the musical act, the efforts of blacks to bring order and meaning to, and explain the significance of, their actions in relation to the systemic violence of the New South. Thus for Bechet, their music, like their new relation to the state, was "a lost thing finding itself."[16]

## Music Was All They Needed

If *Treat It Gentle* focuses on the virtuosity of the jazz act, it does so in terms of "the people who make it, what they have inside them, what they're doing, what they're waiting for."[17] This virtuosity of the act is constructive in that it establishes the most basic logic of relations—the dynamic— between the elements of a musical practice (pitch, tone, and accent) and the act's ideological conditions of production. To study the relation of the jazz act to American ideology is to consider, above all, the question of how jazz was made and who made it, and to place those considerations within the larger context of human being and the human activities of doing and making.[18] As I stated in the introduction, my aim is to analyze the structure of the jazz artifact, to examine the basis of its historical and musical significance, and to understand the manner by which it is situated by its practitioners as a meaningful social and musical act in terms of American exceptionalist ideology. A close analysis of Bechet's narrative enables us, in Elaine Scarry's terms, to build a "more complete account of the interior structure of the act of creating as it is objectified and made knowable in the hidden interior of the created object."[19] What

Bechet delivers, therefore, is an outline of the act of making jazz, and, more important, he articulates what Scarry identifies as the "fundamental framing relation between 'pain and imagining' . . .";[20] *Treat It Gentle* is thus a narrative of human generation that, in its movement from the nineteenth-century slave plantations to Bechet's success in Paris in the 1950s, actualizes the existential form of human ways of imagining. To clarify this narrative framework, I rely on Scarry's analysis of the processes and structures of human making and Wyschogrod's study of the social logic of the modern "death world." Both analyses grasp, in profound ways, the embodied and intentional aspect of human being and how, historically, the abuse, violation, and suppression of human agency was invariably coupled with extraordinary acts of human invention and resistance.[21] In the study of the jazz act, to define the *virtuosic* and *ideological* logic of these ways of making and destroying, of orienting and erasing, is an important step.

Bechet's narrative begins with a fictional account of his enslaved grandfather Omar's death at the hands of a fellow slave. The purpose of this account is to emphasize the fragility of the musical act and affirm the basis of the slaves' collective capacity for psychic survival and creative action. While *Treat It Gentle* has bothered some historians—James Lincoln Collier calls it "self-serving and unreliable"[22]—Bechet's description of slavery is critical for his later attempt to articulate the social character of the jazz act, its relation to the musical practices of the slaves, and the significance of emancipation to the formation of black consciousness. As Bechet remembers: "[Omar] was a leader, he led the music. But still, as an idea, the way he played his horns, the way he beat on his drums, he was still a background music. It was still a music that hadn't broken loose, it hadn't stopped being scared. It was irresponsible in a way to all its worries. It was an awful beginning."[23] The restricted motions of the slaves' existence, the pain and suffering of enforced labor, but also the expressions and orientations of their social situation over time, all these are compressed by Bechet into Omar's struggle against his master. By concentrating on the social basis of the struggle between masters and slaves that Bechet narrates, I follow Scarry in wanting to demonstrate how the "story of expressing physical pain eventually opens onto the wider frame of invention."[24] This invention, for Bechet, was jazz.

Throughout the narrative, the creative structure of the jazz act is divided by Bechet into two axes of material making. The first axis— the horizontal axis—was that of a person's or group's musical efforts, a historical process *constituted within* the social relations of the ex-slave, free black, and Creole communities in New Orleans. This axis relied on the knowledge and the development of common musical practices *among* groups of musicians, some of whom sought to make a living from their music, while others (the bulk of the music-playing population) played music in addition to their working lives. The second axis was defined by the logic of seduction, that is, the performative moment when the collective virtuosity of the musical act *qua* act subsumed all other relations, including the group's own, within its social orbit. On this second axis, the musical act was *constitutive of all* social relations. The subsequent tension between the two axes shaped the direction of Bechet's musical activities and provided the framework for his remythologization of black consciousness.

This framework was divided between the social world of the slaves and that of the ex-slaves, and the synthesis of their musical practices in the form of jazz. As Bechet puts it:

> All the music I play is from what was finding itself in
> my grandfather's time. It was like water moving around
> a stone, all silent, waiting for the stone to wear away.
> Because all the strains that went to make up the spirituals,
> they were still unformed, still waiting for the heart of
> ragtime to grab them up, mix it up in them, bring them
> out of where only a few people could feel the music and
> need it, bring it out where it could say what it had to say.[25]

In this light, Bechet's narrative can be seen to explain how the disparate groups of former slaves who migrated off the plantations later came to act, think, and feel in quite specific and skilled musical ways. It also raises the question of how those musical ways, in turn, affected those who were seduced by the musician's musical powers. As Bechet notes, these musical ways were "a kind of memory that wants to sing itself."[26]

The *logic* of the slaves' musical acts was thus inseparable from the processes of political struggle, legislative emancipation, and wage dependency among southern blacks. For Bechet, however, the transformation in the slaves' lives after emancipation was already mediated by their musical practices, by the collective act of bringing their musical potential into a sense of itself *as a form,* and in the process constituting themselves in *the form* of a people. Emancipation, he recalls, enlarged the feeling, the tone, and intent of the slaves' music as much as it did their lives: " 'Go down Moses, Way down in Egypt land; Tell old Pharaoh, Let my people go.' . . . It was years they'd been singing that. And suddenly there was a different way of singing it. You could feel a new way of happiness in the lines. All that waiting, all that time when the song was far-off music, waiting music, suffering music; and all at once it was there, it had arrived. It was joy music now."[27] Here Bechet directs us to the internal structure of the act itself and its relation to the historical dynamic of slavery and emancipation. For him, the historical truth of the slaves' music—its joy—was evident only once emancipation had taken place. The sense of waiting and suffering in the slaves' music only emerged, as it were, *in retrospect* and in relation to a new sociosymbolic system of meaning, one having to do with the collective struggles during Reconstruction over wage labor, enfranchisement, segregation, black self-determination, and migration. Thus, what was "waiting music" and "suffering music" all at once became "joy music."

On one level, the slaves pass *diachronically* into freedom by way of their acts of musical making, even as those same musical acts were retained as symbols of the conditions of their enslavement. On another level, the phrase "all at once" suggests that the "before" slavery and the "after" slavery coexist *synchronically* in a moment of suspension that is neither one nor the other. In other words, even as the musical act attempted to give a form to the reality of the slave event and its aftermath, it was, on the level of its form, irreducible to that reality and, in these terms, remained in an *impossible* relationship to that reality.

That the musical act stood in an impossible relationship to the reality of the slave event returns us to Maurice Merleau-Ponty's notion of "lived ambiguity." As I understand Merleau-Ponty's phrase, the moment of emancipation (symbolized in Lincoln's Emancipation Proclamation of January 1, 1863) not only involved a fundamental reorganization of the sociosymbolic order of the state, but it also provoked a radical suspension in the orderly progression of history itself: an interruption in the previous social order that was already internal to the *new* order of industrial capital, in that it no longer required slave labor for its production and reproduction.[28] I want to suggest, therefore, that the moment of emancipation, and thus, the musical act itself, occupied an *impossible* point between these two systems of exploitation: slavery and wage labor.

The very impossibility of the situation for the ex-slave—and the documentation on the social agitation and struggles of the period is extensive—demonstrated, in every sense, the lived ambiguity of the slave's and the former slave's relation to the capitalist state. As W. E. B. Du Bois remarked: "The slave went free; stood a brief moment in the sun; then moved back again toward slavery."[29] As with Bechet's comment, we can take Du Bois's remark in both a diachronic sense and synchronic sense. The diachronic sense refers to the period from Lincoln's Emancipation

Proclamation of 1863 until the collapse of Reconstruction in 1877. More specifically, however, it refers to both the enormous promise contained in the Union victory and the magnitude of the failure of Reconstruction. For Herbert Gutman, Du Bois's remark suggests how this period can be approached by the historian. In other words, it is precisely this moment of suspension between two radically different social orders that provides the key to a fuller analysis of slave culture and subsequent developments in black cultural life: the "war and the emancipation fundamentally changed the context that had limited their [the slaves'] behavior. How slaves and ex-slaves commonly behaved at that moment in time (1861–1867)— not fifty years earlier and not fifty years later—is therefore unusually relevant evidence in any assessment of the long-term impact of slavery on slave culture and personality and the subtle interplay between slave beliefs (or values) and slave behavior."[30] Only with this knowledge of how emancipation was lived *ideologically* by the slaves is it possible to articulate the creative character of their social practices and to recognize the collective and individual forms of resistance specific to the slave event and its aftermath.

On the other hand, if we consider Du Bois's statement in its synchronic sense, emancipation—the slaves' brief moment in the sun— occupies the virtual or nonideological (utopian) dimension of the slaves' and ex-slaves' productive labor. Suffice it to recall that the virtual or nonideological dimension remains buried within, or immanent to, the historical modes of human action. Thus, emancipation is the *impossible* form of the slaves' and ex-slaves' historical relationship to the state and to the forms of American ideology. In these terms, the concept of emancipation or freedom has no substantive meaning—either before, during, or, indeed, after the Civil War—except as a tool of domination and ruling class ideology. As Eric Foner points out, "instead of a predetermined category or static concept, 'freedom' itself became a terrain of conflict, its substance open to different and sometimes contradictory interpretations, its content changing for whites as well as blacks in the aftermath of the Civil War."[31] The tragic paradox for Du Bois, however, was that the very form of this conflict—for all its revolutionary potential—ultimately served to reinforce the subsumption of blacks into the institutional structures and modes of production of the industrial state and thus into a new form of enslavement.

The synchronic basis of this paradox meant that the slaves' and ex-slaves' *lived ambiguity,* that is, the relation between their human actions and the historical meaning of those actions, was already internal to the ideology of slavery. I analyze this ideological framework in more detail below. For the moment, however, I want to demonstrate how the paradox of emancipation affected the existential structure of Bechet's narrative. For Bechet, this sense of a *lived ambiguity* and its relation to emancipation was directly expressed in the specific qualities of the spirituals and the blues:

> The spirituals, they had a kind of trance to them, a kind of forgetting. It was like a man closing his eyes so he can see a light inside him. That light, it's far off and you've got to wait to see it, but it's there. It's waiting. The spirituals, they're a way of seeing that light. It's a far off music; it's a going away that takes you with it. And the blues, they've got that sob inside, that awful lonesome feeling. It's got so much remembering inside it, so many bad things to remember, so many losses.[32]

The jazz act arises from the synthesis of these two discrete elements —actualized in the spirituals and the blues—of the slaves' and ex-slaves' being. Indeed, within the very structure of Bechet's narrative the historical value of these elements is defined *retrospectively* as a consequence of the jazz act. However, a third element was required to constitute the jazz act as a *universal expressive form*. For Bechet, this third element was ragtime: "Rag it up, we used to say. You take any piece, you make it so people can dance to it, pat their feet, move around. You make it so they can't help themselves from doing that. You make it so they just can't sit still. And that's all there is to it. It's the rhythm there. The rhythm *is* ragtime."[33] Ragtime thus provided the tempo of the jazz act, the basis of its orientation *in* time (the social conditions of its making) and the act's orienting *of* time (the musical basis of its seduction): " . . . that rhythm and that feeling you put around it, always keeping the melody, that's all there is to it."[34] Thus, the making of the jazz form depended on the transformation of these discrete elements—the spirituals, the blues, and ragtime—into a collectively shared objectification of the slaves' self-consciousness as freed men and women.[35]

The value of Bechet's narrative is that he articulates precisely how, in the act of going for jazz, New Orleans musicians and their audiences were, in Scarry's words, "implicated in each other's sentience."[36] His emphasis is consistently on the *social situation* of the musical act and on music's potential to transform the lives of the ex-slaves. In these terms, the musical act externalized the contents of the ex-slaves' pain and loss, via the blues, and projected the promise of their freedom, via the spirituals, into a logical expression of their ways of musical making. The form of this logical expression was jazz. At the same time, if we take up Scarry's point, the dynamics of the act meant that "not only are the interior facts of sentience projected outward into the artifact in the moment of its making, but conversely those artifacts now enter the interior of other persons as the content of perception and emotion."[37] Thus, the form of the jazz act was already internal to the ways in which the ex-slaves' consciousness of emancipation was "coming into a sense of itself." As Bechet states: "Wherever there was music, a whole lot of people would be there. And those people, they were just natural to the music. The music was all they needed."[38]

## From Jazz Myth to Jazz Life

As a discourse of legitimation, Bechet's text not only carries us into the making and remaking of the jazz artifact, but also into the structures of belief and the logic of seduction on which the social struggle for the jazz act's legitimacy was based. For him, the music of the slaves provided the very condition for a belief in themselves as human beings and in the promise of their emancipation as a social fact: "The only thing they had that couldn't be taken from them was their music. Their song, it was coming right up from the fields, settling itself in their feet and working right up, right up into their stomachs, their spirit, into their fear, into their longing."[39] With emancipation, however, came a pronounced shift in the structures of slave belief and the forms in which that belief was expressed: "All those people who had been slaves, they needed the music more than ever now; it was like they were trying to find out in this music what they were supposed to do with this freedom: playing the music and listening to it—waiting for it to express what they needed to learn."[40]

This notion of belief and its relation to the musical act can be clarified by Scarry's assertion that " 'to believe' is to perpetuate the imagined object across a succession of days, weeks, and years; 'belief' is the capacity to sustain the imagined (or apprehended) object in one's own psyche, even when there is no sensorially available confirmation that the object has any existence independent of one's own interior mental activity."[41] What we find in *Treat It Gentle,* therefore, is a blueprint for the modulation of belief from the "waiting" and "longing" of the slaves—their collective acts of imagining and being—to the "arriving" and "moving" of the freed men and women; a modulation, as I have suggested, that was mediated by the making of discrete black musical practices into the universal form of jazz. In this sense, the "waiting" and "moving" that structured the dynamic between belief and objectification—waiting *for* emancipation, moving *as* freedom—was as much an ideological struggle for control of the musical material as it was an elaboration of the human potential of the ex-slaves.

That this dynamic of "belief" and objectification was, until the 1960s, widely thought to be following a predetermined pattern of assimilation highlights the problems involved when black musical practices are reduced to the assumptions of American exceptionalist ideology.[42] As Gutman argues, so often the study of blacks—either as slaves or as freed men and women—is "encased in snug and static ahistorical opposites such as 'slave' and planter or 'black' and 'white.' "[43] What is neglected are the manifold ways in which black musicians situated themselves, and were situated by others, in relation to the social world, and in terms of which their musical acts were made into meaningful social acts. Jazz historians and critics have repeatedly emphasized the individual moments of musical epiphany that make up jazz history. As a consequence, they have neglected the fundamental relation between the sentient structure of the act and the existential form in which that sentience is cast.[44] Bechet's narrative directs us toward precisely these problems.

As I have suggested, the existential form most commonly identified with the making of jazz is "the jazz life." Some discussion of how this form worked for critics, historians, and musicians is useful in gaining a sense of the inner dynamic of *Treat It Gentle,* but also in clarifying the narrative's relevance for the later analysis of ideology. The jazz life's currency as a means of explanation suggests how a more exact definition of the structure of Bechet's remythologization might be reached, but also the degree to which the state's ideological frame structured the conditions of the act's reception. Nat Hentoff's 1961 study, *The Jazz Life,* although primarily a personal account of his day-to-day interaction with jazz musicians, is one of the few attempts in the 1960s (along with LeRoi Jones's *Blues People*) to explicitly address, rather than simply assume, the particular relations between the musician's social situation and the logic of his or her musical practices. Hentoff's text claims to redefine the structure of the jazz act and the musical feeling associated with it. The basis for this claim is the argument that jazz "is what each musician feels as he plays; and that concatenation of emotions comes from specific experiences in that player's life."[45]

*The Jazz Life* was published in 1961, at the same time as Bechet's narrative. In fact, Bechet was the jazz musician whom Hentoff—as a twelve-year-old growing up in Boston—first encountered in live performance.[46] Both authors situate the jazz life within the same temporal framework of capitalist development and individual progress. Each also offers a penetrating analysis of the social value of human action and the structures of jazz virtuosity. Thus, a discussion of Hentoff's book concerning the social and political conditions of jazz production enables us to gain a deeper understanding of Bechet's argument and a clearer sense of the existential concerns of the jazz musician. For Hentoff, the primary aim is to demonstrate the degree to which, in jazz, the "music reflects the man."[47] He achieves this through a variety of anecdotes and recollections about jazz musicians, and through a range of details about income, recording contracts, and reports from festivals. The various portraits of the jazz life chart the progress of jazz practices from New Orleans to New York and, thus, exemplify the social form of the musician's struggle to create and legitimate the jazz act under conditions of mass consumption.

Hentoff's text is one of a few significant ethnologies of the jazz act and, moreover, offers an invaluable addition to our understanding of its ideological dimension. Two chapters stand out in this regard: one on the financial structure of the jazz world—"The Apprenticeship and the Accounting"—and another—"Studio Time"—a description of two studio sessions involving, first, a 1960 recording by Louis Armstrong and the Dukes of Dixieland, and second, the 1959 recording session of Miles Davis's and Gil Evans's composition *Sketches of Spain*. What concerns us in these descriptions, aside from the dynamics of playing and working, and the overwhelming sense of how musicians have fought as much to make their music heard as to make a livelihood, is Hentoff's argument that the "jazz life, in short, is the total existence of all its players."[48] How this existence, from the 1920s, was determined by increasing "professional standards" and "commercial demands," by booking agents and corporate executives, constituted the social terrain on which the musicians' struggle for recognition and meaning took place.[49]

Hentoff sets out to delineate the conditions of this struggle by dividing his book into two sections: the "background" and the "foreground." Thus, in the early chapter, "The Apprenticeship and the Accounting," the political economy of the jazz life is highlighted by pointing to the role of city police and clerks, liquor licensing officials, and union officials, as well as venue owners and lawyers, in regulating access to the "cabaret cards" that allowed a musician to play in a city's venues. The chapter also gives examples of the limited pay scales offered by club owners once a musician managed to overcome the web of official and unofficial administration. However, while offering in one sense a model of the objective conditions for self-expression, Hentoff's chapters on finance and recording also reinforce an appreciation for the *social situation* of the jazz musician's act; that is, his narrative accentuates the profoundly *social* effort that a musician made to get onto the bandstand. At the same time, so as to accentuate the principle of struggle, Hentoff writes: "[S]ince the jazz life is still very much a part of show business economically, there are absolutely no guarantees."[50]

By focusing on the political economy that structured the jazz life and on the early moments of the jazz act's making, Hentoff details a world of limited possibilities for young apprentice musicians as jam sessions declined in the 1950s, as the focus of popular music shifted toward rhythm and blues and rock and roll, and as capital investment in mass musical production tied up performing and recording opportunities. Other chapters deal with race relations on the bandstand, the influence of drug use and addiction among musicians, and the crisis surrounding the major festival circuit, particularly, the riots at the 1960 Newport Jazz Festival. That there were "no guarantees" is thus presented by Hentoff as the existential horizon—the background—against which the jazz musician was compelled to struggle and as a consequence of which the virtuosity of his or her act of going for jazz—the foreground—was actualized.

The foreground in Hentoff's narrative concerns the moment of musical seduction. To account for the form of this seduction, as distinct from the processes of an act's making, Hentoff inserted a pivotal chapter at the beginning of his "foreground" section entitled "Studio Time." In this chapter, the commercial pressures, the questions of income, and the various other problems that confronted young jazz musicians are subsumed within the struggle among several well-established musicians and their bands, record executives, producers, and technicians for *control* of the act's meaning and value in the course of recording sessions. The structures of the musical act are revealed in the repeated attempts by the musicians and the producers in two recording sessions to get the right "take," that is, the "correct" recording of the music, whether it was scored or memorized. The sense described by Hentoff of moving into the music, and then working through its tempos, melodies, and harmonies, *as a group,* constituted the productive conditions of the act's construction, while the actual finished recording was, in these terms, both the proof and extension of the seductive powers of the act. A comment by Miles Davis points to the orienting force of the act itself, and helps define the basis of its seductive powers: "You know . . . the melody is so strong there's nothing you have to do with it. . . . The thing I have to do now is make things connect, make them mean something in what I play around it."[51] Thus, the structuring and elaboration of Gil Evans's melody required that Davis situate himself in relation to the melody, that he orient himself musically toward it, even as he altered the melody with what he played around it, and that he, in turn, recognize how his playing was altered by the other musicians in the ensemble. Questions of how to direct the ensemble's *collectivity*, its dynamics, as well as the very terms of the musical act's value, were thus fought out on the studio floor, drawing everyone at the session into where and how the melody was going to go (its making), but also into the music's own way of going with the melody (its objectification). As Davis remarked at the end of the session: "That melody . . . is so strong that the softer you play it, the stronger it gets. . . ."[52]

The virtuosity of the act emerged from the level at which the melody defined the relations within the group, or, indeed, we could say that the logic of the group was itself the unfolding of the melody. Seen in this light, Hentoff's account of the "jazz life" is very much an attempt to articulate the value of jazz in terms of other human activities, and to explain how that value is created from the relation of the day-to-day experiences of the musicians to the virtuosic dimensions of their musical making. To emphasize the form of that relation and its corresponding social value, Hentoff identifies two corresponding lines of jazz's development: the evolving virtuosity of the discipline as a national and international phenomenon, and the increasing self-consciousness attached to jazz production by critics, promoters, and audiences. These lines of development provide Hentoff with the narrative framework for demonstrating how the various conversations, interviews, anecdotes, and facts about the musicians lives can be seen as so many symptoms of an underlying *contradiction* between the musicians' ideological background and the act's virtuosic foreground.

What Hentoff's study neglects, however, is sufficient emphasis on what E. P. Thompson has described as "the ideological role of art, its active agency in changing human beings, its agency in man's class-divided society."[53] While his discussion of the relations among musicians, producers, critics, agents, managers, venue owners, recording executives, and audiences does much to articulate the process by which "jazz was evolving into a virtuoso discipline,"[54] in the end he emphasizes the primacy of the musical act's expressive foreground over its sociosymbolic framework, a primacy achieved for the former at the expense of the latter. As Hentoff concludes: "[M]any of the makers of jazz have been larger in life than most people in their generation, and they have transmuted their lives into their music."[55] In this sense, the so-called jazz life was both the result of a contradiction between the individual and his or her social situation, but also—and this is the crucial point—the basis of a resolution. Although the themes of his book are essential to a study of the jazz act, the way Hentoff neutralizes this contradiction succeeds only in turning the jazz life into the ideological form of the jazz act. He does this by defining the central tensions of the musical act primarily as modes of individual expression and then resolving that individuality into the sum of all possible jazz experiences.

Even as Hentoff argues that "jazz, to exist at all, has to be created collectively," his consistent subsumption of the dynamics of the act into the lives of the individual creators precludes serious consideration of the processes of individuation as such.[56] Throughout *The Jazz Life,* the musicians' act is thus characterized by several primary conditions: "their instruments have become extensions of themselves; they "feel much freer in the nightclub"; the act itself is the expression of "specific experiences in each player's life."[57] On the basis of these conditions, the value of the act is understood to emerge from the rising and falling fortunes of the players, that is, from the specific *relation* of the musician to the state's modes of production. In these terms, the obstacles to a musician's significance are the very forces which guarantee the act that same significance. The possibility for his or her transcending such obstacles depends on the ability to direct those forces into the act itself, to turn a historical *lack* of significance—the subject's subsumption by the productive forces of capitalism—into a symbol of the individual's innate productive power.

As Gutman argues, however, the assertion of this productive power conforms to the very ideological form of capitalist relations of production and, as a consequence, privileges self-expression "as the sole device used by . . . groups to overcome their exploitation, inequality, and dependence."[58] Paradoxically, this emphasis on the significance of individual self-expression and freedom emerged during a period of enormous military, bureaucratic, and economic expansion in the American state,[59] historical conditions of production forming the ideological limits of the jazz act and the basis of its social legitimacy. In the following chapters, I further consider how the musical act is structured as a consequence of this ideological frame. For the moment, however, I want to suggest that the overall effect of Hentoff's jazz portraiture is to neutralize the very social struggle on which that act depended for its virtuosic potential. The contradictions that Hentoff focuses on—between jazz musicians and their social situations—are already internal to the structure of the jazz act. Although he wants to redress the imbalances of recognition, of payment, of ignorance, and skill, that is, to give jazz musicians the significance they deserve and their music its real value, the place of jazz within the capitalist system as an ideal form of subjective expression precludes precisely this redress.

## Something Inside You

Hentoff's attempt to account for the contradictions of playing jazz at the height of the Cold War is matched by the eloquence of Bechet's remythologization. Indeed, it is this eloquence that allows Bechet to articulate the deeper social logic at work in the musical act. His narrative has two aims: the first is to *reinsert* musical practices back into the social fabric of black life; the second to manifest a symbolic *reorientation* of the improvised act toward the collective virtuosity of the early jazz musicians, and to find in that collective virtuosity the basis of the jazz act's *social* value. As with Hentoff, we sense an overriding tension between the individual's musical aims and the collective orientation of his or her musical acts. These antagonisms, however, far from being resolved into moments of individual transcendence or productive power, demonstrate the degree to which the social orientation of the act in fact overreaches and complicates the ideological conditions of each musician's individual life.

For Bechet, the "musicianer" is a craftsperson with special gifts of value to his or her community, whose particular ways of musical making situates and orients the collective virtuosity of the act itself, but always in relation to other social and political practices. In this section, I summarize Bechet's understanding of the dynamics of the jazz act. My aim is to demonstrate how the collective virtuosity of the act is framed and reframed by the logic of its remythologization, sometimes in contradictory terms, but also in terms that affirm or complement mainstream beliefs about jazz and the jazz life. For within Bechet's narrative, there is both an emphatic sense of the emergence of a black social consciousness after the Civil War, of which music was just one aspect, but also a tendency, much like that in Hentoff's account of the jazz life, to subsume the social world into the interior structure of the music. This seems to me to be symptomatic of a tendency that characterizes much of the writing on music. Bechet's text, while describing the excesses of racism, poverty, and ignorance about black music, also offers us a way to clarify this tendency and its meaning for historical studies of jazz.

The structure of the jazz artifact and the logic of its making, as described in *Treat It Gentle,* relied upon the multiplication of musical potential, on a modulation in black consciousness, and on the essentially social nature of the musical act itself. Nothing prepares us for the intensity of Bechet's assertion of the dynamic relationship between social situation and musical practices. Much less are we prepared to analyze what is at stake in those collective acts of musical making, or how those acts of musical making reorient the musician toward the wider social contexts of his or her musical sense.[60] As Bechet remarks: "Most people, they think they make themselves. Well, in a way they do. But they don't give enough credit to all the things around them, the things they take from somebody else when they're doing something and creating it . . . things like what you remember, or how you feel, or what you're going to do."[61] By focusing on the relations among social practices, Bechet is able to claim for jazz a fundamental place in black American life—in that music was essential to the ex-slaves' sense of freedom—but also to recognize that jazz is itself determined by other equally significant forces. His account situates the development of black musical practices as part of a larger history in which the figure of the musician has substantial social value and existential import. As I have already noted, the practices of ragtime, the marches, the blues, the spirituals, as well as the popular European dances and songs were an essential part of the social conditions of New Orleans society—its rituals, its daily beliefs, and its sense of human mortality: "That music, it was like where you lived. It was like waking up in the morning and eating, and it was regular in your life. It was natural to the way you lived and the way you died."[62]

At the same time, Bechet recognizes that the ideological relation of blacks to the forms and modes of state power was already internal to the musical act itself: "The conditions, they have to be right, but mostly they're not happening right for Negro music."[63]

What we need to notice here is the assertion of the musical act's "naturalness" in the context of post–Civil War New Orleans society and, likewise, the sense of its timing—the claim made about the "right conditions"—as key motifs in explaining the emergence of black music. For Bechet, the collective virtuosity of the act *qua* act, but also the act's social being, is thus determined by how *well* a group was able to play *together*. His example is the New Orleans brass bands in the early 1900s and their common practice, during the city's regular festivals, picnics, and parades, of entering into "bucking contests":

> Sometimes we'd have what they called in those days
> "bucking contests"; that was long before they talked about
> "cutting contests." One band, it would come right up in
> front of the other and play at it, and the first band it would
> play right back, until finally one band just had to give in.
> And the one that didn't give in, all the people, they'd rush
> up to it and give it drinks and food and holler for more,
> wanting more, not having enough. There just couldn't be

> enough for those people back there. And that band that
> was best that played the best *together.* No matter what kind
> of music it was, if the band could keep it together, that
> made it the best. That band, it would know its numbers
> and know its foundation and it would know *itself.*[64]

This notion that a band could "know itself" serves several purposes in Bechet's narrative. First, it points out the importance to the musical act of the "right conditions" for musical making—that is, it shows how the act's social value was oriented toward the "well-playing" group. Second, it places the significance of the act within the larger economy of exchange and production, of labor and festivity, by linking the virtuosity of the playing to the crowd's act of social reciprocity, that is, the act of offering, in return for music, gifts of drink and food. The form of such an exchange, as we shall see, was bound to what E. P. Thompson has identified (in a different context) as the specific logic of "social norms and obligations, of the proper economic functions of several parties within the community, which taken together, can be said to constitute the moral economy" of New Orleans' working blacks and lower middle class Creoles.[65] And third, it ascribes the act's musical virtuosity to the musicians' consciousness of themselves *as a band.* Thus did Bechet begin to delineate the social logic of the act and the basis of its seductive powers.

To underline the act's double movement, that is, its virtuosic and ideological dimensions, Bechet describes his own attempt in 1907 to perform on the clarinet with one of New Orleans best black bands. At his brother's birthday party, it was the excitement of hearing *how well* Freddie Keppard's band played together that drew him into the music, and inspired him to join in: "There was dancing, people getting together, things being real lively. The people, they were all over the house and the lawn. And the band was in the kitchen. . . . I stood around there hearing them play. I was standing back by myself in the entry to the kitchen, and I couldn't help myself. This was a band that was answering all its own questions. The way they played it got me terrible strong."[66] Again, the idea that the band was "answering all its own questions" situates the musicians' efforts firmly within the group's ability to play, and within the group's relation to *where* and for *whom* they were playing. In asserting this social context of the jazz act, Bechet suggests that the virtuosity of the jazz musician is as much a *virtuosity of the act* as it is mastery of a particular musical instrument or playing technique: "When you're playing *ragtime,* you're feeling it out, you're playing to the other parts, you're waiting to understand what the other man's doing, and then you're going with his feeling, adding what you have of your feeling. You're not trying to steal anything, and you're not trying to fight anything."[67]

What Bechet seems to be saying is that the jazz group is formed from a finely judged and measured musical encounter, a carefully skilled way of "waiting" and "feeling," of doing and adding, and of finding the social limits of each musician's sense of the melody. During the parades and the parties the virtuosity of the musical act thus subsumes the social dynamic of the act's making into a suspended moment of objectification. In this way, the group's seductive powers, its well-playing credentials, are constituted in the moment of its actualization as a "hot jazz" act— when the act appears to both musicians and audience to be effortless, spontaneous, and entirely natural, in spite of the efforts required to maintain such an appearance. For Bechet, it was Manuel Perez's Onward Brass Band that characterized this process:

> Labor Day night in New Orleans, that was always a big celebration. . . . And every year Manuel Perez, he'd be there with the Onward Band. . . . But the interesting thing is that Manuel, *he* was playing music for dancing. It's not easy to dance to a brass band, but Manuel had a way of playing different when it came to the fairgrounds. He'd take his brass and he'd really make it danceable. What he'd do is change the arrangement. He'd play it so it wasn't a matter of everybody taking his chorus; the important thing would be the tempo and the way each player carried the tempo. He'd keep them together and he'd keep them playing with a real swing to it. . . . And when you hear that it would give you a feeling that would be making you want to dance. It would just take your feet and make them go like it was something inside you.[68]

Just as each player carried himself or herself into the act, so to did each player carry the music's tempo and orient the act toward the form of the group itself. Here, once again, we grasp in a precise sense the dynamics of the jazz artifact, but also how deeply embedded it was in the social life of the city. To accentuate this point, Bechet compares a failed recording session with Louis Armstrong in 1940 with an earlier recording he and Armstrong made in the 1920s of the "2.19 Blues" and "Down in Honky Tonk Town." The tension between Bechet and Armstrong in those 1940 sessions emerges from what Bechet considers are two fundamentally opposed ways of going for jazz. Here, Bechet uses the recording session with Armstrong to argue against the competitive developments in music and show how this competition transforms the virtuosic dimension of the musical act itself. At the same time, he describes how the process of "working together for that real feeling"[69] as a band actually takes place:

> In the old days there wasn't no one so anxious to take someone else's run. We were working together. Each person, he was the other person's music: you could feel that really running through the band, making itself up and coming out so new and strong. We played as a group then. . . . And what's changed, you know, it's that hunger. A man now, he's just not a musicianer any more. He's got himself a name and he's got to perform up to that name. It's a demand upon him. His own reputation demands that he become a performer as well as a musicianer. He's got to be a personality. It's what I said at the very beginning when I was talking about Buddy Bolden. If a man can really play where the music is, he's entitled to all the personality they'll give him: but if personality comes first, that's bad for the music. The music, that's for a group to play; the musicianers, they need to be playing together.[70]

Farther on, he insists that it is the nature of the relationships among the musicians in the group that forms the basis of the jazz act's musical value:

> The place where a musicianer is lucky is in having the music. . . . If he's a good musicianer and if he really cares about the music he can stay with it long enough until it begins to come. He can find it. But most of all that don't happen real well in the music unless you're playing with the right people. A man can make a whole lot of music to himself, but what growing the music does, what arriving and what becoming arises from it, that only happens when musicianers play together—really play together with a feeling for one another, giving to one another, reaching out to one another and helping the music advance from what they're doing together. I guess just about the loneliest a musicianer can be is in not being able to find someone he can really play with that way.[71]

From this striking description of the collective orientation of the jazz act, Bechet diagnoses the reasons for the breaking apart of the jazz band's feeling and laments the loss of the act's social context. This theme dominates much of the later part of his book. At the same time, we should be wary of romanticizing the social arrangement of the black bands. I analyze the struggle between jazz musicians and the dominant ideology in more detail in the next chapter. It is significant at this point to note the degree to which Bechet opposes the influence of "personalities" on jazz, and to recognize that, in the context of his remythologization, this opposition is as much about the narrative's political and social impetus, its ideological condition, as about the jazz group's virtuosity:

> Some band leader get himself a reputation for being a
> personality, and that's it. From there on out it has to be his
> personality first and *then* the music. He's busy doing every
> kind of thing *but* the music. "Here's another saxophone,"
> he says. Maybe you don't need that extra sax, it doesn't
> belong, but that's no matter to him. "Here, here's another
> bass," he says. Well there's no reason for it, but there it
> is. And before you know it, you've got eighteen pieces,
> you've got a whole lot of noise, you've got a whole lot
> of something that hasn't got any spirit. All you've got, it's
> something like running a ball through a pinball machine
> and watching all the lights come on. You've got a hell of
> a lot of lights showing themselves off. . . . And all that
> freedom, all that feeling a man's got when he's playing
> next to you—they take that away. . . . All the closeness
> of speaking to another instrument, to another man—it's
> gone. All that waiting to get in for your own chance,
> freeing yourself, all that holding back, not rushing the next
> man, not bucking him, holding right back for the right
> time to come out, all that pride and spirit—it's gone.[72]

Actualizing the oppositions between the personality and the group, Bechet's narrative directs us to the social logic of musical practices and acts, to how they were taken up and used by the black and Creole classes in New Orleans after the Civil War, and to the basis on which those practices and acts acquired or enacted the social value of the classes of which they were an active and generative part. Against the background of the local traditions of musical making, the conditions of labor, and the social practices of New Orleans black culture, Bechet posits a freedom of the act that was constructed from the musicians' ways of *playing together.* Such a "well-playing" signaled a critical modulation in the interior structuring of the act, from the embodied processes of making and remaking to the seductive motions of objectification. This modulation, in turn, suggested that what was made—the jazz form—was, in fact, the very source of its makers—the musicians.

## A Feeling for the Band

Elaine Scarry argues that in "narratives of human generation, there begins to be exposed the mental structure present in the activity of 'believing,' the intensification of the body and the projection of its attributes outward onto a disembodied referent."[73] In *Treat It Gentle,* the "disembodied referent" is the music, and what is increasingly exposed and developed throughout the text—as the focus of a belief in the social value of the musical act—is the "*feeling* for the band."[74] The structuring of this feeling and the structuring of the band are part of the historical process by which the "waiting" of the slaves is turned into the "arriving" of the former slaves. Likewise, the purpose of the music, that is, the basis of its existential value, is premised on the musicians' belief in their ability to turn the collective virtuosity of the act from the pain and frustration of *the slaves'* "waiting" to the joy of *music's* "arriving." Belief in the musical act emerges, in this instance, not from some ulterior force, but from the very conditions in which it is made and consumed.

By describing the transition from his grandfather's slave experience to his own life, Bechet asserts that the social situation of the slaves, as it embodied the ordinary realm of laboring and living, became, through acts of musical making, the disembodied sign of their freedom. The principal aim of the narrative, therefore, is to redirect and restructure the collective intentions of the slaves and, further, to detail the influence of their material labor on the immaterial realm of their freedom; to articulate the process by which the collective feeling of the slave population is in fact turned, via their musical acts, into an image of freedom.

> All those people who had been slaves, they needed the
> music more than ever now; it was like they were trying
> to find out in this music what they were supposed to
> do with this freedom; playing the music and listening to
> it—waiting for it to express what they needed to learn,
> once they had learned it wasn't just white people the

music had to reach to, nor even to their own people, but straight out to life and to what a man does with his life when it finally is his.[75]

Musical acts thus provided the medium through which the experience of slavery was used to remake the horizons of the ex-slaves' world as they confronted the possibilities and the limits of the post–Civil War social and political order. Music, for Bechet, was the basis for a social agency on the part of the slaves that not only forged a radical disjuncture in the slave system itself, but carried with it the potential for a renewal of their world after emancipation:

> It was like they [the slaves] were trying to work the music
> back to its beginning and then start it all over again, start it
> over and build it to a place where it could stop somehow,
> to a place where the music could put an end to itself
> and become another music, a new beginning that could
> begin them over again. There were chants and drums
> and voices—you could hear all that in it—and there was
> love and work and worry and waiting; there was being
> tired, and the sun, and the overseers following behind
> them so they didn't dare stop and look back. It was all in
> the music.[76]

The passage just quoted occupies a definitive point in Bechet's narrative: it demonstrates how the historical experience of emancipation was understood by the ex-slaves. For Bechet, the slaves' collective struggle for life on the plantations was necessarily productive of and preparatory to a new phase in the history of their enslavement in which they were able to grasp their emancipation and their status *as* ex-slave men and women. The historical processes of emancipation and reconstruction were thus constitutive of a new musical phase that, in itself, gave an expressive form to that history—that is, to the historical development over time of the social relations between the slaves and their masters. My interest here is in the way the narrative reorients the form of those relations as they were mediated by music, but also how those relations were subsequently redirected and restructured after slavery as a consequence of music. In other words, while the slaves' musical practices were derived from the specific conditions of their enslavement, the very process of transforming that material existence into acts of musical making also marks the transformation of slavery as such.

In studies such as Eugene Genovese's *Roll Jordan Roll* or John Blassingame's *Slave Community: Plantation Life in the Antebellum South,* the slave system is understood to have offered the chance for limited social and historical meaning to develop among the slaves—enough, that is, to guarantee in the minds of their owners the slaves' effectiveness as laborers.[77] In terms of these structural limitations of the slave system, Bechet focuses on the *journey to freedom* as the orienting force of the slaves' social world. For him, the development of slave musical practices was formed in relation to their work regimes, and in terms of how, for whom, and in what period they labored or, indeed, managed to escape from enforced labor. However, within the terms of the remythologization, it was the journey to freedom—that is, the process of a historical transformation in slave consciousness—that countered and modified the practices of power and the relations of production characteristic of slave life on the plantations.

Throughout Bechet's narrative, emancipation is retained as the virtual dimension of the slaves' collective musical acts and, therefore, the basis of a historical repetition. This collective basis of the acts' repetition provided the means for the slaves to move forward, to stay ahead of their pain, to live at the threshold of their social world. According to Lawrence Levine, the slaves' musical practices, far from simply expressing their condition, were integral to the institutions and beliefs that they developed to sustain themselves in their oppression.[78]

In other words, their music enabled the slaves to subtend the limits of the system, while at the same time pass beyond it into their future as free men and women. Through their musical imaginings, they were able to carry their past into their present, to remember and reconstitute their mythical antecedents as coextensive with a future beyond slavery. Musical acts functioned, in this sense, to both suspend and transform the plantation's social order and the operations of power and violence on which that order was based. To explain the structuring of the musical act as the virtuosic surplus of the slave event, Bechet thus identifies a "mood about the music, a kind of need to be moving. . . . You just can't keep the music unless you move with it."[79]

In this sense, the "birth of jazz" was constituted through the development of musical practices that expressed the ex-slaves' attempts to give meaning to their passage from the slave system to industrial capitalism. That is to say, it was the jazz musician who, through his or her attention to the tempo and the timing of the act, embodied the trauma of the slave event, acting as a cipher for the unconscious realization of black Americans' collective proximity to freedom and, likewise, a critical measure of the distance traveled by the whole of American society from slavery. Bechet links the birth of jazz to a recurrent memorialization of the slave experience that, in turn, reconstitutes the movement from Africa to the New World as the mark of jazz's fundamental originality. The making and remaking of jazz is thus the symbolic means of denying the motions of death and violence, of combating the destructive power of the state and its capitalist mode of production. In other words, under new conditions of industrial production and mass migration, the black musician is increasingly endowed with the cosmic powers of a historical reversal. As a consequence of this reversal, Bechet's jazz myth identifies, in black musical practices, a new feeling for life from which freedom would emerge as a principle of expression. It is not, however, the music that introduces freedom into black life. Rather, it is the musical act, as the condition of change itself, that incorporates black life into this new existential mode and, in the process, transposes the slaves from their enforced period of waiting to their self-created moment of arriving. In other words, the social dynamics of the slaves' collective memory emerged, through acts of musical making, as capable of "structuring the structure" of a modern black consciousness.[80]

The ensuing "crisis" of black emancipation (which found its precise formulation in the ritualized violence of the Ku Klux Klan) emerged from the struggle between the social realities of postbellum society and the dominance of the state's exceptionalist ideology. It was this ideological dominance, furthermore, that was used by the political and financial elites in the North to insist on the transition from the plantation system to industrial capitalism as the necessary condition of the slaves' freedom, a freedom that was, in light of the capitalist dynamics of the American state and given the interests of the ruling classes, already precluded from the start.

## The Structures of the Slave Experience

In his study of blacks in the American economy from 1865–1914, Robert Higgs writes that "[e]mancipation granted black people both very little and a great deal. With freedom came no land or other tangible resources; except for the sporadic, inconsistent and transitory effects of the Freedmen's Bureau and the army of occupation, no protection against the intimidation and violent abuse of Southern Whites; except for the limited effects of missionaries, philanthropists, and the bureau, no education. All that emancipation gave blacks was, in short, themselves."[81] An analysis of this depiction is essential if we are to understand the importance attached to black music in the postbellum period and, particularly, to the relation between black musicians, social mobility, and the historical transformations in the American state after the Civil War. Understanding how blacks situated themselves and were in turn situated within the violent, fragmented, and tumultuous political and social order of southern society enables us to better understand the structuring and orienting of their social and political practices. Indeed, the period from the end of the Civil War until the early 1900s occupies a pivotal position in any analysis of the development of American industrialism, corporate capitalism, and exceptionalist ideology.[82]

On one level, we may consider this period transitory, in the sense that aspects of the social order (particularly in the southern and western states) were either resistant or indifferent to the nationalist project and the consolidation of corporate power in the period from the Civil War to the Franklin D. Roosevelt's New Deal administration in the 1930s.[83] On another level, the forces unleashed by the Civil War and the defeat of the southern slave system found their clearest expression in the rapid consolidation of the Union into a unified political and economic entity that relied on a certain *ideological consistency* between its various shifting and displaced regions, institutions, and mythic forms. How these regions, institutions, and mythic forms were abstracted and reconstituted as necessary signs of the American state's exceptionalist logic underlies in part the following discussion of slave historiography and the dynamics of the slave event.

Between 1900 and 1935, the black intellectual W. E. B. Du Bois provided the initial impetus for the analysis of slave culture and its connections to a more generalized notion of black expression. Du Bois studied the historical basis of slave expression and argued for the substantial importance of black expressive forms to any conception of American society as a whole. He based his argument on the notion that

> the human spirit in this new world has expressed itself in vigor and ingenuity rather than in beauty. And so by fateful chance the Negro folk-song—the rhythmic cry of the slave—stands today not simply as the sole American music, but as the most beautiful expression of human experience born this side of the seas. It has been neglected, it has been, and is, half despised, and above all it has been persistently mistaken and misunderstood; but notwithstanding, it still remains as the singular spiritual heritage of the nation and the greatest gift of the Negro people.[84]

In this way, Du Bois identified a powerful correlation between the form of black musical practices and the "vigor and ingenuity" that characterized the founding of the state. He then used this correlation to argue for a fundamental reorganization of the study of black life in America and of white Americans' relation to the history of slavery.[85] His attempt to understand the encounter between the mythical power of Africa and the historical conditions of African life in America involved expanding the boundaries of American culture to incorporate the specific qualities of black expression. The active synthesis of Africa and America *on the part of the slaves* imparted to their forms of expression a revolutionary potential to resolve the contradictions of industrial capitalism: that is, the disenfranchisement, oppression, poverty, and mechanization specific to the American metropolis.[86]

Du Bois's principal conceptual innovation was the notion of a double consciousness, with which he attempted to encompass the multiple points at which the mythical and ritual elements of African society were drawn into the modernizing forces of the colonial West, and through which black slaves forged the basis for a new myth of regeneration, a baptism, as it were, by song. The ensuing doubled (and doubling) form— identified by Du Bois as the spiritual form of the democratic state—was cast as the catalyst for the black American's becoming a "co-worker in the kingdom of culture."[87]

For Du Bois, it was the historical synthesis of the elemental and modern tendencies in the songs of the freed slave that emerged as the primary cultural expression of the material structures of the New World. The exceptional aspect of the spirituals rested on a recognition of a specifically rhythmic impetus that was the very essence of black musical practices. It was this rhythmic impetus that, according to Du Bois, constituted the existential quality most like America, and from which Americans could properly realize their historical destiny and the form of their civilization. As we have already noted in Bechet's remythologization, the structures of black feeling were situated at the threshold of the slave world and directed their consciousness toward the promise of emancipation. For Du Bois, it was the active tension between the experience of slavery and the promise of emancipation that, ultimately, gave the music of the ex-slaves its historical originality and social value.[88]

Du Bois posited a radical continuity between the historical experience of slavery and the development of the post–Civil War social and political order, particularly in terms of how the ex-slaves who lived and worked in that society understood their past, and how they came to enjoy and partake in musical acts as a consequence of their relation to the past. The constituent elements of the slave world were expanded by Du Bois to encompass the broader structures of the American state, and then folded into a liminal point of black consciousness that guaranteed a black influence on the general course of American life.[89] Historians of slavery, from Du Bois on, have focused on how the slaves' beliefs and social practices were a measure of a slave consciousness. In *The Souls of Black Folk,* Du Bois attempted to describe the historical processes and the political presuppositions that shaped this consciousness after emancipation and to show under what conditions black musical practices were made. His search for a black expressive tradition that was at once timeless, but also deeply historical, positioned black artists as revolutionary figures in the context of American modernity and, at the same time, the repository of an ancient culture that existed prior to Western colonialism. Furthermore, he defined black consciousness as an existential force that enabled the black artist to consciously reflect on the form of the modern democratic state and, likewise, to respond creatively to the exigencies of black Americans' historical experiences.[90] To put it differently, the black musician was both a major exponent of a revolutionary impulse specific to the New World and the inheritor of an ancient expressive tradition rooted in Africa.[91] The black musical act thus indicated the essential modernity of blacks, as they sought to influence the social forms of twentieth-century urban life. In this way, the contributions of black musicians (syncopation, improvisation, the blues, the spirituals, call and response) offered a means of overcoming the traumas of the slave past, but also of signaling the originality of the New World.[92]

The significance and meaning of black music emerged from the various "Africanisms" that were found and retained within its expressive actions. As Du Bois argued, the old plantation and folk songs were "the articulate message of the slave to the world. . . . [They] are the siftings of centuries; the music is far more ancient than the words."[93] Du Bois then divided this underlying temporal frame into three historical phases through which black musical practices passed in the process of becoming expressive forms: the slaves' African past; the world the slaves made; and the combination of African slave experience and the promise of American democracy. Because black musical practices were simultaneously ancient and modern, ritualized and historical, they represented the ideal synthesis of African and European social practices. The emergence of these practices offered Americans a rare opportunity to resolve the internal contradictions between the revolutionary ambitions of "the people" and the historical destiny of the state. Within this context of a transformation in state power, Du Bois opposed Africa to Europe, but in such a way that, through a historical reversal, Europe was now that which was always in the process of becoming African. Africa was both the historical origin of a modern American spirit and the source of black Americans' radical and enduring otherness.[94]

The critical problem for Du Bois was one of attending to the dynamics of making and remaking among the slaves and the ex-slaves: that is, how black vernacular expression was to be understood in terms of the slave experience, and how the musical practices common to the slave experience prefigured the history of jazz as its essential and inevitable artistic destiny. In these terms, Africa was a radical origin that situated the ex-slaves' acts of musical making in entirely new ways, but also gave them a means to struggle against the institutional forces of capitalist exploitation, legislative racism, and state violence. It offered an unusually powerful position from which blacks could begin to exert pressure on the inequalities of American society and to agitate for their "rights" as full citizens. Against the post–Civil War state's refrain "What shall be done with the Negroes?," Du Bois asserted, through his study of the ex-slaves' social and political practices, the significance of "what men and women do with what is done to them."[95]

Throughout both *The Souls of Black Folk* and *Black Reconstruction,* the focus of Du Bois's analysis was on the larger struggle concerning the forms of consciousness, power, agency, ideology, psychology, and resistance on the slave plantations. At issue was the system itself, that is, the very form of social relations in the American South, and the effect of such a system on the American state as a whole. The nature of the problem was effectively stated by Ralph Ellison in his unpublished review of Gundar Myrdal's 1941 book *An American Dilemma.* Myrdal's conclusion to his study was that the "Negro's entire life and, consequently, also his opinions on the Negro problem are, in the main, to be considered as secondary reactions to more primary pressures from the side of the dominant white majority." Ellison's response is crucial for understanding the future analysis of slave ideology:

> But can a people (its faith in an idealized American Creed
> notwithstanding) live and develop for over three hundred
> years simply by *reacting?* Are American Negroes simply
> the creation of white men, or have they at least helped to
> create themselves out of what they found around them?
> Men have made a way of life in caves and upon cliffs, why
> cannot Negroes have made a life upon the horns of the
> white man's dilemma?[96]

The crux of the dilemma, for both Myrdal (and his followers) and for Ellison, was the psychological and social impact of the system on the slaves and their descendants. During the period following the Civil War, the range of disputes concerning the impact of slavery on the slaves, on southerners, and on American society as a whole concentrated on detailing (or, indeed, denying) the brutality and violence of the system. In a discussion of both Myrdal's and Ellison's arguments, Stanley Elkins clarifies the complexity of the problem for historians:

> In surveying the experience of any group subject to radical oppression and stress, and when your principal theme is damage, it is neither easy nor expedient to build an alternative framework that provides adequately for resistance. On the other hand, there is bound to be resistance in *some* form, and this too needs to be recorded. And yet the more you make of it, the more you minimize the impact of brutality and exploitation upon powerlessness as sociological, psychological, and moral fact. Although powerlessness corrupts, just as surely in its way as does power, our sympathies for the powerless puts limits on our tolerance of what their condition has done to them, and upon our willingness to survey the whole damage. Thus as resistance looms larger (both theirs and ours), the damage steadily shrinks; so unavoidably, does the powerlessness; so, even, does the brutality itself. Indeed, it begins to look as though things were generally not so bad, after all, as they had been made out. Much strain in the current state of historical thinking on slavery is a reflection of this dilemma. Is there any resolution in sight? I have my doubts.[97]

Elkins's statement articulates the crucial difficulties in analyzing the structure of ideological conflict and its relation to practices of power and consciousness. A resolution to the dilemma he poses is still far from clear. What does seem possible is that we reconsider our understanding of human phenomena and of the meaning of social acts in terms of the *form* of the social order. In *Weapons of the Weak,* James C. Scott indicates the degree to which the defense or assertion of particular "interests" (defined by a relative distribution of "good sense") has become the measure of social situations, while the concept of ideology refers, not only to a mode of domination in society, but to the very terrain of the social struggle itself. Scott argues that the critical effort in the analysis of ideological conflict "is to grasp the nature of the normative filter through which these self-interested actions must pass and how and why they are socially transformed by this passage."[98] The result of such efforts is to claim for the subjects of exploitation and oppression a *simultaneous* accommodation and resistance to the conditions and terms of their domination.

What such an account of social struggle precludes is the role of unconscious identification in the structuring of social reality. In other words, there is little attention to the *form* of the social struggle and its meaning for human action. For Elkins, this failure is due to the critical limitations of the historiography itself. In the effort to secure the cultural conditions of the slave experience, to demonstrate, unequivocally, the resistant capacities of the slaves on the basis of their position within the slave system, studies that emphasize slave agency at the expense of structural analysis defeat their own best historical intentions. In short, the attempt to assert the primacy of slave cultural experience as the inherent substance of slave resistance precludes the very (distorting) effects of the system on which the slaves' historical experience relied. Thus, the temporal frame on which the continuity of slave culture was premised is equally abstract, a mirror of the progressive or reformist tendencies of the state itself.[99] As Elkins remarks: "Is the passage of time bound to be 'progressive,' and are its effects in the way of cultural change always of a positive character?"[100] The influence of this progressive framework on jazz is further considered in the next chapter.

For the moment, our concern is with the form of the relation of a slave agency to the systemic basis of white domination. Such a systemic analysis finds its strongest advocate in Eugene Genovese. In *The World the Slaveholders Made* and in his later work, *Roll Jordan Roll,* Genovese argues that only by attending to the particular traits of the ruling class in the various slave holding societies of the Americas is it possible to understand the ideology proper to each, and the rationale whereby the ruling class naturalized their own positions in relation to the capitalist world system, of which they were an essential (if contradictory) part.[101] For Genovese, this ideology was paternalism, and from it he seeks to derive and thus positively delineate the slaveholder's worldview from the "world the slaves made," without reducing one to the other. Indeed, Genovese's argument marks a significant challenge to the assumption that slave consciousness merely reflected that of the slaveholders. At the same time, as Elkins points out, Genovese overstates the significance of his own substantive claims about slave society. In a moment of structural blindness, he maintains that, in spite of their differences, slaves and masters were, in the end, the mirrors of each other's limits. This allowed him to retain the essential dignity of both parties in the face of the onslaught of industrial capitalism and northern aggression.[102]

For Genovese, the systemic violence internal to plantation societies was, in the case of the American South, held in check by the ideology of paternalism. Following emancipation, the positive conditions (however difficult) embedded within the master–slave relation were annihilated only to then be restructured according to a wage economy that demanded no terms of "mutual obligation" to the market system itself, but only naked economic interests as such. The ideological framework of paternalism no longer functioned to guarantee the stability of the social order; its subsequent collapse resulted in the abandonment of what Genovese argues was an underlying commitment to a specific conception of social relations. The ideological assumption, in Genovese's analysis, is that in spite of its overriding aims, the plantation system "somehow avoided corrupting either side."[103] Ultimately, what is suppressed in his argument is that slavery relied on a violent appropriation of human labor from the start; that its very structure was already a distortion of human relations. Thus Genovese's argument leads one to a historical impasse that plagues not only those southern conservatives hoping for a "restoration" of sorts, but also those seeking to explain the crisis of black identity in terms of the failure of the Reconstruction period.

The impasse, as it currently stands, turns on the status of the middle passage—the maritime transportation of slaves from African and European ports to the Americas—as the mediating event between Africa and America, the manner by which it was understood and internalized within American ideology, and the ongoing debate that surrounds those elements designated by the anthropologist Melville Herskovits as "African survivals." The influence of slave historiography has critical repercussions for the study of jazz. Among jazz historians, the central issues are related to jazz's synthetic properties: Is jazz expressive of the exceptional history of America? Which elements of the jazz act are African and which derived from European influences? And to what extent does a synthesis of these seeming antithetical elements reflect the social and political structures of the American state itself?[104] In a key historical study, James Lincoln Collier suggests that jazz "is a true fusion, combining principles and elements drawn from both European and African music."[105] This assertion is commonplace, however, finding expression across a range of cultural and musicological discourses. The fundamental problem with this argument, as LeRoi Jones clearly states, is that "to merely point out that blues, jazz, and the Negro's adaptation of the Christian religion all rely heavily on African culture takes no great amount of original thinking. How these activities derive from that culture is what remains important."[106]

Jones's argument along these lines is convincing, particularly his further claim that the "blues could not exist if African captives had not become American captives."[107] This proposition, as with his earlier statement about the radicality of the musical act in the context of formal American culture, must be understood as a statement about the ideological structures that produce the jazz act. In light of Jones's analysis, what is striking about many studies of jazz history (and also those cultural studies of popular music that invoke jazz—often uncritically—as an example of a universal mode of liberation) is the suppression of the very historical processes these studies in fact illustrate and on which they claim to build their argument. Collier's narrative demonstrates this tendency. While he readily acknowledges the origins of jazz as stemming from both Africa and Europe, and begins his study with a description of African music, his ultimate aim is twofold: to confirm his own syncretic power as a historian, and to expand that syncretism to the New World as an *aesthetic principle*. The historical gap—the middle passage—is then relieved of its ideological significance.

What happens to musical practices in the debate over "African survivals" and the impact of the middle passage on the slaves is what Slavoj Žižek terms a "neutralization" of the ideological frame.[108] In other words, positing the coexistence of the two opposed entities—in this case, Africa and Europe—which for many critics and historians constitutes the musical identity of jazz, far from recognizing the deeply traumatic nature of the middle passage presupposes a third, neutral medium—America—through which the two opposed entities find their resolution and thus their common expressive ground. What is also suppressed, however, is the fact that when it comes to "Africanisms" in America, there is in fact no possible point of convergence, no neutral ground shared by Africa and Europe that can simply be resolved by the transcendental movement of American capitalism and its accompanying ideological forms. Rather, the history of black American music is itself symptomatic of a fundamental and irresolvable antagonism between white and black, between master and slave, and finally between Africa and Europe; and this antagonism, as such, is the inexplicable and irreducible fact of the jazz act that few wish, or even bother, to explain. The critical point here is that jazz's meaning, its direction, as an act of collective virtuosity, is in fact as irreducible to either Africa, Europe, or America as is the middle passage the measure of either a successful or unsuccessful cultural transition.

If we expand on Žižek's critique of ideology even further, what was presumed to have been lost in the middle passage, that is Africa, emerged "only at this very moment of loss."[109] "Africa" comes into being at the point when it was no longer possible to know it as such. The very fact of its identification as an object of historical knowledge is the result of the extreme moment of disjuncture produced by the European imagination, new modes of production, and the systemic and sustained violence of the slave trade. The problem of "African survivals" in black music is thus the paradox of a historical narrative that requires a continuity of cultural forms leading to and reconstituting themselves as the unique practices of the New World.[110] But, as Žižek also points out,

> narrativization occludes this paradox (the coincidence of
> emergence and loss) by describing the process in which
> the object is first given and then lost. . . . The conclusion
> to be drawn from this absolute synchronicity, of course,
> is not that "there is no history, since everything was
> already here from the outset," but that the historical
> process does not follow the logic of narration: actual
> historical breaks are, if anything, *more* radical than mere
> narrative deployments, since what changes in them is
> the entire constellation of emergence and loss. In other
> words, a true historical break does not simply designate
> the "regressive" loss (or "progressive" gain) of something,
> but the shift in the very grid which enables us to measure
> loses and gains.[111]

The historical tradition that posed Africa and Europe as the necessary, but contradictory, elements in the creation of a genuinely American expressive form, that is, in the creation of jazz, also sought to resolve the fundamental antagonism of the middle passage as the sign of a crisis at the origins of the New World. It did so by rearranging the terms into a "temporal succession" that dissolved the force of the historical break into the teleological structure of the narrative and then placed the American state as the end of history itself. However, I want to suggest that the middle passage, far from simply providing the teleological conditions for the passage to the New World, reinforced the very act of historical violence on which the American state was founded and, at the same time, underlined the resilience of the slaves in their musical acts.

## Africanisms and Slave Practices

For Melville Herskovits, whose 1941 study of the slaves' and former slaves' culture built on the work of Du Bois and others, the value of black music emerged from a comprehensive understanding of the experience of slavery as a *historical process* that defined and determined the social context of slave beliefs and practices. As Herbert Gutman points out, Herskovits, "who knew a great deal about twentieth-century West African and Afro-American communities, did as much to correct distorted views of these peoples as any scholar of his generation. . . ."[112] Gutman also considers that a great debt is owed to Herskovits by later scholars for his attention to the "extensive relationship groupings" of early-twentieth-century rural southern blacks. The problem with Herskovits's analysis, as Gutman sees it, is that "his failure to study the changing history of enslaved Afro-Americans led him to emphasize direct continuities between discontinuous historical experiences."[113] As already noted, the same problems of static frameworks and ahistorical experience continue to besiege the study of jazz practices and stand in need of substantial revision.[114]

To challenge the accepted terms of slave historiography, Herskovits identified a series of kinship and cultural continuities among different New World black communities and, in the way the slaves structured their beliefs and social practices, a latent African genius for adaptation.[115] The process of documenting these kinship and cultural survivals in the Americas involves overturning the widely accepted notion that "the slaves were merely passive elements in the historical scene."[116] Countering such a view requires that the historian articulate the different levels on which enslaved Africans carried on a dialogue with their African past, and demonstrate how this dialogue transformed the slaves' relationship to the New World societies: "It soon becomes apparent, while Africanisms in material aspects of life are almost lacking, and in political organization are so warped that resemblances are discernible only on close analysis, African religious practices and magical beliefs are everywhere to be found in some measure as recognizable survivals, and are in every region more numerous than survivals in the other realms of culture."[117] By identifying what he saw as "gaps" in the slave system, Herskovits redefined how and why enslaved Africans were able to retain and recreate certain customary beliefs and social practices in spite of the impact of enslavement on their meaning and value. The extent to which this process became the basis for the making of a black consciousness relies upon the disclosure of the exceptional nature of the North American slaves' circumstances within New World slavery as a whole. Herskovits's model for cultural transformation—what he termed "acculturation"—fuses resistance to consciousness in such a way that the *historical* experience of the slaves is recast as the key element of the new slave historiography.[118]

Herskovits overcame the structural focus of earlier historical theories by redirecting the emphasis of enslavement toward the psychological intentions of the slaves and how they collectively grappled with, and transformed, the social and political structures of which they were a significant but subordinate part. He emphasized that the true history of slavery rests on an "invisible" or unconscious history of slave resistance: first, the underlying fear on the part of whites of slave revolt; second, the day-to-day contact between whites and blacks; third, the structural limitations and contradictions of the plantation system itself; and finally, the acts of disruption or disengagement that slowed production down or at times brought the plantation's system of production to a halt. Specific actions available to slaves (such as suicide, escape, "laziness," incompetence, or insurrection) are combined in Herskovits's analysis with the expressive potential of their language, music, and dance to depict the rudiments for the creation of a distinctive slave culture. That is to say, Herskovits provided a model for extending human agency to the subjects of the slave system, an agency (both political and social) that was equivalent in ideological terms to, and that in moral terms surpassed, that of the system itself.

Herskovits's principal achievement was the introduction of an experiential frame into the study of slavery and its post–Civil War aftermath, while the main focus of his argument can be summarized in these terms: Africanisms are to be found both in the cities and in the countryside all over the New World. Because of different social, historical, and economic circumstances, however, these Africanisms differ in intensity, in the structuring of their social and political practices, and in their relation to the slaveholders. In other words, by focusing on *a qualitative analysis of slave practices,* he was able to historicize the transition from slavery to Reconstruction and thereby recognized a "slave intentionality" that found meaning in acts of making and doing beyond the demands of enforced labor and reproduction. Or, in another sense, he expanded the laboring process to encompass the realm of the slaves' nonproductive work. The force of these practices, in orienting and directing the slaves' social consciousness, resulted in an overall pattern of resistance to oppression and exploitation at every level of the slaves' existence.[119] And it was the structures and structuring of these patterns of resistance that constituted the necessary conditions for the making of a discrete slave culture and the subsequent basis of its transformation after the Civil War.[120]

In the music of the slaves, and also that of the ex-slaves, Herskovits identified a direct expression of both an African past and a black American future: "African drums have entirely disappeared in the United States, yet one who is familiar with African music in its original forms cannot hear 'boogie-woogie' piano rhythms without realizing that there is little difference between the two except for the medium."[121] In this sense, the history of the slave experience was not formed through a sharp historical break with Africa, but rather through a subtle change of medium that preserved African social and expressive practices. At the same time, the existential meaning of these practices rested on how they were adapted to the specific conditions of the slave system and, then, to the particular requirements of industrial capitalism. What emerges from all this is a theory of acculturation emphasizing the processes of cultural *bricolage,* and arguing that the slaves be understood as exemplary practitioners of such processes.

In this way, Herskovits posited a theory of black American life in which the habits and customs of the slaves, their social practices and their metaphysics, involved a dual operation: "The realistic appraisal of the problem attempted here follows the hypothesis that this group, like all other folk who have maintained a group identity in this country, have retained something of their cultural heritage, while at the same time accommodating themselves, in whatever measure the exigencies of the historical situation have permitted, to the customs of the country as a whole."[122] On the one hand, what differed about black life was its intractable relation to the New World. On the other hand, the history of slavery in America relied on a continuity of practices that made all cultural objects and acts, by definition, consistent with their origins. The result of this analysis was, in Herskovits's view, to challenge the argument whereby the systemic violence of the middle passage inevitably erased or suppressed the slaves' African past.[123] His assertion was that only by placing the middle passage in a correct perspective in relation to the larger slave event was it possible to recognize the resilience and inventiveness of African cultural practices in the New World.

The combination of political resistance and cultural practices in Herskovits's analysis was used to circumscribe a field of black cultural power that rested on the subsumption of Africa into America as its ontological and mythical horizon. His study determined the essence of an identity that was internal to the residual effects of bondage and also to the presupposition of the future as a time beyond slavery. As with Du Bois's account, this temporal frame posited Africa as the form of a mythical recurrence within, and the source of a radical opposition to, the logic of American capital. What had once appeared to be violently contingent and inexplicable—the middle passage from Africa to America—was now caught in a logic of necessity for which there was an extraordinarily comprehensive and systematic rationale: that is, the scientific and political constitution of the New World and the imperial aims of the West's political and financial elites. In these terms, the "experience of slavery" was increasingly abstracted from the historical reality of the slave system, while the "world the slaves made" was prefigured, not as testimony to the collective or individual agency of the slaves, but as a necessary stage in the realization of the immanent laws of the republic.[124]

While Herskovits sought to position the "world the slaves made" as the temporal horizon of the black experience, he succeeded only in reinforcing the very ideology to which he was opposed from the start. In other words, what was missing from his analysis of black musical practices, what was in fact deferred, was precisely this ideological dimension of the slave experience. That is, in an effort to guarantee a continuity of experience, he precluded an understanding of how the slaves' musical practices were in fact *remade,* and the effect of various migratory passages—middle passage, interregional trade, emancipation, northern migration, and so on—on slave consciousness. Where Herskovits' emphasis on survivals opened the way for more precise and sensitive analyses of the dynamic of slave practices and slave consciousness, it was in the work of historians such as Herbert Gutman, Lawrence Levine, Ira Berlin, Barbara Fields, Eric Foner, and others that the temporal dimension, and its relation to ideologies of class and race, was fully explored. What these studies revealed was how "slaves could transmit and develop their own experiences and general beliefs across generations and over time."[125] In the final section of this chapter, I consider how *Treat It Gentle* articulated this temporal dimension as an ideological struggle for the form of jazz.

### "Free Day"

One of the striking aspects of Bechet's narrative is the way it opens up the question of how and why transformations in black musical practices took place *over time.* In other words, its ideological value as a text rests on how it establishes the relation of the past to the future within the overarching structure of slavery. Moreover, Bechet seeks to give that relation a mythical form that was yet produced within the context of specific social conditions: "All that waiting, all that time when the song was far-off music, waiting music, suffering music; and all at once it was there, it had arrived. It was joy music. It was Free Day. . . .

Emancipation. . . . That music, it wasn't spirituals or blues or ragtime, but everything all at once, each one."[126] The significance of the jazz musical act is here defined by its relation to emancipation. That is, the form of the act emerged from the attempt to repeat the moment of emancipation, which remained buried within the musical act as its virtual power. Indeed, it was through such a repetition that the music became, for Bechet, a "way of living, a blood thing inside you."[127] In other words, the very form of the act's repetition ensured its passage from generation to generation, and from musician to musician. In this chapter thus far, I have argued that Bechet's narrative is a remythologization that seeks, at both an ideological and a musical level, a "solution" to the contradictory and unresolvable *form* of social relations within American capitalist society. I have defined a remythologization, following Kapferer and Wyschogrod, as a reinvention of legendary or mythic constructions of past events in terms of the political and economic circumstances of the present.[128] On this basis, *Treat It Gentle* can be seen to actualize the dynamics of emancipation as a way to explain the relation of the slaves to the American state, but it can also be read as asserting the new powers of vision and action emergent from that relation. For Bechet, these new powers of vision and action emerged from the musical practices of the slaves in such a way that, far from being constrained to a single dimension of the slave experience, the musical act was *constitutive of all* social relations.

While the structure of Bechet's narrative encompasses the unresolvable and contradictory experience of the slave event for black Americans, its underlying purpose is to find a form capable of expressing that experience and, thus, to make that experience the basis for understanding the emergence of jazz. As Bechet says: "I wouldn't tell all this in a story about the music, except that all I been telling, it's part of the music."[129] What *Treat It Gentle* is offering, therefore, is a legitimation of precisely such a form and an outline of the conditions under which the relation of the musical act to that of its form was effectively produced.

The moment of emancipation—"Free Day"—stands as the critical moment in Bechet's text. Around it is organized not only the form of his narrative but the form of the musical act itself. For it is over the meaning of "Free Day" for the slaves, and its subsequent meaning for the former slaves and their descendants, that the struggle between the virtuosic and the ideological dimensions of the jazz musical act is played out. To this end, I argue that within the narrative the moment of emancipation occupies an *impossible* or *irreducible* point between two modes of feeling—the blues and the spirituals; between two existential forms of the musical act—the slave experience and the jazz life; and between two systems of exploitation—

the paternalist system of slave labor and the capitalist system of wage labor. The logic of the relations between the pair in each case constitutes the dynamic of the act's construction, in the sense that the act is both prior to and productive of emancipation itself. Wyschogrod argues that an event such as the slave event carries "blackness" within it as the zero degree of American enlightenment, and thus "requires an ontological counterpoise, a myth which expresses the paradoxes but, at the same time, sublates and overcomes them."[130] Bechet's narrative performs just such a counterpoise. His assertion of a mythical relation between the jazz act and "Free Day" functions to express "the constitutive and generative aspects of practice; that is, practice not as a representation of meanings but the very dynamic of their constitution."[131]

The dynamic of the jazz act's constitution is readily apparent in the extraordinary final chapter of the text, in which past and future coincide on a single plane of musical action. Indeed, the double movement of the act—at once virtuosic and ideological—is already given in the chapter's title: "It's the Music and It's the People." The act is thus neither one nor the other, but rather the constructive movement of one transforming the other in relation to a "Free Day" that remains virtual. In these terms, the act's dual movement is, on the one hand, the movement toward the people on which it depends for ideological meaning and, on the other, toward the music through which that meaning acquires a virtuosic form. Integral to this movement is the mythical figure of Omar: "[I]t was Omar that began the melody of it, the new thing. Behind Omar there was the rhythm and after Omar there was the melody."[132] The figure of Omar is thus the irreducible gap, the inexplicable point, between the people (life itself) and the music (the objectification of that life in a form). His song is cast as the general movement of the slaves into history, while his death signifies both the moment of rupture and the moment of repetition, from the which the jazz form will emerge once historical consciousness of the slave event is achieved. For Bechet, the mark of a great jazz musician is his or her attempt to play with Omar's song, and therefore, to play *after* it. Such an attempt invariably constitutes the dynamic of the jazz act's production and the form of its repetition.[133] In this sense, every jazz act is a return of previous musical practices—the work songs, the chants, the ragtime—and a return of the slave event—the work, the worry, the overseers—but a return within a single form that is itself already a repetition of "Free Day."

As already noted, the argument among historians regarding the slave event circles around two problems that are in fact inseparable: the significance of the middle passage and its effect on the slaves' cultural practices, and the effect of those practices in orienting blacks' relation to the American state after the Civil War. Furthermore, the slaves' practices and the consequences of such practices for an understanding of their behavior, before and after emancipation, are defined by two fundamentally different conceptions of the slaves' relations to slavery: that of accommodation within the system and that of a resistance to the system. The focus on acts of resistance or accommodation, and the resulting social and psychological effects of those actions, constitutes the ideological parameters within which the jazz act is subsequently valued. Its musical significance is thus reduced to an index of its ideological condition, that is, to a measure of black Americans' social and political progress in relation to and as a consequence of the state. The importance of Bechet's narrative, however, is to demonstrate that these ideological parameters are a basis for the social struggle within the act itself. Thus any attempt to value and analyze the act in terms of the progressive logic of the state must distinguish between the ideological form of the jazz life and the virtuosic powers of the act. Bechet's remythologization affects the form of this social struggle within the group, to the point where the narrative becomes as much a blueprint for redefining the form of the jazz act as it is a description of Bechet's jazz life. Only if we understand Bechet's return to "Free Day" in terms of Du Bois's argument about Reconstruction— "The slave went free; stood a brief moment in the sun; then moved back again toward slavery"—is it possible to grasp in what sense there is "something in that song deeper than a man could bear. . . ."[134] It is precisely this depth that functions for Bechet as the ideological limit of the jazz form: "What's Negro music? . . . How could you answer a thing like that?"[135] The very impossibility of an answer, so late in a narrative about Negro music, suspends the field of ideological meaning altogether.[136] In this sense, Bechet's jazz act is made only inasmuch as it is repeated.

We should remind ourselves that Bechet's narrative was transcribed in the 1950s. By this time, jazz was considered a privileged American musical form, useful for underwriting American expansion, and opposing communists and fascists alike. Moreover, it was already internal to the ideological momentum of the Cold War state and the enormous mobilization of capital, as I intend to make clear in the two chapters that follow. For Bechet, the commercialization of the jazz act, its subsumption into the circuits of money and power, constitutes a relation to the state that is purely subjective and without musical significance. The ideological form of this subjective stance or attitude, as we noted in discussing Hentoff's account, is the jazz life, while the social dynamic of the jazz life is one in which personality came to dominate the relations within the band. The effect on jazz, Bechet asserts, is diabolical:

[A]ll that freedom, all that feeling a man's got when
he's playing next to you—they take that away. . . . All
that closeness of speaking to another instrument—that's
gone. . . . A man, he signs a contract and he goes to play
somewhere; and he wants to make music, but he gets up
to play and nobody cares what he plays. That's how it is
in some places. Well, pretty soon he starts playing to *insult*
the audience. That's all he can do. But that's no music.
The music, it's not meant for that; it's for giving.[137]

A remythologization of the jazz act thus becomes a struggle for
the *form* of social relations within the state, and the construction or
giving of an act that will express the logic of those relations musically.
Against the ideological conditions of its production, and its subsumption
within the progressive logic of capitalist consumption, Bechet asserts the
virtuosic powers of the improvising group as *social practice:* "everywhere
you looked there was bands playing and people dancing to them."[138] For
him, the virtuosity of the improvised act, in other words, the orienting
of the group's tempo *toward the musical act itself,* challenges the logic of
consumption and the reduction of the act to the subjective conditions of
the jazz life. While at the level of personality the jazz act is a measure of the
subject's productive relation to capital, at the level of the group the social
logic of the act constitutes the conditions of its repetition. Indeed, it is
the collective repetition of a melody within the jazz group that turns each
musician's sense of timing from the disparate practices of ragtime, brass
music, the blues, and spirituals into a constructive virtuosity of the jazz
act itself. And it is this virtuosity of construction that, for Bechet, endows
the jazz form with the powers of reversal and regeneration: "[T]hat's the
way I'd like to remember the music. That's the way I'd like to have it
remembered: the way it came back from the man's burying and spoke for
him to the world, and spoke the world to him once more."[139]

By concentrating on the act's repetition as the social basis of these
powers of regeneration and reversal, Bechet's narrative offers significant
insights into the multiple practices through which human reality is lived
and relived, made and remade. In the larger context of black Americans'
political struggle against racism and economic exploitation, the narrative
defines the ideological dimension of the jazz act as one of an *impossible*
relation to the state. At the same time, the collective force of Bechet's
remythologization opens the creative potential of black musicians to the
virtuosic powers of their musical acts, all the while pushing jazz toward
claiming new horizons of freedom, new "Free Days."

# 2 Charlie Parker

## The Virtuosity of Speed

> If one shuts up art in the secret reaches of the individual, one can explain the convergence of independent works only by some destiny that rules over them.
>
> Maurice Merleau-Ponty

The subject of this chapter is the alto saxophonist Charlie "Bird" Parker and his role in the "bebop revolution" of the 1940s. It proceeds, however, by way of an analysis of the underlying "progressivism" of American exceptionalist ideology. In many ways, this chapter posed the greatest difficulties in my writing this book, not the least because Parker himself is such an illusive character and the source of a multitude of arguments concerning the identity of black Americans, the significance of jazz, and the value of creative action in American society. But seen in this light, the difficulties of the subject notwithstanding, the story of Parker's jazz life is central to demonstrating the relevance of ideological criticism to the study of the jazz act. As Stanley Crouch reminds us, "[it] was a fully American story of remarkable triumphs, stubborn misconceptions, and squandered resources that tells us as much about the identity of this country as it does about the powers of jazz."[1] Crouch's comment underlines that the essential *tragedy* of Parker's life—his musical brilliance, his imposing influence on jazz from the 1940s, and his early death in 1955—emerged from the social struggle between the ideological and virtuosic dimensions of the jazz act during World War II. I want to extend Crouch's analysis to the structure of the state itself and argue that the tragedy of Parker's life can be seen as a consequence of the progressivism of American exceptionalist ideology; that Parker's virtuosic jazz powers were, in fact, destroyed by the very progressivism to which those powers were ascribed. Thus, we cannot properly understand the tragedy of Parker's jazz life, nor his virtuosity, without setting him in the context of the ideological intensification of the American state's progressive or expansionist phase.

What follows, then, is an analysis of American capitalist expansion in the twentieth century and, in particular, the force of a progressivist ideology in defining and orienting human creative acts in terms of this expansion. In many ways, Parker's untimely death should provide the critical means to analyze and confront the systemic contradictions and social consequences of this ideology. Instead, from Ross Russell's biography *Bird Lives!* to Clint Eastwood's movie *Bird,* Parker has been used to further mystify, and thus often to rationalize, the relentless progress of the state itself. Throughout this chapter, therefore, Parker is an absent presence, a contradictory space, into which all the promise and failure of progressive desire is projected and through which the manifest powers of the liberated individual are affirmed and valued. In fact, an analysis of Parker's music appears only briefly at the end, more a prelude to the analysis of Ornette Coleman in chapter 3. Parker is thus both the point at which the jazz act achieves a radical self-consciousness of its form and the basis of its ideological undoing, its final subsumption *as a style* into the logic of consumption and the circulation of commodities. In this sense, Parker's reputation as an outsider, as a rallying point for dissent, and as the symbol of a natural or primitive expressionism conspires to turn his life from one of tragedy into one of farce.

To understand how such a turn might happen in an individual's life requires attention to how an individual act acquires historical meaning. The relation of individual action to historical meaning within the progressivism of the American state is defined by the social struggle over the *form* of the state itself. In other words, the form of the American state emerged from the struggle to define it's material and spiritual limits. As Richard Slotkin argues,[2] this struggle centered on the significance of the Western frontier. Indeed, the frontier is an immense historical and ontological theme in the making of American consciousness. It encompasses the great westward movements of the European imagination, the struggles for power and social existence that characterize the colonial conquest of the New World, and the structures of consciousness that orient our own conceptions of human being. Its mythical ground is the limits to human reason and reason's radical encounter with the infinite powers of the natural world; its historical logic is that of the forms of human action and belief as they are circumscribed and transformed by the progressive forces of the capitalist state. As the line "between civilization and savagery," the frontier is thus the existential point at which the free individual and exceptionalist state are united in a single purpose: the human struggle with the limits of life itself.[3]

The closure of the geographic frontier during the 1880s and 1890s provoked a profound political and economic crisis among the American ruling and political classes.[4] In fact, the rise of the state's progressivism is fully understandable only as a consequence of such a crisis. In other words, the frontier only finds its ideological meaning at the very moment some-one laments its loss. In this sense, Frederick Jackson Turner's "frontier thesis" functioned to rationalize the loss in terms of a new constellation of power and consciousness that focused on the problem of industrial development and the American metropolis; that is, it introduced an ideological purpose and efficiency to the productive modes specific to the new corporate economy, to the aims of the rising managerial class, to the demographic expansion of the state, and the fierce struggles between mass labor and entrepreneurial capitalists.[5] In this way the "new" metropolitan frontier was defined as both the site of authentic human action and the condition of the act's acceleration toward its own existential limits. My argument, therefore, is that Parker's jazz act was circumscribed and transformed by an immense ideological mobilization designed to wrest control of the metropolis from the labor movement and from the black underclass. At the same time, I also want to show in what way Parker's virtuosic powers were situated in relation to such a mobilization.

While Bechet countered the ideological effect of the slave event with a collective actualization of the jazz form, Parker invested that form with a virtuosic dimension of *relative speeds.* As Crouch puts it, "Velocity was essential to Parker's life. Everything happened fast."[6] This virtuosity of speed was defined by two key changes in musical consciousness: first, a process of melodic substitution (for example, the melodies of popular jazz standards, such as "I Got Rhythm," were replaced by Parker's own melodies); and second, a process of harmonic extension (for example, the chordal structure of "I Got Rhythm" was retained, but its harmonic possibilities extended to the higher overtones of the scale). In themselves, however, these changes were only the most basic elements of Parker's method. To actualize his virtuosic powers in relation to the emergent bebop form, Parker folded his "melodic rhythm" into *speeds* of infinite slowness (exemplified on pieces such as the 1946 recording of "Lover Man" by the Charlie Parker Quintet) and absolute acceleration (exem-plified on the 1946 recording of "Ornithology" by the Charlie Parker Septet).[7] Furthermore, Parker's emphasis on relative speeds *within* a single piece inscribed the *virtuosity* of the bebop act at the very limits of the metropolis itself and, thus, at the limits of the ideological struggle for its control. In light of this struggle, I analyze how bebop was legitimated, in whose terms it was legitimated, and why.

It is this very problem that Scott DeVeaux addresses in his path-breaking study, *The Birth of Bebop,* and that LeRoi Jones also elaborates in *Blues People.* For Jones, the bebop musicians effected a radical moment of black self-consciousness that actively differentiated their musical acts from those of earlier jazz styles, particularly the white swing and Dixieland bands. He sees two reasons underlying this change: their contemporary restatement of the blues impulse and their profound sense of nonconformity in relation to mainstream American life.[8] Likewise, DeVeaux argues that the bebop musicians' break with the dominant practices of the swing bands was a "a crucial moment of definition" in the "progress of jazz from the margins to the center."[9] Unlike Jones, however, DeVeaux exhibits an ambivalence about how to account for the shift from swing to bebop, or whether, in fact, an emphasis on the inherent radicality of bebop is even historically tenable today. To underline this ambivalence, he cites David Stowe's argument in *Swing Changes* that the relationship between swing and bebop was always a distorted one, and that the lines of division were more ideological than historical.[10]

Following these analyses, I argue that the significance of this shift and how it was explained by both the music's practitioners and its critics leads to a more precise sense of the dynamics of the jazz act and the musical ways of the jazz group. Thus, the difference between Count Basie's or Benny Goodman's bands in the 1930s and the small combo groupings of the bebop bands in the late 1940s raises fundamental questions about the *historical formulation* of a major "transformation" in black consciousness and its relation to particular stylistic "dissolutions" within the history of jazz practices. As Stowe suggests, these formulations about the change in jazz styles (and a correlative change in consciousness) gained historical purpose and legitimacy from the influence of American exceptionalism, or, what he calls the ideology of "Americanism."[11]

As I said above, much of this chapter is taken up with a commentary on American exceptionalist ideology. I offer here an extended discussion of Turner's frontier thesis about how Americans dealt with the crisis of the end of "free land" and how they sought a resolution to this problem. Stowe has convincingly argued that the practices of the 1930s swing bands should not be treated independently of an analysis of their social embeddedness in the overarching ideology of the "American way of life" and the specific politics of the Popular Front, the American labor movement, and the New Deal.[12] Likewise, no study of Charlie Parker's influence on jazz practices and on the emergence of a black consciousness following World War II can ignore the "global" aims of the postwar American state nor the pervasive individualism that marked, in Max Harrison's terms, the fascination with Parker's "chaotic genius" and his "instinctive spontaneity."[13] Thus, amid the militarist and anticommunist rhetoric and practices of the Truman administration, of organized labor, and of big business, the black jazz artist was enlisted as a key oppositional figure in the struggle to assert the creative power of the individual in the face of widespread social and political crisis. The main point to keep in mind, at this juncture, is that neither bebop nor the exceptionalist ideology through which it was framed as a meaningful act should be considered analytical constants. Both forms were part of a larger process of social struggle; and this struggle was, as a matter of course, uneven and unstable, fraught with confusion and complications. At no time was the form of bebop, nor that of the state and its ideological framework, reducible to a single moment of theoretical synthesis, a purely structural epiphany in which jazz was equivalent to the state. The historical eventuation of these social and political forms was active and purposive, constrained and constraining, impassioned and destructive, but also incomplete and partial.

All this is to say that bebop's significance as a musical act is not simply to be grasped from the supersession of swing nor in the opposition to mass cultural phenomena; but neither was it simply an assertion of the possibility of the liberated individual, nor indeed the culpability of the state in constraining individual possibility. Squeezed as they were between the dominance of popular dance bands and the elite conditions of the European classical tradition, between the fears of a racist population and the opportunities of mass entertainment, the bebop musicians found ways to the limits of each, and in doing so, reoriented the dynamics of their practices toward *a collective virtuosity of the jazz act*. Dizzy Gillespie put it this way:

> You only have so many notes, and what makes a style is how you get from one note to the other. We had some fundamental background training in European harmony and music theory superimposed on our own knowledge from Afro-American musical tradition. We invented our own way of getting from one place to the next. . . . Our phrases were different. We phrased differently from the older guys. . . . Musically, we were changing the way that we spoke to reflect the way that we felt. New phrasing came in with the new accent. Our music had a new accent.[14]

In this chapter, I argue that the sole reliance on the tenets of exceptionalist ideology to explain the collective virtuosity of the bebop act fails because the very form of that collective virtuosity overreached the progressive symbology of the state and the historical logic of "the American way." Even though Parker's bebop act was in every sense interpellated by the ideological framework of American progressivism, I want to suggest that there was also a dimension to his bebop act that transformed the conditions of its production.

## Only So Many Notes

By 1945, the ideas worked out in jam sessions and a number of small group combos put together by Parker, Gillespie, Thelonious Monk, Max Roach, Oscar Pettiford, and a few others were crystallized into the new musical practices known as bebop. In a 1949 interview, Parker explained that "[b]op is no love-child of jazz," but something "entirely separate and apart" from the older tradition.[15] He went on to explain that the reason for its separation was that the "beat in a bop band is with the music, against it, behind it. It pushes it. It helps it. Help is the big thing. It [bop] has no continuity of beat, no steady chug-chug. Jazz has, and that's why bop is—more flexible."[16]

As noted above, Parker's reputation as a genius is built on the degree to which his music expresses a critical break, a transformation in the conditions of postwar life, not only for black Americans but also for white Americans. Because Parker left so few recorded interviews or coherent statements about his music, we are forced to rely almost entirely on what the musicians he played with thought or remembered about him. At the same time, interest in Parker has prompted, as I suggested at the outset of this chapter, a seeming endless flood of speculation concerning the creative powers of the black musician and his or her role in American society. From jazz critics to poets to intellectuals, Parker's bebop virtuosity encompassed all the contradictions of American society in such a way that, in the words of the novelist Ralph Ellison, it "blew him to the meaningful center of things" from where he captured "something of the discordancies, the yearning, the romance and cunning of the age and ordered it into a haunting art."[17]

Before I discuss the ideological influence of the frontier on American consciousness and then proceed to an analysis of the creative character of the bebop act, I want to establish the sense in which Parker came to symbolize not only the *inevitable* progression from hot jazz and swing to bebop, but also a fundamental shift in the relation of blacks to the American state. As Ross Russell argues in his biography of Parker, "[j]azz style from 1920 to World War II seemed to flow from [Louis] Armstrong. Charlie Parker changed the course of that river and set up a new complex of forces. Almost single-handedly he emancipated time and sound for those to follow."[18] At the same time, the emergence of bebop signaled to educated white Americans such as the novelist John Clellon Holmes that the "quintessential American artist was the Black jazz musician."[19] Likewise, in his influential essay on white middle class disaffection, Norman Mailer writes that the "presence of the Hip as a working philosophy in the sub-world of American life is probably due to jazz and its knifelike entrance into culture, its subtle but so penetrating influence on the avant-garde generation. . . ."[20] Indeed, such was the fervor among the many contributors to Robert Reisner's memorial, *Bird: The Legend of Charlie Parker* that there was every reason to consider bebop to be their "golden age," and Parker their "fertility god."[21]

Scott DeVeaux argues that the pervasive influence of these ideas on historical consciousness suggests that bebop is still very much "the point at which our contemporary ideas of jazz come into focus."[22] In tackling the transition from swing to bebop, his analysis elucidates the sense in which the above statements were symptomatic of an ideological distortion already at work in the social reality of the jazz act, in that they all argue for a particular identification with blackness that displaces any concerns about the domination of blacks *as a class* to the level of the individual musician's capacity for self-expression. DeVeaux's own argument concerning the struggle for recognition by swing saxophonist Coleman Hawkins suggests that what was at stake with jazz's "knife-like entrance" into American culture was not simply the value placed on jazz as such (in relation to other musical forms or in terms of its commercial currency), but the actual suppression of the very social antagonism on which the ultimate ideological *failure* of the American system was premised.[23]

This is precisely the argument pursued by LeRoi Jones in his theory of a dignified and eloquent "blues people," forever struggling against the latent fantasies and dominative practices of the white and black middle classes: plantation owners and club owners, overseers and middlemen, alike. In Jones's analysis, far from being a hipster's playground, the achievement of bebop was to remove the jazz form from the dangers of middle class dilution and understanding: "For one thing, the young musicians began to think of themselves as serious musicians, even artists, and not performers. And that attitude erased immediately the protective and parochial atmosphere of 'the folk expression' from jazz."[24] The decisive break with the structures of mainstream culture came when "Parker, Monk, and Gillespie were all quoted as saying, 'I don't care if you listen to my music or not.' "[25] For Jones, this was the moment of repetition and of renewal; the critical turning point when black musicians asserted that their musical forms were "always radical in the context of formal American culture."[26] I return to Jones's analysis in due course, but first want to consider two justifiably influential essays on jazz by the novelist Ralph Ellison.

Like Jones, Ellison was preoccupied with the bebop player's social sense and how their musical ways transformed the meaning and value of jazz. But, in taking up the problems posed by Jones in *Blues People,* and by the contributors to *Bird: The Legend of Charlie Parker,* Ellison reversed the terms of their analyses in essential ways. In the essay "On Bird, Bird-Watching, and Jazz," for example, he argues that in order to escape the entertainer's role occupied by jazz trumpeter Louis Armstrong, a role which they rejected as a classic case of "Uncle Tomming," the bebop players produced an equally problematic distortion of the "will to expression," and from there, negated the crucial step to a positive black consciousness. Ellison's critique is not in any sense an attempt to deny the significance of bebop. In an earlier piece he praises bebop's "complexity of sound and rhythm and self-assertive passion. . . ."[27] As musicians, the beboppers were at the forefront of defining the character of a black creative practices that were at once resistant to and transformative of the oppressive conditions of postwar American society. But, by labeling Armstrong an "Uncle Tom" with the aim of asserting the authentic nature of their own acts, the bebop musicians confused the virtuosic qualities of Armstrong's playing with the ideological effects of his public persona: "By rejecting Armstrong they thought to rid themselves of the entertainer's role. And by way of getting rid of the role they demanded, in the name of their racial identity, a purity of status which by definition is impossible for the performing artist."[28] For Ellison, Parker was the most visible example of this distortion:

> No jazzman, not even Miles Davis, struggled harder to
> escape the entertainer's role than Charlie Parker. The
> pathos of his life lies in the ironic reversal through which
> his struggles to escape what in Armstrong is basically a
> *make-believe* role of clown—which the irreverent poetry
> and triumphant sound of his trumpet makes even the
> squarest of squares aware of—resulted in Parker's becoming
> something far more "primitive": a sacrificial figure whose

struggles against personal chaos, on stage and off, served as
entertainment for a ravenous, sensation-starved, culturally
disoriented public which had but the slightest notion of
its real significance. . . . In the end he had no private life
and his most tragic moments were drained of human
significance.[29]

Thus, far from attaining the dignity of an art and in an effort to negate
the pervasive influence of the minstrel tradition, the beboppers fell
on their own swords, turning bebop into a "grim comedy of racial
manners. . . ."[30]

Ellison's criticism of Jones's *Blues People* is no less insistent on
the critic's historical accountability to the dynamics of social struggle
among black Americans and a sensitivity to the "cunning of reason"
that determined the social value of human acts: "[H]is [Jones's] theory
founders before that complex of human motives which makes human
history, and which is so characteristic of the American Negro."[31] In his
efforts to accentuate the separatist impulses of the bebop musicians, Jones
"ignores the fact that the creators of the style were seeking, whatever
their musical intentions—and they were the least political of men—a
fresh form of entertainment which would allow them their fair share of
the entertainment market, which had been dominated by whites during
the swing era."[32] Likewise, in seeking to emphasize the political dimension
of black music, Jones's analysis according to Ellison "lacks a sense of the
excitement and surprise of men living in the world—of enslaved and
politically weak men successfully imposing their values upon a powerful
society through song and dance."[33]

Against Jones's opposition of authentic blues (country blues) to the
blues of commercial dilution (city blues), Ellison argues that "any viable
theory of Negro American culture obligates us to fashion a more adequate
theory of American culture as a whole."[34] This involved recognizing the

cruel contradiction implicit within the art form itself.
For true jazz is an art of individual assertion within and
against the group. Each true jazz moment (as distinct from
the uninspired commercial performance) springs from a
contest in which each artist challenges all the rest; each
solo flight, or improvisation, represents (like the successive
canvasses of a painter) a definition of his identity: as
individual, as member of the collectivity and as a link in
the chain of tradition. Thus, because jazz finds its very life

in an endless improvisation upon traditional materials, the
jazzman must lose his identity even as he finds it. . . .[35]

It was, therefore, from "the tension between desire and ability that the
techniques of jazz emerged."[36]

I have summarized Ellison's few articles on jazz at some length not
only because he has mounted a convincing argument for the emergence
of a specific mode of jazz virtuosity, but also because from his arguments
issued a number of the key critical problems concerning Charlie Parker's
significance, and the difficulties of trying to understand the achievement
of this most mercurial of musicians. What Ellison asserts is more suggestive than substantive, sketching the problems (rather than providing the
analysis) for subsequent historians and critics, and all the while demanding
further attention to the structure of the musical act. For him, the making
of jazz was a dangerously negotiated (and continuously renegotiated)
outcome of black Americans' struggle to find their group and individual
identity in modern American society. In this sense, the bebop musician's
politics was never guaranteed, often working to reinforce as much as
decompose the structures of state power and global expansion, to which
the jazz act was attached as sensuous (and, in the case of Parker, tragic)
affirmation. If Parker is to be more than just a sacrificial figure on the altar
of "the American dream," then, in Ellison's view, we must reformulate
the kinds of historical questions that get asked—questions about how to
situate Parker's playing and about the *social intentions* of the jazz act. This
is, in many ways, and in spite of Ellison's polemic, LeRoi Jones's lasting
achievement.

The structuring or situating of the jazz artifact *as an ideological problem*
is clarified by the dispute between Jones and Ellison. While neither explicitly refuted the progressive dimensions of American history, they both
hoped to liberate the musical act from the determinations of entrenched
racism, the consequences of an aversive liberal condescension, and the
constrictive effects of mass commercialism. The difference between them
rests on the burden of explanation placed on black musicians and the
role of history in shaping the forms of black expression. For Ellison,
Jones's attempt to situate the forms of black music within the passageway
from slavery to "citizenship" results in a series of equally problematic
abstractions, none of which can grasp in any but the most limited way the
musician's "will toward expression."[37] The virtuosic powers of the black
musician's practices are compromised by Jones's attempt to "impose an
ideology on this complexity. . . ."[38] A proper grasp of the musical act
would "treat them first as poetry and as ritual."[39] Ellison's objection

here rests on the charge that Jones pays insufficient attention to the interior structure of the act. The actual tension within and between the two arguments thus emerges from a disagreement over not only the dynamics of jazz acts *in practice,* but also how their legitimacy as an artistic form in "the American grain" is to be secured *in theory.* This tension is most evident in what was perhaps Ellison's most important essay, "Living with Music." In the essay, he remembers how, as a youth, the neighbors tolerated his efforts to play the trumpet:

> Despite those who complained and cried to heaven for Gabriel to blow a chorus so heavenly sweet and so hellishly hot that I'd forever put down my horn, there were more tolerant ones who were willing to pay in present pain for future pride. For who knew what skinny kid with his chops wrapped around a trumpet mouthpiece and a faraway look in his eyes might become the next Armstrong? Yes, and send you, at some big dance a few years hence, into an ecstasy of rhythm and memory and brassy affirmation of the goodness of being alive and part of a community? Someone had to; for it was part of the group tradition—though that was not how they said it.[40]

Ellison's argument here places jazz within the social conditions of its production. Instead of the ideological abstractions of the jazz life, he situates musical activity in relation to those for whom such activity constitutes an integral aspect of the social world. Music is thus a means of legitimating the social world as much as the social world gives meaning and value to the musical act. To further emphasize this social dimension to the act and the process of its legitimation, Ellison recalls how the events at Minton's Playhouse in New York in the early 1940s, the small club where many of the early jam sessions that resulted in bebop took place, constituted a "continuing symposium of jazz, a summation of all the styles, personal and traditional, of jazz. Here it was possible to hear its resources of technique, ideas, harmonic structure, melodic phrasing and rhythmic possibilities explored more thoroughly than was ever possible before."[41]

These striking observations direct us toward one of the principal aims of this book: a phenomenology of the jazz act. For example, the virtuosic qualities of the jam session, while no doubt a struggle between musical wills, was in every sense a struggle for the musician's *social* position and status. The assertion of the jazz musician's individual value was, in these conditions, constituted in the aftermath of such events. What counted, however, was the sense in which the musical act formed an attitude toward the social world, a means of orienting the musician and his or her audience, while simultaneously functioning as "entertainment."[42] In this sense, the jazz act was constitutive of social reality, but not as mere evidence of ideological efficiency or commercial success.

To be satisfied with this critique of Jones—in which Ellison argues both for the creative character of the act and against the reduction of the act to ideology—would not only do Jones a disservice but would limit the critical potential of both arguments. Indeed, as we will see, what Ellison neglects is precisely the *form* of the ideological struggle for which he taxes the author of *Blues People*.

Throughout *Blues People,* Jones argues for a disjunctive relation between the ideological *and* practical (and thus, historical) processes of musical making. To demonstrate the logic of this disjunction, he quotes Thelonious Monk on his residency as house pianist at Minton's Playhouse in the 1940s:

> I was just playing a gig, trying to play music. While I was at Minton's anybody sat in if he could play. I never bothered anybody. I had no particular feeling that anything new was being built. It's true modern jazz probably began to get popular there, but some of these histories and articles put what happened over the course of ten years into one year. They put people all together in one time in one place. I've seen practically everybody at Minton's, but they were just there playing. They weren't giving any lectures.[43]

Monk's remark serves as a turning point in Jones's text: How was bebop made? How did it develop? Jones is indecisive here. While he does make a point of comparison between Monk's recollection of the jam sessions and the legend of bebop's sudden emergence that filled Jones's adolescence, there is no sense in which the doubt about bebop's origins is resolved. That he remains indecisive, however, proves crucial to an understanding of bebop: the act itself was constituted in the irreducible gap between "the legend that filled my adolescence" (the ideology of its production) and the ten years that Monk spent "trying to play music" (the logic of its making).[44] To grasp this sense of a disjuncture between the *how* and the *why* of the bebop act, Jones downplays the musical transition from swing to bebop (how did the musicians who played at Minton's Playhouse and other small Harlem jazz clubs arrive at the bebop form?). At the same time, he folds this transition into a larger *ideological* struggle: between "the thirties and the end of World War II, there was perhaps as radical a change in the psychological perspective of the Negro American toward America as there was between the Emancipation and 1930."[45]

Against the tendency to either mystify the bebop act (as, for example, did Andre Hodeir, Norman Mailer, Ross Russell, Robert Reisner) or later attempts to demystify it (as did Ralph Ellison, Scott DeVeaux, David Stowe), Jones asserts a far more radical conception of the musical act. The structural imbalance in his explanatory framework is already internal to the act itself. Indeed, the form of the bebop act was neither the result of the musician's practical struggle to master his or her material, nor that of the act's retrospective ideological mystique. Rather, the bebop act's form was constitutive of, and constituted by, black Americans' new relation toward the American state.

In Jones's terms, the bebop act was both premature (blacks were not ready for it, for its consequences) and came too late (blacks were already caught in the system of capitalist exploitation). The bebop act was thus revolutionary in the sense that it suspended the very terms of its own making and the ideological basis of its future value *as commodity*. In a fine discussion of human action, Harold Rosenberg sketches the paradoxical outline of this revolutionary moment of suspension: "The actors stand at a terminal point of the action, with inevitable destruction before them on one side and an empty space of possibility on the other."[46] We can understand this to mean that for Rosenberg, the revolutionary act is constituted in the process of its enactment, while at the same time, the reasons for acting at all lie buried in the forms of past action. Only in the moment of suspension, when the past is synchronized with the present, does the act produce the conditions for its revolutionary transformation.[47] For Jones, it was the repetition of the blues impulse, in pieces such as Parker's "Now's the Time" or "Cool Blues," that constituted the revolutionary basis of the bebop act, that enabled the musicians to produce a new relation to the jazz form, and thus, to the state.[48]

Jones's emphasis on the gap between the act's history and its future possibilities directs us to the interior structure of the act *qua* act, and the consequences of reducing the act's virtuosic dimension to its reified progressive contents. On the one hand, bebop was determined by the presupposition of an objective historical necessity, persisting independently of consciousness.[49] As Ted Gioia argues, "the rise of a more overt modernism should not be viewed as an abrupt shift, as a major discontinuity in the music's history. It was simply an extension of jazz's inherent tendency to mutate, to change, and to grow."[50] On the other hand, this same objective necessity was coupled with a purely subjective notion of the act. Sacvan Bercovitch puts it this way: "[T]he only plausible modes of American opposition are those that center on the self: as stranger or prophet, rebel or revolutionary, lawbreaker or truth-seeker, or any other adversarial or dissenting form of individualism."[51] In his tribute to Parker, Robert Reisner relies upon exactly this existential mode of explanation: "Bird was the supreme hipster. He made his own laws."[52]

In these terms, bebop can be understood as the synthesis of the objective laws of American history and the subjective desire of the liberated self. To produce such an ideological synthesis, however, the founding gestures of bebop had to be repeated over and over, to the point where even the swing band leader Benny Goodman remade his jazz act as a bebop combo.[53] The struggle among critics and historians to define bebop was a struggle between the individual and history, between the new and the old, between black and white, that would ultimately be resolved by the progressive logic of the state. Even Ellison argues that the very existence of bebop, the logic of its emergence in time as a social act, was evidence of a turbulent level "where human instincts conflict with social institutions; where contemporary civilized values and hypocrisies are challenged by Dionysian urges of between-wars youth born to prosperity, conditioned by the threat of destruction, and inspired—when not seeking total anarchy—by the need to bring social reality and social pretensions into a more meaningful balance."[54] The significance of Jones's analysis of bebop is to question the possibility of ever achieving such a "meaningful balance" within the institutional and ideological framework of the American state. The bebop act already exceeded the historical terms of its subjective making, while the conditions of its historical production were, likewise, already ideological. At this level, the act's very *impossibility* was the also the basis of its radical virtuosity.

## Progress, the Frontier, and American Ideology

From the early period of European colonial settlement in the New World, the western frontier exerted a powerful influence on the development of American artistic practices and American theories of literature, painting, poetry, and music.[55] After the American Revolution in 1776, the development of these practices and their theoretical counterparts in history and aesthetics were intensified through the broader and fiercer debates about national purpose, the form of the new republic, and the character of its citizenry. Much of the discussion was taken up, first, with defining the *unique* qualities of the colonial enterprise—whether religious or mercantile—and then with demonstrating how the subsequent *revolutionary* transformation from British colonial subjects to New World republicans was, in fact, internal to the realization of America's "manifest destiny."[56] It was the *promise* of the frontier as the register of American aspirations, for nineteenth-century and early-twentieth-century American artists, that defined the geographic limits of the state, and thus, the existential limits of individual acts of expression.[57]

I want to develop further my argument concerning the influence of the frontier on the progressivism of the state and its repercussions for the meaning of human creative acts. A significant part of this argument will concern Frederick Jackson Turner's "frontier thesis," which I intend to explain in terms of a dominant "pastoral logic," a notion drawn from Leo Marx's text on the pastoral imagination, *The Machine in the Garden.* I argue that the historical legitimacy of Charlie Parker's music, the fascination with his life, but also the contradictions and confusions evident in studies of Parker stem from a fundamental shift that occurred in the symbolic structure of American ideology after the 1870s. The *form* of this shift, while encompassing the changing modes of production correlative to industrialism and entrepreneurial capitalism, relied upon a pastoral logic to explain and legitimate the dynamics of state expansion, technical and scientific progress, and the exploitation of human labor and natural "resources." Thus, the "fate of the frontier" became the basis of the confrontation between capital and labor, between conservatives and progressives, and between the country and the city; a confrontation, however, that was increasingly centered on a struggle for control of the metropolis.[58]

Before turning to directly consider Turner's argument, however, a further summation of Richard Slotkin's remarkable trilogy of studies (*Regeneration through Violence; The Fatal Environment; Gunfighter Nation*) about the "frontier myth" will help define the relation between American progressive ideology and musical practices. Indeed, any attempt to understand the social value attributed to the jazz act suggests the importance of grasping the paradoxical moment "when 'Frontier' became primarily a term of ideological rather than geographical reference."[59] With *The Fatal Environment*—the second of his studies—Slotkin offers an extended exposition concerning this relation between the frontier myth and its ideological framework during the nineteenth century. Throughout the book, he seeks to demonstrate the centrality of the frontier myth to the problem of maintaining social equilibrium in a society committed irrevocably to expansion.[60] That myth

is arguably the longest-lived of American myths, with
origins in the colonial period and a powerful continuing
presence in contemporary culture. Although the Myth of
the Frontier is only one of the operative myth/ideological
systems that form American culture, it is an extremely
important and persistent one. Its ideological underpinnings
are those same "laws" of capitalist competition, of supply
and demand, of Social Darwinian "survival of the fittest"
as a rationale for social order, and of "Manifest Destiny"
that have been the building blocks of our dominant
historiographical tradition and political ideology.[61]

The relation between mythical consciousness and ideology is the
basis of Slotkin's discussion. For him, myth does not "argue its ideology, it
exemplifies it. It projects models of good or heroic behavior that reinforce
values of ideology, and affirm as good the distribution of authority and
power that ideology rationalizes."[62] The distinction between a myth and
its ideological realization lies in its form: "The language of myth is
indirect, metaphorical, and narrative in structure. It renders ideology
in the form of the symbol, exemplum, and fable, and poetically evokes
fantasy, memory, and sentiment."[63] This is to say, the ideological structure
of human actions actualizes the mythical forms of the society toward
which those actions are oriented. At the same time, the "myths we inherit
carry marks of past reworking, and beneath their smooth surfaces they
conceal the scars of conflicts and ambivalences that attend their making.
All of a culture's ideology is contained in myths: the most opposite
sides and contradictions of belief are registered in mythic discourse and
brought into the frame of its narrative."[64] Myths, therefore, are necessarily
implicated in every act within a given ideological framework, while
ideology is the power of differentiation that systematizes and orients the
historical conditions of the act.

The ideological framework for human action in America was
premised on the mythic notion of an exceptional past actualized in the
movement toward the frontier: "The essence of all that is genuinely
exceptional in American history is embodied in those myths peculiar to
our culture, of which the oldest and most central is the Myth of the
Frontier. If we approach this Myth with the awareness of its function
as a rationalizer of the processes of capitalist development in America,
we can begin to see some of the special characteristics of American
ideology. . . ."[65] In this understanding, the emphasis on the material
conditions for expansion required the frontier to guarantee the cycles of

production and development, of boom and bust, of supply and demand. For Slotkin, this guarantee appeared in the "assertion that the Frontier land had the capacity to work grand transformations on the character, fortunes, and institutions of the inhabitants. Each phase of Frontier development carried its own ideas about the kind of transformations the land offered; but all shared a common implication that transformation would be part of the experience."[66] My argument is that this expectation of a necessary transformation of self, of the self's fortunes, and thus of the state, in terms of a frontier, constituted the ideological basis for the making of authentic human acts.

During the nineteenth century, the struggle for the social and political legitimacy of human action unfolded within an ideological framework that privileged the natural or primitive world of the frontier as the primary basis of material wealth and spiritual renewal. However, the emergence of American capitalism and industrial modes of production in the 1830s and 1840s, and its political correlative in Jacksonian democracy, generated a dramatic crisis of values and a sense of doubt—a pessimism—concerning the future of the state and its revolutionary principles. Examples of the impact of this crisis within American thought extended from Henry David Thoreau's *Walden* to Charles Fourier's phalanxes, from William Lloyd Garrison's abolitionism to Booker T. Washington's Tuskegee Institute. While none of these enterprises was explicitly expansive or aggressive in their relation to the natural world, each was shaped by the idea that the western frontier was the decisive fact in the perpetuity of the American state's independence and for the vitality and success of political suffrage and economic freedom.[67] In Slotkin's terms, this frontier formed "the border between a world of possibilities and one of actualities, a world theoretically unlimited and one defined by its limitations."[68]

The critical articulation of the frontier myth as the basis of the state's material and spiritual power emerged from the early struggle between Federalists and Republicans in the postrevolutionary period, most notably among Thomas Jefferson, Alexander Hamilton, James Madison, Daniel Webster, and Aaron Burr, a debate that reached back to the Massachusetts settlers' "errand into the wilderness." As J. G. A. Pocock reminds us, the political underpinning for the early period of constitutional debates during the 1780s rested on the division between civic virtue and commerce, between a constitutional monarchy and Machiavellian republicanism. The force of the division in shaping the subsequent federative documents, and the initial form of the agrarian capitalist state, illustrated the ideological crisis of the revolutionary generation. For although "Americans had been compelled to abandon a theory of constitutional humanism which related personality to government directly and according to its diversities, they had not thereby given up the pursuit of a form of political society in which an individual might be free and know himself in his relation to society."[69] In this sense, within the ideology of individual equality remained an implicit recognition of political and social hierarchy; in fact, the legal and political structures of the new federal Constitution presupposed and augmented the very inequalities and imbalances its authors sought, in principle, at least to regulate (through reform), if not eradicate (through violence).

The repercussions of this dispute meant that the new political category of "the people" appeared, for a time, to be a socially creative category, but also an undifferentiated and inexplicable revolutionary mass. As Pocock argues, however, this new, republican "people" was yet to be "circumscribed by the definition and distribution of specific qualities. It is of unknown mass and force, and can develop new and unpredicted needs, capacities and powers. All of these can be received and coordinated within the structure of federalism, so that the classical rhetoric of balance and stability is still appropriate, but this structure can be proclaimed capable of infinite expansion."[70] For the new postrevolutionary political class, the central ideological and organizational problem was how to direct this "revolutionary mass" toward the state's productive limits, that is, to liberate its material wealth, without descending once again into the chaos of a Revolutionary War. Thus, interest and faction became the modes in which the abstracted mass—"We the people"—were compelled to identify and pursue their activities in politics.[71] In this way, the new republic of *represented interests* and *factional agency* was cast as a commonwealth for expansion through a logic in which the frontier, by the 1800s, was the definitive principle on which such an expansive enterprise relied.[72]

Following in the wake of a succession of economic and social crises, Turner's "frontier thesis" of 1893 sought to exemplify (and rationalize) this elite and factional commitment to industrial and corporate expansion as the basis of America's political and economic power. The process of making a "democratic people"—a historical act derived from the interests and coalitions in Congress and its relationship to the powerful regional legislatures—expressed both the form of the state and, equally, its material and spiritual limits. By defining the process of westward expansion as a *political fact,* Turner thus argued that the purest examples of democratic consciousness were to be found on the frontier itself: "American social development has been continually beginning over again on the frontier. This perennial rebirth, this fluidity of American life, this expansion westward with its new opportunities, its continuous touch with the simplicity of American society, furnish the forces dominating American character."[73] The future of the American state was predicated on the existence of the frontier; while the *ideal* American character was formed from the promise of that future.

On this understanding, the dynamic relationship of the state to the frontier implied newer and more efficient forms of social and economic organization that required the institutional certainties of centralized government and the enlightened decisions of bourgeois reason and learning:

> The United States lies like a huge page in the history of society. Line by line as we read this continental page from West to East we find the record of social evolution. It begins with the Indian and the hunter; it goes on to tell of the disintegration of savagery by the entrance of the trader, the pathfinder of civilization; we read the annals of the pastoral stage in ranch life; the exploitation of the soil by the raising of unrotated crops of corn and wheat in sparsely settled farming communities; the intensive culture of the denser farm settlement; and finally the manufacturing organization with city and factory system.[74]

The processes of historical development thus expressed the liberal contents of American history—manifested in acts of individual will—as a revolutionary "overcoming of limits" that guaranteed those acts an *exceptional role* in the founding of the American republic.

For Turner, the logic of discovery and expansion "followed the arteries made by geology, pouring an ever richer tide through them, until at last the slender paths of aboriginal intercourse have been broadened and interwoven into the complex mazes of modern commercial lines; the wilderness has been interpenetrated by lines of civilization growing ever more numerous. It is like the steady growth of a complex nervous system from the originally simple, inert continent."[75] American reality was produced in the process of turning inert matter into movement, of turning the "virgin land" into prosperity. Echoing Ralph Waldo Emerson's 1844 lecture on the "Young American," Turner connected the diversity and fecundity of the earth to the image of the brain. Brain and earth were then made one, fused in a series of cerebral and social pathways, that granted a theological primacy to the democratic spirit as it was expressed in the entrepreneurial expansion of trade routes and capital investment. In this way, Turner effectively synthesized individual identity and national productivity.

To achieve this synthesis, however, Turner defined two variables capable of regulating the appearance of an American consciousness and, likewise, guiding the development of the American state as the result of such a consciousness. The first was the size of the population. The second was the frequency with which contradictions or disputes occurred (and were then resolved) within the dominant group or region. These variables enabled Turner to locate the distribution of democratic potential at the frontier itself (in the form of free land) and to outline the terms of individual self-consciousness (in the form of suffrage), but as *part of a single historical process:* the development of the state's statutory and economic power. The American self was then identified with a revolutionary transformation in human history that equated this statutory and economic power of the state with the individual's powers of self-expression and self-transformation.

The focus of the state's power was to regulate the availability of free land—and so guarantee the conditions for the emergence of universal suffrage—and regulate the population—and therefore minimize internal conflict or disorder. These, for Turner, were the essential conditions required to transcend the feudalism of the Old World and consolidate the freedom and prosperity of the New. But, with the West fast approaching its geographic limits and those limits already constitutive of the dynamics of industrial production, Turner was forced to multiply his frontier to infinity, to find a new force immanent to the democratic process.[76] This force was to be found in the expansion of American economic interests abroad and the redemption of nondemocratic (and non-American) peoples. That Americans were capable of further expansion beyond their shores, without undermining their unique institutions, resulted from the fact that they "have been compelled to adapt themselves to the changes of an expanding people—to the changes involved in crossing a continent, in winning a wilderness. . . ."[77] In this way, the frontier was no longer just a geographic boundary denoting freedom, but the symbolic passage from life to art, from experience to expression, and from sense to sensation.

### Turner's Refrain

The critical development in Turner's theory is the subsumption of progress into productivity, and the idealization of a primitive state of being specific to frontier life. Not only did this idea suffuse the institutional and ideological structures of the American state, but as Turner argued, its very logic underpinned the formulation of a theory of American experience and its relation to the state's manifest destiny.[78] The state's progressive crisis emerged when the American "errand into the wilderness" was thrown into turmoil by the geographic limitations of the frontier, and thus, the end of free land. Turner's thesis was, in these terms, symptomatic of the transition in the ideological frame of the American state. He offered an efficient structure through which the analysis of individual expression, and its relation to the experience of life in America, might be pursued; or, as Slotkin argues, Turner's analysis turned the West into a "set of symbols that *constituted* an explanation of history."[79]

In providing a rationale for the emergence of an American historical consciousness, Turner's argument circumscribed the sphere of creative action in relation to the inevitability of expansion. In terms of the logic of exceptionalist ideology, his description was a model of social-evolutionary thought in its attention to how the fundamental tension between expansion and progress might be resolved. In doing so, he implied an absolute correlation between America's unique historical circumstances, as they had developed in relation to the western frontier, and the process of discovery, as the key to consciousness.

In this context, Turner's refrain was: With the end of free land, what then was to become of democracy?[80] Thus the critical question, for Americans, became where to turn—how to proceed, to prosper, and to progress according to the manifest destiny of the state—when the ideological limits of that same state were internal to the very processes of imperial expansion, of technical and scientific progress, of civilization itself. The expressive potential of the frontier offered an answer in the form of a pure relation to nature, a relation grounded in the free individual's inherent capacity for self-identity and self-transformation. In *Virgin Land,* Henry Nash Smith argues that the idea of nature "suggested to Turner a poetic account of the influence of free land as a rebirth, a regeneration, a rejuvenation of man and society constantly recurring where civilization came into contact with the wilderness along the frontier."[81] The frontier allowed for "social development continually to begin over again, wherever society gave signs of breaking into classes. Here was a magic fountain of youth in which America continually bathed and was rejuvenated."[82]

If Smith is correct, the movement toward the frontier and the consequences of human progress as a condition of the frontier were unified by Turner into a single law of production that succeeded in resolving the tension between the origin and development of America, and its statutory validity and historical significance. For him, the frontier, in whatever form it took, was "the line of most rapid and effective

Americanization."[83] In making this claim, Turner prefigured the logic of a transition from the prehistoric geological formations of the "new" continent to the geographical properties of discovery and settlement and, from there, to the democratic, economic, and military institutions of the modern industrial metropolis. The personal history of each individual life was aligned with the general history of the state and its metropolitan centers, such that each moved toward its implicit self-representation (one becoming the mirror of the other). The concept of progress, as the necessary condition of this demand for self-discovery and self-representation, produced a corresponding social order based on the "steady movement away from the influence of Europe, a steady growth of independence along American lines."[84]

The sense of loss generated by the crisis of free land in the 1890s further intensified Turner's argument as to why and how the "men of the Western World turned their backs upon the Atlantic Ocean, and with grim energy and self-reliance began to build up a society free from the dominance of ancient forms."[85] In this way, his very lament effected a radical displacement of progressive thought from the frontier to the city, without giving up the terms of individual identification and regeneration, of national rebirth. His thesis managed to redirect American historians, politicians, and artists toward the problem of the frontier as a limitation of history, rather than its destiny; a logic of displacement, rather than of a radical closure. Far from finding in this crisis of free land evidence of the state's ideological, economic, or political limits, the underlying assumptions of Turner's argument remained intact, while the frontier itself was modified to accommodate the radically altered material dynamics of the industrial state, the corporate aims of entrepreneurial capital, the influx of immigrants from Europe and Asia, and the subsequent expansion (after both World Wars) of the urban working classes.

The significance of the frontier to the historical logic of the American state was grounded in a struggle for control of the metropolis and, more specifically, for *centralized* control of the state's productive forces and material wealth. This struggle, as I have argued, concerned itself with the limits of state power and its relation to individual action. In this sense, we may reconceive Turner's thesis as a theory of human action and an analysis of the individual's struggle for freedom within the state's progressive framework. The frontier is both the site of authentic human action and the condition of the act's acceleration toward its own existential limits: "American democracy is fundamentally the outcome of the experiences of the American people in dealing with the West."[86] The distinctive fact of the frontier was the freedom of the individual to rise under conditions of social mobility. At the same time, this freedom was the very condition of the individual's existence.[87] For Turner, existence was predicated on a mobility that was already inscribed within the limits of the state. The frontier was the horizon against which the *value* of human action was measured and in terms of which the freedom *to act* was ensured. Long after the frontier conditions of a particular region have disappeared, "the conception of society, the ideals and aspirations which it produced, persist in the minds of the people."[88] Without such a mediating ideal, the state itself would inevitably turn from its progressive path to menace the democratic institutions on which it was based.[89] While the closure of the geographic frontier in the 1880s was thus a crisis of action, it was equally about preparing the ground for a new productive relation to the state, about redefining the ideological conditions of the individual's existential limits. In the context of mass industrialism and the emergence of forms of monopoly capital, this existential limit was *mobility itself*, while its productive form was that of *acceleration*.

In *The Visible Hand*, Alfred Chandler defines these new relations of production with the phrase *economies of speed*. What characterized the economies of speed were the dynamics of corporate consolidation, monetary reform, and political centralization:

> In modern mass production, as in modern mass distribution and modern transportation and communications, economies resulted more from speed than from size. It was not the size of a manufacturing establishment in terms of number of workers and the amount of value of productive equipment but the velocity of throughput and the resulting increase in volume that permitted economies that lowered costs and increased output per worker and per machine. . . . Central to obtaining economies of speed were the development of new machinery, better raw materials, and intensified application of energy, followed by the creation of organizational designs and procedures to coordinate and control the new high-volume flows through several processes of production.[90]

This shift to economies of speed comprised a corresponding transformation in historical consciousness that oscillated between a deep pessimism and a wild optimism concerning the value and limits of the modern industrial order, and the relation of the individual to that order. As Dorothy Ross argues in her study of American exceptionalism,

> [t]he urbanizing experience of the early twentieth century
> accentuated the . . . sense of historical dislocation. The
> disorder of the city was a dimension of the disorder
> of history, and the desire for control a measure of the
> disorientation in the changing liberal world. . . . To
> gain perspective one had to look not at the compressed
> foreground, but at the long background of humanity's
> prehistory in nature and forward to the prospect of
> future change.[91]

Moreover, the acquisition of such a perspective required not only the progress of knowledge, but the very *mobility* of the knower.

I suggested at the beginning of this chapter that the transformation in the state's "progressivism," from the vast expanses of the western frontier to the social and psychological conditions of the metropolis, is conceivable only as a consequence of this crisis of historical perspective, the resolution to which is already assumed by the state's *progressive form*. Turner's answer to the rising sense of historical dislocation, and the demand for a renewal of perspective based on the active synthesis of past and future, was to reconstitute the frontier as the virtual form of American consciousness: "The free lands are gone. The material forces that gave vitality to Western democracy are passing away. It is to the realm of the spirit, to the domain of ideals and legislation, that we must look for Western influence upon democracy in our own days."[92] While Turner's refrain was cast in the form of a lament for the loss of the frontier, it was a lament that aimed to rationalize the loss in terms of a new constellation of power and consciousness that turned *acceleration* into an existential principle through which a *new frontier* of industrial production—circumscribed by the realm of ideals and legislation—was to be actualized. This new productive regime of acceleration was founded on an immense corporate-industrial consolidation during the 1880s and 1890s that attempted to grasp the productive process as a whole and sought to control every element of it, without exception.[93] Such a totalizing process, however, risked the collapse of the state's symbolic order. The point of Turner's argument was that, to effectively reproduce its conditions of possibility—that is, to regulate the ideological conditions of social mobility and individual freedom, and thus to moderate class conflict and class relations—the state required the frontier as a virtual limit through which to circumscribe the forms of human action. With the disappearance of the actual western frontier, in relation to which the horizons of individual action had been formed and directed, an ideal frontier became immanent to every act, the basis of the self's new productive relation to the industrial state.

For Richard Slotkin, the very fact of Turner's lament (and its echo in Theodore Roosevelt's saga of American conquest) marks the point at which the frontier became primarily a term of ideological rather than geographical reference, the site of a struggle between social classes rather than between Man and Nature. From the 1860s, the logic of the state's progressivism relied on the fact that, no matter what political party or social class one belonged to, there was substantial agreement "on such central concerns as the exceptional character of American life and history, the necessity and desirability of economic development, the vitality of 'democratic' politics, and the relevance of something called 'the Frontier' as a way of explaining and rationalizing what [was] most distinctive and valuable in 'the American way.' "[94] In this sense, the frontier myth was capable of orienting human action toward the productive limits of the state and, therefore, toward the limits of human action itself. At the same time, the frontier myth was the existential basis for the pursuit of social struggles within the state. The *principle of acceleration,* the reorganization of the social order around economies of speed, constituted the condition under which human acts became meaningful and valued in relation to the new productive powers of the state, but also the basis of a struggle for control of those same powers. The principle of acceleration thus underpinned the systemic relation between the logic of social reform and the dynamics of capital accumulation.

My analysis of Turner in this section (and, by association, Slotkin) concentrates on the *form* of the American state, and the force of progressive ideology in delineating and directing human action toward the material and spiritual limits of the state. On this understanding, the frontier is always virtual to human acts of making and doing. It is the social struggle to actualize the frontier, to find the limits to human action within the state, that constitutes the act's ideological relation to its conditions of production and thus to the logic of history itself. The rapid acceleration of social action toward the frontier in the form of the productive regime of nineteenth-century capitalist enterprise, an acceleration exemplified by the dominance of the railroad monopolies and the midwestern banking trusts from the 1860s, produced a critical reversal in the fortunes of the state, such that the frontier was increasingly internal to the structures of the metropolis, and the metropolis increasingly identified with the state. This reversal had the effect not only of finding in the metropolis new powers of regeneration and rebirth, but of situating the dividing line between savagery and civilization within the confines of the city itself.[95]

The impact of such a dividing line had profound consequences for the mass of black southerners and immigrants who flooded into the northern cities in the early years of the twentieth century, but also for the development of a black underclass whose interests and identities were inseparable from the industrial advances of capitalism and the rise of the American metropolis.[96] Thus, the *acceleration* in the state's productive forces also marked the transition from what Joel Kovel calls the *dominative* racism of the Old South to the *aversive* racism of industrial capitalism and middle class society. The logic of this aversive racism was such that even as the white middle classes celebrated the emancipation of blacks as a sign of the state's inherent progressive—or liberal—powers, they actively segregated them within the confines of the industrial city, limited them to the menial, service, and sharecropping economies, and so radically dehumanized their social conditions. However, the inescapable grip of the slave event on American consciousness meant that the ideological struggle for control of the modern metropolis was as much about race as it was about class. And the existential value of the jazz act as a "primitive" or "natural" mode of expression specific to the city was fundamental to the outcome of this struggle.[97]

## The New Frontier

There is no doubt that Charlie Parker's jazz act encompassed all the ideological contradictions of this struggle, that the tragedy of his life was in every sense a consequence of the new productive powers of the state. There is no more striking example of the argument that the social value of jazz was founded on the conjunction of black musical practices with the social forces unleashed by industrial production and mass consumption.[98] The jazz act seen in this light was integral to the elaboration of a consciousness and social practices specific to the American city. A clear statement of the structure of this consciousness and its effect on practices can be found in John Kouwenhoven's 1948 analysis of the relation of urban forms to jazz. In *Made in America*, Kouwenhoven argued that only by attending to the specific processes of manufacturing in industrial society, and the modes of production that corresponded to those processes, would Americans be able to understand the "inherent qualities of vitality and adaptability, of organic as opposed to static form, of energy rather than repose, that are particularly appropriate to the civilization which, during the brief life span of the United States, has transformed the world. By an accident of historical development it was in America that this tradition had the greatest freedom to develop its distinctive characteristics."⁹⁹

Kouwenhoven's argument is notable because he attempted to secure the relation between jazz and American urban industrial society through the intuitive apprehension of American reality as it emerged from the modern metropolis. The jazz act and industrial society were two sides of the same coin and posed the same problem for American artists: Was it possible to create an American form from the materials at hand? Was it possible to bestow historical value on jazz given the particular dynamics of the American state and its capitalist enterprises? To address this problem, Kouwenhoven asserted that both the playing of jazz and the construction of skyscrapers were "forms of artistic expression which have evolved out of patterns originally devised by people without conscious aesthetic purpose or cultivated preconceptions, in direct, empirical response to the conditions of their everyday environment."¹⁰⁰ Jazz was thus naturalized as evidence of a creative consciousness framed by and enframing the built *forms* of the metropolis.

The congruence of jazz practices and the capitalist social order effected a dynamic in which technological innovation became integral to the processes of creative self-transformation and self-identity. For Kouwenhoven, this congruence displaced the distinction between the inventor-scientist and the artist-entertainer. It also annulled the gap between scientific experiment and aesthetic experience, remaking the *form* of the industrial city into a model for individual artistic self-fulfillment and the basis of the state's power over its working class population. Modern architecture, for Kouwenhoven, involved a radical encounter with the existential limits of industrial society, while jazz musicians expressed the limits of life itself. Thus, the "problems with which [Louis] Armstrong and [Benny] Goodman are concerned have much less to do with the problems of the artist, in the traditional sense, than with those of industrial organization."¹⁰¹ Jazz virtuosity substantiated a modern creative consciousness that was, in its every expression, reconstituted as a sign of progress and refinement, mobility and adaptability, authenticity and self-possession; in other words, the structures of the jazz act were internal to the progressive logic of the state. To explain the relation of jazz to the logic of industrial production, Kouwenhoven urged closer attention to the conditions under which it was produced:

> [T]he microphone of the recording and broadcasting studios has had its effect upon the instrumental and vocal performance of jazz. The vocal techniques of singers

> as diverse as Louis Armstrong and Bing Crosby, Bessie
> Smith and Dinah Shore, have been devised—often with
> remarkable inventiveness and sensitivity—to exploit the
> full range of possibilities in the microphone, and it is
> largely the microphone's limitations and possibilities that
> the typical jazz band owes both its characteristic make-up
> and its distinctive instrumental techniques."[102]

In this description, it was the microphone—as a symbol of industrial progress and technical possibility—that constituted the essence of and the limits to the jazz act. Technical advancement, far from being a barrier to self-expression, was thus the threshold through which the inventive and self-possessed individual passed on his or her way to a fuller sense of self; a self, however, that was already a model of technical progress and efficiency.

Through the integration of social forms within a general acceleration of production and consumption, the jazz act was constituted by the technical innovations and economic structures of the industrial city, while also expressing the sensuous qualities of the new productive conditions.[103] Examples of this conjunction abound. For instance, in 1928 the trumpeter Max Kaminsky recalled that he "was living just being in Chicago."[104] While in the 1930s, the critic J. A. Rogers defined jazz as "a thing of the jungles—modern man-made jungles."[105] And, at the height of bebop's popularity in the mid-1940s, the saxophonist Dexter Gordon described 52nd Street in New York City as the most exciting place in the world.[106] For Gordon, as for many other musicians, 52nd Street (and its immediate surroundings) was a "freely-flowing" realm of movement, language, images, and events that channeled the feelings and emotions of city life into acts of improvised virtuosity.[107] Thus the city was increasingly identified as the jazz musician's "natural" habitat, and the jazz musician as one of its "native" inhabitants. As Leroy Ostransky points out, jazz "did not develop in a vacuum. As a unique American phenomenon, it grew according to its surrounding conditions, environment, and spirit."[108]

Against the background of wartime mobilization and modernization, the existential drama of Charlie Parker's jazz life was turned into a fatal struggle between the "self-made man" of jazz and the chaotic, netherworld of the metropolis; a struggle that, in Slotkin's words, was transferred "from the wilderness to an urban or imperial frontier, where immigrants, strikers, and *insurrectos* were merely allegories of the savage Apache."[109] It was a struggle, moreover, that was acted out at the existential limits of the middle class social world and included all the paradoxes and contradictions identified with these modern, urban *insurrectos*. Within this schema, Parker was heralded as a model of individualized self-expression whose "sacrifice" to the social dynamics of the capitalist state, seemed to embody, at every turn, the conditions for a continual rediscovery and reformation of the same state.[110] For Robert Reisner, it was the very logic of this sacrifice that, ultimately, saved jazz from "death due to oversimplicity and made it into an art form, giving it new dimensions of structure and feeling. Bird was an apt nickname. He was free, and he sang. His music soared, swooped, glided. His fingers flew over the alto sax."[111] At the same time, the "natural" congruence of his music and his life gave immediate expression to the "nervous frenzy of a jungle turned to asphalt."[112]

These descriptions bring us closer to the historical basis of Parker's fame, and the progressive framework through which his achievements were explained as a symbol of both an existential crisis within the state and a productive power directive of the state. In this sense, bebop became the very image of the city itself, and Parker its architect. As Mezz Mezzrow declares: "Modern swing and jump is frantic, savage, frenzied, berserk—it's the agony of the split, hacked-up personality. It's got nothing at all in common with New Orleans, which by contrast is dignified, balanced, deeply harmonious, high-spirited but pervaded all through with a mysterious calm and placidity—the music of a personality that hasn't exploded like a fragmentation bomb."[113] Thus against the dignity and balance of the older players—their constructive virtuosity—Parker was proclaimed as a sociopath with "an ability to produce at a moment's notice a dancing sinuous line that was constantly full of surprises."[114] His life was considered "a passionate act of self destruction: while his music was . . . broken, wild, wandering, giving to the saxophone tone a savagery it had never known. . . . Parker is the supreme master of the nervous forties."[115] And yet, in spite of his self-destructive behavior, "[h]e was, if you will, the bird that seemed to soar with grace and ease along its own flightlines. . . . What Parker and bebop provided was a renewed musical language (or at least a renewed dialect) with which the old practices could be replenished and continued."[116] The brilliance of his playing marked out an expressive terrain full of such unpredictable and virtuosic "cries, swoops, squawks, and slurs,"[117] that his innovations would necessarily "apply to all the instruments of jazz."[118] In short, Parker was the archetypal "American genius," a liberated individual, who not only lived according to his own laws, but created a musical style that "pushed against the limits of art."[119] The heightened sense of discontinuity and fragmentation in his playing, of breaks and percussive "bombs" or dropped beats, seemed to reflect "more accurately the spirit and temper of contemporary emotions."[120]

In spite of differences among the contexts for their writing, each of the authors just quoted argue that the value of Parker's jazz act, and bebop in general, was determined by the degree to which it reflected the circumstances from which it emerged, and the musician's ability to transcend those same circumstances. The focus of such appraisals rarely is on the dynamics of the act itself, but rather, on the processes of negation through which Parker's playing gained its currency as a measure of individual self-expression and the progressive development of jazz. In spite of all the disparities and conflicts that were registered in the music, it was the act's potential to restore a "common culture" to Americans that defines Parker's "ultimate" significance in terms of both the history of jazz and its relation to the state.[121] By situating bebop as an expression of anxiety about the future of jazz (and its traditions) *and* the future of America (and its destiny), Parker's music has been reclaimed by historians and critics as a radical sign of that future, and Parker himself reclaimed—in the form of his (self-willed) sacrifice—as a symbol of the relation "between the facts of American life and the ideals of free liberal enterprise."[122]

In his analysis of these processes, Sacvan Bercovitch argues that the ideological efficiency of the liberal enterprise requires a sense of anxiety about the present to continually reinforce and expand the state's productive powers in the future. While Bercovitch is concerned with the nature and rhetorical influence of the nineteenth-century American literary renaissance, similar tendencies are apparent in the structuring and analysis of Parker's life—that is, in those attempts to find the distinctive Americanness in his music and to emphasize the inherent tragedy of his social world. If the American Renaissance was "a social myth designed to meet the exigencies of modern society in the New World," then the figure of the postwar black jazz musician performed a similar function for disaffected middle class intellectuals, black radicals, and artists during the Cold War.[123] The ideological momentum generated by the state's wartime mobilization, the mounting opposition to communism, and the fears of atomic destruction was organized by politicians, the military, the media, and big business into a system of crisis and control, sparking an apocalyptic urgency that would enforce compliance in such a way that "those who did not join in hope conformed in desperation."[124] The figure of Parker was exemplary in this regard, fulfilling a range of anxieties and hopes, and attracting a range of prophesies and predictions, about the future of America and about the future for blacks in America.

This anxiety about postwar society, the sense of social collapse, found expression among jazz critics and historians in their fascination with Parker's notorious appetite, as though its sheer size accounted for, and contained the key to, his music. As Reisner recalls: "Charlie Parker, in the brief span of his life, crowded more living into it than any other human being. He was a man of tremendous physical appetites. He ate like a horse, drank life a fish, was as sexy as a rabbit. He was complete with the world, was interested in everything. He composed, he painted; he loved machines, cars; he was a loving father. He liked to joke and laugh."[125] To explain Parker's conflicting relationship to the established patterns of mass consumption and middle class culture, Reisner turns to the potent iconography of the nineteenth-century slave as analyzed by George Fredrickson.[126] However, far from settling on what Fredrickson defines as either the figure of "the Negro beast" or that of "the Negro child," Reisner oscillates between the two, as though Parker's behavior managed to exceed the limits of each through a tragic act of *overconsumption*.

While the fascination with this overconsumption contained the key to Parker's complex position within the metropolis, that same fascination soon devolved into an obsession with what critics identified as his "bird-like" qualities—an obsession that merely reinforced the "pastoral logic" that defined the bebop musician's relation to the state. This evocation of Parker as a type of "bird" produced some of the most compelling (and, needless to say, confusing) attempts at historical and musical explanation: that is, his nickname was used to explain everything, from his erratic behavior to his musical abilities, from his relationships to friends and family to his influence on other artists. Critic after critic resorted to metaphors of bird life, of ornithology, and of flight as a way to reconcile Parker's musical virtuosity with his volatile character. Even Ralph Ellison was drawn into this web of hyperbole:

> For although he *usually* sang at night, his playing was
> characterized by velocity, by long-continued successions
> of notes and phrases, by swoops, bleats, echoes, rapidly
> descending bebops—I mean rebopped bebops—by
> mocking mimicry of other jazzmen's styles, and by
> interpolations of motifs from extraneous melodies, all of
> which add up to a dazzling display of wit, satire, burlesque
> and pathos. Further, he was an expert at issuing his
> improvisations from the dense brush as from the extreme
> treetops of the harmonic landscape. . . ."[127]

What we find in Ellison's description is an attempt to encompass all the contradictions, to unite the disparate strands and inconsistencies of Parker's life and music, into an efficient symbolic framework. Such metaphorical exuberance served to underlie the sense that, while Parker's jazz acts were made on the edges of postwar musical culture and his life proof of the exigencies of the postwar existential crisis, his playing offered Americans—in the form of a sacrifice—the key "to a fuller freedom of self-realization."[128] On the basis of this sacrificial offering, however, Parker was incorporated into a progressive logic that, in Reisner's terms, required him "to have sprung full grown from the earth."[129] Commentary of this type not only contributed to the mystification of the improvised jazz act, but recast the social practices of bebop as a mere consequence of Parker's natural genius and black Americans' inherent expressive powers. In opposing the "full grown" genius to an analysis of music as social practice, Reisner (like many other critics and historians of urban culture) manages to erase the social conditions of the jazz act even as he idealizes those same conditions. In this way, he dissolves the making of jazz acts, in fact, the whole system of social relations on which Parker's artistic efforts relied, into an argument about the inevitable "price" of American progress.

The weight of such hyperbole, metaphor, and mystification has completely overwhelmed the analysis of what kind of musician Parker was, what drove him to lead the life he did, or why he chose to play jazz. The resulting confusions and contradictions suggest, however, that descriptions themselves are not up to the task. Which is not to suggest that the actual terms of such descriptions have no meaning, particularly in relation to their use among jazz practitioners, but that as tools of historical explanation they conform to an ideological framework for which jazz is all too often simply a metaphor and means to its own self-affirmation. Thus, the passage from Parker's habits, appetites, and aspirations (so enlarged by gossip and sociological speculation) to the formal study of his musical works is so complicated, and so wrought with misconception, that I am prompted to propose a clarifying and alternative perspective explored in the following section: that the social orientation of Parker's practices disproves the very framework that studies of his life and work depend on for their ideological and historical meaning.

## The Making of Bebop

This move, toward an alternative description of the formation and logic of Parker's act, is buried in scattered remarks by those musicians who were involved in the making of bebop, those musicians who were critical of, or indeed, resisted bebop's claims on the jazz act, and by jazz critics themselves. Furthermore, because of the scarcity of archival material concerning Parker's own ideas about music, our knowledge of his musical practices relies heavily on the comments of those who played or were employed with or by Parker. A critical approach of this type requires that we develop a more precise sense of how the bebop musicians were situated in terms of their relations within the jazz group, but also in terms of the broader situations of which they were a part. For example, the drummer Max Roach explained in an interview that Parker "was kind of like the sun, giving off the energy we drew from him. We're still drawing on it. His glass was overflowing. In any musical situation, his ideas just bounded out, and this inspired anyone who was around. *He had a way of playing that effected every instrument on the bandstand.*"[130] Not only does Roach situate Parker (somewhat metaphorically) within the "orbit" of his own musical situation (as its epicenter), but his comments also suggest that Parker's musical practices were oriented toward and by the musical ways of the groups on which he relied. Likewise, Doris Parker emphasized that "Charlie didn't play by himself. When you take him away from his real musicians, you destroy what inspired him to play what he did."[131]

In a recent essay on Parker's recordings for the Savoy label, the critic Max Harrison asserts the structural basis of this orientation toward the jazz group:

> These recordings find him [Parker] shaping nearly all performances towards specific and consistent ends. Jazz being the kind of music that it is, not all the initiatives are Parker's, of course, and there is creative work here by at least a dozen others. Yet nearly everything played reflects, seldom passively, what is heard from the alto saxophone. This is to suggest that inherent in his music was not just a method for improvising solos but also one for ordering ensembles, and that is a measure of how thoroughgoing his renewal of jazz language was.[132]

Harrison's statement has important implications for studies of Parker's music, but it also directs our attention to the broader dynamics of the jazz act, particularly, its social value. That implicit within Parker's way of going for jazz was a means of ordering ensembles suggests the urgency of further investigation into the structuring and making of the jazz ensemble.

In this final section, I outline how such an investigation might proceed. One aspect of this investigation is that it delimits the process by which bebop musical practices were made and remade, not as a consequence of an ideological consensus that was either imposed from outside or above the musicians, but rather from within a field of conflict and struggle specific to the materiality of their practices and the symbolic formation of those practices as socially meaningful acts.[133] A second aspect of the investigation, therefore, deals with the logic of those practices as they came to be defined in symbolic terms, that is, how the attempts to remake swing in the 1940s and the dynamics of this remaking were socially transformed by the framework of American ideology into an implicit sign of individual freedom specific to the Cold War state.

At issue is the sense, if any, in which we can speak of bebop as a form of resistance to this American ideological framework or, indeed, what the actual basis of the relationship was between bebop musicians, ideology, and the processes of musical making. These questions, in turn, raise the problem of how, precisely, to describe and explain acts of musical making; the sensibilities and agencies generated by, and generative of, such acts; and the basis on which those acts were then valued as socially symbolic forms. In analyzing Parker's bebop acts, I have relied upon Max Harrison's essay quoted above and Carl Woideck's invaluable book *Charlie Parker: His Music and his Life*. Both Harrison and Woideck rightly insist on defining the musical logic of the act in any analysis of Parker's work, and it is from these authors that I have taken my musical illustrations.

The insistence on *struggle* as an orienting force in the making of the jazz act may invite a certain skepticism; after all, jazz is renowned as a cooperative effort. As the bebop drummer Kenny Clarke said: "The most important characteristic of this new style of playing was camaraderie, that was first because everybody, each musician, just loved one another, just loved them so much they just exchanged ideas and would do everything together. That's one characteristic about it I liked very much."[134] The focus on social struggle and social relations, however, is aimed at clarifying the irresolvable antagonism between the ideological and the virtuosic dimensions of the act, and the conditions of their interpenetration. Clarke's description, far from negating the struggle to make music, directs us to how such relations were formed among the bebop musicians and the social basis on which these men and women went from playing swing to making bebop.

Instead of reifying this camaraderie as a precondition of musical activity, the role of the jazz historian is to explain that the *form* of this camaraderie is critical to an analysis of the value of bebop, all the while recognizing that neither the music nor the sense of camaraderie was an inevitable step for those musicians who gathered after hours at Minton's (or any of the other after-hours clubs around New York). The musicians' camaraderie was, in fact, the ideological resolution to social antagonisms within the jazz act itself: between different levels of skill, the different class backgrounds, the racial and sexual antagonisms, and the different political ideas. As Dizzy Gillespie recalled:

> No one man or group of men started modern jazz, but one of the ways it happened was this: Some of us began to jam at Minton's in the early 'forties. But there were always some cats that couldn't blow at all but would take six or seven choruses to prove it. So on afternoons before a session, Thelonious Monk and I began to work out some complex variations on chords and the like, and we used them at night to scare away no-talent guys. After a while, we got more and more interested in what we were doing as music, and, as we began to explore more and more, our music evolved.[135]

Thus, the new musical structure of bebop emerged from an attempt by Monk and Gillespie to reify their act in terms of an implicit definition of musical values. The result of this gesture was to establish the hierarchical basis of the new act's social value *as an authentic mode of expression,* but also to promote the formative role of Monk and Gillespie at the same time. The absence of Parker in Gillespie's account reflects a competitive dimension concerning the "birth of bebop," but also enables us to shift the focus from Parker's heroic powers to the ensemble of relations within the group. Similarly, drummer Kenny Clarke recalled his own discoveries. For him, bebop

> just happened sort of accidentally. . . . We were playing a real fast tune once with Teddy Hill—"Old Man River," I think—and the tempo was too fast to play four beats to the measure, so I began to cut the time up. But to keep the same rhythm going, I had to do it with my hand, and then every once in a while I would sort of lift myself with my foot, to kind of boost myself into it. . . . When it was over, I said, "Good God was that hard." So then I began to think, and say, "Well, you know, it worked." It worked and nobody said anything, so it came out right.

So that must be the way to do it. Because I think if I had
been able to do it [the old way], it would have been stiff.
It wouldn't have worked.[136]

Clarke's bebop act emerged from the very process of trying an action out
and finding that it worked without having the least sense that it would.
The important point, however, is that Clarke could not have stumbled
upon this way of doing rhythm independently of what the group expected
of him as their drummer, the hours spent finding and consolidating those
expectations, and the tension between the jazz form and what was taking
place in the act.

Both Gillespie's and Clarke's accounts reminds us that the bebop
musicians' camaraderie was not given or inclusive, and that neither the
musicians' love of each other's company, nor of their musical ideas, was in
any way inevitable, nor was it a given condition of the musical act. Rather,
the sense of camaraderie and the act of remaking jazz were dynamically
and forcefully related within the larger processes of musical making and
the practical limits of the working lives of jazz musicians.[137] Thus, in the
making of the act, one did not precede the other; and nor was one the
precondition of the other's creating. While the camaraderie obviously
contributed powerfully to the musicians' sense of how the realm of their
musical practices might, in fact, be expanded, or how they were filled
with musical possibility, the camaraderie itself was the ongoing result,
not of a natural affinity, but of prior struggles and compromises that were
continually being challenged within the social conditions of the act's
production.[138] Indeed, in the case of Gillespie and Monk, the camaraderie
was imposed after the fact. The musicians' camaraderie, the discovery of
the social conditions of their musical consciousness, was won from the
act of remaking jazz practices, as much as that process of remaking was
grasped from their attempts to play at jazz together.

Thus, Clarke's sense of the intense camaraderie of the bebop act was
linked to the logic of seduction, that is, to the act's radical objectification
as an expressive act. As such, it occupied what I earlier defined as the
vertical axis of the creative process—that moment when the *ideological*
basis of the act's making is subsumed into the objective moment of its
performance *as an act*. Without the camaraderie, in Clarke's account, the
bebop act would have no social meaning, and the process of going for
bebop would have remained only one possible musical direction, or, in
fact, might never have happened. The remaking of jazz as bebop, and the
making of the musicians' camaraderie in the form of the bebop ensemble,
required an extraordinary effort of social and musical congruence to effect

the act's objectification as a coherent and significant musical form. At the same time, in order to displace the conflicts and divergence among the musicians ("some cats couldn't blow at all"), and legitimate Clarke's and Gillespie's particular ways of musical making, the sense of camaraderie had to appear inevitable, as though internal to the bebop act itself. As Gillespie demonstrated, that camaraderie provided an ideological means to rationalize both the bebop act's radical contingency and the struggle for the form of the act, even as the historical rationalization of the act turned that camaraderie into a technical and political necessity.

The problem for jazz historians, to paraphrase E. P. Thompson, is that far too much attention has been paid to the created jazz artifact, to the consciousness of that artifact in its most refined (and therefore, most seductive) form, and far too little paid to analyzing how the structuring of that form over time related to the act of musical making, the social dynamics of the act, and the elaboration of musical practices specific to the struggle for control of the metropolis.[139] Shifting the emphasis to the processes and logic of making and remaking allows us to recognize, contrary to the arguments of much jazz criticism, that bebop was a *social* and *historical* act, not simply an individual abstraction that mirrored the larger, productive forces of the American state.

To explain this shift of emphasis, I now turn to the field of conflict and struggle specific to the bebop act and its symbolic recognition as a socially meaningful form. In this regard, Scott DeVeaux's *The Birth of Bebop* stands as one of the great works of jazz history, in particular, his discussion of the "jam session" and its role in the general economy of jazz practices, both before and after World War II. I rely on DeVeaux's analysis of this point, especially his argument that the jam session, more than anything else, "underlies all claims for the legitimacy of bebop."[140] I want to test this argument, however, against LeRoi Jones's own argument that between "the thirties and the end of World War II, there was perhaps as radical change in the psychological perspective of the Negro American toward America as there was between the Emancipation and 1930. . . . It was the generation of the forties which . . . began to consciously analyze and evaluate American society in many of that society's own terms."[141] In Jones's analysis, the emergence of bebop was linked to an epochal transformation in black consciousness, and the bebop musicians themselves, in their "rejection" of the jazz "mainstream," were the active embodiments of this struggle for a new relation to the American state. The basis of this assertion brings us back to our initial question of how musical transformations were conceived and oriented, and how they were subsequently analyzed as signs of racial, social, and national progress, while at the same time remaining internal to the larger processes of capitalist commodification and economic expansion.

DeVeaux's study builds on how the social, political, and economic upheavals of the wartime state affected black musicians, but seeks the logic and detail of the jazz act beyond the categorical opposites of commerce and art, conservatism and revolution, acquiescence and rejection. Between these historians, however, the *fact* of a transformation is not an issue; instead, it is the *form* of the change that requires further attention. And the form of that change, as we have noted, was derived from how the jam sessions at clubs like Minton's and Monroe's were to be explained and how the social dynamics of these sessions were then constituted as the essence of a new musical sensibility. While Jones insists on a radical break based on the bebop musicians' rejection of the economy of the swing bands, DeVeaux offers a more ambiguous sense of historical change: for black musicians "at the height of the Swing Era, public performance and after-hours improvising were not separate and antagonistic spheres, reflecting an unbridgeable gulf between the need to put bread on the table and artistic self-respect, but interrelated parts of a larger whole. The jam session was an integral part of the 'art world' that constituted their professional life."[142]

In both accounts, however, there is an emphasis on the efforts by the bebop musicians to direct and expand their musical horizons in whatever ways they could and a guarded recognition (but rarely an acceptance) of the social and economic limits to their professional achievements, and those of black Americans in general. It was at this point that the jam session became critical to changes in jazz practices and, specifically, to the dynamics and focus of the jazz group. Its concrete social aims—that of a distinct and measurable virtuosity of the improvised act, relatively unhindered by the commercial constraints of the mass entertainment industries—meant that the jam session "encouraged techniques, procedures, attitudes—in short, the essential components of a musical language and aesthetic—quite distinct from what was possible or acceptable in more public venues."[143] Thus, the focus on jam sessions, and on the improvised virtuosity they comprised, began to effect a change in the practices of the swing bands themselves; by 1949, as we have already noted, even the "King of Swing" Benny Goodman was appealing to the influence of bebop to legitimate his new group.[144]

The camaraderie described by Clarke can be taken as a statement about how the practices and virtuosity of the bebop act were turned into a meaningful social act, and how a specific social practice that during the 1930s was considered *supplementary* to the main business of entertaining large dance, theater, and radio audiences was, by the end of the 1940s, raised to the level of an art (although still a marginal one) by virtue of this same "supplementarity." DeVeaux identifies several social and historical reasons for this change: the expansion of wartime industries to include large numbers of black workers, the prospects of military service for black musicians, the turmoil within the recording industry, the Office of Defense Transportation ban on bus travel, the emergence of the 52nd Street clubs and the correlative decline of Harlem as an entertainment precinct. He also cites an impatience among younger musicians like Parker, Gillespie, and Monk with the complacency or resistance of the older swing players to new ideas about the jazz form.[145]

What we sense about the jam session, among all the attempts at explanation, is its role in defining the limits of the musical act, of functioning as the point between actualization of the jazz form and the impossibility of the act itself. For DeVeaux, therefore, the transition from swing to bebop was neither as sudden as many critics chose to believe, nor was it as comprehensive as they would have liked. He is backed in this by David Stowe, who argues that "bop was puzzling to contemporaries because it seemed to appear *ex nihilio* and fully formed, its historical roots obscured by conditions in the music industry. Just as the formative preswing years of the 1930s had been elided by the post-Crash collapse of the entertainment business, particularly the recording industry, bebop's lengthy incubation period coincided with the distraction of war."[146] In one sense, Stowe's argument merely states the obvious: those in the midst of a transformation—whether social, political, or artistic—cannot know it as such (even if they sense the novelty of their intent or admit to a general feeling of crisis). In another sense, his statement confirms that the ongoing tension between the bebop musicians' progressive aims and their claims to a common jazz tradition was, in fact, the very basis of jazz's commercial orientation and musical success. The very impossibility of defining the origins of the act—either positively or negatively—became the basis for the act's ideological mystification and its objective rationalization as *historical process.*

To grasp the dimension of the jazz act that challenges such ideological determinations within the capitalist economy—without simply mystifying the act or, indeed, reifying the fact that jazz musicians made their music, worked, and survived in such an economy—requires that we redirect our analysis to the act's virtuosic dimension and to the social dynamics of that virtuosity. As with the camaraderie among the players, the key musical elements that were crystallized into the bebop style— eighth notes, harmonic extensions, substitutions, inversions, and irregular melodies—were not a given set of rules or principles that the bebop musicians suddenly imposed on jazz. As countless oral accounts by the musicians prove, these ideas were instead the raw material through which their musical values and their collective acts were formed, maintained, changed, and above all manipulated by the daily activity of finding regular work, going to sessions, listening to other musicians' playing and recording, and, of course, playing in as many different musical situations as possible. A description by the bass player Milt Hinton provides an outline of the practical logic that informed and constituted the social conditions of the bebop musicians' efforts:

> On Sunday afternoons, in the early forties, some of the guys would get together at my house. Monk, Dizzy, John Collins, Ben Webster, and others. We'd have little sessions listening to records. We'd listen to a lot of Hawk's [Coleman Hawkins] records. He was making some in Europe that we'd get. And we'd play things of our own. There'd often be a guitar, bass, two horns, and my wife would be in the kitchen cooking us something to eat. . . . Then, later that night, we'd go to the Savoy to hear Chick Webb. That was a band that really swung. Then, after the Savoy, we'd go to Puss Johnson's, an after-hours spot at 130th and St. Nicholas, I think. Everybody would come in there. All the guys from the bands downtown. I remember one particular session. Ben Webster and Pres [Lester Young] were there and everybody knew about it. Anyway, at this particular session, each had his individual rhythm section to play for him. A drummer and I played for Ben. Walter Page and Jo Jones played for Pres. The room was filled with smoke and loaded with musicians. Not only that night but many nights guys were so eager to play that bass players would actually line up behind the bass to take turns playing. . . . As for that session with Ben and Lester, there never could be a decision. The house was divided. Most of those there were musicians. There were very, very few outsiders except some real jazz fans. They used to sell lots of chicken and whisky at those sessions. . . . This particular place was especially for Sunday nights, that was the off-night around New York at about that time. It would start about three in the morning and last to about nine or ten [in the morning]. . . . This used to happen like from about 1939 to 1942 or '43.[147]

As with Clarke's description of the musicians' camaraderie, those Sunday afternoon gatherings—to listen to each other's recordings and play—were both oriented by, and orienting of, the social situation of the musicians' practices and the virtuosity of their improvised acts. Thus, the formation of a specific musical virtuosity—a bebop virtuosity—relied upon a range of other social practices and situational constraints: the availability of money and food, sexual divisions and relations within households or between musicians, the broader musical economy within New York before, during, and after World War II, the economic and political state of neighborhoods, and the hierarchy of musical skill and value established prior to and as a consequence of their acts. All these social situations and determinations modified and framed—and in turn were modified and enframed by—the musicians' practice of playing *together*.[148] It is thus impossible to divorce the material basis of the black musician's struggle to make music and survive *as a working musician* from the struggle over values—the ideological struggle.[149] However, neither dimension should be reduced to the other. Rather, they coalesce, one overreaching the limits of the other, and both are transformed in the attempt to actualize the jazz form.

If DeVeaux is right, then it was the jam sessions more than any other event where all the divergent and conflicting factors of the bebop musicians' social existence were brought into focus. Here was the existential ground on which the ideological battle to frame and determine the social and political value of bebop was fought and won. And there is no doubt as to the magnetic appeal of those events and their significance for the development of the new approach. As Clarke recalled: "People dug the music we were playing. They used to come from miles around—from Chicago, from everywhere to hear us play. Most of them were musicians, though there were others who weren't. People would make it a 'must.' Earl Hines and the guys in his band would drop by and play with us. Dizzy would be there and Roy Eldridge, Lips Page, and Georgie Auld."[150] But the basis of that appeal, as I have argued, was consistently rationalized and criticized in terms of whether or not bebop exemplified the historical and existential limits of jazz itself, and whether or not the act's relationship to its conditions of production was constituted progressively. Which explains why the jam session was eventually defined, not as an aberration, an afterthought, but an example of jazz "in its purest state—an uncorrupted, unmediated, and uncommercial form of musical expression."[151]

This kind of progressive argument—when used to sort the authentic players from the inauthentic, the successful from the unsuccessful, the innovators from those who followed—simply obscures the social basis of musical practices and confuses the virtuosity of the act with its conditions of production. As I have suggested, the musicians' attempts to remake jazz and, in the meantime, continue to make a living within a racist society, were reduced to progressive symptoms of the American state's accelerating productive powers. While this ideological dimension no doubt oriented the jazz musician's acts of musical making, I have also suggested that this dimension constituted only one aspect of the field of musical action and was experienced, for the most part, in the localized and limited terms of *need* and *subjectification*. In this sense, Gillespie's and Monk's "complex variations" on chord progressions demonstrated the local "despotic" character, the competitive basis, of the larger systemic framework. Indeed, the bebop musicians regularly mobilized the ideological basis of the capitalist economy to legitimate their actions and their ideas, inasmuch as that ideology was useful for combating or accommodating what they saw as "a basically unjust situation."[152] As Gillespie recalled: "We all wanted to make money, preferably by playing modern jazz."[153] At this level, Gillespie's reduction of the act to the individual basis of need and subjective value—the entertainment criteria—was complicated by the form of the groups on which he relied for his social legitimacy.

However, the ideological terms of the act, the structuring of its economic, political, and social framework, should not be confused with the act's virtuosity which, in its intent and logic, transformed such abstract representations. Instead, our attention should be directed to describing and explaining the historical patterns of everyday making and remaking, the musical economy of the jazz act, in relation to the act's virtuosic powers. Thus, in James C. Scott's words, we should seek "to ground that description in an analysis of the conflicts of meaning and value in which these patterns arise and to which they contribute."[154] Such a phenomenology of the jazz act offers the possibility of overcoming a basic division between the historical description of jazz styles and the musicological analysis of bebop's formal properties, a division that DeVeaux's study goes a long way toward resolving. Max Harrison's argument about Parker's famous Savoy recordings illustrates this problem and, in many ways, points to a further solution. For, although Harrison insists on distinguishing the "shapeless raw material of life from the disciplined form and content of Parker's music," within his analysis itself are the terms of an entirely different explanation.[155]

Harrison's incisive observation is that Parker's playing is "not just a method for improvising solos but also one for ordering ensembles. . . ."[156] At each point in his analysis, the central characteristics of Parker's playing are identified in relation to the musical potential of the other musicians in the studio and to the group's attempts at going for bebop, illustrated by references to the numbers and types of each recorded "take."[157] While Parker is clearly the dominant figure in the recording process, at least as far as Harrison is concerned, his argument also reflects a comprehensive sense of how the *virtuosity* of Parker's improvised acts relied upon precisely who else was playing. At certain points in the argument, the collective nature of the act is implied: "This polyrhythmic aspect is heightened by the irregular punctuations of piano and drums, the latter, in the finest performance, complementing with particular closeness the soloist's invention and the whole emphasizing the need for the bassist in a bop rhythm section to state the underlying pulse more strongly than in earlier styles."[158] At other times, however, Harrison is explicit about with whom and under what conditions the act was being made: "[F]ar from being content with a simple backdrop to his own playing, Parker, because of all the changes he had wrought in the soloist's language, needed answering changes in the ensemble. This is most apparent at the rhythmic level in the close correspondence between alto and drum contributions, the latter showing that Parker's requirements were quite precise."[159]

The inference to be drawn here, one that goes beyond the immediate aims of Harrison's essay, is that getting those "answering changes in the ensemble" was as much about who the musicians were (their class, race, and gender), how they played together as soloists and as a group, and how the act of making these recordings oriented their sense of themselves as musicians. This characterization is underlined in no uncertain terms by Harrison himself in a description of a recording date for the Savoy label in November 1945: the structure of the recording session was arranged "so as to offer as many different but related avenues of expression as possible."[160] What we get from Harrison, briefly and inadvertently, is a sense that the seductive virtuosity of Parker's improvised act was not formed independently of, but *from* the very conditions of his relationship to the other musicians in the group; that it was only in the context of the collective act of going for jazz, that Parker's virtuosity even happened.

The structuring of the group's jazz virtuosity in this sense can be grasped from the justly famous quintet recording of George Gershwin's "Embraceable You," produced by the Charlie Parker Quintet on October 26, 1947, for Dial Records.[161] My analysis of this piece relies on Charles Rosen's great study, *The Romantic Generation,* Slavoj Žižek's essay, "Robert Schumann: Romantic Anti-Humanist," and Theodor Adorno's analysis, *In Search of Wagner.*[162] The quintet's recording of "Embraceable You" has received much critical notice, in that it involved all the elements for which Parker was renowned and, indeed, exemplified what Martin

Williams termed Parker's development of "melodic rhythm."[163] Playing with Parker was Miles Davis on trumpet, Duke Jordan on piano, Tommy Potter on bass, and Max Roach on drums. Their version of the song is unusual in that there is no initial statement from any of the musicians of the Gershwin melody, only Parker's and Davis's solos. Moreover, the Gershwin melody, as Rosen characterizes it, is "inaudible" in the sense that throughout the performance its presence is only implied. The recording begins with a brief eight-bar introduction from Duke Jordan, which establishes the 2/4 meter and a restrained mood and tone to the playing. Parker then enters with a sixty-four-bar solo based on Gershwin's melody without referring to it except through the rhythm section's adherence to the song's harmonic structure. This section is followed by a further forty-bar improvisation by Miles Davis, and then a sharp contraction of the piece in the form of a subdued unison coda between saxophone and trumpet in the final eight bars.

The deceptive simplicity of the song's structure is crucial to how we define the act's virtuosity, as against the struggle with its ideological frame. The social basis of this struggle is apparent in Harrison's comment that Parker's "playing was never mere display but always emotional explosion fused with technical innovation."[164] Here Harrison explains the conditions of Parker's virtuosity in terms of the distinction between the soloist and his or her group. This distinction, however, amounts to an abstraction that relies on a direct correspondence of a reified jazz act—a subject's emotional explosion—with the productive powers of the capitalist state—the forces of technical innovation. What is left out of such formal accounts is that the self-expressive powers attributed to Parker on this recording are already internal to the form of what is played, how it is played, and with whom it is played; that, in the quintet's very attempt to remake Gershwin's song without stating the original melody as such, the act's ideological framework was itself irrevocably altered.

The six-note motif that introduces Parker's "melodying" on "Embraceable You" effects a synchronization of past and present, but only as a consequence of how the act is performed by the other players. Each repetition of the six-note phrase—C, G, F, E, D, E—produces a further intensification of Gershwin's inaudible melody, while at the same time redirecting each player's relation to that very inaudibility on the basis of what will follow. In this sense, the Gershwin melody not only provokes the terms of its own transformation, but also determines the act's relation to the conditions of its production as a commodity.[165] Thus, Williams's comment that Parker "barely glances at Gershwin's melody" misunderstands how this virtuosic dimension of the act worked in terms of the act's ideological frame, that is say, the reality from which it emerged and to which it referred. Although inaudible, Gershwin's melody functioned as the very tempo or timing of the musical act itself. It was the basis of the groups' objectification as a group but also materialized the act's relationship to the American music industry. In Žižek's terms, the melody's "very exclusion guarantees the reality of the remaining elements."[166] Thus the "phantom notes" that were implied in Parker's solo on this piece (and many others), along with his irregular use of accents, while obviously crucial rhythmic devices, also pointed to what was *impossible* in the act—that is, to the jazz musician's struggle with formal American culture and with the endless circulation of commodities.[167] If we recall LeRoi Jones's argument concerning the relation of the act to its virtual or implied form, these *inaudible* notes and Parker's *irregular* accents constitute the jazz musician's fundamental radicality in the context of American capitalism. The initial repetition of the motivic phrase in "Embraceable You" brings about a displacement of its conditions of possibility—the popular melodic style that sustained the profit margins of Tin Pan Alley and Broadway—onto the *form* of the act. The absence of the melody, therefore, is not indicative of an authentic mode of self-expression for each soloist, nor the basis for a pure act of communicative synthesis. Instead, the absence of Gershwin's melody operates on the form of the musical act itself by directing the players toward the problem of how they were to play as a group. In other words, it was the very formation of musical relationships within the group, that is, how the musicians played together—irrespective of their individual abilities—that constituted the bebop act's relationship to Gershwin's song.[168] In this context, the basis of their collective virtuosity was to have asserted the logic of the group's ways over and above its dissolution into the act's ideological abstraction as a sign of progress and profit.

This is not to say that the critical accounts of Martin Williams or those of Max Harrison are wrong. Rather, their accounts have simply not gone far enough into the interior structure of the act's collective making, nor have they adequately addressed the act's relation to its conditions of production. To do this requires a final summation of the logic of Parker's virtuosity of *speed* in terms of the state's productive acceleration toward its material and existential limits. It is helpful to recall LeRoi Jones's assessment that, in positing a new relation of black Americans to the state, bebop was both premature (blacks were not ready for it) and came too late (blacks were already caught in the system of capitalist exploitation). In making this larger historical claim, however, Jones also articulates the double movement of the bebop act itself. In other words, the virtuosic dimension of an act is always premature—one never knows when a new relation to the jazz form will appear—while its ideological dimension is always too late—the act is already surpassed by its repetition under new conditions of production and according to new productive relations.

In this light, Parker's virtuosity of relative speeds was about achieving an absolute acceleration that would reverse the ideological conditions of the act's production and, therefore, transform the act's relation to its future and its past. At the same time, his use of irregular accents, both before and after the beat, his fascination with phantom notes and displaced melodies, and the speed of his improvisations produced a radical disjuncture within the interior of the act. On one level, his harmonic and melodic extensions promised an endless progression of similar acts that ensured the act's reproduction and consumption as a commodity (a prophetic and ironic gift to his countless imitators). On another level, the sheer velocity of his playing was the condition of the act's *impossibility;* that is, Parker's acceleration of the act in all directions, far from conforming to the conditions of its production, changed the very bounds of what it was indeed possible for the jazz musician to do. In the end, this possibility remained unrealized: sacrificed to the racist logic of the "culture industry" and cut short by an untimely death.[169] Parker's failure, therefore, was the failure of progressive history to bring forth a protagonist other than in the state's own productive terms. The tragedy of bebop was thus the tragedy of Charlie Parker's virtuosity: it was both premature and too late.

This consideration of Parker's musical ways, and the contradictions involved in their making, brings us closer to an appropriate terminology for analyzing the historical conditions and the virtuosic character of the jazz act, while reminding us of how the progressivism of exceptionalist ideology framed the bebop act. What is still lacking, however, is some larger explanation of bebop's historical emergence in terms of the "ways of the hand"; in other words, some sense of the situated and situating dynamic of the bebop musicians' collective playing in terms of the embodied force of their human being. David Sudnow argues that such a dynamic was formed in the musician's protracted struggle to master both his or her instrumentality (in Parker's case, the alto saxophone) *and* a way of being with others instrumentally (the dynamics of the act).[170] In the next chapter, I further develop this analysis in relation to Ornette Coleman's free jazz act. The key issue at this point, as Charles Keil makes clear, is that when it comes to improvised music "there is little in the way of a consistent terminology to be grasped. . . ."[171]

# 3     Ornette Coleman

## The Virtuosity of Illusion

He plays all the notes Bird missed. . . .

Thomas Pynchon

L et me recapitulate my argument thus far: the musical act is revealed in a double movement, at once virtuosic and ideological, from which new musical acts arise. My aim is to delineate the logic of that double movement within the jazz form. This chapter's analysis of the musical ways of alto saxophonist Ornette Coleman provides the final link in the chain of the argument, in that it is Coleman who enables us to understand, more fully, the achievements of Bechet and Parker. Only by understanding Coleman's decomposition of the jazz act into the illusion of a pure melody is it possible to grasp not only the virtuosic construction of hot jazz and the virtuosic speed of bebop, but the social conditions of their interpenetration. The logic of this decomposition of the act turns most fully on the question of human freedom and its meaning for the jazz musician. As John Litweiler says, freedom "appears at the very beginning of jazz and reappears at every growing point in the music's history."[1] However, the "history of freedom" embedded within the jazz act is predicated on a claim that is simply assumed rather than explicitly argued: namely, that within the musical performance, there is a freedom that can be expressed.

To make this claim is to assert, at least implicitly, a particular relation between the structure of human action and the social meaning of historical events. The task of a critical analysis of the jazz act is to analyze

the grounds for such an assertion and to measure it against the conditions
of the act's making. To that end I analyze in this chapter Coleman's musical
activities in relation to the institutional and ideological conditions of the
Cold War state. In other words, I consider the situation of Coleman at
the very moment when the nature of his relation to the state, to other
musicians, to his audiences, and friends and family begins to crystallize
through the act of making music. The *form* of this relation between music
practices and the social world occupies much of what follows. It helps
in particular to clarify the basis of the relation between the jazz act and
the immense ideological delirium—Joel Kovel calls it the "black hole of
anticommunism"—that dominated American society from the 1950s.[2]
Furthermore, the power of this delirium over the forms of human action,
and its repercussions for the meaning of human freedom, intensified and
complicated the state's own objective aims, both externally and internally.

These objective aims of the American state, that is, the objective
aims of American political, military, cultural, and economic institutions,
were consolidated through the concentration of centralized administrative power within the executive branch (for example, National Security
Council, CIA, FBI), the Federal Reserve, and the Pentagon. This concentration produced a *contraction* in the form of the world system, even
as the productive capacity of the state was directed toward an expanded
market for American goods and culture.[3] As Mike Davis argues, the "postwar era of American hegemony was inaugurated by a 'revolution from
above.' . . . The crucial precondition, of course, was the unique techno-
military advantage obtained by the United States in the summer of 1945:
the great historical contingency of the atomic bomb was joined to the
more predictable results of the full-scale mobilization of the productive
forces of the giant American economy (which *doubled* its industrial
capacity between 1940 and 1945)."[4]

As we noted in the preceding chapter apropos of Charlie Parker,
the social effect attributed to this "giant American economy" and to mass
productivity as such raises fundamental questions about the ideological
value of the jazz act and its influence on musical practices. However,
detailed attention to these structural transformations after 1945, although
central to any analysis of the postwar American state, only partly explains
what was at stake for the jazz musician. Indeed, to draw simple structural
affinities between the jazz act and larger social transformations within the
state serves only to reinforce the very ideological assumptions we wish
to analyze. At the same time, there is no doubt that such affinities exist
and, to some degree, in fact determine both the virtuosic form of the
jazz act and its ideological value within the state. As Fredric Jameson

suggests, ideology "is not something which informs or invests symbolic production; rather the aesthetic act is itself ideological, and the production of aesthetic or narrative form is to be seen as an ideological act in its own right, with the function of inventing imaginary or formal 'solutions' to unresolvable social contradictions."[5]

It is not enough to define jazz as a history of "freedom players." Such a claim does little more than invoke a static context in which freedom is guaranteed to arise, without alerting us to how that very same guarantee—made just as surely in defense of the "American Way"—was already internal to the Cold War state's activities undertaken in the name of liberal consensus.[6] This defense of freedom was, as Davis demonstrates, the precondition of American power in the postwar period. It provided the rationale for the state's atomic capability and the full-scale mobilization of its productive forces toward an expansion of foreign and domestic consumption. While Davis offers a valuable study of the structural base and the conflicts underlying those changes to the state, particularly as they were implicated in the struggles of the American labor movement and civil rights initiatives, my focus is on the way those structural changes were manifested at the level of musical consciousness and their meaning for musical action.

In his analysis of American consciousness in the wake of the bombing of Hiroshima, Paul Boyer points out that for "a fleeting moment after Hiroshima, American culture had been profoundly affected by atomic fear, by a dizzying plethora of atomic panaceas and proposals, and by endless speculation on the social and political implications of the new reality. By the end of the 1940s, the cultural discourse had largely stopped. Americans now seemed not only to accept the bomb, but to support any measures necessary to maintain atomic supremacy."[7] The degree to which American society had internalized and transformed the violence of the atomic event, turning it into a power of ideological renewal and political control, was matched only by the relentless integration of the political, business, and military elites into a national security state dedicated to the "survival of the free world."[8] That this national security state proceeded to remake its own existential limits through a specifically atomic or nuclear opposition to the Soviet state, but also to communism in general, was directly linked to the collective sublimation of the bomb. As Boyer goes on to argue, the ideological fear "of the Russians had driven the fear of the bomb into the deeper recesses of consciousness."[9]

The effect of the atomic bomb on American society, and its subsequent integration into the American state's ideological and administrative opposition to the Soviet state, produced a fundamental modulation in the forms of human action. What Boyer's analysis demonstrates is that the atomic event increasingly emerged as a *virtual power* against which human action was measured and toward which it was directed. Citing Lewis Mumford's anti-atomic polemics, he outlines the terms in which American society was " . . . entirely geared toward the war that does not come."[10] The formation of the Cold War state, its vast interconnected institutional and bureaucratic framework (that is, government, business, military, educational, artistic, and the various media), was structured around the *impossibility* of the atomic event. And yet, this collective act of restructuring meant that the American state was in some sense becoming the very atomic event it sought to postpone. That is, in the massive effort at all levels of the social order to avert atomic destruction, the power of human making, the ability to act and define one's self in relation to the social world, was transferred to the technocratic interior of the bomb.[11]

Elaine Scarry's analysis in *The Body in Pain* is invaluable for any such consideration as this, and her study has influenced much of the subsequent analysis of Coleman's jazz act. Scarry argues that the virtual power of the atomic event destructures the fundamental integrity of the relation between body and belief, that is, the relation between the act and its form, characterized by precapitalist and capitalist social organization. She distinguishes between the violence of the atomic event and the conventional structures of war and human social practices in which the "relation between body and belief takes many degrees and radiates out over a thousand small acts."[12] It is her understanding that the atomic event displaced the dynamic of belief and corporeal consent that characterized the human will toward form-building from the *actual* domain of human collectivity (however divided and repressive) to the *virtual* power of the atomic event. This migration of human action into the interior of the atomic event effected a radical crisis of action within the state, a social paralysis, to the point where the meaning of action was increasingly defined, or in Scarry's words, reciprocated, by its *simulation* within capitalist consumption and financial speculation.[13]

The effect of this crisis of action and form on jazz is inestimable. An analysis of Coleman's music enables us to grasp the complex ways in which the crisis was worked out among jazz musicians. While some toured the world for the State Department and the CIA-sponsored Congress for Cultural Freedom, others withdrew into embittered isolation or pedagogical obscurity; still others sought to challenge the systemic transformations spurred on by the civil rights and black power movements, the antiwar movement, and the emergence of newer popular musical forms.[14] At the center of the crisis was the problem of the jazz form and the musician's ability to actualize that form in a meaningful way. As was the case with Parker, the influence of progressive ideology on jazz musicians challenged the objective forms of the blues and the popular songs (known as jazz standards) on which jazz depended for musical meaning. While Parker struggled within these objective forms, Coleman and his colleagues aimed to bring a renewed meaning to the jazz act by "liberating" jazz melody from the objective harmonic and rhythmic conditions of the blues or the jazz standards. The result of Coleman's efforts was to focus attention on the musician's powers of subjective expression above all else and to define those powers as a consequence of the "freedom principle" embedded within the act.

This "freedom principle," however, merely expressed the ideological conditions of the act's making and its ultimate collapse into meaningless gestures, into nothing. Far from signaling the end of meaning for jazz, I argue that in taking up what remained buried (or virtual) in Parker's playing—"he played all the notes Bird missed"—Coleman sought to challenge the inertia of the Cold War social order by asserting a new conception of the musical act. Through a radical sublimation of jazz's "objective spirit,"[15] that is, the blues and popular songs, he transposed this objective spirit into the structure of the improvising group itself. I denote the logic of this transposition as the "virtuosity of illusion": a virtuosity that succeeded only by a repetition of what was never there in the first place: pure melody. And yet, the very repetition within the act of such a melodic *impossibility* also constituted the basis of the act's social value. Only if we define Coleman's musical act as a profoundly *social* act is it possible to qualify in what sense we are to understand the specific nature of postwar American society, the musical forms that populated its technobureaucratic spaces, and the practical logics that animated those forms.

## A "Terrifying Freedom"

In *Blues People*, LeRoi Jones asserts that the "implications of this music are extraordinarily profound, and the music itself, deeply and wildly exciting. . . . It is for many musicians a terrifying freedom."[16] The notion of a "terrifying freedom" was implicit in the chorus of responses to Ornette Coleman's first performances in New York City at the Five Spot Cafe in November of 1959. Ambivalent, sometimes hostile, toward the musical and social expectations that dominated postwar jazz practices, the Coleman quartet transformed the ways in which bebop, hard bop, and cool jazz musicians' went for their jazz acts. Not that the works of the pianists Lennie Tristano, Cecil Taylor, or Thelonius Monk, the compositions of bass player Charles Mingus, and the experiments of Carla and Paul Bley, Abby Lincoln, Max Roach, the Art Ensemble of Chicago, and Albert Ayler among others were not equally significant. Rather, it was the scale of Coleman's achievement that provoked so much controversy and uncertainty concerning his musical ideas and his status within the jazz scene. As Mingus recalled:

> Now aside from the fact that I doubt he can play a C scale . . . in tune, the fact remains that his notes and lines are so fresh. So when Symphony Sid played his record, it made everything else he was playing, even my own record that he played, sound terrible. I'm not saying everybody's going to have to play like Coleman. But they're going to have to stop playing Bird.[17]

Mingus's comment offers a precise understanding of the musical problems that informed and structured Coleman's musical ways and the sense of impending crisis associated with his music. My aim in this section is to elaborate the historical context within which this crisis emerged, to demonstrate how Coleman's group actualized their musical practices and their consciousness of those practices, and to theorize more adequately than has been done the ideological framework through which those practices gained meaning and value. If at times I move beyond the scope of Coleman's work to discuss broader musical, social, and political questions, this is not to presume a necessary correlation between historical theory and the particular circumstances of musical performance, but nor do I intend to privilege the minutiae of everyday experience over broader systemic concerns. Rather, I analyze musical practices as social practices that manifest a dynamic and consciousness specific to their ideological frame, while also inflecting upon the social basis of human action and circumstance. Only then is it possible to move beyond a limited interpretive scheme toward the subtle and intricate complexes of human creativity through which postwar jazz musicians established and developed their relationship to the Cold War capitalist state.[18]

Several recent works of scholarship are pertinent to the aims stated above: Paul Berliner's study of improvisation, *Thinking in Jazz;* Ingrid Monson's *Saying Something;* and Ronald Radano's *New Musical Figurations.* Each offers valuable ways to further analyze jazz practices and develop a more rigorous understanding of human creative action.[19] Monson's and Berliner's analyses are notable for the emphasis on the practices, the psychological motivations for the musical act, and the local knowledge of the jazz musician. But their positivist stance also leads them to preclude an adequate consideration of the broader ideological and historical framework of the improvised act; that is, the conditions of the act's production. They tend to rely upon reductive psychological profiles as a mirror of social and political change, and consequently undermine the social processes they wish to understand. Radano, however, achieves an impressive critique of the ideological terms of postwar jazz by identifying, in jazz's crisis of meaning, an infinite series of subversive delinkings and relinkings in the musical practices of postwar artist Anthony Braxton that confounded the progressivist claims of jazz musicians, critics and historians alike. His argument provides an important critical adjunct to the assumptions that inform both Monson's and Berliner's studies.

Still, a deeper understanding is needed of the correspondences among the making of black musical practices, the history of jazz styles, the pursuit of improvised musical acts, and the appearance of those practices, styles, and acts as symptoms of a key ideological struggle within the American state. While Monson places considerable ethical weight on the ethnographic analysis of jazz *as* practice, based on the exploitation of black musicians by whites at all levels of jazz production and distribution, her analysis underplays the historical basis of the processes through which jazz was constituted as a new musical practice and according to which it was also universalized as a sign of America's global political and economic dominance. To her attempt to make of jazz improvisation a metaphor for "more flexible social thinking," I would add that the tendency to reduce the world of human experience either to jazz or improvisation is deeply ideological in itself, and demands closer attention. Only in the wake of such attention is it possible to begin explicating the modes of consciousness ascribed to jazz in the extent of the "jazz life" and, thus, give due consideration to the form of the crisis attributed to Ornette Coleman and the other free jazz musicians.

The social conditions in which free jazz musicians attempted to legitimate their practices developed from the musical problem of bebop's limitations and what those limitations meant for the future of jazz. At the same time, free jazz had important implications for the historical problem of black autonomy and what that meant for the future of American society as an *efficient and productive capitalist state*. The crisis of action produced by the ideological and social forces of the atomic event and the logic of mass consumption meant that, by the late 1950s, there was widespread agreement among the younger, progressive jazz musicians that bebop "had just about destroyed itself as the means toward a moving form of expression."[20] These musicians operated on two fronts: first, they continued to pursue the bebop musicians' attempts to overthrow the image of jazz as mere *entertainment;* and second, they questioned the image of black consciousness as a form of *negation.* For LeRoi Jones, this double engagement functioned to "restore to jazz its valid separation from, and anarchic disregard of, Western popular forms."[21] The crisis of postwar jazz thus provided black musicians with many of the terms with which to confront and transform their relationship to the state.[22]

Jones's overarching aim, as we have already seen, is to demonstrate the social conditions from which jazz practices emerged in the 1920s and how those practices were integral to the form of the struggle among different classes of blacks and between blacks and whites for control of their social world. For him, the questions surrounding the legitimacy of jazz are crucial to any articulation of the emancipatory potential of American society. While the hot jazz of the 1920s and big band jazz of the 1930s determined the framework for the unfolding of black music, it was the making of bebop in the 1940s that provided the conditions for the development of a musical scene in which bebop was not only separate from but opposed to mainstream popular music. This opposition is critical to Jones's argument.[23] It was because of the struggle waged over the value and meaning of bebop that it became possible for musicians such as Coleman, the pianist Cecil Taylor, and the saxophonist John Coltrane to transform the *total area* of jazz practices (pitch, rhythm, and tone) and thus affirm the radicality of the black musician in the context of American culture.[24] For Jones, a radical mode of black consciousness emerged *in the very process* of articulating the logic of the new, "free" jazz practices. Saxophonist Steve Lacy articulates the existential terms of such a radicality in this way: "For me . . . the music always has to be—on the edge—in between the known and the unknown and you have to keep pushing it toward the unknown or it and you die."[25]

Thus the radical impulse in Coleman's music implied a decisive break with the swing ensemble's rhythmic frame. Jones goes on to argue:

> [I]n bop and avant garde compositions it seems as if the
> rhythmic portion of the music is inserted directly into the
> melodic portion. The melody of [Coleman's composition]
> "Ramblin' " is almost a rhythmic pattern in itself. Its
> accents are almost identical to the rhythmic underpinnings
> of the music. . . . One result of this "insertion" of rhythm
> into the melodic fabric of bop as well as the music of
> the avant-garde is the subsequent freedom allowed to

instruments that are normally supposed to carry the entire
rhythmic impetus of the music. Drum and bass lines
are literally "sprung" . . . away from the simple, cloying
4/4 that characterized the musics that came immediately
before and after bop. . . . This is one reason why in a
group like Coleman's it seems as if they have gone back to
the concept of collective improvisation. No one's role in
the ensemble is fixed. . . . Everyone has a chance to play
melody or rhythm.[26]

Coleman's influence, therefore, was manifested in two key transformations in the way free jazz musicians played their instruments. The first
was a shift in the functioning of the jazz ensemble (in particular, the role
of the soloist and his or her relation to the other musicians) as well as
the abandonment of the piano as the main harmonic instrument. This
"unfixing" of the ensemble's usual functioning, and specifically that of
the rhythm section (drums and bass), was necessitated by the expanded
melodic structure of the music itself.[27] The second was the weakening
of the regular "dance" beat in favor of a much more ambiguous idea of
rhythm as it was formed through each musician's use of tone and pitch.
Taken together, these two transformations meant that the fundamental
changes in the organization of his ensembles and Coleman's specific
musical ways were inseparable from the group's new relation to the
musical form of jazz.

In an interview with John Litweiler, Coleman described the basis
of this initial challenge to bebop: "What do you play after you play
the melody and you don't have nothing to go on?"[28] Faced with no
objective harmonic or rhythmic pattern to rely on, his idea was that
the group would develop the melody *together* in such a way that "the
pattern for the tune . . . will be forgotten and the tune itself will be the
pattern, and won't have to be forced into conventional patterns."[29] As
Litweiler shows us, this period in Coleman's development, from 1958–
61, still relied on bebop for diatonic, timbral, and rhythmic meaning,
even if bebop was being challenged and transfigured in the process. At
the same time, the inner dynamic of the jazz group was itself undergoing
a fundamental modulation. This modulation was consolidated on the
major 1960 recording, *Free Jazz*. Not only did Coleman discard explicit
references to blues and jazz standards, he used this recording to develop
his new conception of musical action. By using two quartets which played
the same work *together,* Coleman revealed through a *stereophonic doubling*
the social struggle on which the form of his improvised act depended.

The traces of bebop that remained within *Free Jazz* (the individual solos, a syncopated swing beat, and the walking bass line) functioned as the act's ideological limits, while the musical relation between the two quartets, that is, the act's overall tempo, constituted its virtuosic power. Indeed, the musical transformations evident on this recording enabled Coleman to take the jazz ensemble to a new creative plane and in the process create "a new kind of ensemble music."[30]

## The "Corn-Pone" Musician

Coleman's significance lies in his having located the ideological gestures found in the music of Bechet and of Parker within a different virtuosic dimension: that of an illusion of pure melody. This dimension refers directly to the subsumption of rhythm and harmony into the elaboration of the melody. While in Bechet the melodic line emerged from the combination of the blues and the spirituals into a single expressive act and in Parker's act the melodic line was the differential between his various speeds, for Coleman melody was the very form of the act itself. As the critic Max Harrison wrote in 1965:

> [Louis] Armstrong and Parker did not "change the direction of jazz" because . . . during what we may call its harmonic period, its chief technical moves were pre-set. Rather did they enable it to travel faster: their effect was developmental, not revolutionary. . . . But Coleman indicated a new direction, potentially the most vital move in the music's history . . . toward new ways of musical thought altogether. Coleman's music virtually by-passed harmony in favor of a free modality; it also abandoned equal temperament tuning, which had been a consequence of harmony and its fixed intervals. . . . In effect, Coleman freed the non-European and non-African elements that had always been present in jazz, allowing them a larger part in shaping the new music.[31]

Harrison's understanding of Coleman's work is by far the most insightful among his contemporaries (although it remained undeveloped) and is essential for the analysis that follows. In articles written on Coleman for various jazz journals, his aim is neither to identify in Coleman evidence of African survivals nor to assert the primacy of

European structures; but neither does he assume the efficiency of the act's ideological dimension by claiming its inevitable synthetic qualities. Harrison questions the assumption that Coleman's music merely embodied a modern consciousness that did nothing more than reflect the American state's postwar economic prosperity, political dominance, and military power. Instead, in Coleman he recognizes an effort to redefine human creative action in fundamentally different terms. A situational analysis of Coleman's musical practice thus aims to outline the framework and recognize the complexities of the historical process through which free improvisation was defined as a legitimate musical act, without undermining the originality of Coleman's practice in the restructuring of musical experience.

Harrison's argument has important implications for the study of jazz practices and American ideology. The ongoing difficulty in analyzing free improvisation is due to the uneven state of historical, musicological, and journalistic accounts of Coleman's music, as well as of the improvisational practices of many of his contemporaries. By relying on what Pierre Bourdieu calls a "hagiographic hermeneutic," most studies or critiques of free jazz reduce the music's meaning and legitimacy to the individual's potential for self-identity with the state's progressive or reformist powers. In this light, free jazz is seen simply to have affirmed the transcendent function of all popular music as a purely subjective expression of that same individual's liberation (a liberation conditioned by the rising prosperity of the state and its "progressive" technobureaucratic functions).[32] Such a "hagiography" dissolves the historical specificity of free jazz practices into an ideological form in which the act appears to be both a "naturalized" expression of individual freedom and an abstract representation of a pure communicative exchange. Much of the problem lies in the ambiguous character of Coleman's improvisatory practice, in his uncompromising theories about musical forms and musical history, and, furthermore, in the lack of an analytical frame adequate to the challenges of the musical practices themselves. This lack invariably leads theory, as Marx so aptly put it, away from practices toward an oppressive mysticism of the act.[33]

Ingrid Monson's response to this analytical and historical impasse is to emphasize "what implications musicians' observations about musical processes may have for the rethinking of musical analysis and cultural interpretation from an interactive point of view, with particular attention to the problems of race and culture."[34] As the basis for her study, Monson stresses the perspective musicians contribute to the reshaping of social analysis. To develop a sense of the complexity of this perspective, she suggests that, when it comes to jazz improvisation, "we not be content with identifying structural shapes alone; we should be concerned as well with the interactive processes by which they emerge."[35] The notion of interaction features prominently in Monson's analysis: it functions to explain the source of any conflict between musicians and also accounts for the resolution of such conflicts through an implicit "musicality" of the act. In this way, jazz is both the origin of a "community of sentiment" and its ultimate object.[36]

Likewise, in *Thinking in Jazz*, Paul Berliner wants to focus "on close observation and description of the full range of musical activities that occupied active members of the community known for its expertise in improvisation. . . . The artist's view of the subject became a distinctive focus of this work, one that emerged as imperative for a serious analytical work on jazz improvisation."[37] The impressive scope of Berliner's study takes in the whole life of the jazz musician, from birth to maturity, and aims to demonstrate that "there is a functioning pedagogy of instruction within the tradition."[38] No matter how a musician finds his or her way to jazz, the end result of such a pedagogy—the jazz community—is constituted in relation to the "same basic challenge: to acquire the specialized knowledge upon which advanced jazz performance depends."[39] A significant shortcoming of this argument, however, as with Monson's, is the convergence of ethnographic description with an idealized economy of participation. In this view, the "culture of improvisation" is reified as a first principle from which both musicians and theorists find their ultimate social meaning and, thus, their mutual justification, as free individuals *beyond time*.[40]

Coleman's position within jazz production can be easily reduced to this "culture of improvisation" in which the individual's expressive abilities are reified as the given condition of the act. To counter this tendency I argue for what, in Bourdieu's terms, amounts to the "social history of the struggles for forms which is the life and movement of the artistic field."[41] To recognize the structures and structuring role of *social struggle* in the dynamic of jazz practices is "to reject the subjectivism of theories of aesthetic consciousness."[42] To illustrate this problem, consider how the following incident, recalled by Coleman in a 1984 interview, served to reinforce his reputation as a "naïve" or "natural" musician. In 1959, NBC-TV news anchors Chet Huntley and David Brinkley arrived at a renowned New York jazz club to film his ensemble:

> They came to the Five Spot and asked me, "Can you read?" And I said, "Only the newspaper," because when I told people I could do things like read music, it never helped me. So after that, write-ups always picked up

> on that quote. . . . I realized that my image was sort of
> "corn-pone musician," this illiterate guy who just plays,
> so I started writing classical music.[43]

The journalists' assumption that Coleman was in possession of an innate musical "gift" (rather than Sidney Bechet's more interesting idea of music *as* a gift, and thus, as *social act*) further reinforced the assumptions of an inherent genetic ability that dominates much popular jazz analysis. Such assumptions constitute the ideological basis on which the jazz musician was integrated into American life as both a model of democratic interaction and of a liberated self-consciousness. Far from being an "illiterate guy who just plays," however, Coleman's virtuosity involved in every sense *a situated and historical struggle* with the limits of musical practice and the meaning of the musical act in American society. Indeed, it was precisely his sense of this struggle that enabled Coleman to address the conditions under which the jazz act was made. Furthermore, the orienting aspect of Cold War ideology and institutions, and the pressure to legitimate social practices and artistic forms in terms of these institutions and their ideology, meant that Coleman's attempt to define his musical act as an act of freedom was also an attempt to define the struggle for musical form as an explicitly social struggle.

Central to this struggle was the historical framework of black civil rights and the significance of music to the project of "constructing a new sense of self and of black culture."[44] Richard H. King's analysis of the ideological framework of that movement provides a necessary counterpoint to the larger problems of the Cold War and the atomic event. In defining the theoretical and political bases of the struggle for civil rights, King leads us directly into the social conditions in which free jazz acts were made, and according to which certain musical forms were considered authentic expressions of black consciousness. His initial question about the political concept underlying the civil rights movement leads to the further question of how freedom itself was defined within American society, and how the "repertory of freedom" specific to American historical experience gave to the civil rights movement both its social meaning and the ideological terms for the struggle against segregation.[45] For King, to even raise such questions in the context of Cold War liberal consensus meant that the civil rights movement "failed to fit comfortably, if at all, within the confines of conventional liberal politics."[46]

To pose these questions in relation to the musical practices of free jazz musicians suggests a further stage in the argument. As Ronald Radano illustrates in his study of avant-garde composer Anthony Braxton, from the 1950s the authenticity of the black jazz musician was predicated on whether his or her musical acts effected a significant transformation of black consciousness, and on whether his or her consciousness reflected the concerns of the civil rights movement itself.[47] By the 1960s, "[r]adical black artists sought to construct a new social reality, a new cultural era that would lead blacks away from what they believed to be a materially obsessed and corrupt white world."[48] What Radano's study of Braxton also suggests is that such predicates were infinitely more complicated than most jazz historians or critics would have us believe; that, indeed, the development of specific musical practices by free jazz musicians introduced fundamental antinomies into the jazz act itself that even the movement for civil rights could not contain.

An example of how such antinomies appeared can be found in the series of free improvised jazz concerts organized by trumpet player Bill Dixon in October of 1964. Set in a small cafe in New York City over six nights, the aim of the "October Revolution in Jazz" was to demonstrate that "there was an audience for the new music."[49] Dixon also hoped to liberate jazz from the patterns of commercial dependency and corporate hierarchy that characterized the music industry, and assert the creative power of black musicians in the face of mass consumption. The concerts were so successful that Dixon set up the Jazz Composer's Guild to bargain collectively for jazz musicians and composers in their contractual dealings with venue owners, recording companies, and promoters, and so begin the process of developing "self-respect" among the musicians.[50] A further series of concerts in December of the same year consolidated the project and marked the formation of the Jazz Composer's Guild Orchestra.[51] The organization (but not the Orchestra) fell apart, however, when saxophonist Archie Shepp signed an individual recording contract with the Impulse recording label without telling the other members of the Guild.[52] Shepp's confronting stance, his assertion of economic privilege to further his belief in the powers of musical freedom, shifted the very terms on which that belief was based. Far from producing the conditions for a new relation to the jazz form, however, his jazz act dissolved into purely subjective gestures of freedom (honking, squeals, chants, and so on) and thus into a parody of its own musical possibilities. My point here is that, in each stage of the Guild's efforts to organize and value jazz musicians' labor, the notion of *freedom* was invoked and disputed in the effort to legitimate the actions of the people involved, even when those actions, in the end, undermined the Guild's own objectives.

What was fundamentally at issue in the events surrounding the "October Revolution" concerts was the very social conditions in which the jazz act was made. The musicians who played in them, as was true of other similar events and organizations (for example, the Collective Black Artists in New York, and the Association for the Advancement of Creative Music in Chicago), gave voice to the "rhetoric of freedom" to legitimate their improvised musical acts, while also affecting a transformation in that same rhetoric and in the interior structure of the acts themselves. In this sense, the effort and skill required to legitimate their musical act *qua* act was also a social struggle waged in the context of the state's ideological and institutional forms. On this basis it is possible to seek a deeper understanding of the structure and dynamic of musical groups, beyond the simplistic reduction of the jazz group to a vehicle for individual "self-expression." What is wanted, as Fredric Jameson puts it, "is a whole new logic of collective dynamics, with categories that escape the taint of some mere application of terms drawn from individual experience. . . ."[53]

Coleman's historical situation itself poses key problems for achieving an appreciation of the collective act and its conditions of production. His first quartets were assembled against the background of the vast restructuring of productive power of the American state, and particularly the shift in the productive power of the state's military-industrial base from the northern cities to the southwestern Sun Belt, comprising such states as Texas, California, Nevada, and New Mexico. This background, however, is considered not only fundamental to the subsequent developments in Coleman's ideas but also to his controversial position within the jazz world. As Robert Gordon argues, that a rhythm-and-blues-playing Coleman ended up in Los Angeles rather than New York was significant in terms of both the developing economy of black music practices and the subsequent challenges made to the bebop form by his quartets and trios.[54]

The ideological dimension of the act, its rhetoric of freedom, was determined by a principle of economic distribution. That is to say, the value of the act was wholly dependent on the reversal of one's fortunes within the postwar state. For example, the migration during World War II of blacks from Texas, Kansas, Oklahoma, and Louisiana to the West Coast munitions plants, particularly those in and around Los Angeles, offered many of the black musicians from these same regions some possibility for economic security and even the chance of minor artistic success. The existence of a distinctive southwestern blues tradition combined with a large number of independent studios meant that Los Angeles in the late 1940s was "the capital of R&B [rhythm and blues] recording, while Central Avenue's dazzling 'Main Stem' offered an extraordinary spectrum of jazz, blues and R&B, dominated by musicians from the Southwest circuit of Texas, Oklahoma, Kansas and Louisiana. . . ."[55] The very fact of this regional expansion, however, meant that Coleman and his fellow jazz musicians found it almost impossible to gain recognition or employment other than in menial service jobs. Their approach to jazz and their challenge to the interior structuring of the jazz group resulted in their being identified—and ultimately feted—as very much an "underground within an underground."[56] In this sense, the Coleman quartet's value as "an underground within an underground" became both the basis of its ideological relation to the state and the condition for the virtuosic transformation of that relation.

New York was equally problematic for black musicians and even more competitive, in spite of its financial and institutional status as the "jazz capital" of the world and the fact that, per capita, it offered more opportunities for jazz performance, recordings, artist management, and radio airplay than any other American city. Coleman's arrival there in 1959, although heralded by jazz critics and other musicians, proved as sobering and confrontational as his musical reception was acrimonious and exhausting:

> I haven't had any more success in New York in relation to musical expression than I had anywhere else. New York City has prejudice embedded in wealth as well as color. Wealth is first and color is next; in California color is first and wealth is next. All musical life in New York is determined by the money output it can produce. I'm like a lot of people who come here thinking that they're going to find their fame and fortune and find out that all they're doing is supporting a lot of unsuccessful people and giving wealth to a lot of untalented people.[57]

Coleman's experience, as he describes it, suggests we should be wary about the attempt by some to position black music as a kind of automatic defense, a natural buffer zone, between poverty, racism, and exploitation and the historical conditions of urban black communities.[58] His reference to the forces of racism and money emphasize that musical experiences were actively constituted by, and constitutive of, the social, political, and economic realities of American postwar society, rather than simply a means to its negation. Thus, among black musicians, and between black musicians and nonblack musicians, the dynamics of musical practices and musical acts were as much sites of a struggle to orient the meaning and direction of their social situation as were other social and political practices. And yet, while the improvised musical act was related to other concerns and aspects of human being, it also generated its own singular logic, its own dynamic and rules of engagement, that was not simply a mirror of everyday existence.

## The Virtuosity of the Musical Act

Using transcripts of interviews, articles, and liner notes, along with comments from other musicians and critics, it is possible to grasp the logic and dynamics of Coleman's practices beyond the conventional oppositions that have shaped the study of jazz. While I rely heavily on John Litweiler's invaluable biography of Coleman, I think it is also critical to situate this narrative in its ideological context in order to analyze the influence of free jazz on the jazz act, and clarify its relation to the existential dynamics of postwar American society. The very fact of the free jazz group's musical efforts and the musicians' opposition to the bebop group or the big band presents a critical modification and intensification of the acts and objects of musical perception. A study of the dynamics of the improvising group thus reveals the transformation in musical sensibility as it was developed through the rhythmic and melodic ideas specific to each musician's musical practices. Understanding the formation of Coleman's first free jazz ensemble, a group that was committed to the process of remaking the musical act in every performance, enables us to identify, to some degree, music's very materiality, its sensuous force, within the dynamics of the act itself.

In an interview in 1995, Coleman remarked: "I didn't know you had to know music. I thought everybody just *played* music. . . . No one has to learn to spell to talk, right? You see a little kid holding a conversation with an adult. He probably doesn't know the words he's saying, but he knows where to fit them to make what he's thinking logical to what you're saying. Music is the same way."[59] This emphasis on the act of playing music provides a clear summation of Coleman's theory of the musical act and suggests how we might examine and reconsider the work of other jazz musicians and their music, and likewise explain more precisely the jazz musician's relation to the dynamics of the social world. At the same time, we should refrain from imposing on Coleman's practices the retrospective fantasy of a total revolution or a mystical agency. Comfortable with such fantasies, few critics or historians pay detailed attention to the structures and structuring of Coleman's jazz groups as a significant social form, preferring to ascribe the force of Coleman's ideas to his liberated subjectivity or his unfettered libidinal desire, while attributing the group's success to the individual's capacity for self-expression and self-transformation. For example, Monson sees jazz improvisation as a properly "magical projection of soul and individuality."[60]

To understand musical improvisation as Monson does, however, relies too much on a disembodied principle of creative action. Such analyses tend to overlook the social antagonisms and the materiality of the jazz act: the effort to learn an instrument, to join a jazz group, or to play alone; the passions or moods of the human body; the heated exchanges and arguments between participants; and finally the pleasure of playing an instrument well. In other words, these analyses underestimate to what extent a study of jazz is primarily a study of the historical experience of the improviser as *virtuoso,* and improvisation as an act of *musical virtuosity.*[61]

I now want to consider Coleman and his ensemble in terms of a theory of musical virtuosity. As I mentioned in the introduction to this book, the notion of virtuosity involves a specific domain of human being that here is denoted *musical* and to a form of human consciousness that is analyzed as *musical consciousness.* I oppose the figure of the virtuoso and the act of musical virtuosity to that of the musical genius (or its inverse, the implicit genius of the democratic populace). In European classical music, from Beethoven on (though we may, of course, point to another, virtuosic Beethoven), the musical genius's mastery was considered absolute (and in the image of God), thoroughly individualized, and so privileged as a symbol of the universal law of human reproduction and of the state's divine power. On the contrary, the virtuoso proceeds by and through a ritual of *seduction* and thus always *in relation* to a multitude of others (animate and inanimate)—those to be seduced, those who seduce.

The virtuoso seduces by and because of music, and is likewise seduced by and because of music.[62] He or she is part of an economy of musical practices, but continually short circuits that economy by overreaching the boundaries of good taste, the expectations of music's patrons, the will of the people, and by asserting an extreme passion for the musical act as an act of faith above all else. In entering into and eliciting a musical feeling (however ambivalent), this virtuosity of the musical act thereby guarantees music the radical inequality of its effects and the infinite variability of its enchantment. I owe this notion of the logic of seduction and its relevance to the analysis of musical virtuosity to Jean Baudrillard's book, *Seduction,* which enables me to explicate the idea of musical practices as *the practices and art of seduction.*[63] I intend to test the force of this idea against Coleman's and his group's musical practices, but also to argue for the pertinence of extending such an analysis to other realms of musical practice and to the social and historical conditions wherein those realms of human activity are valued as such.

First, however, to elaborate further the argument for a theory of the virtuosity of the musical act and its logic of seduction, I want to quote a passage from David Sudnow's phenomenology of the jazz act. The significance of Sudnow's work for us, as I suggested in the introduction, lies primarily in detailing the moment of seduction by the improviser, the social conditions of musical production, and the vertiginous motions of the performing body. After many years of trying to develop the musical skills required to do jazz improvisation, Sudnow reached a crucial turning point in his studies, a point he terms "going for jazz." The passage is worth citing in whole because it encompasses many of the problems of analyzing the act of improvisation, as well as the kinds of sociohistorical terms in which these acts might be framed. A faith in the virtuosity of the musical act is here crystallized in the capture (and rapture) of the pianist's hands by the bodily execution of the act and in the realization that technique essentially is not only a matter of knowledge (to learn, to master, to elicit), but equally is of the order of passions, of distraction, of collusion; in other words, of the order of seduction.

> Jimmy Rowles is something of a musician's musician, and in the nightclub in Greenwich Village where he worked, jazzmen from all over New York would gather in their off-hours to hear his marvelous presentations of ballads. He played alone, or with a bass player, and his forte was a most lilting, casual way of playing standard tunes like "Somewhere over the Rainbow," "Body and Soul," "Tenderly," "The Man I Love." To listen to him was to relish each and every place of a luxuriously lingering song. He was a fine improviser, but it was the way he played a ballad that commanded so much professional respect.
>
> Jimmy Rowles had a way with the instrument. He sat rather low down and stretched back, almost lazy with the piano like a competent driver is nonchalant behind the wheel on an open road. Still, there was a taking care with the melody, a caressing of it, a giving each place its due. He was never in a hurry; in fact, it almost seemed as if he would fall behind the beat, but it only seemed that way. It was late-night music, and the song would take its time.
>
> I watched him night after night, watched him move from chord to chord with a broadly swaying participation

of his shoulders and entire torso, watched him delineate waves of movement, some broadly encircling, others subdividing the broadly undulating strokes with finer rotational movements, so that as his arm reached out to get from one chord to another it was as if some spot on his back, for example, circumscribed a small circle at the same time, as if at the very slow tempos this was a way a steadiness to the beat was sustained.

I would at times watch his chordal hand at work, coming in gently for a landing, and even while staying depressed it seemed to take the chord passing, never appearing to come to a final rest, as the elbow and arm displayed a course of elliptical rotation around the engaged keyboard hand. As his foot tapped up and down, his head went through a similar rotational course, and the strict up-and-down tapping of the foot was incorporated within a cyclical manner of accenting his bodily movements. In an anchored heel, you could only see the up-and-down movements of the foot, but in the accompanying head rotation and shoulder swaying, you could see a circularly undulating flow of motion, a pushing and releasing, a thrust and relaxation.

. . . I found over the course of several months of listening to and watching Jimmy Rowles, and starting to play slow ballads myself (which I had previously done chiefly when first learning chord structures at the very beginning), that in order to happen like his, his observable bodily idiom, his style of articulating a beat, served as a guide. In the very act of swaying gently and with elongated movements through the course of playing a song, the lilting, stretching, almost oozing quality of his interpretations could be evoked. It was not that I could imitate his intonation and phrasing with fine success, capture the full richness of his way of moving and pacing and caretaking. His special sense of time was sufficiently distinctive to make him a difficult player to readily imitate. But I found that I could get much of his breathing quality into a song's presentation by trying to copy his ways.

Listening to him, taking notice for the first time of ways of moving at the keyboard, beginning to play slow music, bringing attention for the first time, peculiar

as it was and so much a part of my isolation from the
occupation, to a careful regard for the presentation of a
song, giving that sort of a care to the beat which his bodily
idiom displayed, I began to develop a fundamentally
different way of being at the piano.[64]

Sudnow's attention to the dynamic of the musical act, the virtuosity
of its structures and structuring, brings us closer to how we might
understand the logic of the jazz act's practices, the intentional dimension
of the jazz musician's actions, and the experience of playing and listening
to improvised music. Musical seduction emerges in Sudnow's study as
a singularly embodied experience, an intricate series of tactile displace-
ments and taunts, deceptions and enchantment, between Rowles and his
piano, between the piano and the listener, and between the listener and
Rowles. Sudnow's experience requires the notion of musical seduction
to explain the radical disjuncture between the embodied musician and
the disembodied listener, to define the moment of technical secrecy (the
musician's method) that leads, finally, to an opening up of the virtuosic
ways of the improvised musical act. In the case of Coleman, as I have
argued, the important aspect of his practice—that is, the logic of his
practice—emerged in the process of forming the group as a collective
challenge to the standard division of soloist and rhythm section. What
Sudnow enables us to realize, initially, is the seductive form of the relation
between the techniques of the body and the musical material; that is,
how the act of grasping an instrument's potential as a system of pitches,
textures, and accents was also the basis of a *virtuosity of illusion.*

## A Passion for the Act

Before I return to the internal dynamics of Coleman's jazz act, I want to
address in more detail the problem of virtuosity. In the introduction, I
referred to an essay by the political theorist Paolo Virno entitled "Virtuosity and Revolution." I suggested that Virno's essay poses fundamental
questions concerning the forms of human action and consciousness in
contemporary society. That he does so in terms of a theory of political
revolution and its relation to virtuosic behavior is critical to my argument
about the virtuosic dimensions of the jazz act. The crux of Virno's analysis
is that, before being swallowed up by capitalist production, virtuosic
performance is what qualified *political action* as distinct from (and in
fact opposed to) the various regimes of work (whether slave, peasant,

or waged).[65] However, key developments in contemporary Western experience mean that this distinction is no longer tenable. By becoming virtuosic—that is to say, more like action—work (or production) paralyzes the very realm of action itself. At the same time, work is increasingly defined by its "mass intellectuality," that is, by its command of linguistic or communicative knowledge as such. The resulting crisis of political action has merely served to strengthen the productive powers of the postwar capitalist state and enforce a whole new logic of subjugation and exploitation. This crisis of action and intellect thus underlies an attempt by capitalism "to set to work all those aspects that traditionally it has shut out of work."[66]

What, for Virno, defines a virtuosic act? The virtuosic act is defined by its historical distinction from the activity of productive labor and that of pure thought. It neither exhibits an automatism that makes of it a repetitive and predictable process, like the processes of labor, but nor does it rely on a solitary and nonphemomenal quality, like the processes of thought. It neither creates new objects nor involves itself in intellectual reflection. Rather, virtuosic performances are "activities that find fulfillment in themselves, without being objectivized in a finished work existing outside and beyond them."[67] Virtuosic conduct is therefore an end in itself that "does not have to pursue an extrinsic aim. . . ."[68] In this sense, the virtuoso performer is one who continually modifies the context in which he or she performs. Considered this way, virtuosity is an *attitude* and thus, it constitutes the basis for a specific relation to the world.

The form of the virtuosic relation to the world emerges from two further distinctions: the first between intellectual and manual labor, and the second between productive and nonproductive labor. In making these distinctions, Virno follows Marx in his analysis of intellectual labor in the section of *Capital* entitled "Results of the Immediate Process of Production."[69] For Marx, the *virtuoso performance* is to be distinguished from other immaterial or intellectual activities (such as writing or painting) that result in the limited production of commodities. Positioned at the level of luxury services, the result of the labors of the pianist or dancer, but also such occupations as orators, priests, and doctors, is that "the product is not separable from the act of producing."[70] At stake, in both Marx's and Virno's accounts, is the value of nonproductive labor, its relative insignificance (Marx defined this activity as peripheral) in terms of the "mass of capitalist production," and the conditions for its subsequent transformation into productive labor.[71]

For Virno, this transformation is the fundamental *political* problem of what he terms the "post-Fordist era" in capitalist production, that is, the transition to a new global regime of accumulation during the 1970s. The organizational and productive premise of this new regime is no longer the figure of the manual laborer or factory worker, but rather that of the intellectual virtuoso. Thus, the

> pianist and the dancer stand precariously balanced on a
> watershed that divides two antithetical destinies: on the
> one hand, they may become examples of "wage-labor that
> is not at the same time productive labor"; on the other,
> they have a quality that is suggestive of political action. . . .
> So far . . . each of the potential developments inherent
> in the figure of the performing artist—poiesis or praxis,
> Work or Action—seems to exclude its opposite. . . . From
> a certain point onward, however, the alternative changes
> into complicity . . . the virtuoso works (in fact she or he is
> a worker par excellence) not despite the fact, but precisely
> because of the fact that her or his activity is closely
> reminiscent of political praxis. . . . Within post-Fordist
> organization of production, activity-without-a-finished-
> work moves from being a special and problematic case to
> becoming the prototype of waged labor in general.[72]

However, the form of this virtuosic performance is not that of "a specific kind of composition (let us say, Bach's Goldberg Variations) as played by a top-notch performer (let us say Glenn Gould, for example)."[73] Rather the contemporary logic of social relations in capitalist economies is determined by a demand placed on labor for a sequence of variations on a theme, performances, improvisations, an "acting-in-concert" with others that has no end in itself. This virtuosity "is nothing unusual, nor does it require some special talent."[74] It simply implies the transformation of communicative and cognitive attitudes into a force of production that now "figures as capital's most eminent resource."[75] Once transformed, or in fact in the process of such a transformation, these newly productive capacities become the technical prerequisites for work as a whole and thus are "subjected to the kinds of criteria and hierarchies that characterized the factory regime."[76]

In other words, the post-Fordist conditions of production are built on the surplus value of a "global social knowledge" or a "scientific capacity" as it appears in public and through which the new regime of accumulation guarantees its perpetual reproduction. The form of this appearance is that of a "general Intellect" (or what Virno terms "linguistic services") that, far from giving rise to a final product, exhausts itself "in the communicative interaction that [its] own performance brings about."[77] Examples of this would be the vast distribution of clerical functions within the corporate or state sectors, or the telecommunications infrastructure that facilitate the "decentralized" forms of financial speculation and consumption.[78] The epicenter of production is now the tasks of overseeing and coordination, functions that effect the administrative *modulation* of the social order via the postmodern state. Within the new "linguistic economy," such tasks are called upon "to exercise the art of the possible, to deal with the unforeseen, to profit from opportunities."[79] In this sense, virtuosity becomes a generalized condition of human subservience within capitalist society.

Against this subsumption of virtuosic performance into the post-Fordist relations of production, and against its subservience to the administrative structures of the state, Virno argues for a form of *nonservile virtuosity*.[80] The political basis of his distinction between a servile and nonservile virtuosity has striking implications for a study of the jazz act, particularly in terms of how he defines the *form* of the event. For Virno, a nonservile virtuosity is not an event shrouded in mystery, a "primitive experience," that displays no relation to the post-Fordist economic system, but rather an event that is "awaited and yet unexpected. " In this sense, it is "an exception that is especially surprising to the one who was awaiting it. It is an anomaly so potent it completely disorients our conceptual compass, which, however, had precisely signaled the place of its insurgence. We have here a discrepancy between cause and effect, in which one can always grasp the cause, but the innovative effect is never lessened."[81] Through what Virno defines as an implicit "right to resistance," the nonservile act short circuits the very ideological and productive conditions in which it is made, while, in a single gesture, it effects a precise summation of virtuosic constructions, speeds, and illusions.

The contemporary distinction between a servile and a nonservile virtuosity in post-Fordist society can be broadened to encompass the history of the jazz act and its engagement with the conditions of its production. Indeed, an analysis of the structures of virtuosity as they are constituted within the jazz act defines the very ideological terrain on which the struggle for the value and form of the jazz act takes place. Virno's analysis, as he suggests, is only an outline, an attempt to posit a theoretical "score" for the renewal of political action. My efforts here are directed toward the creative character of the improvised act and the basis of its virtuosic relation to the Cold War state. Adopting the terms of Virno's analysis, I suggest that within the historical development of jazz practice, the virtuosic "surplus" referred to above is precisely this moment of nonservility. However, far from superseding its opposite, a nonservile virtuosity, as practiced by the improvising group, is already constituted ideologically in the image of the capitalist state—that is, in the form of individuals freely expressing themselves—and therefore is already internal to the operations of power and consciousness.

The improvising group's collective act of melodying modifies both the ideological (or servile) and virtuosic (or nonservile) dimensions of the jazz form, as it does the situation in which the musical act takes place. In the very process of going for a pure melody the act is no longer what it was, even as it is returned, through its ideological dimension, to the conditions of its production as a sign of the state's historical progress. To analyze the virtuosity of the act, in the words of Maurice Merleau-Ponty, is to grasp "that strange overlapping of means and ends which makes the choice of means already a choice of ends—making the justification of the means by the ends absurd."[82] Understood in this way, a nonservile virtuosity circumvents the logic of the act's material making even as it affirms the act's relation to a past that is perpetually ready to be remade. It is, to use another of Merleau-Ponty's phrases, a "coherent deformation" imposed on the musical material that manages "to distend the dimensions of our experience and pull them toward new meaning."[83] A nonservile virtuosity is thus the improvised act's own ebb and flow without which the act would merely appear as a series of abstract technical details about tone, timbre, pitch levels, volumes, and so on.

The structure of Virno's analysis suggests the difficulties in moving from the order of events to that of expression, a difficulty that is equally apparent in Sudnow's description of Jimmy Rowles. Virno's sense of an *unexpected waiting,* that is, the virtuosic moment that eludes the domain of ideology, is concretely displayed in Sudnow's encounter with Rowles. Sudnow's description allows us to discover that this unexpected waiting is, in actual fact, the *amorous* form of the musical act. Consider the focus of Sudnow's description, his concentration on Rowles's hands, his arms and back; the close attention to the piano's setting, to how Rowles sat at the piano, and the modulations in rhythm. It is a description suffused with desire and passion: a love letter addressed to the musical act, to the form of the act, to what is possible and impossible in acting just so. The motions of acting and being are thoroughly intertwined, inseparable from Sudnow's efforts at playing, his sense of already knowing, and his self-objectification as someone who is played upon by musical desire. And yet, while Sudnow watched Rowles "night after night, watched him move from chord to chord," his own ardor for the act was not that of one who would be an imitator but rather one who would copy, the form of the act becoming one of repetition:

> It was not that I could imitate his intonation and phrasing with fine success, capture the full richness of his way of moving and pacing and caretaking. His special sense of time was sufficiently distinctive to make him a difficult player to really imitate. But I found that I could get much of his breathing quality into a song's presentation by trying to copy his ways.[84]

The musical act, as an unexpected waiting, a moment of virtuosic suspension, emerged from a series of postures and dispositions: Sudnow's frustration at his own ways of "melodying"; his encounter with Rowles in the New York club; the realization that Rowles "had a way with the instrument"; the view that to play like Rowles would prove, at some level, impossible; the decision to take Rowles as a role model in spite of that impossibility; the transference of Sudnow's own musical desire onto Rowles; and finally, the understanding of how Rowles actually got his jazz going. By repeating Rowles's gestures, his piano-playing ways, by trying to do as he did at the piano, Sudnow was able "to develop a fundamentally different way of being at the piano." But this "different way," that is, the power to create something new by copying it, relied on the difficulty of imitating Rowles's "special sense of time." This irreducible gap, between Rowles's act and Sudnow's attempted repetition of it, was the very condition of Sudnow's emergent virtuosity.

The ardent qualities of Sudnow's description directs us to the interior structure of Coleman's ensembles, so as to enter more fully into the musical character of the improvised act. In arguing for an understanding of musical practices as the practices and arts of seduction, I am not ignoring the technical nor the imaginative efforts required to improvise. Rather I argue that through the logic of seduction a virtuosity of illusion, a play of appearances, enters into the interior structure of the improvised act itself. A theory of seduction, as Baudrillard points out, requires the "beauty of an artifice," and the musical virtuoso, as both seducer and seduced, requires the extraordinary artifice of the act, but an act constituted in the social struggle of its making.[85] Within the collective improvisations pursued by Coleman and his ensemble, what counted most of all, in spite of the deliberate, elaborate, and often confrontational nature of their musical efforts, was in fact how to effect a sense of the act's spontaneity and an ease of going for jazz within the act itself.[86]

This leap from the making of an act to its "spontaneous" repetition is given detailed attention by Paul Berliner. Berliner's analysis of spontaneity adds an additional qualification to how the making of the improvised act is constituted through its seductive motions. For him, the effort that goes into making and remaking the act is determined by a musician's or a group's "habits of musical thought." These habits constitute the outer limit of what is musically possible during any one performance, and circumscribe the kinds of musical phrases that are practiced and learned prior to the performance. It is the structuring of those habits—how and in what order notes are played—that form the pathway from merely "playing the changes" to acts of "spontaneous" improvisation. The act's spontaneity results from an amorous or impassioned moment of breakthrough, that point when a player "can be affected by his [or her] 'own notes.' "[87] The improvised act's character is thus defined and valued by the unexpected potency (and pleasure) experienced by the musician on hearing what he or she in fact played. In this way, the spontaneity of the act confronts the musician with his or her capacity for musical activity and, in the process, opens up new regions of creative action, new powers of repetition.[88]

Elaine Scarry's analysis of an act's objectification can assist us in refining the notion of seduction and in appreciating more fully how a sense of spontaneity was achieved by free jazz musicians. What is immediately apparent on listening to a work such as Coleman's "The Ark" is the level of tension between the embodied motions of the musicians' making and the seductive moment of the act's playing.[89] That is, internal to the act was the contradiction between the musicians' efforts at playing together and the disappearance of such efforts. Our task, then, as historians of the musical activities of the improviser, is to follow the "path of the object back to its sentient source"[90] and, in doing so, to recognize that, far from being resolved, the tension of making and playing constituted the actual dynamic of the group's virtuosity. Where the object of free jazz is the act itself, the moment of seduction implies, in Baudrillard's terms, "another space of refraction. Seduction does not consist of a simple appearance, nor a pure absence, but the eclipse of presence. Its sole strategy is to be-there/not-there, and thereby produce a sort of flickering, a hypnotic mechanism that crystallizes attention outside all concern with meaning."[91] This is the amorous moment that suspends the field of ideological significance.

Such a suspension of the act's ideological significance occurred for the free jazz musicians in the very process of trying to play together. That is to say, the virtuosity of Coleman's groups resulted from the displacement of the musical meaning from the objective forms of the blues and popular standards onto their efforts at playing together as an improvising ensemble. The structuring and making of the act—its ideological dimension—was refracted in the degree of spontaneity and freedom implied by the act's contingency, while the act's very artificiality was made to appear, through the organization of its rhythmic cycles and melodic motifs, as though internal to the musical ways of the group. The logic of their musical ways *as a group* thus became the grounds for positing a "natural" harmonic and rhythmic sense through which the group was, in fact, constituted as both act and object in the same instance. The moment of seduction, the virtuosity of illusion, was that point when the struggle to play was no longer felt to be preparatory to, but rather a consequence of, the motions of playing.

These virtuosic efforts—to organize the collective musical act through a group of musicians committed to pursuing the melodic, harmonic, and rhythmic limits of the jazz standards and bebop—first appeared on two recordings made by Coleman in Los Angeles in 1958 and 1959, respectively: *Something Else!!!!* and *Tomorrow Is the Question!* While the recordings betray structural and historical links to bebop, particularly in the interplay of saxophone and trumpet, the very dynamic of the group was already in the process of altering the way the music was played, just as the musicians' unique ways of going for their improvised act began to alter the form of the group itself. As Walter Norris, the pianist on *Tomorrow Is the Question!,* recalled: "Each time we played the tunes we'd change them around a different way. We did everything possible we could do to them."[92] Far from implying a "raw" state of musical practice, founded on a "magical projection of the individual," Norris's statement should be understood in its correct historical sense: the virtuosic form of the improvised jazz act emerged on the basis of the act's repetition. The social conditions required of such a repetition, that is, the group's efforts to "get it right" are further clarified in a comment by the saxophonist Lee Konitz. For Konitz, the aim is "to relate as fully as possible to every sound that everyone is making. . . . But whew! It's difficult for me to achieve."[93]

Konitz's comment suggests that although historical accounts of Coleman's quartets or trios focus on each individual's success within the act, the moments when a musician disagreed or had difficulty with Coleman's ideas or the larger aims of the group were of equal significance. It was these moments within the act's making that demonstrate the ideological limits of a musician's struggle to turn his or her musical ways into a socially meaningful act, and to give that act a form.[94] In other words, the conflicts within the group point to the structural insufficiency of the act in relation to its form. In this sense, the act is always inadequate to its form, the conditions of which remain buried within the movement of history itself as its nonhistorical dimension. Indeed, the form of the act always remains symbolically "unconsummated" (the very aim of a musical seduction) or "unrepresentable" (the historical dynamic of musical practices as practices of repetition).[95] Any attempt to symbolize the Coleman quartet as *an idealized or consummated unit of expression* presupposes a level of subjective transparency for the musical act that abstracts the group in its totality, thereby effacing the dynamics of its practice *qua* practice and, likewise, reducing the act's virtuosic dimension to meaningless subjective gestures and thus to the inertia of the Cold War state itself.[96] On the contrary, the dynamic of the group, the virtuosity of its musical act, was necessarily unstable and displaced with regard to itself and to any assumption of an immanent expressionism. What historians such as Monson and Berliner accept as primordially given in jazz, that is, the fact of an "essential communication," a pure exchange, between the musicians, was actually the thing at stake in each and every one of the group's performances. As Martin Williams said, the radical *impossibility* within the group's virtuosity—that the group might *fail* or disband as a group—was in fact the form of the musical act itself.[97]

## Virtuosic Excess and Seductive Motions

In the early recordings and performances, what shocked or excited other musicians and listeners was the way Coleman used his saxophone to turn the relation between his playing and the objective forms of bebop into a continuous development of a melody's pitching; that is, into a relentless play of pitches, tones, and accents among all the players in the ensemble and between the specific timbral qualities of their instruments.[98] As with Sudnow's description of Rowles, the trumpeter Don Cherry (who began playing with Coleman in Los Angeles in the 1950s) ascribed the attraction of Coleman's music to the very materiality of Coleman's saxophone and his bodily feeling for and control of tone and pitch:

> Ornette always writes and plays how he feels. You'll notice too that he uses a plastic alto; it has a drier warmer sound without the ping of metal. He also has a special mouthpiece that together with the #1 reeds he uses has enabled him to develop his tone so that he can control it. He has real control of pitch, and pitch is so important to

him. He can now express on his horn what he hears, and
he has a very unusual ear.[99]

The preoccupation with Coleman's "instrumentality" stems from a
double and extreme polyvalence: that of the act (all musical positions or
roles may be changed at any moment) and that of the notes themselves
(there are no octaves and scales, but rather, just notes—the pitch, the
tone, and their accentuation). As Nat Hentoff explained, "Ornette's
concern with pitch is part of the dominant characteristic of his work—his
conviction that the way the line is going and the pitches in which the
notes of the lines are played should primarily determine the harmonic
progressions."[100] Similarly, the saxophonist Julian "Cannonball" Adderley
located Coleman's virtuosity in the form of movement between pitches,
tones, and rhythms:

> Ornette says he has discovered that the alto saxophone
> has 32 available pitches, from D-flat in the lower middle
> register to A-flat in the second upper middle register of
> the piano. He does not think in octaves. Each tone to
> him is a separate sound. . . . He respects Charlie Parker
> as the only musician, of those who play changes, who
> really exploited the sound of the instrument; and he has
> the unique idea that the alto voice should be thought of
> in the alto clef. Consequently, his E-flat alto C-natural
> concert [pitch] is really B-flat in the alto clef.[101]

This modulation from an octaval or tempered scale to a pitched-
based tone system meant that Coleman's effort to redefine the dynamic
of the improvised act was as much an attempt to remake the jazz group
itself as it was about a transformation of the bebop and swing styles.
Thus his concern with liberating pitch and tone from the tempered
scale, and with separating rhythm from the 4/4 beat, was productive
of an entirely new set of social relations within the group that, in turn,
shifted the social circumstances (the technical, political, and economic
hierarchies, the modes of domination and symbolic power, the systems
of belief and knowledge, and so on) within which the jazz group had
meaning and value.

Several key questions arise as a consequence of Coleman's concerns:
How were the activities of his quartets and trios related to and constitutive
of their immediate situation in terms of the making and remaking of jazz
practices? How was it possible for the quartet or trio to move from the

domain of its creative activities to the larger domain of human action and objectification in such a way that one was not reducible to the other? And how was the social and historical relation between the two domains recognizable and effective in terms of a given order of existence? The sociologist Erving Goffman's solution to this problem is a useful one: in a specific situation, the already given structures and the historical structuring of the primary framework (the range of conjectures and expectations we bring to every act, event, or idea) circumscribes the active or intentional basis of human being. In other words, it is the definition of a framework for human actions that in turn constitutes the meaning and organizational premise of those actions (historically, socially, and practically) and, in so doing, remakes the logic of the framework itself.[102]

The important aspect of Goffman's proposal for the present analysis is the experiential "rim" or edge of the framework such that the musician's capacity to isolate or extract the improvised musical act from other socially charged acts, to find a value and order specific to that act, was in itself a necessary constituent of the *virtuosity* of the particular musical act. In the attempt to understand the ideological frame for the act of free improvisation and to explain the logic of seduction that inspires and directs this virtuosity, the key point is to analyze where the claims and demands of the ongoing social world leave off and where the musician's claims and demands for the act's virtuosic powers begin.[103] In Goffman's words, the

> very points at which the internal activity leaves off
> and external activity takes over—the rim of the frame
> itself—become generalized by the individual and taken
> into his framework of interpretation, thus becoming,
> recursively, an additional part of the frame. In general,
> then, the assumptions that cut the activity off from the
> external surroundings also mark the ways in which this
> activity is inevitably bound to the surrounding world.[104]

The jazz act therefore is situated at the *midpoint* in the unfolding of the musical experience: caught between the projective intentions of the player and the reciprocal encounter with other musicians, previous jazz acts, and the jazz form itself.[105] In other words, only through the musician's virtuosic comings and goings, that is, through his or her intensively embodied and organized projection of tones, pitches, and accents, do these acts gather musical sense. The gathering of the act into the way of its playing then returns to the players a sense of themselves as musicians who are "filled" or "enlarged" with and by musical possibility, and thereby capable of continuing to act in this way. Such a reciprocity of the act, this amplitude and abundance of the musical encounter, relies on an alteration in the act's experiential frame. The musical act, far from being reduced to an expression of the liberated individual, constitutes a way of orienting the world, a means of overreaching the limitations of human being through the encompassing of the creative act within the social dynamic of framing and reframing. This, in Elaine Scarry's terms, is the logic of music's virtuosic excess and the form of its seductive appearance.[106]

For Coleman, this dynamic of framing and reframing—we will call it enframing—was centered on the melodic limits of the improvising group and what those limits meant for the form of the improvised act. As we have seen, before the *Free Jazz* recording session of 1960, Coleman still relied on a loose harmonic structure, but one that privileged the melodic direction taken by the members of the group in terms of the variability of pitch, tone, and accent. What in fact was notable on early recordings such as "Ramblin'," "Bird Food," or "Chronology" was that the rhythm section of Charlie Haden on bass and Billy Higgins on drums had already developed a very different conception of how the tempo was applied to the timing of a melody's pitch and the overall direction of the melody. This new conception in turn shifted their relation to Coleman's saxophone and Don Cherry's trumpet. For Coleman, in this context, rhythm patterns were "more or less like natural breathing patterns. I would like the rhythm section to be as free as I'm trying to get, but very few players, rhythm or horns, can do this yet. Thelonious Monk can. He sometimes plays one note, and because he plays it in exactly the right pitch, he carries more music in it than if he had filled out the chord."[107]

By playing a single note and striking that note in certain way, Monk was able to induce a performative ellipsis such that what was played was heard as much more than a single note, as an excess of the musical act, that was also the form of the act's displacement from the realm of the ideological to that of the virtuosic. The ellipsis thus functioned to situate the virtuosity of the improvised act within the realm of the act's timing, or specifically, its tempo. What was important was not the interpretation of the song, but the timing, the tempo, of striking (and being struck, enchanted, and finally overcome by) the material limits of the keyboard; and this act of striking is what David Sudnow defines as the moment of "going for jazz."[108] I am defining tempo here as more than just the division of accents and their interpretation (whether notated or extemporized); it is also the dynamic of pitch, tone, and accent that orients and drives the musical act toward the limits of its frame, toward its appearance as symbolic form with social, historical, and existential consequences. The result of this aspect of Monk's playing, his excessive virtuosity, traversed a double horizon of reaching for the "right" note and striking the "right" key. In this way he defied the form of the improvisation to exist beyond the sheer immediacy of the sound itself, opposing the seductive opacity of the act to the abstract transparency of technique.[109] Monk's pianistic astringency sustained the illusion of a pure melody that was nevertheless *impossible* within the ideological conditions of its own making.

Taking up Monk's provocation, Coleman posited a whole other order of the musical act that proceeded through all the pitfalls of a group of musicians attempting to play *together* without using the stock of objective jazz forms—which is not to say, however, that they played without structures or rules. Rather, the form of their virtuosity produced a method for warding off internal collusions or antagonisms, the deceit or fear, the mistakes or banality, implicit in their attempts to realize precisely what was *unexpected* within the act. As Coleman was quoted as saying:

> Perhaps the most important new element in our music is our conception of *free* group improvisation. The idea of group improvisation, in itself, is not at all new; it played a big role in New Orleans' early bands. The big bands of the swing period changed all that. Today, still, the individual is either swallowed up in a group situation, or else he is out front soloing, with none of the other horns doing anything but calmly awaiting their turn for *their* solos. Even in some of the trios and quartets, which permit quite a bit of group improvisation, the final effect is one that is imposed beforehand by the arranger. One knows pretty much what to expect.[110]

For Coleman, free improvisation was the irreducible point at which the virtuosic and the ideological dimensions of the act intersected, at once the subjective conditions of the act's production and the basis of its collective possibility. This double movement enabled him to assert a series of melodic obligations within the act itself, such that the bass and drums were now held as accountable to the form of the melody as the conventional melodic or lead instruments (saxophone, trumpet, or violin).[111] Examples of this collective logic are especially evident on the 1960 recording *Change of the Century*. On each of the pieces recorded by the quartet, the form of the act emerged from an extended counterpoint between two unison melodies, which was interspersed by a series of improvised duets between trumpet and bass, saxophone and bass, bass and drums, and by unaccompanied bass or drum solos. This splitting of the act into two unison melodies not only intensified the musicians' struggle with the act's ideological limits, but hinted at the developments that took place on *Free Jazz* a year later.

In the liner notes to *Change of the Century*, Coleman clarified how the form of the act oriented the ensemble's musical ways:

> When our group plays, before we start to play, we do not have any idea what the end result will be. Each player is free to contribute what he feels in the music at any given moment. We do not begin with a preconceived notion as to what kind of effect we will achieve. When we record, sometimes I can hardly believe that what I hear when the tape is played back to me, *is* the playing of my ensemble. I am so busy and absorbed when I play that I am not aware of what I am doing at the time I'm doing it.[112]

Hence, the dynamic of improvisation was formed from the virtuosity of the act itself, such that even the musicians were seduced by their own passion for the act and by their efforts to remake the horizons of their musical experience. Coleman's disbelief when the tape was played back to him, far from asserting an innate musical sense, a pure mode of self-expression, instead marked the irreducibility of the act to the conditions of its production, that is, to its ideological frame.

At the same time, the capacity for self-expression was already implied in the musicians' recognition of the "freedom principle," such that the principle formed the very basis of the act's ideological meaning. So while the freedom principle was invoked by Coleman to orient the dynamics of the group, it also functioned as the ideological limit against which the group's virtuosic powers were tested. On the one hand, the freedom principle was the musical condition of the group's transformation of bebop and swing, and on the other hand, it became the ideological basis of the act's commodification, that is, its effective circulation within the capitalist economy. A comment by the saxophonist Jackie McLean demonstrates how this principle transformed the dynamics of the act itself: "Ornette Coleman has made me stop and think. He has stood up under such criticism, yet he never gives up his cause, freedom of expression. The search is on."[113] The "search for freedom," far from being outside the improvised act, was thus internal to and directive of the virtuosity of Coleman's groups; it galvanized the collective aspects of their musical experience without ever being actualized as such. In other words, the "search for freedom" was the act's ideological relation to its conditions of possibility, that is, to the Cold War state and to the position of black Americans within that state. Closer attention to the dynamics of the act reveals that this "freedom principle" was an object of the act only inasmuch as it defined the musician's subjective relation to the capitalist system (how he or she was marketed, his or her value as a commodity) and the institutions of state power (his or her procedural rights as an individual). Such a subjective relation, however, falls short of what actually transpires within the act; in fact, the act is already prior to and beyond its subjective realization.

To explain this complicated logic, Coleman divided his improvisations into two movements:

> I don't tell the members of my group what to do. I want
> them to play what they hear in the piece for themselves.
> I let everyone express himself just as he wants to. The
> musicians have complete freedom, and so, of course,
> our final results depend entirely on the musicianship,
> emotional make-up and taste of the individual member.
> Ours is at all times a group effort and it is only because we
> have the rapport we do that our music takes on the shape
> that it does. A strong personality with a star-complex
> would take away from the effectiveness of the group, no
> matter how brilliantly he played.[114]

This statement, coming as it did just prior to the recording of *Free Jazz*, and with so much at stake for the group of musicians, all of whom were on the verge of successful careers (by jazz standards), amounted to a declaration of Coleman's faith in the potential of the group; a faith that was also a challenge to each musician to effect a "coherent deformation" of his or her subjective limitations in relation to the demands of the ensemble. This challenge, to the subjective limitations of the act, emerged from Coleman's insistence that the group "play the music not the background."[115] To play the music was to offer a virtuosity that was also a tearing away from the subjective conditions of such a virtuosity.

At the same time, the distinction between the music and its background indicated that the way the music was to be played also determined each musician's relation to how the act became musical—that is, in what sense each musician's practice was to be aimed for and arrived at within the group. The risk in every attempt to play as a group was that the subjective conditions of the act, its ideological background, would subsume and thus destroy the virtuosic potential of the act itself. Against the act's subsumption, Coleman proposed that "we have to make breaks with a lot of jazz's recent past, just as the boppers did with swing and traditional jazz. We want to incorporate more musical materials and theoretical ideas— from the classical world, as well as jazz and folk—into our work to create a broader base for the new music we are creating."[116] This broadening of the musical horizons was as much a means of intensifying the group's virtuosic reach as it was about the subjective relation of the musicians to the musical economy.

Having established the double movement of the act, I now want to examine how the Coleman quartet actualized the group's virtuosic potential and what was at stake in this process. This examination requires, as Charles Keil has suggested, "careful, even microscopic, observation of the movements associated with music making. . . ."[117] These musical movements are not easily detailed, and the terminology for such observations, as Keil has also reminded us, is inconsistent and imprecise. Indeed, the analysis of such movements as they were formed over time is even more difficult. But if we are to go any way toward gaining a sense of the oriented and orienting character of jazz creativity and the structuring of the jazz artifact, attention to the act's material undertaking—to how and with whom certain musical, technical, and organizational problems were worked on while others were discarded or simply forgotten—is crucial.

### Alive or Dead?

When Coleman arrived in New York, one of the things that raised doubts about the quality of his playing was that he used a white plastic saxophone. Often dismissed as a cheap gimmick, the saxophone was in fact integral to the ways in which the virtuosity of Coleman's musical making was achieved. His description of how he acquired the instrument illustrates the material processes by which his musical practices were worked out:

> I bought it [the saxophone] in Los Angeles in 1954. . . .
> I needed a new horn badly but didn't have much money.
> A man in the music store said he could sell me a new
> horn—a plastic model—for the price of a used Selmer. I
> didn't like it at first, but I figured it would be better to have
> a new horn anyway. Now I won't play any other. They're

made in England, and I have to send for them. They're only good for a year the way I play them. The plastic horn is better for me because it responds more completely to the way I blow into it. There's less resistance than from metal. Also, the notes seem to come out detached, almost like you could see them. What I mean is that notes from a metal instrument include the sounds the metal itself makes when it vibrates. The notes from a plastic horn are purer. In addition, the body of the horn is flat, like a flute keyboard, whereas a regular horn is curved. On a flat keyboard I can dig in more.[118]

The logic of Coleman's description here crystallizes the material universe of the act's making. To reiterate my argument in chapter 1 concerning the two axis of creativity—the horizontal or ideological axis of making, and the vertical or virtuosic axis of seduction—I now want to focus on the situational context of Coleman's jazz act and how the ways of his and his group's musical makings indicate the historical experience of jazz practices. The acquisition of the plastic saxophone points us toward the historical form of Coleman's musical act. Without such a sense of how a musician developed his or her playing over time, or how he or she came to jazz, it is not possible to describe and analyze what was meant by the act of going for jazz, the basis of the act's collective virtuosity, or the logic of its seductive powers. Only with further consideration of this material dimension can we hope to grasp how these musicians got at a musical feeling of jazz and, furthermore, will we gain a sense of what was at stake for the musicians in the making of their jazz.

Coleman's account of the ways of his hands on the saxophone, offers us both the tools for a phenomenology of the musical act and a means to analyze the jazz musician's practices. In recalling how he came to play a plastic saxophone and what it did for his playing, not only did he effect an intensification in the processes of learning, of trying certain musical patterns or phrases out, and of playing music with others, but these music-making efforts were also indicative of the larger structures of the musical economy. That the decisive factor in Coleman's decision to buy the plastic saxophone was its price in comparison to a secondhand Selmer (the famous French-made saxophone) transposes the usual terms of the jazz debate from an ideological preoccupation with "soul" to the social processes of its material making and the dynamics of its virtuosic ways. The passage from wanting to (or imagining one would like to) play music, to playing in a certain way just to be able to play at all, and then to actively playing the way one wants is later repeated in the process of how to get the right musical instrument to do the right things at the right time: in rehearsal, on stage, in front of an audience, or in the recording studio.

Thus, a passion for the jazz act itself—what I defined earlier as the act's tempo—cannot be detached from how the relationship to the musician's instrument developed, how it was paid for, and how the instrument itself was subsequently remade from the act of playing it—that is, how the feeling for the instrument's instrumentality evolved over time and became necessary to the moment of performance. That Coleman focused on the actual feeling of the notes from the plastic instrument, on how they sounded—"the notes seemed to come out detached"—demonstrates the way in which the very materiality of the saxophone, far from being simply a medium for his expressive self, was thoroughly entangled with and constitutive of the processes of his musical making. In other words, as much as Coleman sought to find a saxophone adequate to his musical aims, the actual process of finding such an instrument, paying for it, and then learning and directing its instrumental ways also reoriented his consciousness of the act itself. Contained within the effort of finding such a material object that he could afford and seeking to use it in a musical way—"I didn't like it at first, but I figured it would be better to have a new horn anyway"—were, in fact, manifold possibilities for expanding the realm of human being, of extending and reextending the reach of human sentience.

Seen in this light, Coleman's musical act privileged neither the intentions of the individual musician, nor his instrument, nor the musical ensembles in which he played, nor the audience for whom he played. Instead, the act was constituted by and constitutive of the form of the relations between all the people and objects involved in the act, oriented by what was possible in the moment of the act's making, but also contained by the subsumption of its materiality into its objectification as an act. At work, therefore, in Coleman's passage from a Texas-based rhythm-and-blues musician to an acclaimed free jazz musician in New York was an emphatic sense of the ways of making the act valuable and the social conditions of that value, but also the potential for the act's virtuosic dimension to seduce the world of its making.[119]

By focusing on the saxophone, Coleman was able to explain how the ways of his playing—"There's less resistance than from metal" and "I can dig in more"—turned an inanimate plastic object (with none of the mythical power of the metallic instrument and its European antecedents) into a seductive object of musical experimentation and bodily extension. At the same time, he divided his musical ways into two orders of value:

one, the monetary value of the musical instrument in capitalist society; and the other, the musical value of improvisation as it was formed in relation to the group. In the first of these, the hierarchy of value turned on the status of owning a new instrument as against the more traditional value of a secondhand instrument. That distinction, however, was complicated by the comparison between a plastic instrument (which carried a connotation of vulgarity, cheapness, and mass production) with the regal qualities assigned to the French-made Selmer (which implied an intimate, if ambivalent, relation to the traditions and forms of European music). In the end, however, buying the new plastic instrument outweighed the regality of the antique instrument. At the same time, this moment of purchase, while initially scorned by other musicians and critics as a joke, lead to an intensification and extension of the musical material itself.[120]

It was in the second order of musical value, an order that corresponds to the vertical axis of seduction, that Coleman's decision to buy a plastic instrument had its most significant influence. As we have seen, Coleman did not like the plastic instrument at first, but the desire to have a new instrument overwhelmed any desire to have the already valuable secondhand Selmer. We can only guess at the reasons why his valuation of new objects guided his decision to have the plastic instrument. In any case, Coleman's decision affected an unexpected transmutation in the values and the structures of feeling associated with bebop and hard bop. As with Dizzy Gillespie's and Thelonius Monk's discovery of harmonic substitutions as a way to exclude certain musicians from the jam sessions at Minton's in the 1940s, Coleman's use of the plastic saxophone, as a way into his musical practices and the collective musical motions that proceeded from them, only happened once *a decision had been taken for other reasons.*

Once the plastic instrument was recognized and objectified as a means to the jazz act's musical enlargement and became a way of working out the logic of a method—"Now I won't play any other"—Coleman's subsequent transmutation in musical values could then be stated in precise terms: "The plastic horn is better for me because it responds more completely to the way I blow into it. There's less resistance than from metal. . . . What I mean is that notes from a metal instrument include the sounds the metal itself makes when it vibrates." The specific musical feeling engendered by the plastic material, the particular qualities of the notes produced by his playing of the "flat keyboard," were thus inseparable from Coleman's efforts to orient his playing in time and to find those "ways of the hand" adequate to the task of playing with other musicians.

The purchase of the plastic instrument, while initially indicative of the inequalities of postwar capitalism and the competitive aspect of playing jazz, was used by Coleman to "break through the wall that those [bebop] harmonies have built and restore melody. . . ."[121]

This "wall" was the subjective limit of the act itself, that is, it stood for all the historically conditioned forms of musical practice, but also constituted the basis of the act's virtuosic powers and its seductive logic. As saxophonist Steve Lacy recalls:

> [Don Cherry] used to come over to my house in '59
> and '60, around that time, and he used to tell me, "Well,
> let's play." So I said "O.K. What shall we play?" And
> there it was. The dilemma. The problem. It was a terrible
> moment. I didn't know what to do. And it took me five
> years to work myself out of that. To break through that
> wall. . . . It was a process that was partly playing tunes
> and playing tunes and finally getting to the point where
> it didn't seem to be important and it didn't do anything
> for you, to play the tunes. So you just drop the tunes.
> And you just played. It happened in gradual stages. There
> would be a moment here, a fifteen minutes there, a half
> hour there, an afternoon, an evening, and then all the
> time. . . . But it all had to do with musical environment.
> You have to have some kindred spirits. And at the time
> that was in the air. It was happening everywhere.[122]

Lacy's description is an exemplary statement of the interior structure of the act: there is the sense of waiting, of continually trying to find the means to expression, the coming and going of the musicians, and then unexpectedly the act itself appears. Thus the combination of Cherry's casualness—"Well, let's play"—with Lacy's fear of not knowing what to do next—"It was a terrible moment"—exemplifies the experiential arc of the jazz musician's musical consciousness, but it also leads us to see the conditions of the act's impossibility. Lacy's description demonstrates how the structure of his and Cherry's virtuosity was constituted in the gap between the act and its form; that the very repetition of their attempts to "play free" produced a new materiality of the act itself and a new relation to the jazz form. We see then, that Lacy's encounter with Cherry oriented and circumscribed the conditions of musical value as they were grasped from the actual ways of their playing together. The social conditions of the act's making were likewise made palpable in their commitment to decomposing the motions of bebop and hard bop and their rediscovery of the thrill of trying "to just play."

The desire to just play should not, however, be confused with an attempt to just play anything, that is, with a psychological projection of the surrounding reality. While a spontaneity of the act was their aim, how the musicians actually got to that point, as Lacy's narrative suggests, involved a conscious process of trying to shift the act toward a new understanding of musical structure, even as that structure preceded its unconscious realization in the act. Consider, for example, the assessment of John Snyder, who studied with Coleman:

> I studied theory, and Ornette's is the opposite of everything they teach you. It's the sound in the instrument. It's the structure he's built around his feelings. You cannot play anything you want with Ornette. It takes the same work—more work, if anything—as playing bebop. You cannot hide in Ornette's music. You have to know his structure. It can be a scale or three notes or a little movement. It can be a tonality, a melody, a feeling, a rhythm. This structure will allow you to play, to reveal yourself on your instrument. I've come to think that the only way to learn how to play Ornette's music is to study with him every day for seven years. Once learned, his music would free a lot of people. It lets a musician take what he is and make music with it. You go where the improvisation is. It's already there, and you explore it.[123]

The paradoxical point here is that, in the context of a free improvisation, one does not just play anything. In other words, the act's subjective value, its freedom principle, is already caught in the double movement, at once ideological and virtuosic, for which the musical structure is both the preparation and the condition of the act's repetition.

The effect of this repetition on the jazz act was such that it produced a significant reversal in the order of the act itself. As Charlie Haden recalls, "Ornette and I used to talk about making music as though it were something completely new, as though we'd never heard music before. Only a few musicians are inspired in this way. And you know, the more I became sure of my mission in this respect, the closer it brought me to my reverence for the chord structure. The inspiration I developed for playing *on* the changes opened up. . . ."[124] In seeking to make something completely new, Coleman and Haden remade the very form of the jazz act itself; or, to put it in Haden's terms, they brought the act into a new relationship to the jazz form and thus opened up new possibilities for musical action. This radical break constitutes a reversal in the order of time such that the virtuosity of illusion now precedes the virtuosities of construction and speed. However, the musical potential of this reversal depends on redefining the social relations within the group. To achieve a new relation of the act to the jazz form, Coleman required that the musicians play "on a multiple level. I don't want them to follow me. I want them to follow themselves, but to be with me."[125] To play at all meant to play with the group, so that each musician remained virtuosic only so long as his or her playing was seduced by the presence of others, and thus by the act itself.

In recalling his first encounter with Coleman, the drummer Shelley Manne has described the result of this process:

> I've always been bugged by having to stay within certain boundaries. Here is a guy that came along that was able to free me . . . of all those things I wanted to throw off. Meter structure, for example. Sometimes Ornette ignores it. He makes you listen so hard to what he's doing in order to *know* where he is in the tune and what he's trying to express. It's just complete freedom from every way you might have been forced to play before.[126]

Although it is commonplace to assess a musical act's success or failure on the basis of each musician's technical and expressive abilities, Manne's description enables us to revise such a view and to focus instead on how Coleman's groups overreached this structural limitation. In the process of getting the group to "listen so hard" to *what* and *how* he was playing, that is, to his pitching, tones, and accents, Coleman enveloped the players' musical ways within the form of the melody, only to have them find, in the obliquity and delirium of their playing, that they had developed a new passion for musical action. As if to underline Manne's point, Coleman offered an equally precise explanation for the act's embodied effect on the musicians:

> I know exactly what I'm doing. I'm beginning where Charlie Parker stopped. Parker's melodic lines were placed across ordinary chord progressions. My melodic approach is based on phrasing, and my phrasing is an extension of how I hear the intervals and the pitch of the tunes I play.

> There is no end to pitch. You can play flat in tune and sharp in tune. It's a question of vibration. My phrasing is spontaneous, not a style. A style happens when your phrasing hardens. Jazz music is the only music in which the same note can be played night after night but different each time. It's the hidden things, the subconscious that lies in your body and lets you know: you feel this, you play this.[127]

This is a crucial description of the conditions under which a new conception of the jazz act was produced. For Coleman, the relationship within the act, between the conscious effort to direct how and where the melody was placed and phrased—its rhythmic acceleration—and the unexpected or unconscious sense of what happened to that melody —its harmonic construction—was one of a repetition *between* different acts. The repetition emerged from a double movement: that of the act—its ideological dimension—and that of the notes within the act—its virtuosic dimension. However, as I suggested above, this double movement was contained within a third repetition of what was never there in the first place, that remained virtual: a pure melody, or the jazz form itself. This third repetition, in Gilles Deleuze's words, "ensures the order, the totality of our series."[128] It also brings us to our conclusions.

My argument is that Ornette Coleman's musical practices were constituted in the process of remaking the jazz act into a virtuosic illusion, where that virtuosity was *nothing but* the form of the musical act in its most seductive yet unstable condition. This virtuosic dimension was formed from the act's relation to the ideological forces that demarcated it and gave it a social meaning as an act, and the social interplay of its most basic practical elements—namely, pitch, tone and accent. For Coleman, free improvisation was not defined by an escape *from* musical form (via either its transgression or its transcendence), nor a reduction of the jazz form to a static mirror of its immanent sociality. Rather, the form of the improvisation emerged from its virtuosic or unexpected relation to time, to history, and to the horizons of our musical experience. As he said, in an interview in 1965,

> [it] is not easy to find ways to become involved with existence in its relation to the history that one has been exposed to, to use that history to become better, and not to let it fence you in from anything else that could possibly exist. The menace in America is that everyone—black

> or white—is enslaved in history. This enslavement tends
> to make you remember history more than to think of
> what you could do if you were nothing but history. . . .
> In music, especially, I have yet to hear a composer or
> performer who doesn't give me the feeling that he is
> trying to eliminate some of history or dominate the
> present—as a reason for doing it, not because that's where
> he was going.[129]

This passage clarifies the transformations produced by Coleman, both in terms of the postwar state and in relation to the jazz form. Thus, against the slave event, he asserted the power of history; against history, he asserted the passion of the virtuoso; and against the virtuoso, he asserted the virtuosity of the act itself. In other words, against the inertia of the atomic event and its reification within the circuits of postwar state power and capitalist consumption, Coleman's achievement was to have opened an inexhaustible field of musical actions, to have brought to jazz a new passion for the musical act. And the measure of this achievement was that he managed to remake the jazz act and reorient the jazz group despite the allure of what Scarry terms "corporeal engulfment." That is, when he played, he played in the face of the impending chaos of a "dangerous bodily absorption," the sheer subjectivism of the act, that haunts any "throwing back" onto the human struggle for, and making of, musical acts.[130]

# Epilogue

## "A Tune beyond Ourselves"

And then they said, "But play, you must,
A tune beyond ourselves, yet ourselves. . . ."

Wallace Stevens

In his essay on Charlie Parker, Max Harrison argues that inherent in Parker's musical practice "was not just a method for improvising solos but also one for ordering ensembles, and that is a measure of how thoroughgoing his renewal of the jazz language was."[1] While Harrison's focus remains with Parker's individual achievements as a soloist, the invaluable research undertaken by Paul Berliner and Ingrid Monson suggest that only with meticulous attention to the dynamics of the improvising group in the making and remaking of the jazz act can we arrive at a precise historical sense of the act's virtuosity and the musical intentions of its practitioners. A shift of this type throws the historical stakes wide open. My aim in this book has been to chart this shift in terms of American exceptionalist ideology and to explain the influence of the jazz act on the formation and development of this ideology. On another level, my purpose has been to find evidence of a virtuosic surplus within the very dynamics of the act, that is, within the jazz act's collective making, that provided grounds for an active struggle not only with the commodity form of popular music and the dominance of mass entertainment, but with the deep assumptions of the social order.[2]

These assumptions extend most forcefully to the musical act's making and remaking. The effort to articulate and qualify the practical logic of the jazz act requires more than merely inverting the dominant, institutional idea of musical creativity while retaining all its conventional criteria of value. The legitimacy accorded trumpet player Wynton Marsalis's program at Lincoln Center in New York City or the music driving the events of Robert Altman's 1998 film *Kansas City* was not inevitable. Rather, the value of the jazz act—as a preeminently *social act*—was the result of a long process of developing musical skills and technical inventiveness, of musical compromise and social misdeed, of political coercion and economic destruction, all of which were continually altered in the very act of making music. That is, the musical, social, and political value of the jazz act emerged from a historical struggle to make those acts count, on the part of its practitioners, its supporters, but also among its detractors.

I have already detailed my admiration for, but also my concerns with, Berliner's and Monson's work. Their arguments emerge from an ethnographic tradition that, in seeking to privilege the activities and intentions of non-Western cultures, tends to anatomize and suspend musical practices in a condition of theoretical stasis. This occurs less from a willingness to engage in spurious abstractions than to prove the historical limitations of the Western intellectual's own constructions. However, such tendencies, if too relentless, would seem to encourage self-defeat (and, on the part of some, self-promotion). The displacement from the historical process to that of static description undermines the very historicity and the value that these practices acquire in social situations. It also enforces the fallacy that in the complex process by which musical practices are passed from generation to generation, or from social group to social group, or from individual to individual, the jazz act itself remains constant.[3] Berliner argues that the "configuration of musical personalities and talents within each band establishes its fundamental framework and determines its unique possibilities for invention."[4] What he fails to emphasize is the historical contingency of these configurations; that the improvising group is not a container into which so many musical ingredients are poured to procure the right mixture, but the site of a struggle to make musical and social sense over time; a resource and a stance, useful for sometimes opposing while at other times affirming the constraints of the social order, and sometimes doing both at once.

At the same time, the dynamic of the act *qua* act, its practical orientation, subsumes all prior and future attempts to rationalize it and give it an abstract meaning beyond its social and political consequences and as a consequence of its happening.[5] In this sense, the act is its own anchoring in time, made and remade in the attempt to actualize the jazz form to which it endlessly refers. As the bass player Chuck Israels remarked in a recent interview with Berliner: "No matter what you're doing or thinking about beforehand . . . from the very moment the performance begins, you plunge into that world of sounds. It becomes your world instantly, and your whole consciousness changes."[6] To gain a sense of the act's historical dynamic and the dynamics of musical practice, however, we should shift our attention from the static imagery of the "world of sounds" to the act of plunging or throwing oneself into the music; that is to say, we should attend to the manifold ways of grasping the virtuosic dimensions of the act that, in turn, remakes the ways in which musical acts are done.

A musician's attempts at "going for jazz," his or her musical motions and elaborations, are constituted in the process of finding and learning through practice the "right" musical pathways, the "correct" postures and gestures, and the "adequate" means necessary to convey melodic, rhythmic, or harmonic motifs consonant with the musical practices of others.[7] On this basis, jazz did not make itself nor was it latent in the black or national psyche prior to its making and remaking. It was not created in a sociohistorical vacuum nor was it patched together from fixed or timeless elements of a musician's or a people's past. To paraphrase E. P. Thompson, we might say that observers of jazz, even sympathetic ones, often write as though jazz sprang from some submusical "raw" instinct on the part of its players combined with a natural affinity for adapting to their environments (as though any values they might have held as a group were simply the result of an accident of fate—in other words, the "world the slaveholders made").[8] Contrary to such views, jazz was made by groups of musicians confronting and reacting to known and contingent circumstances, and crafted according to a range of historical expectations and feelings about why things worked, how things worked, and in what way they might continue to work. It was formed from the immediate experience of playing in groups, initially using what available and affordable musical instruments there were (brass instruments, voices, drums, strings, and so on) and also using the most familiar musical forms of the time (dances, marches, rags, hymns, and the blues). Such a congruence of collective making turned the practice of "jazzing" into both a distinct musical form and a virtuosic act with decisive social, political, and economic consequences.[9]

Thus, from the orienting force of "going for jazz" we might distinguish a further problem for the historical analysis of jazz practices: the process of coming to jazz or finding out about jazz, of knowing it and feeling it as a meaningful act and then aiming to go and play it somewhere and with someone. For Berliner, this is a critical phase in the life of the musician, crucial to how jazz players were in fact able to recognize what they were doing as "going for jazz."[10] This process may be protracted or sudden; it may be intentional, a slow process of realization, or indeed accidental; or it might happen in fits and starts, interrupted by the demands of work or family or the constraints of money or time. It could happen only late in life or the desire to play jazz might be there from a very young age. Wynton Marsalis's description of how he came to jazz in the 1970s is significant in this regard in that he attests to a historical shift in the relation of social situation and musical practices: "I know if it weren't for the fact that my father [New Orleans jazz pianist Ellis Marsalis] is a jazz musician, for the fact that he has jazz records, I know that I would not play jazz, because there was nothing. None of my surroundings, none of my peers, nothing on the radio, nothing I got at school gave me any input."[11] For Marsalis, a critical aspect of coming to jazz was thus a process of learning "to put my experience in the proper context, because I was educated away from my strength."[12] This required an understanding of the jazz musician's historical situation within black communities, an attention to the formal properties of jazz, as well as an understanding of the logic of its practices. When asked to clarify the role of New Orleans pianist Jelly Roll Morton, Marsalis pointed out that

> [w]hen you look past all his prejudices and things, past the
> jive about how he invented it, into the heart of what he's
> saying—that's jazz. When I first heard those tapes [in the
> Library of Congress], I knew what jazz was. I could see
> how they put it together: the organization of the band,
> the riffs, the breaks, how to orchestrate. Jelly Roll gave
> me a way to understand Ellington. I could see how Duke
> organized things, how he used shout choruses and riffs
> and breaks and contrapuntal lines.[13]

Much the same might be said of Marsalis: once we look past all his "prejudices and things," past the "jive" about how he saved jazz from obscurity, what in fact becomes critical to this analysis is his attention to the interior structure of the jazz act and to the organization of the jazz group—that is, to the question of how and why people choose to play *in a group,* and the circumstances and constraints that define the value and meaning of a jazz performance as *a social act.* Much is made of Marsalis's provocative status in the mainstream media as well as in the specialist jazz press. The argument over Marsalis's projected aims, however, seems limited to asserting the power of critics to arbitrate taste, or of musicians to command institutional and financial backing in the face of declining funds for jazz recording and the small number of viable jazz venues. But we mustn't lose sight of the fact that the success of Marsalis in generating a substantial argument over the value of jazz to American culture cannot be understood independently of Bechet's, Parker's, or Coleman's struggle to legitimate the conditions of their virtuosity, and nor should his arguments for a definitive *jazz form* be detached from the larger ideological struggle over the value of creative acts within the capitalist state. As Gary Giddins observes, the "violent expressionism of the 1960s made the current wave of neo-classicism possible."[14]

But to limit the problem of jazz history to that of a progressive struggle between traditionalists and innovators, and the subsequent post-modern "resolution" in moments of either reversal or parody, is only a partial statement of the problem. Correlative to this struggle was the historical emergence of the jazz group. Bechet, Parker and Coleman all created, in the dynamics of their improvisation and composition, a means of reordering and remaking the jazz act and, in particular, the dynamics of the group. What we find in their musical practices is the discrete form of the improvising group, put together under specific historical and social circumstances, through which they actualized their musical virtuosity as an attitude toward the world. Thus, while Bechet's, Parker's and Coleman's music is comprehensible in terms of the development of each other's practices as jazz practices, the dynamic of each of their groups was constituted through the irreducibility of the act itself. In coming to and going for jazz, it was the ways of these groups—sometimes a quartet or a duo, sometimes a quintet or trio or large band—that effectively challenged and reoriented the idea of jazz as an orderly succession of innovators whose groups functioned only as support for the particular genius of the individual.

The form of this challenge meant that there was an active tension between the development and dominance of a progressive ideology that hypostatized the individual as the source of all historical change, and a jazz act that required the dynamics of an improvising group for the conditions of its practice and the basis of its virtuosity. This was not a tension easily deflected or directed by jazz musicians nor readily absolved, especially as that progressive ideology was hardened from 1947 into its Cold War form and violently turned against anyone who struggled with and actively countered the state functionaries and technocratic institutions that guaranteed and enforced such an ideological frame.[15] Likewise, the constraints on where and when a jazz group performed, including the income derived from and the social orientation of those performances, meant that it was often more effective to "sell" a group to a club owner, to that club's potential audience, or to a record company executive on the basis of one or two players, whether on the reputation of the group's leader or that of the "rising" talents of individual players. Even Ornette Coleman "headlined" at the Five Spot in 1959, despite the fact that his playing and the virtuosity of the Coleman group's collective act required the specific musical affinities developed over time among Don Cherry, Charlie Haden, and Billy Higgins.

In coming to and going for jazz, the often difficult process of organizing a group and finding a way to circumscribe the potential of any player's motivic, harmonic, or rhythmic sensibility in terms of the group's limits is clarified by Paul Berliner's proposition, quoting Kenny Barron, that jazz performance is a "matter of give and take."[16] This is both an active and a restrictive means of understanding the seductive powers of the jazz act and the jazz musician's virtuosity. In *Thinking in Jazz,* Berliner devotes several chapters to it and for good reason.[17] The problem that his analysis poses for the historical study of jazz is unavoidable: What were the circumstances in which musicians came together in New Orleans and decided to make jazz, and how and on what terms did they decide to relate to each other as musicians who were able to play music? What was the mode of consciousness, the gestures and habits, specific to such practices, and how were those practices transformed into the virtuosic improvised acts we today consider jazz to be? Ingrid Monson's interview with drummer Kenny Washington clarifies the critical scope of the problem: "When you listen to jazz, you have to go beneath all that and find out *why* the drummer is playing like he's playing. . . ."[18] For Berliner, the answer to this question is to detail the considerations that enter into the jazz act at any given moment: a shared sense of the beat, a musician's technical consistency, the collective transparency of sound in which each part is discernible, various kinds of imitative interplay, the interpretation and management of musical preferences and models, and the ability to control and direct errors. In other words, what constitutes the jazz act for Berliner is a mutuality of musical exchanges that "continually cross-fertilize and revitalize one another. . . . It is this dynamic reciprocity that characterizes improvisation as both an individual and collective music-making process."[19] Likewise, Monson's analysis of Washington's comment confirms the "inherent tension within the jazz ensemble between individual and group."[20]

Neither of these approaches to Washington's question—why and how do musicians play in the way they do with or in relation to other musicians?—fully grasps the act's double movement: that is, its virtuosic and ideological dimensions. The intentions and requirements of the musicians, the ways in which they make and remake their collective acts, simply appear as abstracted functions of the music, a guarantee of the music's inherent unity as a form and as a symbol of a timeless democratic process. In seeking to demonstrate the jazz act's general equilibrium, how it functions as a form that expresses the sum of all individual contributions, Berliner and Monson place too little emphasis on the social relations among and the various traits and values brought by the musicians to any jazz performance; they overlook the kind of embodied dynamic and musical consciousness that the group effects *in its virtuosic realization*. As a result, the emphasis on the "mutuality of musical exchange" reifies the individual's experience of coming to the group as the only means of evaluating the success of the group's work. Individual consciousness remains intact and, in these terms, constitutes the ideological precondition of any act, the ultimate basis of its exchange value as a commodity.

A comment by pianist Cecil McBee further articulates this point: "We are all individuals. . . . When we approach the stage . . . we are collectivized there. . . . I mean history is about to take place right?"[21] For Monson, McBee's comment encapsulates the moment at which jazz musicians constitute the collective form of their musical acts: to walk onto the stage "ensures that each individual must adjust to the presence and activities of the other band members."[22] If the moment of walking onto the stage marks the division between individual and group, the "individual" in this case functions as the basic unit of value from which the jazz group derives its "original" historical and musical meaning. At the same time, Monson claims an essential sociability for jazz practices that produces and reproduces itself, through "conversation" and "intermusicality," as a fluid exchange of ideas, positions, and techniques that are carried into a performance from other social situations. The structure of this sociability, however, was already a given condition of the reception of jazz in America, and thus jazz performance becomes simply a reflection of the limits of individual self-expression. But, as E. P. Thompson reminds us, "[w]e cannot construct our historical or economic knowledge by first positing 'individuals' as isolates."[23]

The historical implications of jazz practices and the jazz act, and the logic of relations through which those practices and acts were valued and made meaningful as *social practices* and as *social acts,* suggests a more complicated dynamic. While Monson's and Berliner's respective accounts of the tension between individual and group point to this dynamic, far more is at stake in the structuring of the jazz act than simply finding and maintaining an ideal balance between the demands of the soloist and his or her group. The weakness in their discussion of the jazz musician's "communicative praxis" is the attempted resolution of the force of this tension into a fluid, interactive model of a "musical conversation." Although their studies recognize the implicit danger of the jazz act, either as a conversation (it often fails) or as a purposive social act (it may not happen or, indeed, it might go terribly wrong), the structure of their arguments preclude that danger (and what it means for the social order as such) from receiving any serious or sustained consideration.[24] And so, in the process of highlighting a "verbal" analogy to grasp the form of jazz improvisation, Monson collapses the virtuosic "surplus" into a single, stable point of individual self-expression—a rarefied moment of "intermusicality"—from which the active and embodied practices of language, and their unstable relation to the historical development of jazz musical practices, are then removed. How this moment occurs, that is, how the transition takes place from the process of musical making to the moment of the musical artifact's actualization as an object and as a social practice, is left unexplained.

There are, of course, aspects of Monson's and Berliner's rich body of work that require further detailed discussion. Their respective insights and research into the dynamics of the improvising group are of particular significance to our understanding of the jazz act and the processes through which black and nonblack musicians acquired and then asserted their knowledge of and feeling for the making of jazz practices. But to analyze the *making* of jazz practices and the jazz act *in precise historical terms,* further attention must be directed to understanding the complexity of desire and feeling, of values and expectations, as these are seen in light of the improvising musician's class status, gender, and race, in other words, his or her social situation in terms of the state. To explain this social process of coming to jazz, I emphasized that the relation between jazz musicians and the jazz act's ideological dimensions emerged from a "world in tension." That is, the jazz act emerged from a fundamental impossibility in relation to its form and to the conditions of its production. Such a view displaces the common tendency, as Ira Berlin sees it, to idealize jazz musicians (black and white) as a "prefabricated community of brothers."[25] Herbert Gutman makes a similar argument in his analysis of black miners in the 1890s: "[W]hen you freeze a moment in time to examine a structural relationship, you cannot neglect the process by which that relationship was formed, how it developed."[26] A historical focus of this type relies upon demonstrating how a person became a jazz musician and how the making of jazz practices and a jazz virtuosity oriented groups of musicians not only toward the form of the act itself but also toward the conditions of the act's production.

Some repetition of my basic argument is in order. I have attempted to situate the virtuosity of the jazz act in terms of three ideological dimensions that are central to the course of American history: the struggle between masters and slaves, the influence of the frontier on American history, and the significance of musical practices to notions of human freedom. My aim has been to analyze and develop a sense of the jazz musical act's social situation, and from there, to define and explicate the virtuosity of the improvised act in terms of the musical ways of a jazz group's performances. The specific conditions for the making of Bechet's, Parker's, and Coleman's jazz acts depended on the collective virtuosity of their groups and relied, for a sense of that virtuosity, on the logic of seduction and the powers of repetition. As distinct from the making of its practices in time, the musical act is an act of seduction, such that the musician's virtuosity is considered as the art and practices of seduction: his or her own self-seduction, the seduction of other musicians and the listener, and the seductive powers of the act itself. At the same time, without a consideration of the ideological frame of both the act and the virtuosity of its practices, the social and political value of jazz to an understanding of human creative practices is reduced to a mere index of the American state's global ambitions. Thus a sense of the influence and dominance of progressive ideology on jazz practices is countered by an analysis of the repetition of the jazz act's virtuosic surplus in terms of and against which such ideological determinations functioned. This repetition of the musical act in relation to its form, through the musician's effort and desire to *improvise together* is, finally, what we must continue to explain.

My concern with the musical act is to account for two radically different aspects of its performance: the process of gaining musical knowledge and technique—that is, its contingent historical and social context; and the moment of *going for* jazz—that is, the intensive singularity of the musical act, its radical objectification as a human artifact set free in the world. My distinction between the ideological dimension and the musical act's virtuosic dimension seeks to define what, for Marx in *Capital,* amounted to the violent and distorting abstraction of the maker from what was made, of labor from the artifact, so as to ascribe to the artifact its sense of "magical projection." While it is the very form of a musical seduction that makes the act appear effortless and spontaneous, a given fact of human existence, this same seductive power also carries within its folds the potential for a reversal in the act's subsumption by money and power. This art of the seducer gives to the musical act its danger, but also its necessity as a style, its immutability as a form and, most important, its virtuosity in the face of the widespread social and technical inertia of the state. While the force of a musician's or group's virtuosity extends into the orders of feeling and thought, buried within the jazz virtuoso's seductive motions and pitched against the impossibility of the form itself is the sentient structure of the artifact in time—that is, the human pandemonium, the living conflict and potential of history, work, morality, and politics, that constitutes its active and willed reality.

In this sense, the making of jazz is to be distinguished from the virtuosity of the act, although both aspects require the same attention to the dynamics of performance and the act's consequences in time. A precise statement of this is to be found in a comment by Miles Davis: "Play what you hear, not what you know."[27] Such a comment indicates the form of the conflict between "the long labor of symbolic construction"[28] and the assumption of a "spontaneity" internal to the jazz musicians' way of acting musically in relation to themselves and to others. Through his distinction between the ear and cognition, Davis demonstrates how this conflict, between acting musically and the subsequent historical recognition and rationalization of jazz as a self-conscious mode of knowledge, was already constitutive of the act's social value as a free act. In other words, in the process of going for jazz, the group members' virtuosity—that is, their ability to listen to each other and orient the motions of their act beyond themselves—necessarily erased any sense of the act's ideological limitations. However, the logic of this virtuosic movement also required an ideological limit—a sense of *impossibility*—for the act to exist as a meaningful event in American society. This social struggle, to turn the act's ideological limits into a virtuosic power, is the condition of the jazz act's happening and the source of its impassioned repetition.

# N O T E S

## Introduction

1. "Mediation is the classical dialectical term for the establishment of relationships between, say, the formal analysis of a work of art and its social ground, or between the internal dynamics of the political state and its economic base." Fredric Jameson, *The Political Unconscious: Narrative as Socially Symbolic Act* (London: Routledge, 1989), p. 39.

2. Theodor W. Adorno, *Sound Figures,* trans. Rodney Livingston (Stanford: Stanford University Press, 1999), p. 4.

3. John Chilton, *Sidney Bechet: First Wizard of Jazz* (New York: Da Capo Press, 1996); Carl Woideck, *Charlie Parker: His Music and Life* (Ann Arbor: University of Michigan Press, 1996); John Litweiler, *Ornette Coleman: A Harmolodic Life* (New York: William Morrow, 1992).

4. To define jazz expression as a "unity of self-expression" reduces it to the abstract laws of commodity exchange that rely on a division between manual and intellectual labor.

5. To this end, I will follow Slavoj Žižek in his argument concerning the potential for resistant acts: "[O]ne should maintain the crucial distinction between a mere 'performative reconfiguration,' a subversive displacement which remains *within* the hegemonic field and, as it were, conducts an internal guerrilla war of turning the terms of the hegemonic field against itself, *and* the much more radical act of a thorough reconfiguration of the entire field which redefines the very conditions of socially sustained performability." Slavoj Žižek, *The Ticklish Subject: The Absent Center of Political Ontology* (London: Verso, 1999), p. 264.

6. I use the term *series* to mean the particular ensemble of relations to which each musician belongs. The series is a type of human gathering in which historical relationships are organized in statistical anonymity and "lived separately as identical instances of the same act." Jean-Paul Sartre, *The Critique of Dialectical Reason: Theory of Practical Ensembles,* trans. Alan Sheridan-Smith (London: Verso, 1991), p. 1:262.

7. To paraphrase Charles Rosen, what unites Bechet, Parker, and Coleman is not personal contact or even mutual influence and interaction, but their common understanding of the musical language they did so much to formulate and change. In other words, they were united by their specific relation to the

jazz form. Charles Rosen, *The Classical Style* (New York: W. W. Norton, 1972), p. 23.

8. Paolo Virno, "Virtuosity and Revolution: The Political Theory of Exodus," in *Radical Thought in Italy: A Potential Politics,* ed. Paolo Virno and Michael Hardt (Minneapolis: University of Minnesota Press, 1996), pp. 189–91.

9. Maurice Merleau-Ponty, *The Phenomenology of Perception,* trans. Colin Smith (London: Routledge, 1989), p. 171 n. 1.

10. Lewis A. Erenberg, *Swingin' the Dream: Big Band Jazz and the Rebirth of American Culture* (Chicago: University of Chicago Press, 1998), p. 81.

11. Lawrence Levine, *Black Culture and Black Consciousness* (New York: Oxford University Press, 1977), pp. 30–55, 191–297; Charles Joyner, *Down by the Riverside* (Urbana: University of Illinois Press, 1984); Eugene Genovese, *Roll Jordan Roll: The World the Slaves Made* (New York: Vintage Books, 1976); Barbara J. Fields, "Slavery, Race and Ideology in the United States of America," *New Left Review* 181 (May–June 1990).

12. Eileen Southern, *The Music of Black Americans: A History* (New York: W. W. Norton, 1971).

13. For example, see the wide-ranging analysis of black music in the publication by the Center for Black Music Research, *Black Music Research Journal.*

14. The idea of a situational analysis has two immediate tributaries: one anthropological and the other sociological. The first was developed in Manchester by the likes of J. Clyde Mitchell and Max Gluckman, and later by Erving Goffman, Nathan Glaser, and Ansell Strauss, to name a few key figures. My interest in a situational approach to historical problems was stimulated by Erving Goffman's classic study of situations and their framing, *Frame Analysis* (Cambridge: Harvard University Press, 1974), as well as Bruce Kapferer, *The Feast of the Sorcerer: Practices of Consciousness and Power* (Chicago: University of Chicago Press, 1997), and J. Clyde Mitchell, *Cities, Society, and Social Perception: A Central African Perspective* (Oxford: Clarendon Press, 1987), pp. 1–33.

15. Richard Slotkin, *Gunfighter Nation: The Myth of the Frontier in Twentieth-Century America* (New York: HarperCollins, 1992), pp. 88–122.

16. David Stowe, *Swing Changes: Big Band Jazz in New Deal America* (Cambridge: Harvard University Press, 1994), p. 9.

17. Ibid., p. 73.

18. Adorno, *Sound Figures,* p. 6.

19. "[H]istorical change eventuates, not because a given 'basis' must give rise to a correspondent 'superstructure,' but because changes in productive relationships are experienced in social and cultural life, refracted in men's ideas and their values, and argued through their actions, their choices and their beliefs." E. P. Thompson, "History and Anthropology," in *Persons and Polemics: Historical Essays* (London: Merlin Press, 1994), p. 224.

20. The aim of reconstituting all possible views at all possible times has a bad habit of mutating into the best possible view at the best possible time, depending of course on the ideological orientation of the author.

21. Kapferer, *The Feast of the Sorcerer*, p. xiv.

22. Goffman is instructive because his arguments pertain directly to American society, although with a less defined sense or consideration of historical change than the anthropologists. Goffman, *Frame Analysis*.

23. Bruce Kapferer, *Legends of People, Myths of State: Violence, Intolerance, and Political Culture in Sri Lanka and Australia* (Washington, D.C.: Smithsonian Institution Press, 1988), p. 233 n. 6.

24. Mitchell, *Cities, Society, and Social Perception,* pp. 278–313; Kapferer, *Legends of People, Myths of State,* p. 114.

25. Mitchell, *Cities, Society, and Social Perception,* pp. 8–9.

26. The taped transcription of Bechet's narrative was made in the late 1950s by Joan Reid and Desmond Flower.

27. Lawrence Levine notes that Bechet's story of his slave grandfather, Omar, closely follows the New Orleans legend of Bras Coupe. Levine, *Black Culture and Black Consciousness,* p. 388.

28. Ira Berlin, *Many Thousands Gone: The First Two Centuries of Slavery in North America* (Cambridge: Harvard University Press, Belknap Press, 1998), pp. 1–3.

29. Herbert G. Gutman, *Power and Culture: Essays on the American Working Class,* ed. Ira Berlin (New York: Pantheon Books, 1987), p. 349.

30. Eileen Southern, *The Music of Black Americans: A History* (New York: W. W. Norton, 1971), pp. 245–77; Levine, *Black Culture and Black Consciousness,* pp. 190–297.

31. Edith Wyschogrod, *Spirit in Ashes: Hegel, Heidegger, and Man-Made Mass Death* (New Haven: Yale University Press, 1985), p. 28; Bruce Kapferer, "Remythologizing Discourses: State and Insurrectionary Violence in Sri Lanka," in *The Legitimation of Violence,* ed. David E. Apter (London: Macmillan Press, 1997), pp. 159–88.

32. Lerone Bennett Jr., "Charlie (Bird) Parker—Madman or Genius?" *Negro Digest* 10, no. 11 (September 1961): 70.

33. One only has to glance at Philip Foner's study of black workers and the American labor movement to recognize the social restrictions placed on blacks during and after the war, the expansion of wartime industries notwithstanding, but also the equally prominent (although extremely difficult) position accorded black musicians in the American entertainment industry. Philip S. Foner, *Organized Labor and the Black Worker, 1619–1973* (New York: International Publishers, 1974), pp. 204–92.

34. Frederick Jackson Turner, *The Frontier in American History* (New York: Henry Holt, 1920).

35. Dorothy Ross, *The Origins of American Social Science* (Cambridge: Cambridge University Press, 1991), pp. 257–300. William Cronon, George Miles, and Jay Gitlin argue that critics of Turner missed the point. The "problem they thought they saw in his definition of western history was, in fact, the central problem of that history." William Cronon, George Miles, Jay Gitlin, "Becoming West: Towards a New Meaning for Western History," in *Under an Open Sky: Rethinking America's Western Past,* ed. William Cronon, George Miles, and Jay Gitlin (New York: W. W. Norton, 1992), pp. 3–27; Patricia Nelson Limerick, *The Legacy of Conquest: The Unbroken Past of the American West* (New York: W.W. Norton, 1987), pp. 20–32.

36. Ross, *The Origins of American Social Science,* p. 270–74; Cronon, Miles, and Gitlin, "Becoming West," p. 6.

37. F. Scott Fitzgerald, "Echoes of the Jazz Age," in *The Crack-up, with Other Pieces and Stories* (Harmondsworth: Penguin Books, 1965), p. 17.

38. Ross, *The Origins of American Social Science,* p. 272.

39. Sudnow, *Ways of the Hand,* pp. 81–152.

40. Gilles Deleuze, *Difference and Repetition,* trans. Paul Patton (New York: Columbia University Press, 1994), p. 90.

41. Slavoj Žižek, *The Plague of Fantasies* (London: Verso, 1997), p. 211 n. 3.

42. Charles Rosen, *The Romantic Generation* (London: Fontana Press, 1999), p. 7.

43. Nat Hentoff, *The Jazz Life* (New York: Da Capo Press, 1978), p. 184.

44. LeRoi Jones, *Blues People* (New York: William Morrow, 1963), p. 142.

45. It is possible to point to deeper forms of expression that are not reducible to subjective interpretation, but of the order of the passions and of seduction. This is addressed in chapter 3.

46. Jones, *Blues People,* p. 142.

47. Žižek, *The Plague of Fantasies,* p. 217.

48. "[A]ll class consciousness—or in other words, all ideology in the strongest sense, including the most exclusive forms of ruling-class consciousness just as much as that of oppositional or oppressed classes—is in its very nature Utopian." Jameson, *The Political Unconscious,* p. 289.

49. For a critical analysis of the racist capitalist state and, in particular, an account of the state's metaracist practices, see Joel Kovel, *White Racism: A Psychohistory* (New York: Columbia University Press, 1994), pp. 177–230.

50. Rosen argues for two senses of virtuality, or what he calls "inaudibility": "In Bach the notation implies something beyond the reach of every realization, but in Schumann the music is a realization which implies something beyond itself." Rosen, *The Romantic Generation,* p. 10. For a further statement of this problem of virtuality in musical form, see the discussion of the violin concerto in Žižek, *The Ticklish Subject,* pp. 101–3.

51. Susan Langer, *Feeling and Form: A Theory of Art* (New York: Charles Scribner's Sons, 1953), pp. 69–119.

52. Ibid., p. 109.

53. The couple virtual/actual is developed comprehensively in Gilles Deleuze, *Bergsonism,* trans. Hugh Tomlinson and Barbara Habberjam (New York: Zone Books, 1991), pp. 42–43.

54. "[T]he insistence of blues verse on the life of the individual and his individual trials and successes on earth is a manifestation of the whole Western concept of man's life, and it is a development that could only be found in an American black man's music." Jones, *Blues People,* p. 66.

55. "Blues issued directly out of the shout and of course the spiritual. The three-line structure of blues was a feature of the shout. The first two lines of the song were repeated, it would seem, while the singer was waiting for the next line to come. Or, as was the character of the hollers and shouts, the single line could be repeated again and again, either because the singer especially liked it, or because he could not think of another line. The repeated phrase also carries into instrumental jazz as the *riff.*" Ibid., p. 62.

56. Ibid., p. 235.

57. For a valuable discussion of resistance and human acts, see Žižek, *The Ticklish Subject,* pp. 260–64.

58. Henri Focillon argues that an artistic style passes through four stages: the experimental, the classical, the stage of refinement, and finally, the baroque stage (which he considers the freest stage in the development of a style.) If we discard Focillon's diachronic model, we might divide the artistic act into three modes—the experimental, classical, and refined modes—that are constituted, synchronically, within a single, continuous form—that of the baroque. The manner of their arrangement in relation to this form defines the act's virtuosity. Henri Focillon, *The Life of Forms in Art,* trans. Charles B. Hogan and George Kubler (New York: Zone Books, 1989), pp. 31–63.

59. Citing Marx's sixth thesis on Feuerbach, Thompson, "History and Anthropology," p. 216

60. The virtuosic stance or attitude is productive of the "structures of feeling" of which that virtuosity is itself a product and from which it derives social meaning and value. The phrase "structures of feeling" is used by Raymond Williams to grasp "meanings and values as they are actively lived and felt . . . the specifically affective elements of consciousness and relationships." Raymond Williams, *Marxism and Literature* (Oxford: Oxford University Press, 1977), p. 132.

61. Rossana Dalmonte and Balint Andras Varga, *Luciano Berio: Two Interviews,* trans. David Osmond-Smith (New York: Marion Boyars, 1985), p. 23.

62. Ibid., p. 90.

63. Berio's sense of this problem is exemplary: "I hold a great respect for virtuosity even if this word may provoke derisive smiles and even conjure up

the picture of an elegant and rather diaphanous man with agile fingers and a rather empty head." Ibid.

64. Elaine Scarry, *The Body in Pain: The Making and Unmaking of the World* (Oxford: Oxford University Press, 1987), p. 176.

65. E. P. Thompson, *The Poverty of Theory* (London: Merlin Press, 1978; reprint 1995), p. 116.

66. This is the critical argument of phenomenology as developed by Edmund Husserl: the relation between act and object is one of intent. As Peter Koestenbaum argues in his introduction to a collection of Husserl's Paris Lectures, the object "is said to be an intention: the object is meant and intended by the act. The act of apprehension constructs, fashions, *constitutes* the object." Edmund Husserl, *The Paris Lectures,* trans. with an introductory essay by Peter Koestenbaum (The Hague: Martinus Nijhoff, 1964), p. xxii.

67. Scarry, *The Body in Pain,* p. 162.

68. Ibid., p. 175.

69. Sudnow, *Ways of the Hand,* p. xiv.

70. Ibid., p. xiii.

71. Edward Said, *Musical Elaborations* (London: Chatto & Windus, 1991), p. 25.

72. Ibid., p. 28.

73. Scarry, *The Body in Pain,* p. 253.

74. Pierre Boulez, interviewed in *Boulez in Rehearsal,* dir. Felix Breisach (Vienna: Spectrum TV/Rm Arts in association with ZDF/ARTE, 1998).

75. Sudnow, *Ways of the Hand,* p. xiii.

76. Ibid., pp. 1–80.

77. Ibid., p. 64.

78. Ibid., p. 86.

79. Ibid., p. 83.

80. Ibid., p. 103.

81. Ibid., p. 146.

82. Jean Baudrillard, *Seduction,* trans. Brian Singer (London: Macmillan Press, 1990).

83. Ibid., p. 47.

84. Ibid., p. 81.

85. Seduction "does not consist of a simple appearance, nor a pure absence, but the eclipse of a presence. Its sole strategy is to be-there/not-there, and thereby produce a sort of flickering, a hypnotic mechanism that crystallizes attention outside all concern with meaning." Ibid., p. 85.

86. Rosen, *The Romantic Generation,* p. 5. The notion of a musical act's impossibility is developed in Rosen's brilliant analysis of the music of Chopin,

Schumann, Mendelssohn, Liszt, and Berlioz. Rosen maintains the significance or *pathos* of the gap between the musical idea or form and the musical act's realization. The distinction he makes is between an *audible* and *inaudible* dimension to the act.

87. In a superb analysis of postmodern politics, Žižek points to the "well-known definition of politics as the 'art of the possible': authentic politics is, rather, the exact opposite, that is, the art of the *impossible*—it changes the very parameters of what is considered 'possible' in the existing constellation." Žižek, *The Ticklish Subject*, p. 199. My use of the concept of the "impossible" draws on this analysis.

88. Thelonious Monk quoted in Dalmonte and Varga, *Luciano Berio: Two Interviews*, p. 84.

89. Gigi Gryce recalls precisely this impossibility in relation to playing with Monk: "I had a part he wrote for me that was impossible. I had to play melody while simultaneously playing harmony with him. In addition, the intervals were very wide besides; and I told him I couldn't do it. 'You have an instrument, don't you?' he said. 'Either play it or throw it away.'" Gryce quoted in Hentoff, *The Jazz Life*, p. 183.

90. Merleau-Ponty, *The Phenomenology of Perception*, p. 173.

91. "Neither the appointed order, not the free act which destroys it, is represented; they are lived through in ambiguity." Ibid., p. 445.

92. The concept of "ideological interpellation" is developed in Louis Althusser, "Ideology and Ideological State Apparatuses (Notes towards an Investigation)," in *Mapping Ideology*, ed. Slavoj Žižek (London: Verso, 1994), pp. 100–141. For Althusser, ideological "interpellation" describes the process whereby ideology is materialized in the entire organization of a given society. In this way, ideology is not something imposed from above, by the ruling class, on the working class—that is, a false consciousness—but is already internal to the capitalist division of labor itself. The moment of interpellation is both a subject's own self-recognition of his or her allotted symbolic place within this division of labor, and the systematic preparation of such a place in advance.

93. Hentoff, *The Jazz Life*, p. 255.

94. Karl Marx and Frederick Engels, *The German Ideology*, ed. C. J. Arthur (London: Lawrence & Wishart, 1970). For further comprehensive expositions of ideology, see Louis Dumont, *From Mandeville to Marx: The Genesis and Triumph of Economic Ideology* (Chicago: University of Chicago Press, 1977); Williams, *Marxism and Literature;* Alfred Sohn-Rethel, *Intellectual and Manual Labor: A Critique of Epistemology* (London: Macmillan, 1978); and Maurice Godelier, *The Mental and the Material: Thought, Economy and Society,* trans. Martin Thom (London: Verso, 1986).

95. Louis Althusser and Etienne Balibar, *Reading Capital,* trans. Ben Brewster (London: New Left Books, 1975), pp. 174–81.

96. Althusser's central point is that the "relations of production" necessarily implies an analysis of the relation between *people* and *things;* that is, an analysis of the processes of material making—the laboring process—cannot repress the "thingness" of material acts. "[T]he *relations of production* necessarily implies relations between men and things, such that the relations between men and men are defined by the precise relations existing between men and the material elements of the production process." Ibid., pp. 174–75.

97. The notion of the jazz act as an act of self-expression within an idealized intersubjective situation is, almost without exception, the basis for the study of jazz practices. For example, see Ted Gioia, *The History of Jazz* (Oxford: Oxford University Press, 1997); Berliner, *Thinking in Jazz;* Monson, *Saying Something.*

98. Slavoj Žižek, "Introduction: The Specter of Ideology," in *Mapping Ideology,* ed. Žižek, p. 12.

99. Žižek, *The Sublime Object of Ideology* (London: Verso, 1989), p. 89.

100. Ibid., p. 30.

101. Richard Slotkin, *The Fatal Environment: The Myth of the Frontier in the Age of Industrialization, 1800–1890* (New York: Atheneum, 1985), p. 22.

102. Fredric Jameson, *Marxism and Form* (Princeton: Princeton University Press, 1971; reprint 1974), p. 224.

103. Jameson, *The Political Unconscious,* p. 22.

104. Ross, *The Origins of American Social Science,* pp. 22–30.

105. James Livingston, *Origins of the Federal Reserve System: Money, Class, and Corporate Capitalism, 1890–1913* (Ithaca: Cornell University Press, 1986); Harry Braverman, *Labor and Monopoly Capital: The Degradation of Work in the Twentieth Century* (New York: Monthly Review Press, 1974; reprint 1998); Gutman, *Power and Culture.*

106. J. A. Rogers, "Jazz at Home," in *The New Negro,* ed. Alain Locke (New York: Johnson Reprint, 1968), pp. 216–17.

107. Jonathan Yardley, "Jazz, Most Glorious of Mongrels," *Guardian Weekly* 157, no. 25 (December 21, 1997), p. 18.

108. Slotkin, *The Fatal Environment,* p. 34.

109. Sacvan Bercovitch, *The Rites of Assent: Transformations in the Symbolic Construction of America* (London: Routledge, 1993), p. 56.

110. Ibid., p. 49.

111. Ibid.

112. Ibid., p. 366.

113. Ibid., p. 355.

114. Žižek, *The Sublime Object of Ideology,* pp. 87–129.

115. Christopher Lasch, *The Culture of Narcissism: American Life in An Age of Diminishing Returns* (New York: W. W. Norton, 1979; reprint 1991), pp. 222–36. For further accounts of the key elements of American

exceptionalist ideology, see Ross, *The Origins of American Social Science;* Bercovitch, *The Rites of Assent;* Slotkin, *The Fatal Environment;* and Michael Paul Rogin, *Ronald Reagan, The Movie, and Other Episodes in American Demonology* (Berkeley: University of California Press, 1987), pp. 134–89.

116. Louis Dumont, *Essays on Individualism: Modern Ideology in Anthropological Perspective* (Chicago: University of Chicago Press, 1986), p. 77.

117. Michael Hardt and Antonio Negri, *Labor of Dionysus: A Critique of the State-Form* (Minneapolis: University of Minnesota Press, 1994); Dumont, *Essays on Individualism;* Louis Dumont, *German Ideology: From France to Germany and Back* (Chicago: University of Chicago Press, 1994); Kapferer, *The Feast of the Sorcerer;* Pierre Clastres, *Society against the State,* trans. Robert Hurley (New York: Urizen Books, 1977).

118. Kapferer, *The Feast of the Sorcerer,* p. 274.

119. Ibid., pp. 274–82; Clastres, *Society against the State,* pp. 159–86.

120. The notion of a logic of practice is different from, say, the theoretical logic of calculus, in that the logic of calculus itself is part of a larger praxology gathered under the social domain of mathematics. As numerous historians and anthropologists have argued, practice has a "logic which is not that of the logician." Pierre Bourdieu, *The Logic of Practice,* trans. Richard Nice (Stanford: Stanford University Press, 1990), p. 86. Kapferer, expanding upon and transforming Bourdieu's analysis, points out that logic encompasses the "diverse ways in which human beings through their practices (practices that have various historical influences working on them and are always specific to situations) put their worlds together and generate and continually alter the structures of their contexts and lives." Kapferer, *The Feast of the Sorcerer,* p. 325. Cornelius Castoriadis emphasizes that human consciousness is essentially a *practical* consciousness. Cornelius Castoriadis, *The Imaginary Institution of Society,* trans. Kathleen Blamey (Cambridge, U.K.: Polity Press, 1997), p. 21.

121. Bourdieu, *The Logic of Practice,* p. 81.

122. Ibid.

123. Fredric Jameson, "The Antinomies of Postmodernity," in *The Cultural Turn: Selected Writings on the Postmodern, 1983–1998* (London: Verso, 1998), p. 58.

124. "The first task of analysis is therefore to isolate, in a given ideological field, the particular struggle which at the same time determines the horizon of its totality—to put it in Hegelian terms, the species which is its own universal kind." Žižek, *The Sublime Object of Ideology,* p. 89.

## Chapter One

1. Sidney Bechet, *Treat It Gentle* (New York: Da Capo Press, 1978).

2. Eric Foner, *Nothing but Freedom: Emancipation and Its Legacy* (Baton Rouge: Louisiana State University Press, 1983), pp. 39–73.

3. Ibid., p. 44.

4. Burton W. Peretti, *The Creation of Jazz: Music, Race, and Culture in Urbanizing America* (Urbana: University of Illinois Press, 1992); William J. Schafer, *Brass Bands and New Orleans Jazz* (Baton Rouge: Louisiana State University Press, 1977); Eileen Southern, *The Music of Black Americans: A History* (New York: W. W. Norton, 1971); Donald Marquis, *In Search of Buddy Bolden: First Man of Jazz* (Baton Rouge: Louisiana State University Press, 1978).

5. Southern, *The Music of Black Americans*, pp. 244–77.

6. Schafer, *Brass Bands and New Orleans Jazz*, p. 8.

7. Peretti, *The Creation of Jazz*, pp. 22–38, Southern, *The Music of Black Americans*, pp. 134–42.

8. Peretti, *The Creation of Jazz*, p. 25.

9. Schafer, *Brass Bands and New Orleans Jazz*.

10. The Jim Crow laws were designed by regional legislators to limit ex-slaves' social and political participation in the various regimes of the "New South."

11. Peretti, *The Creation of Jazz*, p. 31.

12. Ibid., p. 32.

13. E. P. Thompson, "Time, Work-Discipline and Industrial Capitalism," in *Customs in Common* (Harmondsworth: Penguin Books, 1993), p. 382.

14. Bruce Kapferer, "Remythologizing Discourses: State and Insurrectionary Violence in Sri Lanka," in *The Legitimization of Violence*, ed. David E. Apter (London: Macmillan, 1997), p. 165

15. Ibid., p. 167; Edith Wyschogrod, *Spirit in Ashes: Hegel, Heidegger, and Man-Made Mass Death* (New Haven: Yale University Press, 1985), pp. 28–33.

16. Bechet, *Treat It Gentle*, p. 48.

17. Ibid., p. 209.

18. To paraphrase E. P. Thompson, we cannot have music without musicians. E. P. Thompson, *The Making of the English Working Class* (Harmondsworth: Penguin Books, 1963; reprint 1991), p. 8.

19. Elaine Scarry, *The Body in Pain: The Making and Unmaking of the World* (New York: Oxford University Press, 1985), p. 176.

20. Ibid., p. 178.

21. This is not to argue, as Scarry warns us, that artists are the most authentic sufferers. Rather, the intertwining of acts of making and those of destruction or unmaking is part of a complex social movement that often permits intensely creative acts, such as a work of art, to be made in the midst of terrible acts of violence and exploitation (often without the knowledge or the interest of the artist, or indeed, perhaps because of their lack of interest). One is reminded of the fact that the huge corporate sponsorship of current artistic institutions (for example, British Petroleum and the Tate Gallery in London) is made possible

by the corporation's ability to extract enormous surplus value from their low-wage/high-yield strategic operations that rely on the labor power of the Third World's poor and a range of diversified investments that further complicate the logic of exploitation. See James C. Scott, *Domination and the Arts of Resistance: Hidden Transcripts* (New Haven: Yale University Press, 1990).

22. James Lincoln Collier, *The Making of Jazz: A Comprehensive History* (London: Macmillan, 1978), p. 79.

23. Bechet, *Treat It Gentle,* p. 44.

24. Scarry, *The Body in Pain,* p. 22.

25. Bechet, *Treat It Gentle,* p. 46.

26. Ibid., p. 124.

27. Ibid., pp. 47–48.

28. Maurice Merleau-Ponty, *The Phenomenology of Perception,* trans. Colin Smith (London: Routledge, 1989), p. 438.

29. W. E. B. Du Bois, *Black Reconstruction in America* (New York: Russell & Russell, 1935), p. 30.

30. Herbert G. Gutman, *The Black Family in Slavery and Freedom, 1750–1925* (New York: Vintage Books, 1976), pp. 365–66.

31. Eric Foner, *Reconstruction: America's Unfinished Revolution, 1863–1877* (New York: Harper & Row, 1988), p. 77.

32. Bechet, *Treat It Gentle,* p. 213.

33. Ibid., p. 212.

34. Ibid., p. 213.

35. Scarry, *The Body in Pain,* p. 288.

36. Ibid., p. 176.

37. Ibid., p. 176.

38. Bechet, *Treat It Gentle,* p. 213.

39. Ibid., p. 30.

40. Ibid., p. 50.

41. Scarry, *The Body in Pain,* p. 180.

42. Herbert G. Gutman, *Power and Culture: Essays on the American Working Class,* ed. Ira Berlin (New York: Pantheon Books, 1987), p. 344.

43. Gutman, *The Black Family in Slavery and Freedom,* p. 335.

44. Gutman, *Power and Culture,* p. 353.

45. Nat Hentoff, *The Jazz Life* (New York: Da Capo Press, 1978), p. 142.

46. Ibid., p. 16.

47. Ibid., p. 184.

48. Ibid., p. 255.

49. Ibid., p. 33.

50. Ibid., p. 57.

51. Miles Davis, cited in ibid., pp. 134–35.

52. Miles Davis, cited in ibid., p. 137.

53. E. P. Thompson, *William Morris: Romantic To Revolutionary* (London: Merlin Press, 1955; reprint 1977), p. 657.

54. Hentoff, *The Jazz Life,* p. 33.

55. Ibid., p. 255.

56. Ibid., p. 74.

57. Ibid., pp. 16, 142.

58. Gutman, *Power and Culture,* p. 404.

59. Joel Kovel, *Red Hunting in the Promised Land* (New York: Basic Books, 1994); C. Wright Mills, *The Power Elite* (New York: Oxford University Press, 1956), pp. 298–324; Noam Chomsky, *Deterring Democracy* (London: Vintage Books, 1992), pp. 9–68; Noam Chomsky, *Rethinking Camelot: JFK, the Vietnam War, and U.S. Political Culture* (London: Verso, 1993), pp. 1–38; Joyce Kolko and Gabriel Kolko, *The Limits of Power: The World and United States Foreign Policy* (New York: Harper & Row, 1972), Theodor W. Adorno and Max Horkheimer, *The Dialectic of Enlightenment,* trans. John Cumming (London: Verso, 1997), pp. 120–67; Ernest Mandel, *Late Capitalism,* trans. Joris de Bre (London: Verso, 1999); Michael Hardt and Antonio Negri, *The Labor of Dionysus: A Critique of the State Form* (Minneapolis: University of Minnesota Press, 1994).

60. To find a language adequate to her study of the made artifact as a social act, Scarry poses this fundamental question: What is at stake in material making? Scarry, *The Body in Pain,* p. 185.

61. Bechet, *Treat It Gentle,* p. 139.

62. Ibid., p. 217.

63. Ibid., p. 209.

64. Ibid., p. 64.

65. E. P. Thompson, "The Moral Economy of the Crowd," in *Customs in Common* (Harmondsworth: Penguin Books, 1993), p. 188.

66. Ibid., p. 71.

67. Ibid., p. 141.

68. Ibid., p. 216.

69. Ibid., p. 176.

70. Ibid.

71. Ibid., p. 177.

72. Ibid., pp. 210–11.

73. Scarry, *The Body In Pain,* p. 197.

74. Bechet, *Treat It Gentle,* p. 143.

75. Ibid., p. 50.

76. Ibid., p. 30.

77. See also Gutman, *The Black Family in Slavery and Freedom*, pp. 261–64; and Eugene D. Genovese, *The World the Slaveholders Made: Two Essays in Interpretation* (London: Penguin Press, 1970), p. 125.

78. Lawrence Levine, *Black Culture and Black Consciousness* (Oxford: Oxford University Press, 1977), pp. 3–83.

79. Bechet, *Treat It Gentle*, p. 95.

80. The concept of "structuring the structure" is taken from Kapferer's work on Sinhalese rituals. Bruce Kapferer, "Performance and the Structuring of Meaning and Experience," in *The Anthropology of Experience*, ed. Victor Turner and Edward M. Brunner (Urbana: University of Illinois Press, 1986), pp. 188–220. In an analysis directly concerned with musical practices, Stephen Friedson uses this idea of "structuring the structure" to explore the process of imparting meaning and resolving oppositions, conflicts, and crises within a particular lifeworld. Stephen M. Friedson, *Dancing Prophets: Musical Experience in Tumbuka Healing* (Chicago: University of Chicago Press, 1996), p. 89.

81. Robert Higgs, *Competition and Coercion: Blacks in the American economy, 1865–1914* (Cambridge: Cambridge University Press, 1977), p. 118.

82. See Herbert Gutman, *Work, Culture, and Society in Industrializing America: Essays in American Working Class and Social History* (New York: Knopf, 1976), pp. 3–78; Christopher Lasch, *The True and Only Heaven: Progress and Its Critics* (New York: W. W. Norton, 1991); Alfred Chandler, *The Visible Hand: The Managerial Revolution in American Business* (Cambridge: Harvard University Press, Belknap Press, 1977); James Livingston, *Origins of the Federal Reserve System: Money, Class, and Corporate Capitalism, 1890–1913* (Ithaca: Cornell University Press, 1986). See also Giovanni Arrighi, *The Long Twentieth Century: Money, Power, and the Origins of our Times* (London: Verso, 1994; reprint 1996), p. 240: "Railway companies had pioneered most of the organizational innovations that were to revolutionize the structure of accumulation in the United States, and along with those innovations went a thorough reorganization of distribution through the rise of mass marketeers (the mass retailer, the advertising agency, the mail order house, the chain store), who internalized a high volume of market transactions within a single enterprise."

83. Chandler, *The Visible Hand*; Livingston, *Origins of the Federal Reserve System*; and Gabriel Kolko, *The Triumph of Conservatism: A Reinterpretation of American History, 1900–1916* (New York: Free Press, 1963). Kolko's argument is critical to any analysis of the consolidation of corporate power and its relation to the state: "The theory of the national government as a neutral intermediary in its intervention into the economic process is a convenient ideological myth, but such a contention will not survive a serious inquiry into the origins and consequences of such intervention. The rhetoric of reform is invariably different than its structural results. Such mythology is based on the

assumption that those who control the state will not use it for their own welfare." Ibid., p. 302.

84. W. E. B. Du Bois, *The Souls of Black Folk* (New York: Signet Classic, 1969), p. 265.

85. This is emphasized by Richard Cullen Rath, "Echo and Narcissus: The Afrocentric Pragmatism of W. E. B. Du Bois," *Journal of American History* 84, no. 2 (September 1997): 461–495.

86. One of the most important points raised by Louis Dumont concerning modern ideology is the degree to which the diagnosis of fragmentation, alienation, and technologization is itself *part of economic ideology,* that is, part of a one-sided, abstract economism. Louis Dumont, *From Mandeville to Marx: The Genesis and Triumph of Economic Ideology* (Chicago: University of Chicago Press, 1977; reprint 1983), pp. 33–39.

87. Du Bois, *The Souls of Black Folk,* p. 46.

88. Rath, "Echo and Narcissus," pp. 466–70.

89. Ibid., p. 490.

90. James Baldwin, *The Fire Next Time* (Harmondsworth: Penguin Books, 1963), pp. 74–78.

91. Archie Shepp, "A View from The Inside," *Down Beat,* Year Book, 1965, p. 44.

92. See Peretti, *The Creation of Jazz,* pp. 105, 216–17; LeRoi Jones, *Blues People* (New York: William Morrow, 1963), p. 120; Gunther Schuller, *Early Jazz: Its Roots and Musical Development* (New York: Oxford University Press, 1968), pp. 3–88.

93. Du Bois, *The Souls of Black Folk,* p. 267.

94. See Rudi Blesh, *Shining Trumpets* (London: Cassell, 1954), pp. 3–16. Levine, *Black Culture and Black Consciousness,* writes that "it was in the spirituals that slaves found a medium which resembled in many crucial ways the cosmology they had brought with them from Africa and afforded them the possibility of both adapting to and transcending their situation." Ibid., p. 19.

95. Gutman, *Power and Culture,* p. 346.

96. Gundar Myrdal quoted by Ralph Ellison, "An American Dilemma: A Review," in *Shadow and Act* (New York: Vintage Books, 1972), pp. 315–16.

97. Stanley Elkins, "Two Arguments on Slavery," in *Slavery: A Problem in American Institutional and Intellectual Life* (Chicago: University of Chicago Press, 1959; reprint 1976), pp. 267–68.

98. James C. Scott, *Weapons of the Weak: Everyday Forms of Peasant Resistance* (New Haven: Yale University Press, 1985), p. 306.

99. Gutman's argument was developed in later work, particularly his interest in discontinuity: "The movement of slaves in North America, between 1790 and 1860, from the Upper South to the Lower South was probably the largest

single internal forced migration in the world in the nineteenth century." Gutman, *Power and Culture,* p. 355.

100. Elkins, "Two Arguments on Slavery," p. 287.

101. Genovese, *The World the Slaveholders Made,* pp. 3–9; Eugene Genovese, *Roll Jordan Roll: The World the Slaves Made* (New York: Vintage Books, 1976).

102. Elkins, "Two Arguments on Slavery," and Genovese, *The World the Slaveholders Made,* pp. 4–11, 151–64.

103. Elkins, "Two Arguments on Slavery," p. 292.

104. These same questions also pertain to other styles of black music (and also now to India and the Middle East): that is, their universal application as symbols of liberation and the subsequent "mixture" of these traditions into a series of timeless ethnic motifs understood to be inherently resistant to the structures of American corporate culture and the logic of postmodern capitalism.

105. Collier, *The Making of Jazz,* p. 6.

106. Jones, *Blues People,* p. 10.

107. Ibid., p. 17.

108. For a precise exposition of this idea see Slavoj Žižek, "Introduction: The Specter of Ideology," in *Mapping Ideology,* ed. Slavoj Žižek (London: Verso, 1994), p. 23.

109. Slavoj Žižek, *The Plague of Fantasies* (London: Verso, 1997), pp. 12–13.

110. Robin Blackburn, *The Making of New World Slavery from the Baroque to the Modern, 1492–1800* (London: Verso, 1997).

111. Žižek, *The Plague of Fantasies,* p. 13.

112. Gutman, *The Black Family in Slavery and Freedom,* p. 212.

113. Ibid.

114. See James Lincoln Collier, *The Reception of Jazz in America: A New View* (Brooklyn, N.Y.: Institute for Studies in American Music, 1988). For a critique of the assumptions in Collier's work, see Toni Morrison, *Playing in the Dark: Whiteness and the Literary Imagination* (Cambridge: Harvard University Press, 1992), p. 5.

115. Melville J. Herskovits, *The Myth of the Negro Past* (Boston: Beacon Press, 1958), p. 263.

116. Ibid., p. 95.

117. Ibid., p. 11.

118. Herbert Gutman, W. E. B. Du Bois, Ira Berlin, Lawrence Levine, and Charles Joyner stand as exemplary historians in this regard.

119. Genovese refines this argument further by comparing the different patterns of slave resistance and analyzing why certain revolutionary actions were limited or nonexistent in the Old South, while in the Caribbean and the Spanish and Portuguese South American colonies slave rebellion and revolt was

far more sustained and successful. Eugene Genovese, *From Rebellion to Revolution: Afro-American Slave Revolts in the Making of the New World* (New York: Vintage Books, 1981).

120. Herskovits, *The Myth of the Negro Past*, p. 125.

121. Ibid., p. 142.

122. Ibid., p. 145.

123. We can still see this idea at work in mass media productions like Steven Spielberg's *Amistad*.

124. It is in this sense that we might refer to the *heretical* aspect of black music, in that the very idea of progress implicitly makes a heresy of any position that would hinder, through "mere subjectivity," the immanent result of the logic of American history. This problem of progress goes some of the way toward explaining the ways in which black music was assimilated to the dominant logic of American progressivism and the structure of those discourses that sought to legitimate jazz practices as signs of a democratic spirit. For further exposition of the role of the heretic in modern thought, see Hans Blumenberg, *Work on Myth*, trans. Robert M. Wallace (Cambridge: MIT Press, 1990), pp. 215–62.

125. Gutman, *Power and Culture*, p. 349.

126. Bechet, *Treat It Gentle*, p. 46.

127. Ibid.

128. Kapferer, "Remythologizing Discourses," p. 165.

129. Bechet, *Treat It Gentle*, p. 201.

130. Wyschogrod, *Spirit in Ashes*, p. 39.

131. Kapferer, *The Feast of the Sorcerer*, p. 178.

132. Bechet, *Treat It Gentle*, p. 202.

133. Ibid.

134. Ibid., p. 204.

135. Ibid.

136. Slavoj Žižek, *Enjoy Your Symptom! Jacques Lacan in Hollywood and Out* (New York: Routledge, 1992), p. 35.

137. Bechet, *Treat It Gentle*, pp. 210–15.

138. Ibid., p. 216.

139. Ibid., pp. 210, 217.

## Chapter Two

1. Stanley Crouch, "Bird Land: Charlie Parker, Clint Eastwood, and America," *The Charlie Parker Companion*, ed. Carl Woideck (New York: Schirmer Books, 1998), p. 251.

2. Richard Slotkin, *Gunfighter Nation: The Myth of the Frontier in Twentieth Century America* (New York: HarperCollins, 1993), pp. 29–62.

3. Henry Nash Smith, *Virgin Land: The American West as Symbol and Myth* (Cambridge: Harvard University Press, 1978), pp. 3–48, 251.

4. Slotkin, *Gunfighter Nation,* pp. 29–62.

5. Ibid., pp. 22–26; Harry Braverman, *Labor and Monopoly Capital: The Degradation of Work in the Twentieth Century* (New York: Monthly Review Press, 1974; reprint 1998), pp. 107–200; Fredrick Jackson Turner, *The Frontier in American History* (New York: Henry Holt, 1920), pp. 1–38.

6. Crouch, "Bird Land," p. 258.

7. These recordings of "Lover Man" and "Ornithology" are both collected on Charlie Parker, *The Legendary Dial Masters,* vol. 1 (New York: Stash Records, 1989) ST-CD-23. The notion of "rhythmic melodying" is from Martin Williams, "Charlie Parker: The Burden of Innovation," *The Charlie Parker Companion,* ed. Woideck, p. 16.

8. LeRoi Jones, *Blues People* (New York: William Morrow, 1963), pp. 194, 188.

9. Scott DeVeaux, *The Birth of Bebop: A Musical and Social History* (Berkeley: University of California Press, 1997), pp. 15, 445.

10. Stowe's argument is worth stating in full:

> The incongruity of Goodman as a standard bearer for bebop arises from a distorted notion of the relationship between swing and bebop. Because of the apparent contrasts between these two genres, both as music and as cultural style, historians and others have seen them as polar opposites often attributing differences where similarities should be emphasized, and vice versa. Swing has been depicted as primarily a white phenomenon, bop as African-American; swing as widely popular functional music performed by big bands, bop as small-group art music that spurned commercial success; swing as participatory, bop as detached; swing as embodying the politics of consensus, bop as militant harbinger of the race consciousness that would bloom in the 1950s. . . . Such characterizations are as misleading about swing as about bop.

David Stowe, *Swing Changes: Big Band Jazz in New Deal America* (Cambridge: Harvard University Press, 1994), p. 204.

11. Ibid., pp. 52–53, 73–74.

12. Ibid., p. 10.

13. Max Harrison, "A Rare Bird," *The Charlie Parker Companion,* ed. Woideck, p. 206.

14. Dizzy Gillespie and Al Fraser, *Dizzy: The Autobiography of Dizzy Gillespie* (London: W. H. Allen, 1980), pp. 140–41.

15. The interview between Parker and journalists Michael Levin and John S. Wilson is reproduced in *The Charlie Parker Companion,* ed. Woideck, p. 70.

16. Ibid., p. 70.

17. Ralph Ellison, "On Bird, Bird-Watching, and Jazz," in *Shadow and Act* (New York: Vintage Books, 1972), p. 230.

18. Ross Russell, *Bird Lives! The High Life and Hard Times of Charlie "Yardbird" Parker* (London: Quartet Books, 1988), p. 366.

19. John Clellon Holmes, *The Horn* (Berkeley: Creative Arts Book Co., 1980), p. ii. Indeed, Holmes says that he made the "arduous transition from Dixie to Bop with the help of Kerouac and Bird [Charlie Parker]. . . ."

20. Norman Mailer, "The White Negro," *Advertisements for Myself* (London: Flamingo Modern Classics, 1991), p. 292.

21. With reference to bebop, the phrase, of course, is Ellison's. Ralph Ellison, "The Golden Age, Time Past," in *Shadow and Act,* pp. 199–212; Robert Reisner, *Bird: The Legend of Charlie Parker* (London: Quartet Books, 1962)

22. DeVeaux, *The Birth of Bebop,* p. 3.

23. These questions are also addressed in Joel Kovel, *White Racism: A Psychohistory* (New York: Columbia University Press, 1984), p. 53, and Slavoj Žižek, *The Sublime Object of Ideology* (London: Verso, 1989), pp. 124–29.

24. Jones, *Blues People,* p. 188.

25. Ibid.

26. Ibid., p. 235.

27. Ellison, "The Golden Age, Time Past," p. 204.

28. Ellison, "On Bird, Bird-Watching, and Jazz," p. 227.

29. Ibid., pp. 226–27.

30. Ibid., p. 225–27.

31. Ellison, "Blues People," in *Shadow and Act,* p. 253.

32. Ibid., p. 252.

33. Ibid., p. 256.

34. Ibid., p. 253.

35. Ellison, "The Charlie Christian Story," in *Shadow and Act,* p. 234.

36. Ellison, "Blues People," p. 254.

37. Ibid., p. 255.

38. Ibid., p. 256.

39. Ibid.

40. Ellison, "Living with Music," in *Shadow and Act,* pp. 192–93.

41. Ellison, "The Golden Age, Time Past," p. 210.

42. Ellison, "Blues People," p. 257.

43. Thelonious Monk quoted in Jones, *Blues People,* p. 198, from Nat Hentoff, *The Jazz Life* (New York: Da Capo, 1978), p. 195.

44. Jones, *Blues People,* p. 198.

45. Ibid., p. 179.

46. Harold Rosenberg, *The Tradition of the New* (London: Thames and Hudson, 1962), p. 156.

47. Ibid., p. 156; Žižek, *The Sublime Object of Ideology*, pp. 140–41.

48. Jones, *Blues People*, p. 200.

49. Žižek, *The Sublime Object of Ideology*, p. 61.

50. Ted Gioia, *The History of Jazz* (Oxford: Oxford University Press, 1997), p. 200.

51. Sacvan Bercovitch, *The Rites of Assent: Transformations in the Symbolic Construction of America* (New York: Routledge, 1993), p. 215.

52. Reisner, *Bird: The Legend of Charlie Parker*, p. 13.

53. Stowe, *Swing Changes*, pp. 202–4.

54. Ellison, "On Bird, Bird-Watching, and Jazz," pp. 227–28.

55. Leo Marx, *The Machine in the Garden* (Oxford: Oxford University Press, 1964), pp. 141–44; Michael Paul Rogin, "Nature as Politics and Nature as Romance," in *Ronald Reagan, the Movie, and other Episodes in Political Demonology* (Berkeley: University of California Press, 1987), pp. 169–89.

56. Ernest Lee Tuveson, *Redeemer Nation: The Idea of America's Millennial Role* (Chicago: University of Chicago Press, 1968), pp. 90–136; Bercovitch, *The Rites of Assent*, pp. 29–67, 168–245; Daniel Boorstin, *The Lost World of Thomas Jefferson* (Chicago: University of Chicago Press, 1948; reprint 1981), pp. 227–32; Rogin, "Nature as Politics and Nature as Romance," p. 182.

57. Robert Hughes, *American Visions: The Epic History of Art in America* (London: Harvill Press, 1997), pp. 137–205.

58. "[The] assimilation of the machine to the garden in the nineteenth century imagination helped prolong the life of pastoralism in the twentieth century. The harmoniously functioning machine would bring order to, or even replace, nature." Rogin, "Nature as Politics and Nature as Romance," p. 183. See also Slotkin, *The Fatal Environment: The Myth of the Frontier in the Age of Industrialization, 1800–1890* (New York: Atheneum, 1985), p. 45: "The Frontier theory of development offers both a theory of capital development and a theory of social relations. It sees the sources of wealth as lying outside society, in an unappropriated natural wilderness, rather than as products of social labor; and it sees acquisition of that sort of wealth as an antidote to social conflicts within the Metropolis."

59. Slotkin, *Gunfighter Nation*, p. 4.

60. Slotkin, *The Fatal Environment*, p. 109.

61. Ibid., p. 15.

62. Ibid., p. 19.

63. Ibid., p. 22.

64. Ibid., p. 23.

65. Ibid., p. 34.

66. Ibid., p. 40.

67. Marx, *The Machine in the Garden,* pp. 227–65; Bercovitch, *The Rites of Assent,* pp. 307–52; George M. Fredrickson, *The Black Image in the White Mind: The Debate on Afro-American Character and Destiny, 1817–1914* (New York: Harper & Row, 1971), pp. 1–129; Herbert G. Gutman, *The Black Family in Slavery and Freedom: 1750–1925* (New York: Pantheon Books, 1976), p. 357.

68. Slotkin, *The Fatal Environment,* p. 45.

69. J. G. A. Pocock, *The Machiavellian Moment: Florentine Political Thought and the Atlantic Republican Tradition* (Princeton: Princeton University Press, 1975), p. 527.

70. Ibid., p. 523.

71. Ibid., p. 522.

72. Ibid., p. 534. Pocock goes on to argue against the idea that the American state constituted a radical break with the past. Instead, the "dialectic of virtue and commerce was a quarrel with modernity, most fully articulated—at least until the advent of Rousseau—within the humanist and neo-Harrington vocabularies employed by the English-speaking cultures of the North Atlantic; and it was in those cultures that American self-consciousness originated and acquired its terminology" (p. 546). We should, of course, be specific about the class consciousness Pocock was referring to: the North Atlantic political and landowning elite.

73. Frederick Jackson Turner, *The Frontier in American History* (New York: Henry Holt, 1920), pp. 2–3.

74. Ibid., p. 11. This understanding preempts F. W. Taylor's argument that "the greatest prosperity can exist only when [the] individual has reached his highest state of efficiency. . . ." Frederick Winslow Taylor, *The Principles of Scientific Management* (New York: Harper & Brothers Publishers, 1915), p. 11.

75. Turner, *The Frontier in American History,* pp. 14–15.

76. Smith, *Virgin Land,* p. 258.

77. Turner, *The Frontier In American History,* p. 2. Joel Kovel notes how the notion of adaptation was crucial to the development of the racist state: "According to postwar American psychoanalysis, either one was a brute or a well-adapted bourgeois. With no other possibility presented, the average citizen could be much more easily reconciled to his or her fate. A psychology of 'adaptation' facilitates submission to unfreedom." Kovel, *White Racism,* p. xli.

78. Christopher Lasch, *The True and Only Heaven: Progress and Its Critics* (New York: W. W. Norton, 1991), pp. 21–81.

79. Slotkin, *Gunfighter Nation,* p. 61.

80. Turner, *The Frontier In American History,* pp. 243–68, Smith, *Virgin Land,* p. 257.

81. Smith, *Virgin Land,* p. 253.

82. Turner quoted in ibid., p. 254.

83. Turner, *The Frontier In American History,* pp. 3–4.

84. Ibid., p. 4.

85. Ibid., p. 253.

86. Ibid., p. 266.

87. Ibid.

88. Ibid., p. 264.

89. Ibid., p. 267.

90. Alfred Chandler, *The Visible Hand: The Managerial Revolution in American Business* (Cambridge: Harvard University Press, Belknap Press, 1977), p. 244.

91. Dorothy Ross, *The Origins of American Social Science* (Cambridge: Cambridge University Press, 1991), pp. 312–14.

92. Turner, *The Frontier in American History,* p. 261.

93. Braverman, *Labor and Monopoly Capital,* p. 118.

94. Slotkin, *Gunfighter Nation,* p. 24.

95. Kovel, *White Racism,* pp. 24–41, 60–92.

96. Gutman, *The Black Family in Slavery and Freedom,* pp. 450–75; Florette Henri, *Black Migration: Movement North, 1900–1920* (Garden City, N.J.: Anchor Press, 1975).

97. The idea of jazz as a "primitive" or "untamed" form of expression and the social struggle that surrounded that idea is well documented in Kathy J. Ogren, *The Jazz Revolution: Twenties America and the Meaning of Jazz* (New York: Oxford University Press, 1989); Neil Leonard, *Jazz and the White Americans: The Acceptance of a New Art Form* (Chicago: University of Chicago Press, 1962; reprint 1970); and David Levering Lewis, *When Harlem Was in Vogue* (Harmondsworth, England: Penguin, 1979; reprint 1997).

98. Burton W. Peretti, *The Creation of Jazz: Music, Race, and Culture in Urbanizing America* (Urbana: University of Illinois Press, 1992), p. 38.

99. John Kouwenhoven, *Made in America: The Arts in Modern Civilization* (New York: Doubleday, 1948), p. 268.

100. Ibid., p. 267.

101. Ibid., pp. 264–65.

102. Ibid., p. 259.

103. Leroy Ostransky, *Jazz City: The Impact of Our Cities on the Development of Jazz* (Englewood Cliffs, N.J.: Prentice-Hall, 1978), pp. 42–59, 102–21, 148–72, 200–230, 252; Ogren, *The Jazz Revolution,* p. 86; Henri, *Black Migration,* pp. 49–92.

104. Max Kaminsky and V. E. Hughes, *My Life in Jazz* (New York: Da Capo Press, 1963), pp. 30–31.

105. J. A. Rogers, "Jazz at Home," in *The New Negro,* ed. Alain Locke (New York: Johnson Reprint, 1968), p. 218.

106. Quoted in Ira Gitler, *Jazz Masters of the 1940s* (New York: Macmillan, 1966), p. 208.

107. To have experienced "52nd street between 1945 and 1949 was like reading a textbook to the future of music." Miles Davis and Quincy Troupe, *Miles: The Autobiography* (London: Macmillan, 1990), p. 42.

108. Ostransky, *Jazz City*, p. xii.

109. Slotkin, *Gunfighter Nation*, p. 125.

110. Rogin, "Nature as Politics and Nature as Romance," p. 170; and Wilfrid Mellers, *Music in a New Found Land: Themes and Developments in the History of American Music* (London: Barrie & Rockcliff, 1964), p. 339.

111. Reisner, *Bird: The Legend of Charlie Parker*, p. 20.

112. Mellers, *Music in a New Found Land*, p. 333.

113. Mezz Mezzrow and Bernard Wolfe, *Really the Blues* (New York: Citadel Press, 1990), p. 327.

114. James Lincoln Collier, *The Making of Jazz: A Comprehensive History* (London: PaperMac, 1981), p. 373.

115. Mellers, *Music In A New Found Land*, p. 339.

116. Martin Williams, *The Jazz Tradition* (New York: Oxford University Press, 1993), pp. 133, 136.

117. Jones, *Blues People*, p. 30.

118. Russell, *Bird Lives!*, p. 22.

119. Murray Kempton quoted in Reisner, *Bird: The Legend of Charlie Parker*, p. 234.

120. Ross Russell quoted in Jones, *Blues People*, p. 193.

121. Bercovitch, *The Rites of Assent*, p. 61.

122. Ibid., p. 59.

123. Ibid.

124. Ibid., pp. 62–63.

125. Reisner, *Bird: The Legend of Charlie Parker*, p. 15.

126. Fredrickson, *The Black Image in the White Mind*.

127. Ellison, "On Bird, Bird-Watching, and Jazz," p. 223.

128. Ellison, "The Golden Age, Time Past," p. 205.

129. Reisner, *Bird: The Legend of Charlie Parker*, p. 17.

130. Ibid., p. 194.

131. Doris Parker quoted in Crouch, "Bird Land," p. 255.

132. Max Harrison, "A Rare Bird," p. 207.

133. This point is drawn from James C. Scott, *Weapons of the Weak: Everyday Forms of Peasant Resistance* (New Haven: Yale University Press, 1985), p. 308.

134. Kenny Clarke quoted in Gillespie and Fraser, *Dizzy*, p. 100.

135. *Hear Me Talkin' to Ya: The Story of Jazz as Told by the Men Who Made It,* ed. Nat Shapiro and Nat Hentoff (London: Souvenir Press, 1992), p. 337.

136. Kenny Clarke quoted by DeVeaux, *The Birth of Bebop,* p. 218.

137. Ibid., pp. 202–35.

138. Scott, *Weapons of the Weak,* pp. 326, 336 n.69.

139. E. P. Thompson, "Eighteenth Century English Society: Class Struggle without Class?" *Social History* 3, no. 2 (May 1978): 149:

> In my view, far too much theoretical attention (much of it plainly ahistorical) has been paid to "class" and far too little to "class-struggle." Indeed, class struggle is the prior, as well as the more universal, concept. To put it bluntly, classes do not exist as separate entities, look around, find an enemy class, and then start to struggle. On the contrary, people find themselves in a society structured in determined ways (crucial, but not exclusively, in productive relations), they experience exploitation (or the need to maintain power over those whom they exploit), they identify points of antagonistic interest, they commence to struggle around these issues and in the process of struggling they discover themselves as classes, they come to know this discovery as class-consciousness. Class and class-consciousness are always the *last,* not the first, stage in the real historical process.

140. DeVeaux, *The Birth of Bebop,* p. 202.

141. Jones, *Blues People,* p. 179.

142. DeVeaux, *The Birth of Bebop,* p. 207.

143. Ibid., p. 217.

144. Stowe, *Swing Changes,* pp. 203–4.

145. DeVeaux, *The Birth of Bebop,* pp. 167–317.

146. Stowe, *Swing Changes,* p. 206.

147. *Hear Me Talkin' To Ya,* ed. Shapiro and Hentoff, p. 336.

148. There are, of course, many references to musicians' *woodshedding,* that is, the practice of isolating oneself so as to work on instrumental technique (Parker's summer spent in the Ozark Mountains is always cited in this instance). But even that practice itself was premised on a musician's *sensing* what had already happened, and *anticipating* what might happen, among the other players on the bandstand.

149. See the discussion concerning social being and ideological struggle in Scott, *Weapons of the Weak,* p. 297.

150. *Hear Me Talkin' To Ya,* ed. Shapiro and Hentoff, p. 339.

151. DeVeaux, *The Birth of Bebop,* p. 204.

152. Gillespie and Fraser, *Dizzy,* p. 296.

153. Ibid., p. 297.

154. Scott, *Weapons of the Weak,* p. 38.

155. Harrison, "A Rare Bird," p. 205.

156. Ibid., p. 207.

157. A "take," in recording jargon, is one of a number of recordings of the same piece made during a recording session.

158. Harrison, "A Rare Bird," p. 209.

159. Ibid., p. 215.

160. Ibid.

161. Charlie Parker, *The Legendary Dial Masters,* vol. 1, Stash Records, 1989, ST-CT-2, track 23.

162. Slavoj Žižek, *The Plague of Fantasies* (London: Verso, 1997), pp. 192–212; Charles Rosen, *The Romantic Generation* (London: Fontana Press, 1999); Theodor Adorno, *In Search of Wagner,* trans. Rodney Livingstone (London: Verso, 1991). All three analyses stand as significant developments in the sociology of musical practices.

163. Williams, "Charlie Parker: The Burden of Innovation," p. 14.

164. Harrison, "A Rare Bird," p. 214.

165. For a transcription of the six-note motif with which Parker began his solo on "Embraceable You," see Carl Woideck, *Charlie Parker: His Music and Life* (Ann Arbor: University of Michigan Press, 1996), p. 152. The notion of an inaudible or absent melody is Rosen's. Rosen, *The Romantic Generation,* pp. 7–40.

166. Žižek, *The Plague of Fantasies,* p. 207.

167. For references to these phantom notes or the melody's "platonic ghost," see Russell, *Bird Lives!,* p. 250, and Harrison, "A Rare Bird," pp. 209, 214.

168. Miles Davis recalled the way in which Parker's groups were put together and the *imbalance* that was already internal to the jazz act:

> We argued half the night about what we were going to play and who was going to play what. There had been no rehearsal for the recording date, and the musicians were pissed because they were going to be playing tunes they were unfamiliar with. Bird was never organized about telling people what he wanted them to do. . . . Nothing was written down, maybe a sketch of a melody. . . . Bird would play the melody he wanted. The other musicians had to remember what he wanted played. . . . I loved the way Bird played. I learned a lot from him that way. It would later help me with my own musical concepts. . . . Bird would get guys in who couldn't handle the concept. He did it in the recording studio and when they

> were playing a live performance. That's what a lot of the argument was about. . . .

Davis and Troupe, *Miles,* p. 79.

169. Ellison, "On Bird, Bird-Watching, and Jazz," p. 227. "Culture industry" is the shorthand term used by Theodor Adorno and Max Horkheimer to describe the social structures and technical phenomena that produce human consciousness in consumer society. Theodor Adorno and Max Horkheimer, *Dialectic of Enlightenment,* trans. John Cumming (London: Verso, 1997).

170. David Sudnow, *Ways of the Hand: The Organization of Improvised Conduct* (Cambridge: MIT Press, 1978; reprint 1995), pp. 85–96.

171. Charles Keil and Steven Feld, *Music Grooves: Essays and Dialogues* (Chicago: University of Chicago Press, 1994), p. 73.

## Chapter Three

1. John Litweiler, *The Freedom Principle: Jazz after 1958* (New York: Da Capo Press, 1984), p. 13.

2. Joel Kovel, *Red Hunting in the Promised Land* (New York: Basic Books, 1994), p. 121.

3. "The national security state was formalized with the National Security Act of 1947, which created the National Security Council, centralized the military into the Department of Defense, and fashioned the Central Intelligence Agency from the shards of the wartime intelligence services." Ibid., p. 168.

4. Mike Davis, *Prisoners of the American Dream: Politics and Economy in the History of the American Working Class* (London: Verso, 1986), p. 182.

5. Fredric Jameson, *The Political Unconscious: Narrative as a Socially Symbolic Act* (London: Routledge, 1981; reprint 1996), p. 79.

6. C. Wright Mills, *The Power Elite* (New York: Oxford University Press, 1956), pp. 3–29; Kovel, *Red Hunting in the Promised Land,* pp. 39–136.

7. Paul Boyer, *By the Bomb's Early Light: American Thought and Culture at the Dawn of the Atomic Age* (New York: Pantheon, 1984), p. 334.

8. The basic Cold War document, the National Security Council Document No. 68 from April 1950, announced that "the cold war is in fact a real war in which the survival of the free world is at stake." Quoted in Noam Chomsky, *Deterring Democracy* (London: Vintage Books, 1992), p. 10.

9. Boyer, *By the Bomb's Early Light,* p. 339.

10. Ibid., pp. 286–87.

11. Elaine Scarry, *The Body in Pain: The Making and Unmaking of the World* (New York: Oxford University Press, 1985), p. 152.

12. Ibid., pp. 152–53.

13. In a fine essay on globalization, Jameson argues that the supreme form in which American economic interests and America cultural interests coincide is not that of individualism or crass materialism (which he finds too moralistic), but that of *consumerism*. Fredric Jameson, "Globalization as Philosophical Issue," in *The Cultures of Globalization,* ed. Fredric Jameson and Masao Miyoshi (Durham: Duke University Press, 1998), p. 64.

14. LeRoi Jones, *Blues People* (New York: William Morrow, 1963); Ronald M. Radano, *New Musical Figurations: Anthony Braxton's Cultural Critique* (Chicago: University of Chicago Press, 1993); David H. Rosenthal, *Hard Bop and Black Music, 1955–1965* (New York: Oxford University Press, 1992); Brian Ward, *Just My Soul Responding: Rhythm and Blues, Black Consciousness, and Race Relations* (Berkeley: University of California Press, 1998).

15. "Objective Spirit" is Theodor Adorno's phrase for musical form. Theodor Adorno, *Sound Figures,* trans. Rodney Livingstone (Stanford: Stanford University Press, 1999), p. 159.

16. Jones, *Blues People,* p. 227.

17. Charles Mingus quoted in Rosenthal, *Hard Bop,* p. 152.

18. A study of jazz improvisation by ethnomusicologist Paul Berliner is perhaps the most significant attempt to study the logic of jazz practices. However, Berliner's study is compromised by an overbearing psychologism that fails to account for the historical eventuation of jazz practices and, likewise, neglects the ideological frame in which jazz musicians organized their social experiences over time.

19. See also Steven M. Friedson, *Dancing Prophets: Musical Experience in Tumbuka Healing* (Chicago: University of Chicago Press, 1996).

20. Jones, *Blues People,* p. 223.

21. Ibid., p. 225.

22. Ralph Ellison, "Blues People," in *Shadow and Act* (New York: Vintage Books, 1972), pp. 247–58.

23. Jones, *Blues People,* p. 193

24. "Negro music is *always* radical in the context of formal American culture." Ibid., p. 235.

25. Steve Lacy quoted in Derek Bailey, *Improvisation* (London: British National Sound Archive, 1992), p. 54.

26. LeRoi Jones, *Black Music* (London: MacGibbon & Kee, 1969), pp. 74–76. The reference to 4/4 means that the basic organizing unit of Western rhythmic notation—the bar line—is divided by four beats of equal length.

27. John Litweiler points out that "Lennie Tristano and his small circle created an even more fragile idiom out of bop's romanticism. Pure spontaneity was their objective; their materials were bop's potential ensemble unity, bop's displaced, irregular accenting, and the rhythmic effervescence of the late swing

era." John Litweiler, *The Freedom Principle* (New York: Da Capo Press, 1984), p. 15.

28. Interview with Ornette Coleman in Litweiler, *The Freedom Principle,* p. 33.

29. Ornette Coleman in the liner notes to *Something Else!!!! The Music of Ornette Coleman,* Contemporary, 1958 CD 7551.

30. Litweiler, *The Freedom Principle,* p. 106.

31. Max Harrison, *A Jazz Retrospect* (London: David & Charles, 1976), pp. 105–10.

32. Pierre Bourdieu, *The Logic of Practice,* trans. Richard Nice (Stanford: Stanford University Press, 1990), p. 34.

33. "All social life is essentially *practical.* All mysteries which lead theory to mysticism find their rational solution in human practice and the comprehension of this practice." Karl Marx, *Early Writings,* trans. Rodney Livingstone (Harmondsworth: Penguin Books, 1975; reprint 1984), p. 423.

34. Ingrid Monson, *Saying Something: Jazz Improvisation and Interaction* (Chicago: University of Chicago Press, 1996), p. 5.

35. Ibid., p. 139.

36. Ibid., pp. 178–91.

37. Paul Berliner, *Thinking in Jazz: The Infinite Art of Improvisation* (Chicago: University of Chicago Press, 1994), p. 5.

38. Ibid., p. 12.

39. Ibid., p. 35.

40. Jazz studies often begin with a description of a bar or club, or a statement of musical intent on the part of the ethnographer, as a means of establishing the legitimacy of the ethnographic act in entering into and commenting on the lives of jazz musicians. This results in the ethnographer's production and reproduction of the logic of the field as the underlying principle of the analysis, thereby affirming the ethnographer's own transcendence in relation to the object.

41. Pierre Bourdieu, *The Field of Cultural Production,* trans. Randal Johnson (Cambridge: Polity Press, 1993), p. 266.

42. Ibid., p. 304, n. 8.

43. Ornette Coleman quoted in John Litweiler, *Ornette Coleman: A Harmolodic Life* (New York: William Morrow, 1992), p. 104.

44. Richard H. King, *Civil Rights and the Idea of Freedom* (New York: Oxford University Press, 1992), p. 5.

45. Ibid., pp. 39–87.

46. Ibid., p. 6.

47. Radano, *New Musical Figurations,* pp. 85–99.

48. Ibid., p. 95.

49. Valerie Wilmer, *As Serious as Your Life: The Story of the New Jazz* (London: Allison & Busby, 1977), p. 213.

50. Ibid., p. 214.

51. Ibid.

52. Ibid., pp. 214–15.

53. Jameson, *The Political Unconscious,* p. 294.

54. Robert Gordon, *Jazz West Coast: The Los Angeles Scene in the 1950s* (London: Quartet Books, 1986), p. 199.

55. Mike Davis, *City of Quartz: Excavating The Future in Los Angeles* (London: Verso, 1990), p. 64.

56. Gordon, *Jazz West Coast,* p. 183.

57. Ornette Coleman quoted in A. B. Spellman, *Four Lives in the Bebop Business* (New York: Limelight Editions, 1990), p. 129. Comparatively, black musicians in New York attained a level of economic leverage (however fragile) unthinkable for most young blacks in the city. Philip Foner cites a report in which the New York City Youth Board, based on the 1960 Census, spelled out what the Civil Rights Commission's data meant to black youth. The proportion of unemployed nonwhite youth in New York City was more than twice that of unemployed whites. It also made clear that, at a time of "increased demand for skilled and educated workers and a decrease in opportunities for the unskilled and uneducated," black youth coming out of both general and vocational high schools were untrained, unskilled, and ill prepared for anything but menial work. Apprenticeship training was dismissed as a viable means to alleviate the acute unemployment among black youth. Of approximately 15,000 registered apprentices in New York State, fewer than 2 per cent were blacks, and these were almost all in "New York City." Philip S. Foner, *Organized Labor and the Black Worker, 1619–1973* (New York: International Publishers, 1974), p. 341.

58. As found, for example, in George Lipsitz, *Class and Culture in Cold War America* (South Hadley, Mass.: J. F. Bergin, 1981), p. 197.

59. Quoted in Michael Jarrett, "Ornette Coleman: Interview," *Cadence* 21, no. 10 (October 1995): 7.

60. Monson, *Saying Something,* p. 1.

61. For an analysis of the disembodied and reembodied structures of creating, see Scarry, *The Body in Pain,* pp. 181–277; David Sudnow, *Ways of the Hand: The Organization of Improvised Conduct* (Cambridge: MIT Press, 1978; reprint 1995), pp. 81–152. Likewise, Bourdieu argues that art is "a 'bodily thing,' and music, the most 'pure' and 'spiritual' of the arts, perhaps simply the most corporeal. Linked to *etats d'ame* which are also states of the body or, as they were once called, humours, it ravishes, carries away, moves. It is pitched not so much beyond words as below them, in gestures and movements of the body, rhythms . . . quickening and slowing, crescendo and decrescendo, tension and

relaxation." Pierre Bourdieu, *Distinction: A Social Critique of the Judgment of Taste,* trans. Richard Nice (Cambridge: Harvard University Press, 1984), p. 80.

62. Consider the complex relationship in the eighteenth- and early-nineteenth-century European courts between the virtuosity of fencing or swordsmanship and that of the violinist in terms of how a virtuosity of the musical act is to be conceived. For example, one can hear in the development of Beethoven's sonatas for piano and violin a duel of sorts, in which each instrument, and the virtuosi themselves, enter into a arch game of seduction and abandonment.

63. Jean Baudrillard, *Seduction,* trans. Brian Singer (London: Macmillan, 1990). To argue that music is the art and practice of seduction is not to trivialize musical acts but to situate them within a different framework that refuses to undermine the pleasure of musical experience in the name of an abstract economy of musical meaning or social function.

64. Sudnow, *Ways of the Hand,* pp. 80–83.

65. Paolo Virno, "Virtuosity and Revolution: The Political Theory of Exodus," in *Radical Thought in Italy: A Potential Politics,* ed. Paolo Virno and Michael Hardt (Minneapolis: University of Minnesota Press, 1996), p. 192.

66. Ibid., p. 193.

67. Ibid., p. 191.

68. Ibid., p. 192.

69. Karl Marx, *Capital: A Critique of Political Economy,* trans. Ben Brewster (Harmondsworth: Penguin Books, 1976; reprint 1990), pp. 948–1084.

70. Virno, "Virtuosity and Revolution," p. 191, Marx, *Capital,* p. 1048.

71. Virno, "Virtuosity and Revolution," p. 191, Marx, *Capital,* p. 1048.

72. Virno, "Virtuosity and Revolution," pp. 192–93.

73. Ibid., p. 195.

74. Ibid.

75. Ibid.

76. Ibid.

77. Ibid., p. 193.

78. Harry Braverman, *Labor and Monopoly Capital: The Degradation of Work in the Twentieth Century* (New York: Monthly Review Press, 1974), pp. 203–47; Saskia Sassen, *The Global City: New York, London, Tokyo* (Princeton: Princeton University Press, 1991), pp. 90–167.

79. Virno, "Virtuosity and Revolution," p. 193.

80. Ibid., p. 200.

81. Ibid., p. 209.

82. Maurice Merleau-Ponty, "The Indirect Language," in *The Prose of the World,* trans. John O'Neill (Evanston: Northwestern University Press, 1973), p. 84.

83. Ibid., p. 91.

84. Sudnow, *Ways of the Hand,* p. 83.

85. Baudrillard, *Seduction,* p. 76.

86. Nat Hentoff cites composer George Russell in this regard, who observed that a composer may write an idea that will sound so improvised it might influence improvisers to play something they have never played before. Nat Hentoff, *The Jazz Life* (New York: Da Capo Press, 1978), p. 225.

87. The sense of being affected by one's *own notes* is described by Lee Konitz and quoted in Berliner, *Thinking in Jazz,* p. 270.

88. For Jimmy Robinson, that an improviser might have bad night "is understandable because that's the way your body is. It doesn't respond the same way every night, and you can't be consistent as you would like. Some nights are real good, and others you just can't do a thing." Robinson quoted in Berliner, *Thinking in Jazz,* p. 272.

89. Ornette Coleman, *Town Hall, 1962,* Get Back, 1998, GET1002.

90. Scarry, *The Body in Pain,* p. 176.

91. Baudrillard, *Seduction,* p. 85,

92. Walter Norris quoted in the liner notes to Coleman, *Something Else!!!!*

93. Lee Konitz quoted in Berliner, *Thinking in Jazz,* p. 362.

94. For a discussion of various groups, in particular, the Jazz Composers Guild and the Jazz and People's Movement, see Wilmer, *As Serious as Your Life,* pp. 213–40. For the history of the Chicago-based Association for the Advancement of Creative Musicians (AACM), see Radano, *New Musical Figurations,* pp. 77–139. An example of this failure was the dispute between Coleman and bass player Red Mitchell during the recording of *Tomorrow Is the Question!* over the issue of how to play the harmonic changes. See Gordon, *Jazz West Coast,* pp. 194–95; Spellman, *Four Lives in the Bebop Business,* p. 121.

95. Susan Langer, *Philosophy in a New Key: A Study in the Symbolism of Reason, Rite, and Art* (Cambridge: Harvard University Press, 1996), p. 240.

96. In his otherwise useful analysis of Coleman, Martin Williams continually refers to a "telepathy" between Coleman and Don Cherry to explain their exemplary unison passages or their "dialogue," or he points to Coleman's natural melodic sense, comments that only serve to to suppress and mystify their acts of musical making. Martin Williams, *The Jazz Tradition* (New York: Oxford University Press, 1993), pp. 236–48.

97. "[T]here is a moment at the end of *Chronology* when Coleman is ready for the closing 'head' but Don Cherry does not respond, so the saxophonist uses a few bars to give him a guttural saxophone yell and call him in." Ibid., p. 243.

98. Scarry, *The Body in Pain,* p. 176.

99. Don Cherry quoted in the liner notes to Coleman *Something Else!!!!*

100. Nat Hentoff, ibid.

101. Julian "Cannonball" Adderley, "Cannonball Looks at Ornette Coleman," in *Down Beat* 27, no. 11 (26 May 1960): 21.

102. Erving Goffman, *Frame Analysis: An Essay on the Organization of Experience* (Cambridge: Harvard University Press, 1974), pp. 247–300.

103. Ibid., p. 249.

104. Ibid.

105. Scarry argues that the dynamic of projection and reciprocity constitutes the form of the artifact. Scarry, *The Body in Pain,* pp. 307–26.

106. Ibid., p. 318.

107. Coleman quoted in the liner notes to *Something Else!!!!*

108. Sudnow, *Ways of the Hand,* p. 80.

109. For Miles Davis also, the jazz act was all about "timing and getting everything in rhythm. It can sound good . . . as long as things are in the right place." Miles Davis and Quincy Troupe, *Miles: The Autobiography* (London: Macmillan, 1989), p. 386.

110. Coleman quoted in the liner notes to Ornette Coleman, *Change of the Century,* Atlantic, 1960, 1962 CD 81341.

111. In an interview with Ingrid Monson, Billy Higgins spoke of the *obligation* he felt toward others in the band, and thus the responsibility that emerged from such improvised musical acts. Monson, *Saying Something,* p. 63.

112. Coleman quoted in the liner notes to *Change of the Century.*

113. Jackie Mclean quoted in the liner notes to *Let Freedom Ring,* Blue Note, B21Y-46527.

114. Coleman quoted in the liner notes to *Change of the Century.*

115. Coleman quoted in the liner notes to Ornette Coleman, *Free Jazz,* Atlantic, 1961, CD 1364.

116. Coleman quoted in the liner notes to *Change of the Century.*

117. Charkes Keil, "Motion and Feeling through Music," in Charles Keil and Steven Feld, *Music Grooves: Essays and Dialogues (Chicago: University of Chicago Press, 1994),* p. 73.

118. Coleman quoted in Hentoff, *The Jazz Life,* p. 243.

119. "[I]t is the basic work of creation to bring about this very projection of aliveness. . . ." Scarry, *The Body in Pain,* p. 286.

120. Litweiler, *Ornette Coleman,* p. 46.

121. Martin Williams, liner notes to Ornette Coleman, *The Shape of Jazz To Come,* Atlantic, 1959, CD 1317.

122. Steve Lacy quoted in Bailey, *Improvisation.*

123. John Snyder quoted in Whitney Balliet, *Jelly Roll, Jabbo, and Fats: 19 Portraits in Jazz* (New York: Oxford University Press, 1983), p. 197.

124. Howard Mandel, "Charlie Haden's Search For Freedom," *Down Beat* 54, no. 9 (September 1987): 22.

125. Jarrett, "Ornette Coleman: Interview," p. 6.

126. Shelley Manne quoted in the liner notes of Ornette Coleman, *Tomorrow Is The Question! The New Music Of Ornette Coleman!,* Contemporary Records, 1959, 1988, OJCCD 342.

127. Coleman quoted in Joe Goldberg, *Jazz Masters of the Fifties* (New York: Macmillan, 1965), p. 243.

128. For an analysis of the three forms of repetition, see Gilles Deleuze, *Difference and Repetition,* trans. Paul Patton (New York: Columbia University, 1994), pp. 91–96.

129. Coleman quoted in Dan Morgenstern, "Ornette Coleman: From the Heart," *Downbeat* 32, no. 8 (8 April 1965): 17.

130. Scarry, *The Body in Pain,* p. 167.

## Epilogue

1. Max Harrison, "A Rare Bird," in *The Charlie Parker Companion: Six Decades of Commentary,* ed. Carl Woideck (New York: Schirmer Books, 1998), p. 207.

2. A similar way of thinking about this virtuosic surplus can be found in the many references to Antonio Gramsci's notion of an antihegemonic struggle within the social order. *Anti*hegemonic tendencies can be identified only when, in E. P. Thompson's view, we accept that

> in most societies we can observe an intellectual as well as an institutional hegemony, or dominant discourse, which imposes a structure of ideas and beliefs—deep assumptions as to social proprieties and economic process and as to the legitimacy of relations of property and power, a general "common sense" as to what is possible and what is not, a limited horizon of moral norms and practical possibilities beyond which all must be blasphemous, seditious, insane or apocalyptic fantasy—a structure which serves to consolidate the existent social order, enforce its priorities, and which is itself enforced by rewards and penalties, by notions of "reputability."

E. P. Thompson, *Witness against the Beast: William Blake and the Moral Law* (Cambridge: Cambridge University Press, 1994), pp. 108–9.

3. E. P. Thompson makes this point in terms of property inheritance in Thompson, "The Grid of Inheritance," in *Persons and Polemics: Historical Essays* (London: Merlin Press, 1994), p. 263.

4. Paul Berliner, *Thinking in Jazz: The Infinite Art of Improvisation* (Chicago: University of Chicago Press, 1994), p. 416.

5. James Lincoln Collier's claims for the "inevitability of jazz in America" is an example of such teleological arguments. James Lincoln Collier, *Jazz: The American Theme Song* (New York: Oxford University Press, 1993), pp. 3–4.

6. Chuck Israels quoted in Berliner, *Thinking in Jazz,* p. 348.

7. Berliner, *Thinking in Jazz,* pp. 21–94; Ingrid Monson, *Saying Something: Jazz Improvisation and Interaction* (Chicago: University of Chicago Press, 1996), pp. 26–72; David Sudnow, *Ways of the Hand: The Organization of Improvised Conduct* (Cambridge: MIT Press, 1978; reprint 1995), pp. 34–80.

8. Even "sympathetic observers often write about miners as if their solidarity sprang from some sub-intellectual sociological traditionalism, a combination of muscles and moral instincts." E. P. Thompson, "A Special Case," in *Writing by Candlelight* (London: Merlin Books, 1980), p. 71. For Herbert Gutman's critique of similar examples of primitivism concerning slavery and black culture, see Herbert Gutman, *Power and Culture: Essays on the American Working Class,* ed. Ira Berlin (New York: Pantheon Books, 1987), pp. 356–79.

9. William J. Schafer, *Brass Bands and New Orleans Jazz* (Baton Rouge: Louisiana State University Press, 1977), p. 45.

10. Berliner devotes two chapters to this phase. However, he tends to idealize the ways in which a musician came to jazz, sketching a mythical moment of discovery that "begins at birth" and then describing the musician's abilities as a *function* of their static environment, where musical sense was directly attributable to the musicality of the environment, which in itself was a function of the musician's inherent creativity. The circularity of this argument closes off the actual historical conditions in which jazz was made and the dynamic of its making. Berliner, *Thinking in Jazz,* pp. 21–94.

11. Wynton Marsalis quoted in David H. Rosenthal, *Hard Bop: Jazz and Black Music, 1955–1965* (New York: Oxford University Press, 1992), p. 176.

12. Tony Scherman, "What is Jazz? An Interview with Wynton Marsalis," *American Heritage,* October 1995, p. 81.

13. Ibid., p. 74.

14. Gary Giddins, *Rhythm-a-ning: Jazz Tradition and Innovation in the '80s* (New York: Oxford University Press, 1985), p. xiv.

15. Michael Paul Rogin, *Ronald Reagan, the Movie and Other Essays in American Political Demonolgy* (Berkeley: University of California Press, 1987), pp. 44–80.

16. Kenny Barron quoted in Berliner, *Thinking in Jazz,* p. 348.

17. Berliner, *Thinking in Jazz,* chaps. 13–15.

18. Kenny Washington quoted in Monson, *Saying Something,* p. 64.

19. Berliner, *Thinking in Jazz,* pp. 348–86.

20. Monson, *Saying Something,* p. 66.

21. Ibid., p. 67.

22. Ibid., p. 90.

23. E. P. Thompson, *The Poverty of Theory* (London: Merlin Press, 1978; reprint 1995), p. 204.

24. Fredric Jameson draws attention to the comical aspect of intentionality (for example, slipping on a banana peel) and suggests that "something has been

gained when we restore to human action and thought this ineradicable dimension of clumsiness. . . ." Fredric Jameson, *Postmodernism, or, the Cultural Logic of Late Capitalism* (London: Verso, 1991), p. 219. With an improvised act, the potential for mistakes is great. Part of the virtuosity of the jazz act—its seductive power—is to make those mistakes appear as intended and generative, rather than destructive.

25. While the world of the twentieth-century jazz musician and that of the nineteenth-century black miner obviously are radically different, the tendency to divide the analysis of American society into either an "interracial utopia or an Oceania of racial warfare" is still the mainstay of consensus history of one kind or another, whether dealing with music or labor. Ira Berlin, "Herbert G. Gutman and the American Working Class," in Gutman, *Power and Culture,* p. 30.

26. Herbert Gutman, "The Negro and the United Mine Workers of America," in *Work, Culture, and Society in Industrializing America* (New York: Knopf, 1976), pp. 121–208, and Gutman, *Power and Culture,* p. 353.

27. Miles Davis quoted in Berliner, *Thinking in Jazz,* p. 263.

28. Pierre Bourdieu, *Pascalian Meditations,* trans. Richard Nice (Cambridge, U.K.: Polity Press, 1999), p. 124.

# BIBLIOGRAPHY

## Books and Articles

Adams, James Truslow. *The Tempo of Modern Life*. Freeport, N.Y.: Books for Libraries Press, 1931; reprint 1970.

Ade, George. "Where Is Jazz Leading America?" *Etude* 42, no. 8 (August 1924).

Adderley, Julian "Cannonball." "Cannonball Looks at Ornette Coleman." *Down Beat* 27, no. 11 (May 26, 1960).

Adorno, Theodor W. *Aesthetic Theory*. Translated by Robert Hullot-Kentor. Minneapolis: University of Minnesota Press, 1997.

———. *In Search of Wagner*. Translated by Rodney Livingstone. London: Verso, 1991.

———. *Sound Figures*. Translated by Rodney Livingston. Stanford: Stanford University Press, 1999.

Adorno, Theodor W., and Max Horkheimer. *The Dialectic of Enlightenment*. Translated by John Cumming. London: Verso, 1997.

Althusser, Louis. "Ideology and Ideological State Apparatuses (Notes towards an Investigation)." In *Mapping Ideology,* edited by Slavoj Žižek. London: Verso, 1994.

Althusser, Louis, and Etienne Balibar. *Reading Capital*. Translated by Ben Brewster. London: New Left Books, 1975.

Ambrose, Stephen E. *Rise to Globalism: American Foreign Policy since 1938*. London: Penguin Books, 1971.

Anderson, Jervis. "Medium Cool." *New Yorker,* 12 December 1994.

Anderson, Perry. *The Origins of Postmodernity*. London: Verso, 1998.

———. *A Zone of Engagement*. London: Verso, 1992.

Armstrong, Louis. *Satchmo: My Life in New Orleans*. New York: Da Capo, 1986.

———. *Swing That Music*. New York: Da Capo, 1993.

Arrighi, Giovanni. *The Long Twentieth Century: Money, Power, and the Origins of Our Times*. London: Verso, 1994; reprint 1996.

Backus, Rob. *Fire Music: A Political History of Jazz*. Chicago: Vanguard Books, 1978.

Bailey, Derek. *Improvisation*. London: British Library National Sound Archive, 1992.

Baker, Houston A., Jr. *Modernism and the Harlem Renaissance*. Chicago: University of Chicago Press, 1987.

Baldwin, James. *The Fire Next Time*. Harmondsworth: Penguin Books, 1963.

————. "Of the Sorrow Songs." In *The Picador Book of Jazz and Blues*. Edited by James Campbell. London: Picador, 1996.

Balibar, Etienne. "Politics and Truth: The Vacillation of Ideology, II." In *Masses, Classes, Ideas: Studies on Philosophy before and after Marx*. New York: Routledge, 1986.

Balliet, Whitney. *Jelly Roll, Jabbo, and Fats: 19 Portraits in Jazz*. New York: Oxford University Press, 1983.

————. "King Louis." *New Yorker*, 8 August 1994.

Barker, Danny. *A Life In Jazz*. New York: Oxford University Press, 1986.

Baudrillard, Jean. *Seduction*. Translated by Brian Singer. London: Macmillan, 1990.

Bechet, Sidney. *Treat It Gentle*. New York: Da Capo Press, 1978.

Bell, Daniel. *The End of Ideology: On the Exhaustion of Political Ideas in the Fifties*. New York: Collier Books, 1961.

Bennett, Lerone, Jr. "Charlie (Bird) Parker—Madman or Genius?" *Negro Digest* 10, no. 11 (September 1961).

Bercovitch, Sacvan. *The Puritan Origins of the American Self*. New Haven: Yale University Press, 1975.

————. *The Rites of Assent: Transformations in the Symbolic Construction of America*. New York: Routledge, 1993.

Berlin, Ira. *Many Thousands Gone: The First Two Centuries of Slavery in North America*. Cambridge: Harvard University Press, Belknap Press, 1998.

Berliner, Paul. *Thinking in Jazz: The Infinite Art of Improvisation*. Chicago: University of Chicago Press, 1994.

Blackburn, Robin. *The Making of New World Slavery from the Baroque to the Modern, 1492–1800*. London: Verso, 1997.

Blesh, Rudi. *Shining Trumpets*. London: Cassell, 1954.

Blumenberg, Hans. *The Legitimacy of the Modern Age*. Translated by Robert M. Wallace. Cambridge: MIT Press, 1995.

————. *Work on Myth*. Translated by Robert M. Wallace. Cambridge: MIT Press, 1990.

————. "On a Lineage of the Idea of Progress." *Social Research* 41, no. 1 (1974).

Boorstin, Daniel J. *The Lost World of Thomas Jefferson*. Chicago: University of Chicago Press, 1981.

Bourdieu, Pierre. *Distinction: A Social Critique of the Judgement of Taste*. Translated by Richard Nice. Cambridge: Harvard University Press, 1984.

————. *The Field of Cultural Production.* Cambridge, U.K.: Polity Press, 1993.

————. *The Logic of Practice.* Translated by Richard Nice. Stanford: Stanford University Press, 1990.

————. *Pascalian Meditations.* Translated by Richard Nice. Cambridge, U.K.: Polity Press, 1999.

Bourdieu, Pierre, and Loic J. D. Wacquant. *An Invitation to a Reflexive Sociology.* Cambridge, U.K.: Polity Press, 1992.

Boyer, Paul. *By the Bomb's Early Light: American Thought and Culture at the Dawn of the Atomic Age.* New York: Pantheon, 1984.

Braverman, Harry. *Labor and Monopoly Capital: The Degradation of Work in the Twentieth Century.* New York: Monthly Review Press, 1974; reprint 1998.

Breton, Marcel, ed. *Hot and Cool: Jazz Short Stories.* London: Bloomsbury, 1991.

Brett, E. A. *International Money and Capitalist Crisis: The Anatomy of Global Disintegration.* London: Heinemann Educational Books, 1983.

Carby, Hazel. "In Body and Spirit: Representing Black Women Musicians." *Black Music Research Journal* 11, no. 2 (1991).

Cassirer, Ernst. *The Myth of the State.* New Haven: Yale University Press, 1974.

————. *The Problem of Knowledge: Philosophy, Science, and History since Hegel.* Translated by William H. Woglom and Charles W. Hendell. New Haven: Yale University Press, 1950; reprint 1978.

Castoriadis, Cornelius. *The Imaginary Institution of Society.* Translated by Kathleen Blamey. Cambridge, U.K.: Polity Press, 1997.

Chandler, Alfred. *The Visible Hand: The Managerial Revolution in American Business.* Cambridge: Harvard University Press, Belknap Press, 1977.

Chilton, John. *Sidney Bechet: The Wizard of Jazz.* New York: Da Capo Press, 1996.

Chomsky, Noam. *Deterring Democracy.* London: Vintage Books, 1992.

————. *Rethinking Camelot: JFK, the Vietnam War, and U.S. Political Culture.* London: Verso, 1993.

Clastres, Pierre. *Society against the State.* Translated by Robert Hurley. New York: Urizen Books, 1977.

Collier, James Lincoln. *Jazz: The American Theme Song.* New York: Oxford University Press, 1993.

————. *The Making of Jazz: A Comprehensive History.* London: PaperMac, 1981.

————. *The Reception of Jazz in America: A New View.* Brooklyn: Institute for Studies in American Music, 1988.

Coleman, Ornette. "Prime Time for Harmolodics." *Down Beat* 50, no. 7 (July 1983).

Coltrane, John, and Don DeMichael. "Coltrane on Coltrane." *Down Beat* 27, no. 20 (September 1960).

Condon, Eddie. *We Called It Music.* New York: Da Capo Press, 1992.

Coss, Bill. "Cecil Taylor's Struggle for Existence." *Down Beat* 28, no. 22 (1961).

Crouch, Stanley. "Bird Land: Charlie Parker, Clint Eastwood, and America." In *The Charlie Parker Companion: Six Decades of Commentary.* Edited by Carl Woideck. New York: Schirmer Books, 1998.

Cronon, William, George Miles, and Jay Gitlin, eds. *Under an Open Sky: Rethinking America's Western Past.* New York: W. W. Norton, 1992.

Dalmonte, Rossana, and Balint Andras Varga. *Luciano Berio: Two Interviews.* Translated by David Osmond-Smith. New York: Marion Boyars.

Davis, Mike. *City of Quartz: Excavating the Future in Los Angeles.* London: Verso, 1990.

———. *Prisoners of the American Dream: Politics and Economy in the History of the American Working Class.* London: Verso, 1986.

Davis, Miles, and Quincy Troupe. *Miles: The Autobiography.* London: Macmillan, 1989.

Deleuze, Gilles. *Bergsonism.* Translated by Hugh Tomlinson and Barbara Habberjam. New York: Zone Books, 1991.

———. *Cinema 1: The Movement-Image.* Translated by Hugh Tomlinson and Barbara Habberjam. Minneapolis: University of Minnesota Press, 1986.

———. *Cinema 2: The Time-Image.* Translated by Hugh Tomlinson and Robert Galeta. Minneapolis: University of Minnesota Press, 1989.

———. *Difference and Repetition.* Translated by Paul Patton. New York: Columbia University Press, 1994.

Deleuze, Gilles, and Felix Guattari. *A Thousand Plateaus: Capitalism and Schizophrenia.* Translated by Brian Massumi. Minneapolis: University of Minnesota Press, 1987.

DeMichael, Don. "John Coltrane and Eric Dolphy Answer the Critics." *Down Beat* 29, no. (April 1962).

DeVeaux, Scott. *The Birth of Bebop: A Musical and Social History.* Berkeley: University of California Press, 1997.

———. "Jazz in the Forties: A Conversation with Howard McGhee." *Black Perspective in Music* 15, no. 1 (spring 1987).

Dickstein, Morris. *Gates of Eden: American Culture in the Sixties.* New York: Basic Books, 1977.

Douglas, Ann. *Terrible Honesty: Mongrel Manhattan in the 1920s.* New York: Farrar, Strauss & Giroux, 1995.

Du Bois, W. E. B. *Black Reconstruction in America.* New York: Russell & Russell, 1935.

————. *The Souls of Black Folk.* New York: Signet Classic, 1969.

Dumont, Louis. *Essays on Individualism: Modern Ideology in Anthropological Perspective.* Chicago: University of Chicago Press, 1986.

————. *From Mandeville to Marx: The Genesis and Triumph of Economic Ideology.* Chicago: University of Chicago Press, 1977; reprint 1983.

————. *German Ideology: From France to Germany and Back.* Chicago: University of Chicago Press, 1994.

Dyer, Geoff. *But Beautiful: A Book about Jazz.* London: Vintage Books, 1991.

Elkins, Stanley. *Slavery: A Problem in American Institutional and Intellectual Life.* Chicago: University of Chicago Press, 1959; reprint 1976.

Ellison, Ralph. *Going to the Territory.* New York: Vintage Books, 1987.

————. *Invisible Man.* London: Penguin Books, 1965.

————. *Shadow and Act.* New York: Vintage Books, 1972.

Erenberg, Lewis A. *Swingin' the Dream: Big Band Jazz and the Rebirth of American Culture.* Chicago: University of Chicago Press, 1998.

Esman, Aaron H. "Jazz—A Study in Cultural Conflict." *American Imago* 8, no. 2 (June 1951).

Feather, Leonard. *Earwitness to an Era.* London: Picador, 1988.

Fields, Barbara J. "Slavery, Race and Ideology in the United States of America." *New Left Review* no. 181 (May–June 1990).

Finkelstein, Sidney. *Jazz: A People's Music.* New York: Da Capo Press, 1975.

Fitzgerald, F. Scott. *The Crack-up, with Other Pieces and Stories.* Harmondsworth: Penguin Books, 1974.

Focillon, Henri. *The Life of Forms.* Translated by Charles Beecher Hogan and George Kubler. New York: Zone Books, 1989.

Foner, Eric. *Nothing but Freedom: Emancipation and Its Legacy.* Baton Rouge: Louisiana State University Press, 1977.

————. *Reconstruction: America's Unfinished Revolution, 1863–1877.* New York: Harper & Row, 1988.

————. "The Meaning of Freedom in the Age of Emancipation." *Journal of American History* 81, no. 2 (1994).

Foner, Philip S. *Organized Labor and the Black Worker, 1619–1973.* New York: International Publishers, 1974.

Fredrickson, George M. *The Black Image in the White Mind: The Debate on Afro-American Character and Destiny, 1817–1914.* New York: Harper & Row, 1971.

Friedson, Steven M. *Dancing Prophets: Musical Experience in Tumbuka Healing.* Chicago: University of Chicago Press, 1996.

Gabbard, Krin. *Jazz among the Discourses.* Durham: Duke University Press, 1995.

Gates, Henry Louis, Jr. *The Signifying Monkey.* Oxford: Oxford University Press, 1988.

Gennari, John. "Jazz Criticism: Its Development and Ideologies." *Black American Literature Forum* 25, no. 3 (fall 1991).

Genovese, Eugene D. *From Rebellion to Revolution: Afro-American Slave Revolts in the Making of the New World.* New York: Vintage Books, 1981.

———. *Roll, Jordan, Roll: The World the Slaves Made.* New York: Vintage Books, 1976.

———. *The World the Slaveholders Made: Two Essays in Interpretation.* London: Penguin Press, 1970.

Giddins, Gary. *Rhythm-a-ning: Jazz Tradition and Innovation in the 1980s.* New York: Oxford University Press, 1985.

Gillespie, Dizzy, and Al Fraser. *Dizzy: The Autobiography of Dizzy Gillespie.* London: W. H. Allen, 1980.

Gioia, Ted. *The History of Jazz.* Oxford: Oxford University Press, 1997.

Gitler, Ira. *Jazz Masters of the 1940s.* New York: Macmillan, 1966.

———. *Swing to Bop: An Oral History of the Transition in Jazz in the 1940s.* New York: Oxford University Press, 1985.

Godelier, Maurice. *The Mental and the Material: Thought, Economy and Society.* Translated by Martin Thom. London: Verso, 1986.

Goffman, Erving. *Frame Analysis: An Essay on the Organization of Experience.* Cambridge: Harvard University Press, 1974.

Goldberg, Joe. *Jazz Masters of the Fifties.* New York: Macmillan, 1965.

Gordon, Robert. *Jazz West Coast: The Los Angeles Jazz Scene of the 1950s.* London: Quartet Books, 1990.

Guilbaut, Serge. *How New York Stole the Idea of Modern Art: Abstract Expressionism, Freedom, and the Cold War.* Translated by Arthur Goldhammer. Chicago: University of Chicago Press, 1983.

Gutman, Herbert G. *The Black Family in Slavery and Freedom: 1750–1925.* New York: Pantheon Books, 1976.

———. *Power and Culture: Essays on the American Working Class.* Edited by Ira Berlin. New York: Pantheon Books, 1987.

———. *Work, Culture, and Society in Industrializing America: Essays in American Working Class and Social History.* New York: Knopf, 1976.

Harding, Vincent. *There Is a River: The Black Struggle for Freedom in America.* New York: Harcourt Brace Jovanovich, 1981.

Hardt, Michael, and Antonio Negri. *The Labor of Dionysus: A Critique of the State Form.* Minneapolis: University of Minnesota Press, 1994.

Harrison, Max. *A Jazz Retrospect.* London: David & Charles, 1976.

———. "A Rare Bird." In *The Charlie Parker Companion: Six Decades of Commentary*. Edited by Carl Woideck. New York: Schirmer Books, 1998.

Hartz, Louis. *The Liberal Tradition in America*. New York: Harvest/HBJ, 1983.

Heckman, Don. "Inside Ornette Coleman." *Down Beat* 32, no. 19 (September 1965).

———. "Way Out There." *Down Beat* Yearbook (1963).

Henri, Florette. *Black Migration: Movement North, 1900–1920*. Garden City, N.Y.: Anchor Press/Doubleday, 1975.

Hentoff, Nat. *The Jazz Life*. New York: Da Capo, 1978.

———. "Jazz and Reverse Jim Crow." *Negro Digest* 10, no. 8 (1961).

———. "Just Call Him Thelonious." *Down Beat* 23, no. 15 (July 1956).

———. "The Life Perspectives of the New Jazz." *Down Beat* Yearbook (1966).

———. "The Truth Is Marching In." *Down Beat* 33, no. 33 (November 1966).

Herskovits, Melville J. *The Myth of the Negro Past*. Boston: Beacon Press, 1958.

Higgs, Robert. *Competition and Coercion: Blacks in the American Economy, 1865–1914*. Cambridge: Cambridge University Press, 1977.

Hobsbawm, Eric. "Jazz Comes to Europe." In *Uncommon People: Resistance, Rebellion, and Jazz*. London: Weidenfield & Nicolson, 1998.

———. *The Jazz Scene*. London: Weidenfield & Nicolson, 1989.

Holmes, John Clellon. *The Horn*. Berkeley: Creative Arts Book Company, 1958.

Hughes, Robert. *American Visions: The Epic History of Art in America*. London: Harvill Press, 1997.

Husserl, Edmund. *The Paris Lectures*. Translated with an introductory essay by Peter Koestenbaum. The Hague: Matinus Nijhoff, 1964.

Jameson, Fredric. *The Cultural Turn: Selected Writings on Postmodernism, 1983–1998*. London: Verso, 1998.

———. *Marxism and Form*. Princeton: Princeton University Press, 1971; reprint 1974.

———. *The Political Unconscious: Narrative as a Socially Symbolic Act*. London: Routledge, 1981; reprinted 1996.

———. *Postmodernism, or, The Cultural Logic of Late Capitalism*. London: Verso, 1991.

———. "Globalization as Philosophical Issue." In *The Cultures of Globalization*. Edited by Fredric Jameson and Masao Miyoshi. Durham: Duke University Press, 1998.

Jarrett, Michael. "Ornette Coleman Interview." *Cadence* 21, no. 10 (October 1995).

Jeske, Lee. "The Cherry Variations." *Down Beat* 50, no. 6 (June 1983).

Johnson, James Weldon. *Black Manhattan*. New York: Da Capo Books, 1991.

Jones, LeRoi [Amiri Baraka]. *Black Music*. London: MacGibbon & Kee, 1969.

——. *Blues People*. New York: William Morrow, 1963.

——. "Archie Shepp Live." *Jazz* 4, no. 1 (1965).

——. "Don Cherry: Making It the Hard Way." *Down Beat* 30, no. 30 (November 1963).

——. "Voice from the Avant-Garde: Archie Shepp." *Down Beat* 32, no. 1 (January 1965).

——. "We Are Our Feeling: The Black Aesthetic," *Negro Digest,* Volume 18, Number 11, September, 1969

Joyner, Charles. *Down by the Riverside*. Urbana: University of Illinois Press, 1984.

Kaminsky, Max, and V. E. Hughes. *Jazz Band: My Life in Jazz*. New York: Da Capo Press, 1963.

Kapferer, Bruce. *The Feast of the Sorcerer: Practices of Consciousness and Power.* Chicago: University of Chicago Press, 1997.

——. *Legends of People, Myths of State: Violence, Intolerance, and Political Culture in Sri Lanka and Australia*. Washington, D.C.: Smithsonian Institution Press, 1988.

——. "Performance and the Structuring of Meaning and Experience." In *The Anthropology of Experience*. Edited by Victor Turner and Edward M. Brunner. Urbana: University of Illinois Press, 1986.

——. "Remythologizing Discourses: State and Insurrectionary Violence in Sri Lanka." In *The Legitimization of Violence*. Edited by David E. Apter. London: Macmillan, 1997.

Keil, Charles, and Steven Feld. *Music Grooves: Essays and Dialogues.* Chicago: University of Chicago Press, 1994.

Kerouac, Jack. *On The Road*. New York: Signet Classics, 1955.

——. *Scattered Poems*. San Francisco: City Lights Books, 1971.

King, Richard H. *Civil Rights and the Idea of Freedom*. New York: Oxford University Press, 1992.

Kofsky, Frank. *Black Nationalism and the Revolution in Music*. New York: Pathfinder Press, 1970.

Kolko, Gabriel. *The Triumph of Conservatism: A Reinterpretation of American History, 1900–1916*. New York: Free Press, 1963.

Kolko, Joyce, and Gabriel Kolko. *The Limits of Power: The World and United States Foreign Policy*. New York: Harper & Row, 1972.

Kouwenhoven, John. *Made in America: The Arts in Modern Civilization*. New York: Doubleday, 1948.

Kovel, Joel. *Red Hunting in the Promised Land*. New York: Basic Books, 1994.

———. *White Racism: A Psychohistory.* New York: Columbia University Press, 1994.

Lasch, Christopher. *The Culture of Narcissism: American Life in an Age of Diminishing Expectations.* New York: W. W. Norton, 1991.

———. *The True and Only Heaven: Progress and Its Critics.* New York: W. W. Norton, 1991.

Langer, Susan. *Feeling and Form: A Theory of Art.* New York: Charles Scribner's Sons, 1953.

———. *Philosophy in a New Key: A Study in the Symbolism of Reason, Rite, and Art.* Cambridge: Harvard University Press, 1996.

Leonard, Neil. *Jazz and the White Americans: The Acceptance of a New Art Form.* Chicago: University of Chicago Press, 1962; reprint 1970.

———. *Jazz: Myth and Religion.* Oxford: Oxford University Press, 1987.

Levine, Lawrence. *Black Culture and Black Consciousness.* Oxford: Oxford University Press, 1977.

———. "Jazz and American Culture." *Journal of American Folklore* 102, no. 403 (January–March 1989).

Lewis, David Levering. *When Harlem Was in Vogue.* New York: Oxford University Press, 1989.

Limerick, Patricia Nelson. *The Legacy of Conquest: The Unbroken Past of the American West.* New York: W. W. Norton, 1987.

Lipsitz, George. *Class and Culture in Cold War America* (South Hadley, Mass.: J. F. Bergin Publishers, 1981.

———. *Time Passages.* Minneapolis: University of Minnesota Press, 1990.

Litweiler, John. *The Freedom Principle: Jazz after 1958.* New York: Da Capo Press, 1984.

———. *Ornette Coleman: A Harmolodic Life.* New York: William Morrow, 1992.

Livingston, James. *Origins of the Federal Reserve System: Money, Class, and Corporate Capitalism, 1890–1913.* Ithaca: Cornell University Press, 1986.

Locke, Alain. *The Negro and His Music.* Port Washington, New York: Kennikat Press, 1936; reprint 1968.

Lomax, Alan. *Mister Jelly Roll.* London: Virgin Books, 1991.

Lowith, Karl. *Meaning in History.* Chicago: University of Chicago Press, 1949.

Mache, Francois-Berhard. *Music, Myth, Nature.* Translated by Susan Delaney. Chur, Switzerland: Harwood Academic Publishers, 1992.

Mailer, Norman. *Advertisements for Myself.* New York: Flamingo Modern Classics, 1994.

Mandel, Ernest. *Late Capitalism.* Translated by Joris de Bre. London: Verso, 1999.

Mandel, Howard. "Charlie Haden's Search for Freedom." *Down Beat* 54, no. 9 (September 1987).

Margolis, Norman, "A Theory on the Psychology of Jazz." *American Imago* 11, no. 3 (fall 1954).

Marquis, Donald. *Searching for Buddy Bolden: First Man of Jazz*. Baton Rouge: Louisiana State University Press, 1978.

Marx, Karl. *Capital: A Critique of Political Economy*. Vol. 1. Translated by Ben Brewster. Harmondsworth: Penguin Books, 1976; reprint 1990.

———. *Early Writings*. Translated by Rodney Livingstone. Harmondsworth: Penguin Books, 1975; reprint 1984.

Marx, Karl, and Friedrich Engels. *The German Ideology*. Edited and translated by C. J. Arthur. London: Lawrence & Wishart, 1970.

Marx, Leo. *The Machine in the Garden*. New York: Oxford University Press, 1964.

Mason, Daniel Gregory. "The Jazz Invasion." In *Behold America!* Edited by Samuel D. Schmalhausen. New York: Farrar & Rinehardt, 1931.

Mehegan, John. "Bill Evans: An Interview." *Jazz* 4, no. 1 (January 1965).

Mellers, Wilfrid. *Music in a New Found Land: Themes and Developments in the History of American Music*. London: Barrie & Rockcliff, 1964.

Meltzer, David, ed. *Reading Jazz*. San Francisco: Mecury House, 1993.

Merleau-Ponty, Maurice. *The Phenomenology of Perception*. Translated by Colin Smith. London: Routledge, 1989.

———. *The Prose of the World*. Translated by John O'Neill. Evanston: Northwestern University Press, 1973.

Mezzrow, Mezz, and Bernard Wolfe. *Really the Blues*. New York: Citadel Press, 1990.

Mills, C. Wright. *The Power Elite*. New York: Oxford University Press, 1956.

Mingus, Charles. *Beneath the Underdog: His World as Composed by Mingus*. New York: Vintage Books, 1991.

Mitchell, J. Clyde. *Cities, Society, and Social Perception: A Central African Perspective*. Oxford: Clarendon Press, 1987.

Monson, Ingrid. *Saying Something: Jazz Improvisation and Interaction*. Chicago: University of Chicago Press, 1996.

———. "Doubleness and Jazz Improvisation: Irony, Parody, and Ethnomusicology." *Critical Inquiry* 20, no. 2 (winter 1994).

———. "Oh Freedom." In *In the Course of Performance: Studies in the World of Improvisation*. Edited by Bruno Nettl. Chicago: University of Chicago Press, 1998.

Moore, Macdonald Smith. *Yankee Blues: Musical Culture and American Identity*. Bloomington: Indiana University Press, 1985.

Morgan, Edmund S. "Slavery and Freedom: The American Paradox." *Journal of American History* 59, no. 1 (June 1972).

Morgenstern, Dan. "Ornette Coleman: From the Heart." *Down Beat* 32, no. 8 (April 1965).

Morrison, Toni. *Playing in the Dark: Whiteness and the Literary Imagination.* Cambridge: Harvard University Press, 1992.

Mumford, Lewis. *The City in History: Its Origins, Its Transformations, and Its Prospects.* Harmondsworth: Penguin, 1963.

Nanry, Charles. "Jazz and Modernism: Twin-Born Children of the Age of Invention." *Annual Review of Jazz Studies* no. 1, 1982.

Neal, Lawrence P. "The Black Musician in White America." *Negro Digest* 16, no. 5 (March 1967).

——. "Some Reflections on the Black Aesthetic." In *The Black Aesthetic.* Edited by Addison Gayle. New York: Anchor Books, 1972.

Nettl, Bruno. "Thoughts on Improvisation: A Comparative Approach." *Musical Quarterly* 60, no. 1 (January 1974).

Nietzsche, Friedrich. *The Birth of Tragedy and the Genealogy of Morals.* Translated by Francis Golffing. New York: Doubleday, 1956.

Ogren, Kathy J. *The Jazz Revolution: Twenties America and the Meaning of Jazz.* New York: Oxford University Press, 1989.

Osgood, Henry O. *So This Is Jazz.* Boston: Little, Brown, 192.

Ostransky, Leroy. *Jazz City: The Impact of Our Cities on the Development of Jazz.* Englewood Cliffs, N.J.: Prentice-Hall, 1978.

Owens, Thomas. *Bebop: The Music and Its Players.* New York: Oxford University Press, 1995.

Patterson, Michael. "Archie Shepp: A Profile-Interview." *Black World* (November 1973).

Peretti, Burton W. *The Creation of Jazz: Music, Race, and Culture in Urbanizing America.* Urbana: University of Illinois Press, 1992.

Pocock, J. G. A. *The Machiavellian Moment: Florentine Political Thought and the Atlantic Republican Tradition.* Princeton: Princeton University Press, 1975.

Radano, Ronald M. *New Musical Figurations: Anthony Braxton's Cultural Critique.* Chicago: University of Chicago Press, 1993.

Rath, Richard Cullen. "Echo and Narcissus: The Afrocentric Pragmatism of W. E. B. Du Bois." *Journal of American History* 84, no. 2 (September 1997).

Rexroth, Kenneth. *The Alternative Society: Essays from the Other World.* New York: Herder & Herder, 1970.

Riesner, Robert. *Bird: The Legend of Charlie Parker.* London: Quartet Books, 1962.

Rogers, J. A., "Jazz at Home." In *The New Negro*. Edited by Alain Locke. New York: Johnson Reprint Corporation, 1968.

Rogin, Michael Paul. *Ronald Reagan, the Movie and Other Essays in American Political Demonology*. Berkeley: University of California Press, 1987.

Rosen, Charles. *The Classical Style*. New York: W. W. Norton, 1972.

———. *The Romantic Generation*. London: Fontana Press, 1999.

Rosenberg, Harold. *The Tradition of the New*. London: Thames & Hudson, 1962.

Rosenthal, David H. *Hard Bop: Jazz and Black Music, 1955–1965*. New York: Oxford University Press, 1992.

Ross, Dorothy. *The Origins of American Social Science*. Cambridge: Cambridge University Press, 1991.

———. "Historical Consciousness in Nineteenth-Century America." *American Historical Review* 89, no. 4 (October 1984).

Rossellini, Roberto. *My Method: Writings and Interviews*. New York: Marsilio Publishers, 1995.

Russell, Ross. *Bird Lives: The High Life and Hard Times of Charlie "Yardbird" Parker*. London: Quartet Books, 1972; reprint 1980, 1988.

Said, Edward W. *Musical Elaborations*. London: Chatto & Windus, 1991.

Sargeant, Winthrop. *Jazz: Hot and Hybrid*. New York: Da Capo Press, 1975.

Sartre, Jean-Paul. *The Critique of Dialectical Reason: Theory of Practical Ensembles*. Vol. 1. Translated by Alan Sheridan-Smith. London: Verso Books, 1991.

Sassen, Saskia. *The Global City: New York, London, Tokyo*. Princeton: Princeton University Press, 1991.

Scarry, Elaine. *The Body in Pain: The Making and Unmaking of the World*. New York: Oxford University Press, 1985.

Scherman, Tony. "What Is Jazz? An Interview with Wynton Marsalis." *American Heritage* (October 1995).

Schuller, Gunther. *Early Jazz: Its Roots and Development*. New York: Oxford University Press, 1968.

Scott, James C. *Domination and the Arts of Resistance: Hidden Transcripts*. New Haven: Yale University Press, 1990.

———. *The Moral Economy of the Peasant: Rebellion and Subsistence in Southeast Asia*. New Haven: Yale University Press, 1976.

———. *Weapons of the Weak: Everyday Forms of Peasant Resistance*. New Haven: Yale University Press, 1985.

Shapiro, Nat, and Nat Hentoff. *Hear Me Talkin' to Ya: The Story of Jazz as Told by the Men Who Made It*. London: Souvenir Press, 1992.

Shepp, Archie. "A View from the Inside" *Down Beat* Yearbook (1965).

Skvorecky, Josef. "Red Music." In *The Picador Book of Blues and Jazz*. Edited by James Campbell. London: Picador, 1995.

Slobin, Mark. "Micromusics of the West: A Comparative Approach." *Ethnomusicology* 36, no. 1 (winter 1992).

Slotkin, Richard. *The Fatal Environment: The Myth of the Frontier in the Age of Industrialization, 1800–1890*. New York: Atheneum, 1985.

———. *Gunfighter Nation: The Myth of the Frontier in Twentieth-Century America*. New York: HarperCollins, 1993.

Smith, Frank. "Music and Internal Activities: Contacting Greatness in Art and the Music of Ornette Coleman." Part 1. *Jazz* 5, no. 4 (April 1966).

Smith, Henry Nash. *Virgin Land: The American West as Symbol and Myth*. Cambridge: Harvard University Press, 1950.

Sohn-Rethel, Alfred. *Intellectual and Manual Labor: A Critique of Epistemology*. London: Macmillan, 1978.

Spellman, A.B., *Four Lives In The Bebop Business* (New York: Limelight Editions, 1990)

Stewart, James T. "The Development of the Revolutionary Black Artist." In *Black Fire: An Anthology of Afro-American Writing*. Edited by LeRoi Jones and Larry Neal. New York: William Morrow, 1968.

Stowe, David. *Swing Changes: Big Band Jazz in New Deal America*. Cambridge: Harvard University Press, 1994.

Southern, Eileen. *The Music of Black Americans: A History*. New York: W. W. Norton, 1971.

Sudnow, David. *Ways of the Hand: The Organization of Improvised Conduct*. Cambridge: MIT Press, 1978; reprint 1995.

Szwed, John F. "Musical Style and Racial Conflict." *Phylon* 27, no. 4 (winter 1966).

Taylor, Arthur. *Notes and Tones: Musician-to-Musician Interviews*. New York: Da Capo Press, 1993.

Taylor, Frederick Winslow. *The Principles of Scientific Management*. New York: Harper & Brothers Publishers, 1915.

Thomas, Hugh. *The Slave Trade: The History of the Atlantic Slave Trade, 1440–1870*. London: Picador, 1997.

Thompson, E. P. *Customs in Common*. Harmondsworth: Penguin Books, 1993.

———. *The Making of the English Working Class*. Harmondsworth: Penguin Books, 1991.

———. *Persons and Polemics: Historical Essays*. London: Merlin Press, 1994.

———. *The Poverty of Theory*. London: Merlin Press, 1978; reprint 1995.

———. *William Morris: Romantic to Revolutionary*. London: Merlin Press, 1955; reprint 1977.

————. *Witness against the Beast: William Blake and Moral Law.* Cambridge: Cambridge University Press, 1993.

————. *Writing by Candlelight.* London: Merlin Press, 1980.

————. "Eighteenth Century English Society: Class Struggle without Class?" *Social History* 3, no. 2 (May 1978).

Tomlinson, Gary. "Cultural Dialogics: A White Historian Signifies." *Black Music Research Journal* 11, no. 2 (1991).

Turner, Frederick Jackson. *The Frontier in American History.* New York: Henry Holt, 1920.

Turner, Victor, and Edward M. Brunner, eds. *The Anthropology of Experience.* Urbana: University of Illinois Press, 1986.

Tuveson, Ernest Lee. *Redeemer Nation: The Idea of America's Millennial Role.* Chicago: University of Chicago Press, 1968.

Virno, Paolo. "Virtuosity and Revolution: The Political Theory of Exodus." In *Radical Thought in Italy: A Potential Politics.* Edited by Paolo Virno and Michael Hardt. Minneapolis: University of Minnesota Press, 1996.

Ward, Brian. *Just My Soul Responding: Rhythm and Blues, Black Consciousness, and Race Relations.* Berkeley: University of California Press, 1998.

Weinberg, Albert K. *Manifest Destiny: A Study of Nationalist Expansionism in American History.* Chicago: Quadrangle Books, 1935.

White, Shane, and Graham White. *Stylin': African American Expressive Culture from Its Beginnings to the Zoot Suit.* Ithaca: Cornell University Press, 1998.

Williams, Martin. *The Jazz Tradition.* New York: Oxford University Press, 1993.

————. "Charlie Parker: The Burden of Innovation." In *The Charlie Parker Companion: Six Decades of Commentary.* Edited by Carl Woideck. New York: Schirmer Books, 1998.

Williams, Raymond. *Marxism and Literature.* Oxford: Oxford University Press, 1977.

Wilmer, Valerie. *As Serious as Your Life.* London: Allison & Busby, 1977.

Woideck, Carl. *Charlie Parker: His Music and Life.* Ann Arbor: University of Michigan Press, 1996.

Woideck, Carl, ed. *The Charlie Parker Companion: Six Decades of Commentary.* New York: Schirmer Books, 1998.

Wolf, Eric R. *Europe and the People without History.* Berkeley: University of California Press, 1982.

Wyschogrod, Edith. *Spirit in Ashes: Hegel, Heidegger, and Man-Made Mass Death.* New Haven: Yale University Press, 1985.

Yardley, Jonathan. "Jazz, Most Glorious of Mongrels." *Guardian Weekly* 157, no. 25 (21 December 1997).

Žižek, Slavoj. *Enjoy Your Symptom! Jacques Lacan in Hollywood and Out.* New York: Routledge, 1992.

———. *The Plague of Fantasies.* London: Verso, 1997.

———. *The Sublime Object of Ideology.* London: Verso, 1989.

———. *The Ticklish Subject: The Absent Center of Political Ontology.* London: Verso, 1999.

Žižek, Slavoj, ed. *Mapping Ideology.* London: Verso, 1994.

## Selected Discography

Bechet, Sidney. *Summertime: 1932–1941.* Giants of Jazz, 1991, CD 53104.

———. *Revolutionary Blues: 1941–1951.* Giants of Jazz, 1992, CD 53106.

Coleman, Ornette. *Something Else!!!! The Music of Ornette Coleman.* Contemporary, 1958, CD 7551.

———. *Tomorrow Is the Question! The New Music of Ornette Coleman!* Contemporary Records, 1959, 1988, OJCCD 342.

———. *The Shape of Jazz to Come.* Atlantic, 1959, CD 1317.

———. *Change of the Century.* Atlantic, 1960, 1992, CD 81341.

———. *Free Jazz.* Atlantic, 1961, CD 1364.

———. *Town Hall, 1962.* Get Back, 1998, CD GET1002.

———. *Ornette on Tenor.* Atlantic/Rhino, 1962, 1993, R2 71455.

———. *Chappaqua Suite.* Sony Music, 1965, SRCS 9192.

———. *At the "Golden Circle" Stockholm.* Vol. 1. Blue Note, 1965, CDP 7 84224.

———. *At the "Golden Circle" Stockholm.* Vol. 2. Blue Note, 1965, CDP 7 84225.

———. *Broken Shadows.* Sony Music, 1982, SRCS 9373.

———. *Sound Museum.* Harmolodic, 1996, CD531 914.

Coleman, Ornette, and Pat Metheny. *Song X.* Geffen Records, 1986, CD 9 24096.

Coleman, Ornette, and Prime Time. *Virgin Beauty.* CBS, 1988, RK 44301.

Coleman, Ornette, Howard Shore, and the London Philharmonic Orchestra. *Naked Lunch: Music from The Original Soundtrack.* Milan America/BMG, 1992, CD 73138/35614.

Coleman, Ornette, and Prime Time. *Tone Dialing.* Harmolodic/Verve, 1995, CD 527 483.

Coleman, Ornette, and Joachim Kuhn. *Colors.* Harmolodic, 1997, CD 537 789.

McLean, Jackie. *Let Freedom Ring.* Blue Note B21Y-46527.

Mingus, Charles. *Mingus Ah Um.* Columbia, 1959, CK 40648.

Monk, Thelonious. *The Complete Genius.* Blue Note, 1976, BN–LA579–H2.

Parker, Charlie. *The Legendary Dial Masters.* Vol. 1. Stash Records, 1989, ST-CD-2.

## Videography

Felix Breisach, director. *Boulez in Rehearsal.* Vienna: Spectrum TV/Rm Arts in association with ZDF/ARTE, 1998.

# INDEX

Adderley, Julian "Cannonball," 152
Adorno, Theodor, 1, 6, 119; commodity
  character of music, 6
Africa, 59, 66–68, 71–72
Althusser, Louis, 24; ideological
  interpellation as defined by, 24, 26,
  183n. 92, 184n. 96
Altman, Robert, 168
American exceptionalism, 27, 38, 44,
  77–78, 80–82, 167; doctrine of
  the state, 27–30; frontier, 90–102;
  ideology of Americanism, 80;
  manifest destiny, 97. *See also*
  freedom; frontier; slavery; Turner,
  Frederick Jackson
American historical consciousness, 24, 31;
  American history, 24, 95; "slave
  event," 41
American ideology, 1, 27–30, 37, 91, 176;
  Africa, 66; civil rights movement,
  135; elements of, 30; frontier,
  26, 78–79, 90–102, 175; human
  freedom, 26, 124, 125, 175; jazz
  life as ideological form of, 26–27,
  129; powers and properties of, 26;
  progressivism of, 30, 77–79, 100,
  117–18, 171; relation to the state,
  77–78; slavery, 26, 37, 42, 59–72,
  175; Slotkin, Richard, and theories
  of, 25. *See also* Bercovitch, Sacvan;
  ideology; Žižek, Slavoj
American state, 26, 27–30, 133; American
  metropolis, 79; anticommunism,
  124; black Americans and the, 38,
  42, 51, 74–76, 89, 106, 121, 130;
  Civil War, 34, 42, 50, 59, 70; Cold
  War and the, 123–127, 135, 151,
  171; dynamics of emancipation

and, 33, 59, 60; Emancipation
  Proclamation (1863), 40, 41; jazz
  musicians and the, 25, 30, 49, 113,
  128, 174; New South, 38; objective
  aims of, 124; power of, 28, 62,
  175; Reconstruction, 33, 35, 42,
  62; relation of slaves to, 51, 73, 75;
  theory of, 5, 27–30; and World War
  II, 77. *See also* capitalism; slavery
Armstrong, Louis, 46, 84, 103; and
  Bechet, Sidney, 53–54
Arrighi, Giovanni, 189n. 82
Art Ensemble of Chicago, 128
Ayler, Albert, 128

Basie, William "Count," 80
Baudrillard, Jean, 16, 22, 140, 148, 149;
  *Seduction,* 16, 22, 140. *See also*
  seduction
Bechet, Sidney, 2, 8, 33, 38–59, 72–76,
  123, 132, 134, 171; "Free Day,"
  72–76; Omar, 39, 74; slavery
  and slave music, 43, 72–76; *Treat
  It Gentle,* 8, 33, 36 38–39 (*see
  also* discourse of legitimation;
  remythologization); virtuosity of
  construction, 33, 38–44, 50–59
Beethoven, Ludwig van, 140
Bercovitch, Sacvan, 29, 90, 106; *The Rites
  of Assent,* 29; ritual of consensus, 29
Berio, Luciano, 16; theory of virtuosity,
  16–17
Berlin, Ira, 72, 174; consensus history and
  black music, 210n. 25
Berliner, Paul, 16, 128, 129, 134, 149, 151,
  168, 169, 172, 173, 174, 209n. 10
black consciousness, 8–9, 36, 50, 80, 130,
  135

**227**

Gordon, Dexter, 104
Gordon, Robert, 137
Gutman, Herbert G., 8, 9, 37, 49, 69, 72; on black miners, 174; on Herskovits, 69; on slavery, 42

Haden, Charlie, 154, 163–64
Hardt, Michael, 30; theory of the state, 30–31
Harrison, Max, 81; and Ornette Coleman, 132–33; and Charlie Parker, 109–10, 118–21, 167
Hawkins, Coleman, 83
Hentoff, Nat, 14, 24, 45–50, 75, 152; on Miles Davis, 46, 47; *The Jazz Life,* 14, 45–50. *See also* ideology; jazz
Herskovits, Melville J., 9, 37, 69–72; African survivals and Africanisms, 69–70; middle passage, 9; *The Myth of the Negro Past,* 9
Higgins, Billy, 154, 172
Higgs, Robert, 59
Hinton, Milt, 116
Hiroshima, 125. *See also* Boyer, Paul
historical consciousness, 11–12. *See also* American historical consciousness; frontier, myth of; ideology; Ross, Dorothy; Slotkin, Richard; Turner, Frederick Jackson
Holmes, John Clellon, 83
human action, 3, 17, 89, 98–99, 126, 133; creative forms of, 12, 82, 128; creative structure of, 39; historical forms of, 3–4; musical forms of, 37, 76, 166; New World and, 78–79. *See also,* Scarry, Elaine
Husserl, Edmund, 182n. 66

ideology, 25, 26, 92; Althusser on, 24; ideological interpellation, 183n. 92; *The German Ideology* (Marx and Engels), 25; mediation, 1, 27, 177n. 1; and social struggle, 25, 64–65, 134; *The Sublime Object of Ideology* (Žižek) and the theory of, 25–26, 67–68; task of an ideological analysis, 26; unconscious, 25. *See also* American exceptionalism;

American ideology; American state; jazz, jazz life

Jameson, Fredric, 27, 32, 124, 137, 177n. 1, 180n. 48; American power, 202n. 13; intentionality and accident, 209n. 24
jazz, 1, 13–16, 27; artifact, structure and dynamics of, 27, 38, 44, 53; bebop, 80–90, 105–22, 130, 132, 158, 162; black consciousness, 50; capitalism, 78, 115, 174, 191n. 104; collective basis of, 48, 50, 51, 55, 56, 81; creativity, axes of, 39, 112–13, 159–62; hot jazz, 105, 130, 158; ideological form of, 13, 24, 48, 51, 72, 86, 111, 112, 124, 123–25, 133, 134, 137, 149, 174, 175 (*see also* American ideology); jam session, 87, 113–17; jazz act, 13, 38, 39, 41, 87, 121, 124, 139–51, 153–54, 158–66, 172–76; jazz form, 15, 74, 123, 153–54; jazz group, the structure and dynamics of, 51–56, 131–32, 137, 139, 149–51, 169–74; jazz life, 24, 25, 45–49, 73, 75, 76; musical practice, 1–2, 167; radical impossibility of the jazz act, 23–24, 176; social act of, 2, 46–49, 52, 73, 76, 87, 103–22, 162, 168, 170; swing, 80, 130, 158; tempo of, 53, 58, 61, 131, 154–55; theory of, 13, 51–56, 153–54; virtuosity of, 48, 86–90, 103, 119–22, 124, 151–66, 175. *See also* music; virtuosity
Jazz Composer's Guild, and Jazz Composer's Guild Orchestra, 136
Jones, LeRoi (Amiri Baraka), 7, 14, 23, 66, 80, 83–90, 127, 130–31; blues impulse, 7, 14,15; *Blues People,* 14, 45, 80, 88, 127; jazz and ideology, 14, 90, 113–14; jazz as radical act in context of American culture, 15, 90, 121; the riff, 15

Kaminsky, Max, 104
Kapferer, Bruce, 6–7, 31, 73; discourses of legitimation, 36–37; practice, theory of, 185n.